FOREVER
MY BROTHER

Journeys through the Game of Life

ISAIAH BEALER

ISBN: 978-1-4834-8501-0 (sc)
ISBN: 978-1-4834-8500-3 (e)

Lulu Publishing Services rev. date: 10/22/2018

Contents

Summer before sophomore year

The crowd was roaring with pandemonium as the last twenty-five seconds counted down in the 15-year-old division championship AAU game.

"Push the ball, push the ball Malachi!" Coach Joe yelled as his son dribbled up the court in a track star pace.

Malachi approached the three-point line rising up over two Hoyas defenders personifying Kobe Bryant in his prime. Malachi made the shot as the basketball fell smoothly through the net. The Flyers team switched up to their defensive formation after the successful three-point shot made by Malachi.

"Man up, man up full court!" Coach Joe's voice echoed over the tumultuous crowd noise.

The Hoyas coach called a timeout when he noticed that Coach Joe's team the Flyers were playing full court defense.

"Huddle up," Coach Joe said waving his arms. "Alright now, it's a tie game 62 to 62, so let's play smart ball and execute!" he demanded.

"Coach, who you want to take the last shot once we get the ball back?" T.C. the other Flyers guard asked.

Coach Joe gave T.C. the laser eye replying, "Any one of y'all. All of y'all are stars. All right now bring it in!" The team put their right hands in the huddle and yelled out "Victory" as the timeout buzzer rang.

The five Flyer players walked back onto the court with championship poise as their teammates from the bench encouraged them. Malachi, J.B., Rob and Heavy all stood over 6 feet with T.C.

inching beneath them at 5'10. As the two teams lined back up on the court, J.B. matched up with Snoop who was the number one ranked fifteen-year-old in the state of Ohio. The ref blew the whistle as he handed the ball to the Hoyas center. He threw the ball into the Hoyas point guard who took two dribbles and passed the ball to Snoop at midcourt. Snoop dribbled the ball slowly waving his hands signaling everyone to spread the court, so he could isolate J.B. one on one. Malachi wanted to play off of his man and help J.B. but he knew better, knowing the man he was guarding was capable of making the game winning shot. Snoop was at the top of the key glancing at the clock tick down from 14 to 13 seconds as the sweat dripped off of his brown face. Snoop made a quick move to his left before J.B. anticipated and crossed over to his right at the free throw line pulling up for the jump shot. J.B. lunged in the air to alter Snoop's shot but ended up hitting his elbow. Snoop missed the shot, but the ref blew the whistle hastily calling a foul on J.B..

"Bullshit, bullshit ref," were the chants from some of the Flyer fans.

J.B. yelled, "Damn" mad at himself because he had fouled Snoop.

"You cool bro. We still in the game," Rob the Flyers forward said to J.B. as they lined up for the free throws.

Snoop walked to the free throw line standing at 6'4 looking confident as ever. He resembled a young Iverson as his braids hung to the back. The ref bounced the ball to him and he cuffed it in his left arm and flicked his right wrist practicing his shooting motion. Snoop made his first free throw easily.

"It's 63 to 62. Let's make sure we box out!" Coach Joe yelled out from the opposite sideline.

Snoop made his second free throw. Heavy ran to the ball to take it out quickly passing it into T.C.. T.C. pushed the ball up the court looking at time tick off from eight seconds to seven seconds. Passing midcourt, he seen nobody open, so he decided to drive into the paint for the shot. Fearing T.C. was going to score, Snoop slid off of J.B. to block the driving lane. T.C. noticing Snoop playing help defense threw the ball to J.B. in the corner. J.B. took a dribble backwards stepping behind the 3-point line releasing the shot. The ball spinned through the air gracefully going straight through the net as the game buzzer went off. The whole crowd flooded the court as the whole team ran over to J.B. bombarding him in excitement. T.C., Malachi and the rest of the Flyer team instantly joined in the celebration also.

Chants of "Yeah bro" and "Flyer squad" was all anybody heard as they celebrated in the midst of the moment.

"Line up champs so we can shake the Hoyas hands," Coach Joe spoke with a big smile on his face.

The Flyers lined up single file to shake the Hoyas hands. Even though the two teams were rivals their was no animosity because the two coaches ensured that the players respected each other.

"Man y'all see that shot though!" J.B. asked rhetorically impersonating his shooting motion.

T.C. butted in, "Ay that shot wouldn't have happened without my immaculate assist."

"Yeah bro, that whole play was live. I thought you was gone take it all the way," Rob added.

"Trust me, I was but as soon as I seen Snoop playing off it was just natural instinct to dish the ball off to bro," T.C. replied grinning ear to ear.

As the young men conversed the tournament director walked over with a large team trophy that stood about three feet high plated in gold.

"Coach Joe I need everyone to line up, so I can get a picture of the championship team," Mr. Rucker said in a raspy voice.

"Y'all heard Mr. Rucker lets lineup so he can get this photo." The starting five players lined up behind the other five players on the team. Heavy being the tallest at 6'4, 210 pounds lined up directly in the middle. He had a full chinstrap goatee and was dark skin with a mini fro. Standing to the right of him was Rob. Rob was 6'3 and weighed about 190 pounds. His pigment was that of a yellow complexion. Everyone said the braids he wore made him resemble Big Meech from the BMF crew. J.B. stood on the other side of Heavy at 6'1 weighing about 175 pounds. J.B. was brown skin and rocked a bald fade. Malachi stood next to be J.B. at 6'2 and weighed about 180 pounds. He was also brown skin but wore a jet black even Steven haircut. The light mustache Malachi had growing in gave him a slightly older look. T.C. stood beside Rob at 5'10 weighing about 170 pounds. He had a dark brown skin complexion and had short black dreads. The long scar he had on his neck made him easy to spot out in a crowd of people. Coach Joe stood at the end at the height of 6'7 weighing about 250. He had a low haircut and a thick mustache with a couple of grey hairs in it. Coach Joe had an old tattoo on his right forearm that read "OG".

"Alright, y'all ready for this picture?" Mr. Rucker asked. He pointed a vintage black Polaroid camera at the team starting to take pictures. As the young men smiled Mama Kelley and Mama J came running up snapping pictures with their android phones.

"Y'all get enough pictures yet? Damn, I'm tired of smiling," Coach Joe said aggressively. Mama Kelley Coach Joe's wife made a disgruntled face at him before she responded. "Yeah Joe, we got em now!"

Mama J, who was J.B.'s mother, noticed that her son and his other three friends had merged off into their own conversation. "Alright, let me get some photos of all my sons," she said holding her android phone backup.

Malachi, T.C., J.B. and Rob started doing several poses like they were posing for an album cover.

"Ay y'all we need to come up with a name for the squad," T.C. shouted out still posing.

"We definitely do need a name, so we can be official," Malachi added.

"Shit, what about the Lion squad?" Rob spoke confidently. J.B. squinted his face up looking in Rob's direction.

"The Lion squad? Nigga this ain't the Animal planet!" J.B.'s comical remarks had made everyone laugh including his mama.

"What about N.W.A.?" T.C. shouted feeling like that was a good choice.

"What that mean bro, niggas with attitude?" Rob asked.

T.C. replied, "Na we got to put our own twist on it. We should call it Niggas with Ambition."

"I'm feeling that," Rob replied as he pounded T.C.'s fist.

"Man N.W.A.? Hell na, we don't got no jerry curls and this for damn sure not Compton," J.B. remarked over Malachi's laughter.

Rob and T.C. both looked at Malachi frowning their faces because he was laughing so hard.

"You laughing Mal but you ain't came up with nothing," T.C. stated.

"You right but I got a name for the squad." Malachi paused for a second as his demeanor became serious again. "F.M.B.. Yeah, that's it. It should be F.M.B.."

"What that stand for bro?" Rob questioned curiously.

"It stand for forever my brother."

"Yeah, I'm feeling that," T.C. replied. Rob thought about it and then shook his head in agreeance.

"Yeah, that's 100 bro. I'm feeling it too!" They all turned to J.B. anticipating another silly remark.

Instead, J.B. raised his arms up in a flexing position and yelled out the phrase "F.M.B. for life!" His voice was so loud it echoed throughout the gymnasium. Big Rob walked up as J.B. yelled out F.M.B.

"What F.M.B. mean?" Big Rob asked.

"It mean forever my brother. That's our new name for the squad," Rob said answering his daddy.

"That's live, I like that. Y'all rolling with me to LaRosa's? Coach Joe and me gone treat everybody for that epic championship win."

"Oh yeah, we in the Caddy truck Big Rob," T.C. said ecstatically.

"Is that cool Jade?" Big Rob asked Mama J.

"That's cool. I have to work third shift tonight, so I won't be able to make it."

"Go ahead and get to that money," Big Rob replied.

Mama J cracked a smile as she said, "You know it."

The four of them grabbed their gym bags and walked towards the gym exit. The amount of handshakes and "good game" remarks were overwhelming as they walked to Big Rob's truck. One man separated himself from the crowd and made a valiant effort to shake all of their hands including Big Rob's and Mama J's. He pulled a clean 100-dollar bill out of his pocket and handed it to Malachi who was the closest to him.

"Make sure y'all split this up evenly and make sure Heavy gets his cut also."

"What's this for?" little Rob asked confused as to why he was giving them money.

"Y'all boys won me 500 dollars today. I had a bet with somebody else that y'all was gone get the win. When J.B. hit the game winner, I made dude pay up asap," the man affirmed in a high-pitched voice.

The four of them looked at each other still astonished that the man was breaking bread with them.

"Shut, bra we should be getting four hundred dollars and you should only be getting a hundred. We the ones who was on the court putting the work in!" T.C. iterated sharply.

The man looked at T.C. like he was half crazy. "Na young buck, if I never would have initiated the bet none of us would be getting paid right now!"

"It's cool bro. Thanks for showing us love," Malachi spoke extending his hand to the man to exchange dap.

"I don't see why no grown ass man betting on my son's anyway! They not playing in the damn NBA," Mama J vented with an attitude.

"Come on Jade, you know wherever sports is being played, it's most likely some type of money or gambling involved," Big Rob spoke walking to the driver side of his car.

Mama J flared her nostrils up at Big Rob in response to what he said. "Whatever! I will see y'all when I get off in the morning." She gave her son Jerome a kiss and walked to her car.

"Shotgun!" Rob yelled as he hopped into the passenger seat of his daddy's candy painted blue Escalade.

Big Rob had his truck sitting on 26-inch rims with pitch black tint on his windows. His interior was coated with all leather seats with 10-inch TV's in the headrests. The 380 handgun was partly visible being tucked in a space on the right side of his driver's seat. Big Rob started the car mashing down on the gas making his duel pipes roar. He turned on some old school 8ball & MJG to the maximum volume as they proceeded to the next destination. The four of them loved riding with Big Rob not only because he was Rob's father but because he was one of the most notorious figures in the city of Cincinnati.

Big Rob was 38 years old, 6'5 in height and weighed about 250 pounds. He rocked an even-Steven haircut and was known for wearing extravagant iced out jewelry that attracted a lot of attention. If one was being stereotypical he definitely fit the image of a major drug dealer, which he was. Everyone knew who Big Rob was. He carried the reputation of being one of the biggest cocaine distributors not only in Ohio but the Midwest. He was always on the move and every time the young men were with him they felt like they were with a celebrity.

"So how y'all feel winning it all this year?" Big Rob asked lowering his music volume.

"It feel good. We definitely had to grind it out this year," T.C. replied first.

"Big Rob since we the champs and all, can you buy us a couple bottles of champagne, so we can pop some bottles?" J.B. asked confidently.

Big Rob looked in his rear-view mirror locking eyes with J.B. "Jerome Messiah Barnes if you don't shut ya young ass up. I'll buy you young kings some wine coolers and y'all can pop them!" Big Rob exclaimed making everyone laugh. "How you feel back there Malachi?"

"I feel like it was God destined for us to win it all this year, especially after that loss we took last year in the championship," Malachi answered.

"Well, that's the true mark of a champion. Every man takes a loss, but you validate what type of man you are by how you bounce back from defeat," Big Rob explained giving them wisdom. The young adolescents looked at Coach Joe & Big Rob as father figures taking heed to every piece of advice they gave.

-

"Man where y'all been at?" I thought y'all might have went to play another game," Coach Joe said in a joking manner.

Big Rob and the F.M.B. clique walked into the LaRosa's dining area as the rest of the team waited for them. Coach Joe and Big Rob went in half on buying every player on the team their own personal large pizza. Seeing everyone was present Coach Joe decided to go ahead and pray over the food.

Coach Joe cleared his throat. "Lord we thank you for this food and for this day. We thank you for prospering this team to stick together and win a championship. I thank you for every player and parent on this team. Amen."

"Good prayer coach," J.B. spoke already devouring his pizza.

"Boy you couldn't wait until I got done praying. Damn!"

"The Lord knoweth my heart," J.B. said in a joking manner.

"You better stop playing with the Lord!" one of the player's mamas said giving J.B. a serious look.

Coach Joe stood up as everyone filled their plates with pizza. "I just want to say to my team that I am proud of you. I admire you guy's hard work and dedication this season. I have watched all of you evolve on and off the court. I look to all you young men as sons and any of you can personally come to me for anything. I love all of you."

"We love you too coach," the players and parents repeated simultaneously.

"Do you need anything else sir?" the young waitress asked Coach Joe.

"No mam, I think we're good for right now."

"Okay sir, I'll be back to check on you guys."

As the young waitress walked away, T.C. made sure he made eye contact with her, making her smile at him.

"Nigga you can't get her T," Heavy challenged stuffing a piece of pepperoni pizza in his mouth.

"Who said I was trying to get her bro?"

"Man, you dang near stared her down," Heavy replied.

"Yeah, you know T be thirsty. He don't got any game for real," Rob spoke as if he was challenging his brother also.

T.C. looked at Rob with a stale expression on his face. "More game then you nigga!" he replied.

"Don't none of y'all got more game then big Mal," Malachi elaborated chiming in.

"Yeah, yeah it ain't nothing. I bet y'all I get her number before we leave. I put my twenty on it!" T.C. pulled out his twenty-dollar bill and slapped it on the table like he was playing dominos.

Rob reached in his pocket and threw his forty dollars on the table. "I bet twenty you can't and another twenty that I get her friend that's working with her!"

T.C. turned to Malachi and the rest of his teammates. "Y'all hear him though? He flexing like he the man."

"I don't think either one of y'all gone get either one of them," Malachi spoke as he also pulled twenty dollars out of his pocket.

"Oh, you getting in this too bro?" T.C. inquired thinking Malachi was challenging him also.

"Nah bro, this for Heavy," Malachi confirmed as he slapped the twenty dollars into Heavy's hand.

"What's this for bro?" Heavy asked.

"Some dude after the game ran up to us saying he won five hundred dollars off of us winning the game. He broke us off a hundred and told us to split it five ways."

"Oh yeah, that's watsup!" Heavy commented with a smile on his face.

"One of y'all about to lose dough though. I don't know why y'all betting anyway. I'm the pretty boy out the squad," J.B. spoke rubbing the peach fuzz on his chin.

"Yeah alright, we gone see," T.C. commented ending the conversation temporarily.

"Mama Kelley can we stay at your house tonight?" Rob asked wrapping his arm around her shoulder.

"I don't care Rob, as long as it's all right with Joe," she replied.

Coach Joe wiped some of the pizza sauce from his mouth. "I don't care either, as long as y'all don't tear the house up. See if y'all daddy can drop y'all off. Kelley and I got a run to make before we go home."

"Pops can you take us over to Coach Joe spot?" Rob yelled to the other end of the table.

"I drove us over here, didn't I?" Big Rob asked rhetorically in a mild voice of anger. Big Rob was on the phone and his son knew better than to interrupt him. He knew his occupation and knew he was most likely conducting business if he was on the phone.

"In fact, we can roll out now," Big Rob said in a commanding voice.

Big Rob got up and the F.M.B. gang followed suit. They all gave dap to the other players and said their farewell to the other parents. T.C. walked past the waitress he had been staring down as if cupid had shot an arrow through his heart.

"See bro, I knew you wasn't gone bust a grape," Rob ranted after they had walked out of hearing distance of the young waitress.

"Men shut up. You ain't say nothing to her either!" T.C. said silencing Rob for the moment.

"Both of y'all talked all that stuff and didn't even shoot the shot. Both of y'all owe down!" Malachi vented in a rowdy voice.

Big Rob had let the four of them walk out. He stopped at the front counter giving the impression that he was purchasing something else. They all observed him from a distance as he talked to the young waitress.

Big Rob turned around and walked out of the restaurant turning to T.C. "I set it up for you. Now go ahead and shoot your shot young buck." T.C. looked a little hesitant but ended up taking out his six-piece gold grill and throwing it in the bottom of his mouth. He walked back through the door nervous but confident.

"Why you help him out Big Rob? He wasn't even gonna say nothing to her," J.B. questioned.

"Don't be no hater J. Everybody need a little help every once in a while. Now let's see if he can capitalize on his opportunity," Big Rob explained.

Rob walked a short distance behind T.C. to watch him in action. As T.C. approached the counter he was in awe of her appearance. Reading her name badge he seen her name was Kandi. Kandi was 5'6 with a caramel brown complexion. She had black hair that had tint of bronze in it that hung to her shoulder.

"Watup with you," Kandi said before T.C. was able to get a word out.

"I'm good. What up with you? Kandi that's a nice name," T.C. replied back trying to break the ice.

"Thank you and I'm ready to get off. Your coach told me that you like me. Is that true?" she asked as if she was interviewing him.

"Yeah, that's true. I haven't seen a face as pretty as yours in a while." T.C.'s statement made Kandi smile which helped boost his confidence. "Do you stay around here?" he asked her.

"Yup, I stay in Woodland. I just moved back out here from downtown. I used to go to elementary school out here. Where you stay at?" she asked returning the question back.

"I stay in Rolling Heights, right across the track." "Oh okay, that's what's up," she said smiling at him again.

"You got a number I can hit you up on?" T.C. asked pulling his phone out of his pocket.

"Yeah, it's 513-348-2402. Text me so I can save your number."

T.C. was feeling like he just hit the lotto on the inside as he put the number in his phone. "Ima definitely hit you up boo," he said smiling showing off his six-piece grill.

"Do your boy behind you like my cousin?" she asked referring to the other waitress.

"Who the dude with the braids?" T.C. mentioned as if he didn't know she was talking about Rob.

"Yeah, him right there." Kandi waved her hand towards Rob motioning him to come to the counter. "You like my cousin, don't you? Don't lie because we both already been seeing you look at her!"

"Yeah, I do," Rob tried to reply smoothly.

"That's what's up. Well her number is 513-348-9244. Make sure y'all hit us up."

"We definitely will boo," T.C. voiced as he seen her manager start to walk up. T.C. & Rob both walked out of the restaurant feeling like players.

"Bro they both super thick," Rob boasted.

"Yeah, they both power ball thick but you owe down bra. I won the bet!"

"What you mean bro! I got her cousin number too, just like I said I was. I ain't lose nothing, fuck u mean!" Rob vented with passion.

"Man, your Big Meech looking ass wouldn't have won nothing if I never would have started talking to Kandi. You was just standing there looking silly!" T.C. proclaimed.

"Ay, get y'all asses in the car!" Big Rob shouted from his driver's side window.

T.C. and Rob got into the back with J.B. because Malachi was already sitting in the front. "Ay, who won that bet? Tell this fool I won that bet Mal," T.C. spoke as he hit Malachi's shoulder.

"I don't know. J who you think won?" Malachi questioned with a smirk on his face.

"Let me first say this! Neither one of y'all scrubs got more chicks than J, but I don't know who won honestly. Both of y'all got they numbers, right?"

"Yeah, we both did," Rob remarked. Rob wasn't mad, but his yellow face started to turn red from the disagreement.

"Let's ask the head honcho Big Rob. Big Rob who you think won?" J.B. asked seeking counsel from the OG.

Big Rob took his time to respond as he moved the red Bic lighter in a back and forth rotation over his freshly rolled blunt. "If you ask me neither one of y'all won," Big Rob confirmed as he lit his blunt.

"How is that?" J.B. commented curiously trying to decode Big Rob's logic.

"Because neither one of them won off their own strength. If I never would have assisted T, he never would have talked to shorty. As for Rob he wasn't about to bust a grape until he seen T was about to get the number. T fed off of my energy and Rob fed off of my energy. So, in all essence both of yall little niggas owe me!" Big Rob took a strong hit from the blunt and let out a couple of coughs.

"You good Big Rob?" Malachi asked as he seen Big Rob's body jolt back and forth from the weed.

Big Rob let out a couple of more coughs. "I'm good. This that thunder! You hear me!"

"So, we both got to pay you daddy?" Rob asked from the backseat.

"Na, son I don't want your money. I need y'all to take heed and listen to what I'm about to tell y'all though."

Big Rob took another hit from the blunt as he stopped at the red light. He turned his left turn signal preparing to turn into the Woodland community.

"Right now, y'all are young and really haven't got your dick wet yet. The four of you are going to have more than your fair share of women. Women come a dime a dozen and I don't want anybody in this car falling out over a woman. In fact, the only women y'all should ever put before F.M.B. is y'all mamas, and future wives. Y'all hear me?" Big Rob looked in his rear-view mirror and then turned to look at Malachi to make sure he had their full attention.

"Yeah, we feel you," Malachi answered as he looked at Big Rob's ketchup red eyes. The rest of them responded with the same reply as Malachi.

Malachi turned and looked out the window as they rode to his house. The song "We Gone Make it" by Jadakiss and Styles P was playing through the speakers. Malachi was envisioning himself in the NBA with a Los Angeles Lakers jersey on, his favorite team. The vision was so vivid to him that he started to think it had already came to pass until the pause of the song threw him out of his trance. It was so much smoke in the car that Malachi knew he had caught some serious contact and was more than likely high. Regardless of the influence of the marijuana the drive to achieve his vision was strong in his heart and he knew God himself had put it there.

"Rob, call me in the morning. I'ma probably have you help your grandma out with some yard work early tomorrow."

"Alright daddy, I will," his son replied as they pulled into Malachi's driveway.

"Yall be safe and don't be getting into any trouble," were the last words of Big Rob before they hopped out of his truck. The growl of Big Rob's pipes on his Escalade dominated the quiet scenery of Woodland as he rode down the street.

I think I caught contact from all that loud smoke your daddy was boothing in the whip," Malachi said turning towards Rob.

"I think all of us did. Shit it felt like I needed a gas mask!" J.B. added in.

Rob was laughing as he said, "Man y'all know how my daddy do. He a stoner!"

"We all little faded but that's not no excuse for me busting y'all asses on this 2K!" T.C. boasted strongly as they entered the three-story house.

"You ain't said nothing but a word T! We can get it in. Just make sure y'all high asses don't knock nothing over in the house. Y'all already know my mama be trippin," Malachi spoke walking up the steps to his room. Malachi turned on his PS4. "Who want it on these sticks?" Malachi yelled out.

T.C. always accepting a challenge picked up the joysticks. "Who you got Mal?" he asked.

"It don't matter. I should bust you with the Bulls, but Ima run you with his squad." Malachi pointed to the Kobe Bryant poster that was on his wall next to the Michael Jordan poster.

"Both you and T wack for real," J.B. said talking shit.

"Don't worry you gone get this work too bro," T.C. voiced cutting his eyes over at J.B.

The game started and at the end of the first quarter the score was 20 to 15 in favor of Malachi. "This game trash for real!" Rob spoke standing up with a basketball in his hand.

T.C. paused the game and said, "We can get it in on the real court sap! The real court ain't nothing but five minutes away down the street."

"Let's go then!" Rob replied.

The teenagers ran down the steps outside into the humid August air. "Me and Rob vs. you and Malachi," J.B. selected as they stepped onto the cement court.

"Ball up then," Malachi yelled as he squared up with Rob to play defense on him.

It was eleven pm at night, but the crew played hard under the court night lights like it was one pm in the afternoon. They lived to play basketball. Basketball was life for them.

First quarter of Sophomore year

The first day of school was exactly what they had been anticipating. They were only sophomores, but they felt like the school was already theirs. Their prestigious reputation was already well known in the school and had started to spread city wide.

"Damn summer went to quick. We back in here already," Rob commented as they coasted through the main hallway.

"We fresh as hell though, so I'm not even tripping," J.B. spoke brushing his hair.

J.B. had a fresh bald fade. Malachi had a fresh even Steven cut. Rob braids were fresh and T.C. had some newly twisted short dreads. The four of them had on black t shirts with the letters "F.M.B." spray painted on them in gold. All of them had the new all black Jordan editions of the 10's that had just been released.

"T, I thought you said you wasn't copping the tens because you said ain't have the dough?" Rob asked.

"Bro you know Ima hustler. I sold my last pair of J's and mowed a couple of lawns to come up with the dough."

"That's what's up!" Rob commented admiring his brother's hustle.

Changing the subject, J.B. asked what everybody's first class was as he stared at a group of senior girls walk by in short skirts.

"I gotta computer class," Malachi replied as he leaned up against a locker.

"I gotta computer class too bro," J.B. added.

"I got study hall," T.C. commented as bent down lacing up his Jordan sneakers.

"Shit, y'all lucky. I got environmental science," Rob spoke shaking his head as the bell rang for first period.

Noticing the main hallway was starting to clear out they gave each other dap and dispersed their separate ways. T.C. and J.B. yelled out their squad name "F.M.B." as they went down the hallway.

"What's up big bro," Malachi spoke extending his hand towards the upper classmen Sean Mays.

Locking hands with Malachi, Big Sean replied, "What up little bro. You good?"

"Yeah, Ima hundred. I'm on my way to this computer class."

"I hear you. So, you ready to run the court this year little bro?" Big Sean asked Malachi the question, but he already knew what type of mentality he played with.

"You already know Ima terrorize the court but it's your team as long as you here big bro. You already know that!"

"I know that, but I wouldn't be a true leader if I didn't pass the torch to you in the right way. You'll be passing it off to someone else in a couple years yourself."

Big Sean was 6'10 and weighed about 240 pounds. He had accepted a full scholarship to play for Ohio State. "Mark my words Malachi, they'll be calling you the greatest player to ever come through this school," Big Sean spoke with genuineness.

Malachi looked at Big Sean with a look of amazement at the words that he spoke.

"I'm serious little bro. I'm too real to sit here and gas you up. As long as you stay focused and don't get caught up in the bs that's gone come your way the next 3 years, you'll be cool."

"Ima definitely stay focused. Ball is all I know!" Malachi voiced.

"That's what I like to hear little bro," Big Sean responded extending his hand to dap Malachi's fist.

"I'ma holler at you Mal."

"Alright big bro."

Malachi walked to his first class with a strong vibration of confidence. It felt good to receive that type of love from somebody he looked up to on and off of the court.

-

The first day flew by and the main hallway was flooded with students as they prepared to get on their buses.

"What's up shorty, what's your name?" J.B. asked to a young redbone standing with her friend. She was smiling and he was smiling back at her as he stroked his hair with his brush.

"Look at J over there scheming," Rob said as him, T.C. and Malachi stood in the midst of the students.

"Shut, I'm bout to go get her friend," T.C. commented fixing his black Nike headband he was wearing around his dreads. He wasted no time because in the blink of an eye he was standing next to J.B. running game on her friend.

"What up Rob. You ready for Friday?" an unfamiliar face from the crowd asked him.

"Of course, I'm not bringing anything but the best out on the field!" Rob answered in a voice of surety.

Malachi looked at Rob waiting for the foreign face to leave before he spoke. "You sure you ready for Friday bro? I'm not doubting your skills but I'm just saying we been hooping all summer."

Rob looked at Malachi disturbed that his brother questioned his preparation. "Come on Mal, you know how I get down on that field. You and T.C. run the court but you know I'm king on the field," Rob confirmed with authority.

"I know you gone do your thing bro. I'm just making sure you on point," Malachi spoke in return.

J.B. and T.C. walked back over rejoining the conversation. "What's popping today?" T.C. questioned as the sun glistened off of his gold grill.

"We need to go over to the hood and get it in at the Dungeon. I know it's gone be thick outside today," Malachi spoke in anticipation to go the hoop court.

"Y'all go head and ball out. I'ma ring yall line after I get out of football practice," Rob spoke as he picked up his sports bag.

"Okay bro," they said as he walked away.

Malachi turned to J.B. and T.C. asking, "Y'all going to my spot? We can go to the hood from there."

"That's cool. Ima run to the crib and change my clothes," J.B. affirmed as they started to get on the bus.

The bus ride was short as the community of Woodland was only about ten minutes away from the high school. "I'm about to change real quick and I'll be at your house in like twenty minutes bro," J.B. said as they exited the bus.

"Ay, bring some of your mama cookies when you come back out here. I know she got some on deck in the kitchen," T.C. shouted out.

"Na bro, make your own damn cookies!" J.B. replied back.

"Bring me some cookies nigga," T.C. repeated again jokingly.

"Na, I ain't bringing you no cookies bro but I got something else for you!" J.B. threw two quick slap punches at T.C. One of the slap punches missed T.C. but the second one grazed his face.

T.C. threw two slap punches in return before Malachi stepped in between the two of them. "Man gone head and shoot to the house! Y'all already know the court gone be thick," he told them.

As J.B. approached his doorstep he heard the vocals of Mary J Blige ringing from his mama's stereo speakers. Entering his house Mama J was sitting on the couch with a glass of wine.

"How was school J?" she asked him as she vibed to the song.

"It was cool. Here is a list of all my classes." He handed her his course schedule and ran upstairs to change his clothes. He threw on some red hoop shorts, a black t shirt and some old Nike hoop shoes he had from a couple of years back.

"This is a solid schedule. All college prep and advanced classes. If you make all A's and B's this year that will help position you to start receiving scholarship offers next year Jerome." Mama J took a sip of her wine as she continued to look at the paperwork.

"I'ma definitely be on it mama. You know your son cheap so I'm in no way trying to pay for college!" Jerome's statement made Mama J laugh.

"Right, son! You know our motto. Educate, accelerate and elevate!" she stated as she stood up to give her son a high five.

Mama J was only 5'3 so she had to reach up to her son's 6-foot frame. She was an attractive brown skin woman with black orangish hair that hung to her shoulder. She took on the responsibility of raising J.B. by herself ever since he had been born.

"What kind of cupcakes is these mama?'" J.B. asked he walked into the kitchen.

"Vegan cupcakes J. I didn't use any dairy products in them," she commented.

J.B. stuffed one of the cupcakes into his mouth. "They good ma. I'm about to head to the court."

"Okay, be safe son. I might go into work tonight but dinner is already made."

As he was leaving out he noticed a pack of Newport 100's on the table. "Ma, I thought you quit smoking?"

"Stay out of my business J. I got this!" she said projecting her voice over the music.

J.B. walked out of the house shaking his head. He hated the fact that his mama was still smoking cigarettes. He would have thought his mom would be more cautious because his grandpa had passed away from cancer a couple years prior.

-

Malachi and T.C. were sitting on the porch waiting for J.B. as he walked up. T.C. had changed into some hoop shorts and just left his school clothes at Malachi's house. Coach Joe and Mama Kelley didn't mind him leaving T.C. leaving his clothes there because they often helped out Grandpa Gus and Grandma Lois, T.C.'s grandparents.

"We ready to roll out?" T.C. asked dribbling the ball through his legs.

"Yeah, let's go," Malachi replied already walking up the street.

The journey from Woodland to Rolling Heights was a short one. It took about five minutes by car and about twenty minutes walking. They approached the train tracks that separated the two communities quickly. The humid August weather had them sweating halfway into their walk.

"It's hotter than the devil's nipples out here. We need a car sap!" J.B. said as he brushed his hair.

"Man put that damn brush down. You ugly no matter how many times you brush your head!" T.C. commented with a grin on his face.

"Yeah, whatever bro. I got that pretty boy Floyd swag! Don't get the big head just cause you got them short ass dreads re twisted," J.B. mentioned firing back his verbal assault.

They walked upon the first corner store in the hood. "Let's hit the store real quick y'all," J.B. suggested.

Malachi turned around with the ball in his hand. "Na bro, let's keep it moving. We can hit the store on our way back." J.B. listened to Malachi and decided to stay with his team.

The distance from Woodland to Rolling Heights was a short but observing the change in the scenery was inevitable. Walking past the corner store there were numerous Flamin Hot Cheeto bags, Grippo's bags and empty cigarillo wrappers scattered on the ground. The air was a little denser and the houses were closer together looking more run down. Some of the cars sitting in the driveway were tireless cars sitting on top of bricks. Passing Terrance Street, a main street in the community they saw a flood of people. Most of them were young males and females trying to be on the scene.

Walking past the block they heard shouts of "Watup y'all". T.C. knowing the most people in the neighborhood replied, "Watup, watup F.M.B. nigga." T.C. stayed two streets over with his grandma and grandpa. Walking down the hill to Memphis Street they seen the local bootleg man in the hood making back and forth rides transporting local residents. Memphis Street was the street the Dungeon was on and also the prime location to get whatever you wanted. Memphis Street provided everything from drugs, basketball, gambling, women and even a healthcare clinic at the end of the street.

"What up Heavy." "Watup Mal. Y'all bout to hoop?" Heavy asked.

"You know it bro," T.C. answered as he dribbled the ball behind his back.

"You gone get out there and hoop with us?" Malachi asked Heavy.

"Na, I got to get the rest of this pack off first." Heavy was referring to the pack of weed he had concealed in his pocket.

"What your big ass gone do if they raid the block? You know you too slow to run nigga," J.B. spoke with a serious face.

"Everybody fast when it come to getting away from them blue uniforms plus I know where to run to!" Heavy explained as if he had been hustling for years.

"Man, I bet if I hopped out here on the block I would have this whole strip jumping!" T.C. stated boldly having dope boy ambitions.

As he was talking an all red candy painted Monte Carlo pulled up behind them. The tinted window on the passenger side of the Monte Carlo rolled down.

"What y'all young negroes out here doing?" It was Heavy's brother Tank that spoke from the driver seat.

"I'm out here trying to get it bro. They out here trying to hoop," Heavy said referring to his three friends.

"Oh yeah, well you should be out here hopping too nigga. How much you got left in your pack?" Tank asked turning down the Gucci Mane playing in his radio.

"I got about a twenty-bag left," Heavy replied.

Tank reached in his pocket and pulled out a twenty-dollar bill and handed it to Heavy through his passenger window. Heavy threw the last of his pack in the car to his big brother.

"Now get off this block and go hoop!" Tank commanded as he drove his car down the street parking it. Tank knew his little brother wanted to be just like him. Tank earned his nickname for taking over and moving people out of the way. He was respected in Rolling Heights for being an enforcer and supreme drug dealer.

-

"Let's hit this court though," Malachi commented seeing that a game was just ending.

They walked onto the court that was surrounded by a tall caged fence on all four sides of it. "Y'all young boys don't want this work!" an old head on the court shouted.

"What's up old head," T.C. hollered back in retaliation.

The old heads looked at each other with a smirk on their faces. "These young boys probably can't even touch rim yet," one of the old heads said laughing.

Malachi, J.B., and T.C. looked at each other almost in disbelief at how reckless the old heads were insulting their skills.

"Yeah right, me and bro will out jump anybody out here right now!" Malachi boasted arrogantly. He was referring to him and T.C.

"Oh yeah, you boys can jump huh? Well grab these twenty dollar bills off the top of the backboard. To make it even better, if y'all can grab em off, y'all can keep the money!" the old head proclaimed.

The challenge was too good to pass up, plus their reputation was on the line, so they had to accept the challenge. "Shit, that ain't nothing! I'll jump first and then bro will jump after me," Thomas elaborated tightening up his sneakers.

The old head who made the bet started to laugh. "Na young blood, y'all jumping at the same time. We'll set the twenty-dollar bills on opposite sides of the rims." Somebody from the hood had climbed up onto the rim and placed the bills directly on top of it. The man put a quarter on top of both the twenties to make sure they didn't fall off.

"Go head and snatch that shit!" J.B. shouted having full confidence in his brothers.

The participants in the dice game that was going down on the outside of the court had took a pause to watch Malachi and T.C. attempt the difficult bet. T.C. and Malachi looked at each other as they both lined up on opposite sides of the three-point line. Both of them took off running at the same time. Taking off for flight they both soared in the air like Vince Carter in his prime. Malachi stretched his right arm out grabbing the twenty with his hand. T.C.

was a half second behind him focusing in on the bill, grabbing it with his left hand.

"Oh shit, oh shit," were the yells from the crowd as Malachi and T.C. landed on the ground. J.B. ran up to Malachi and dabbed. Heavy ran up to T.C. and hit the dab with him.

"Anymore bets? Who else wanna lose they job money today?" T.C. shouted testing the whole hood. Malachi and T.C. fist bumped each other boasting over the fact that they just made an almost impossible bet look easy.

"Yall young boys still ain't shit! Check the ball up. Let's get this real game started!" the old head shouted out irately.

The four older men lined up as Heavy and the three brothers matched up on who they wanted guard. The dice game that had paused had now resumed again. The game started off on the physical tip because the older crew was still upset for losing the bet. Every point the young crew scored was a jump shot. It was almost impossible for them to get a shot off in the paint because they got fouled every time they drove the ball in. Heavy and J.B. grabbed most of the rebounds as they stayed down in the post wrestling with the stronger old heads.

"Y'all gone score in the paint or shoot jump shots all game? Soft ass young boys!" T.C.'s defender shouted out.

The trash talk had made T.C. irate. "Ball bro," T.C. called out to Malachi as he walked the ball up the court.

Malachi passed the ball to T.C. He caught the ball squaring up with his opponent. He drove to his right side and spinned off of his defender to the middle of the paint. It was a nice move, nevertheless, he was met by a massive body knocking him to the ground.

"Foul!" T.C. yelled out as he got up from the ground. The whole game stopped.

"Hell na, that wasn't no foul! You just took some contact!" his defender spoke fiercely.

"Man, that was a foul. That's why I called the shit!" T.C. exclaimed with a voice of hostility.

"Give bro his foul call," Heavy said joining the argument.

Aside from the feud on the court, there was a bigger conflict going down in the dice game. J.B. overheard someone accusing somebody of cheating them out of money. Between the hoop court and chaos from the dice game nobody could hardly hear each other. Out of nowhere a sudden "bang, bang, bang" sounded off! Three loud shots rang out which sounded like they came from a cannon. It was pandemonium as everyone at the dice game diversified their own separate ways. The players on the court got down unsure of where exactly the gun shots were coming from. "Bang, bang!" Two more shots rang out not quite as loud as the first ones but they still had everyone paranoid. Car tires started to screech as some of the parked cars started to pull off rapidly.

"Y'all good?" Malachi hollered out to his teammates.

"We good. Let's get up through!" T.C. yelled noticing more people were starting to evacuate the vicinity.

The three of them got up and ran following T.C. to his grandma house but Heavy went his own separate way. Running as fast as they could, they heard four more shots pop off which sounded like they were still down near Memphis Street.

"Oh shit!" J.B. yelled out dropping to the ground as if he had been hit.

"J, you good?" Malachi asked in a worried state.

"Yeah, I'm good," J.B. responded.

"Well come on then nigga!" Malachi instructed.

-

Finally arriving at T.C.'s house they ran through the door like they were running backs.

"What in God's green earth is going on out there?" Grandma Lois asked. She came out of the kitchen with her bible in one hand and 22 caliber pistol in the other hand.

"Grandma why you got your pistol out?" T.C. asked.

"Well baby, I heard shots so I was ready to let shots go off my damn self. I was praying to the Lord that I didn't have to do that though."

Malachi and J.B. let out a slight laugh but they knew Grandma Lois was as serious as a heart attack. Grandma Lois was only 5'2 and about 140 pounds. She had grayish black hair and a sweet grandma voice.

Grandma Lois put her possessions away as she asked, "You all wasn't involved in that mess out there today was y'all?"

"No, mam. It did get crazy out there on the court today though," Malachi told her.

"I'm just glad you boys is safe. Y'all want something to eat. I made meatloaf, cabbage and cornbread."

"Now grandma you already know we hungry plus you got the best cornbread I ever had," J.B. told her as they walked in the kitchen. J.B.'s compliment made the elderly lady grin.

"Thanks Jerome, you always have the nicest things to say. Thomas go downstairs in the basement and see if your grandpa ready to eat."

T.C. walked through the kitchen to the basement door. Walking down the stairs his ears were overwhelmed by the obnoxious snoring coming from Grandpa Gus. Grandpa Gus was leaned back in his all black recliner with his mouth wide open. His massive 6'2, 230-pound frame filled all of the recliner. Seeing that Grandpa Gus was sleep T.C. went back up the steps.

"He sleep grandma, knocked out," T.C. said walking back in the kitchen.

Grandma Lois stood over her stove shaking her head. "Lawd, that's all that man do is sleep and watch them damn sport shows." Grandma Lois prepared their plates with the meatloaf, cabbage, mac and cheese and cornbread. She complimented their meals with cold glasses of lemonade.

"What the hell happened down there at the court? Something went left at that dice game," Malachi said.

"I don't know but I looked over and seen at least four stacks on the ground. Whenever it's some major dough involved somebody always feel played," J.B. added in.

"That's why I don't bet. I'd rather just hustle for mine," T.C. spoke stuffing his mouth with cornbread.

"I don't mind betting. I just try to make sure the odds are in my favor," J.B. said.

"That's the thing though, in the hood, the odds is never in anybody's favor," T.C. spoke again.

Malachi nodded his head in agreeance as his android phone started to ring. "Watup Rob," Malachi said speaking to Rob.

"Nothing just got out of practice. What's the word?" Rob asked.

"We at Grandma Lois house smashing something to eat right now. They was down there shooting at the court today."

"Yeah, I heard they was popping off, you know word spread fast. They said Tank & Cory G got into it over some dough," Rob added.

"Yeah, we really ain't get to see what exactly went down because we was on the court running the score up on some old heads when everything popped off."

"Speaking of that! I heard you and T was getting y'all Jordan on out there, grabbing money off of backboards and shit!" Rob expressed.

Malachi had put Rob on speakerphone so Jerome and Thomas could hear the convo also.

"Man what! These dudes was out there looking like them dudes from the old school And 1 highlights!" J.B. exclaimed giving them high compliments.

"Real spill, we was out there getting our Earl Manigoat on," T.C. commented paying homage to the vintage basketball legend.

"That's what's up though. I'ma holla at you when we get to school tomorrow though," Rob spoke.

"Okay bro, we'll see you tomorrow," Malachi spoke hanging up the phone.

"Let's head back over to Woodland before it get dark out here. Y'all know the police be tripping when the sun go down out here," T.C. mentioned finishing the plate.

"Y'all leaving?" Grandma Lois asked from her sewing chair.

T.C. bent down to kiss his grandma on her cheek. "Yeah, we bout walk over back to Woodland grandma."

"Okay, make sure you boys be safe. I love you all."

"We love you too," the three of them said as they walked through the screen door out onto the porch.

All of the mayhem from earlier had settled but the air was still hot even though the sun was setting. They walked at a mild pace but stayed alert knowing that anything could pop off at any time.

"See this why we need the strap. What if some drama popped off our way?" T.C. asked in a rant as they walked past the block on Terrance Street.

"Shit, I got these hands if anybody want smoke," Malachi mentioned putting his hands up in a boxing posture.

"We all got hands but our hands can't beat bullets Mal," T.C. confirmed in a grave voice.

"He right though, our hands can't hit harder than bullets and damn sure not faster than bullets. Only thing is that with guns come cases and dead bodies. I know I'm not ready to catch a body honestly," J.B. commented sharing his perspective.

"As long as we ride for each other, we unbeatable no matter what extent we got to go to when we got drama," Malachi spoke validating the squad's loyalty. The three of them finished out their journey politicking on how to handle the various issues in the street.

-

The first day of school flew by. It was Friday and the last class of the day was now in session. Rob, T.C. and Malachi all shared the same African American studies class taught by Mr. Smith. Mr. Smith turned around from the whiteboard fixing his black tie.

He asked his predominantly black class, "So class have you learned anything valuable from this class this week?" T.C. raised his hand. "Go head Mr. Crawford," he said pointing to T.C.

"Mr. Smith why you call us kings and queens when it says in these books our history started off in slavery?"

Mr. Smith grinned at his student. "I am glad you asked that Thomas. You see the history books we have here in America never say that our history started there. Certain historians have only chosen to start our story of African history here when we were already captive in slavery under Europeans. You see students before we touched these shores our ancestors had countless empires and civilizations in Africa. We created fully operating civilizations, understood the laws of science, mathematics and astrology. In fact, Greeks and other groups of Europeans came to Egypt to be taught in Egyptian schools."

Mr. Smith raised his eyebrows with a slight grin on his face as he knew that he had dropped new found knowledge on the young students. The students looked with faces of amazement in reaction to what he spoke. Not too long after the bell rung and the students snapped out of their state of awe.

"Rob, Malachi, Thomas do you have a minute?" Mr. Smith questioned as the other students dashed for the door.

"Watup, up Mr. Smith?" T.C. inquired interested.

Mr. Smith was sure all of the students had cleared out of the room before he started to talk. "I know you all are great athletes and most likely are going to the next level athletically but I want to urge you to study your history and acquire knowledge of self. As a black man it is critical that you know your true roots and identity."

"My daddy always tells us that it's important that we know who we are and where we came from," Malachi chimed in.

Mr. Smith nodded his in agreeance as he looked up to the teenagers. Mr. Smith was a smaller man standing at 5'6 and was yellow in complexion. He always kept a well-groomed beard and a nice even-Steven haircut.

"He is right. Whether you have locks like you Thomas, a haircut like you Malachi or braids like you Robert, we are all kings. It is imperative that we conduct ourselves like the royalty we are." Changing the topic, he directed his attention towards Rob. "You ready to lead the team to victory tonight Rob?"

"You know I am. I been waiting all week for this game," Rob spoke confidently.

"That's what I like to hear. I'll see you kings at the game tonight."

"Alright Mr. Smith," the teens said walking out of the classroom. J.B. was waiting for them as they stepped into the hallway.

"I was wondering where y'all was at. Everybody that one-way hype about the game tonight."

"Oh yeah, what everybody saying about the game tonight?" Rob asked knowing J.B. would tell him the truth.

"Real talk bro, everybody know u can ball but then again you still a sophomore starting varsity tonight. You already know you gotta ball out to shut the haters up," J.B. mentioned.

Walking through the midst of the thick hallway crowd the four of them could feel people's attention shifting towards them. "Throw a touchdown tonight for me Rob," a random girl shouted giving him a hug.

"I will baby," Rob replied not shying away from the attention.

"Ay Rob, you gone get the W tonight for us?" another random student approached asking.

Rob paused, "No doubt we gone get it bro!"

"You not nervous, are you?" the miscellaneous upperclassmen asked.

T.C. sensing that the upperclassman was trying to throw shade replied before Rob could. "Na bro, he not nervous. My nigga gone put up hall of fame numbers. You can miss us with that sucka shit!"

Feeling the hostility in T.C.'s voice the upperclassmen responded saying, "My bad bro, I was just asking. What you gonna do on that court this year Malachi?"

Malachi looked at the student with a stale face. "I'm gone ball out bra, me and my squad," Malachi vouched with surety referring to F.M.B..

"That's what's up. I can feel that," the upperclassmen responded. He lifted his hand to shake theirs but nobody returned the favor so he just walked off.

"Who the hell was dude? I wasn't feeling his energy from jump," Malachi pondered.

"Just another hater and nothing but more motivation for me to run that stat sheet up tonight. What y'all about to do?" Rob asked.

"I'm about to slide to my grandma house and chill for a little bit.

Mal, is your pops still gone be able to pick me up for the game?" T.C. asked.

"He should. Just be ready about seven."

"Cool, just shoot me a text when y'all on the way," T.C. said starting to walk towards his bus.

"We a see you after the game bro," J.B. said to Rob as him and Malachi got onto the bus. Rob saluted them and walked back into the school.

-

Malachi walked through the doors being greeted by his parents dancing in their living room. The old school 80's song "Computer Love" was playing off of Mama Kelley's Ipad through their surround sound speakers. Malachi started to laugh as he seen his parents slow grind and sing the lyrics to the song.

"Hey son, you home a little early, aren't you?" Mama Kelley asked.

"Na ma, I'm here at the regular time. I didn't expect to walk in on an episode of Soul Train though!"

"Son, if you pay attention to your daddy I'll teach you how to sweep your woman off her feet," Coach Joe spoke as he gripped Mama Kelly's waist.

Malachi stood stationary taking in the moment of seeing his parents enjoy each other's company. "Daddy you ain't sweeping nothing dressed like that!"

Coach Joe had on an old white beater and dingy old grey sweats which was his typical lounge wear around the house. Coach Joe waived Malachi off as he walked up the steps to his room. Tired from the first school week he walked into his room plopping face down on his bed.

-

"Wake up, wake up boy. We bout to be late for the game," Coach Joe said shaking his son by his shoulders. Coach Joe was already dressed wearing his Flyer team apparel with the Flyer hat to top it off.

Hopping up from his bed, Malachi asked, "What time is it daddy?"

"It's about seven pm. Don't we still got to get J.B. and T.C. still?"

"Yeah, we do. I'ma be ready in about 5 minutes."

"Alright, I'll be waiting in the car," Coach Joe told him leaving the room.

Malachi checked his phone and seen he had two missed calls. One from T.C. and the other from J.B. He went to his closet and threw on his red and black Akoo shirt with his red and black Nikes. He grabbed his wallet off the dresser before he jetted outside where his dad was waiting for him in his Dodge Durango. Jerome was already on the porch waiting, gliding the brush over his hair as they pulled into his driveway.

"Dang Coach Joe you almost made us late for the game," J.B. mentioned as he got in the car.

"Blame that on sleepy head over here," Coach Joe commented slapping his son on the head.

"I hope bro put up big numbers tonight," Malachi commented from the front seat.

Coach Joe slowed down to cross the tracks to Rolling Heights. "He will be fine out there tonight. Y'all know football is Rob's better sport anyway."

"Yup! Rob live and breathe for football. Mal and T live and breathe for hoop. I'm the super smart nigga who happened to just be athletic," J.B. spoke analyzing the whole crew.

Coach Joe honked the horn twice pulling up in front of Thomas grandparent's house. T.C. came running out like he was running from the police in his all black tee.

Slamming the door, he yelled, "Watup with y'all!"

Coach Joe looked in his rear-view mirror at him. "I know what's not up. You slamming my damn car door like you crazy!"

"My bad coach, I ain't mean to," T.C. mentioned in a calmer voice.

Coach Joe turned up the ESPN radio station as he drove to the stadium. Arriving at the stadium the parking lots was thick with cars parked back to back. It had to be at least 1500 people in attendance at the game. Coach Joe bought all of their tickets as they walked in.

"I should have played football this year. I definitely could have been out there playing receiver," J.B. elaborated.

Coach Joe turned and looked at J.B. "Yeah, you should have. You got some good hands on you and the build for it."

T.C. butted in the conversation. "This dude not bout to touch the field. He already think he a pretty boy."

"You exactly right T, plus I'm cool on practicing twice a day in the summer!" J.B. exclaimed as they walked up the bleacher steps.

Malachi spotted Big Rob waiving his hand at the top of the bleachers. "There go Big Rob y'all," he said.

"We can go sit with Rob at the top so we can get a good view of the game," Coach Joe instructed walking past the capacity crowd in the bleachers.

"Watup Joe! What it do!" Big Rob shouted over the noisy crowd. Big Rob was dressed in simple attire but was sporting an iced out watch that you only see rappers or flashy pro players wear.

"How much you want for that ice Big Rob?" J.B. questioned with a smirk on his face knowing he couldn't afford it.

"The price is irrelevant young g. You can get this watch if you put in the hard work for it. Before you ask though, yeah, these is real diamonds. I just copped it from my jeweler yesterday."

"Mann, I need your plug Big Rob!" T.C. added in. T.C. had a grin on his face but he was serious on the inside.

"Welcome to tonight's Friday night high school football game. Our own Princeton Bearcats are taking on the Winton Woods Tigers," the announcer on the intercom spoke overpowering everyone's personal conversations. "Let's give it up for our Bearcats." The Bearcats football team was lined up behind a long white paper sign that read "Go Bearcats" in red letters. They performed their notorious team chant before they stampeded through the long white paper sign like wild animals.

"That boy Rob super hype!" T.C. spoke looking at Rob run up and down the sideline hitting his teammate's shoulder pads.

"It looks like the Bearcats will be starting on their own twenty-yard line with Robert Pounds leading them down the field at quarterback," the commentator notified.

"F.M.B., F.M.B. Do your thang bro!" the three brothers shouted out.

The bright stadium lights made Rob look even more massive than he already was. Rob had grown and was now 6'3 weighing 195 pounds. He looked like a titan in his red and black uniform.

"Blue 42, blue 42, hike, hike," Rob yelled as his voice projected throughout the field. He handed the ball off to their running back who gained 3 yards. The next play the Bearcats ran a no huddle offense. Rob hiked the ball and faked the handoff to his running back. He pump faked like he was going to throw the ball to his left and rolled out the pocket to his right side cuffing the ball beginning to dash with it. Rob's braids that hung from under his helmet bounced around as he ran the ball.

"Pounds off to the 35, 40, 45, 50! Pounds to the Tigers 48-yard line being tackled by the Tigers safety," the announcer said.

"Good run Rob!" Coach Joe shouted from the bleachers.

The next play Rob completed a pass to one of his receivers for 8 yards. The Bearcats were moving easily down the field under Rob's leadership. On the next down he handed it off to his running back who rushed for 7 yards.

"The Bearcats are now on the Tigers 33-yard line, soon to be in field goal range," the commentator announced.

Between the crowd noise, coaches yelling and cheerleaders cheering it was extremely loud.

Walking up to his offensive line, Rob scoped the defense looking side to side. "Red 38, red 38, hike, hike!" he called out.

The center snapped the ball to him and he rolled out to his left scrambling from a defensive lineman who got a quick jump on the snap. He did a Barry Sanders juke on the bigger, slower, defensive lineman and threw a 6-yard pass to his tight end. His tight end ended up running down the field accumulating a 20-yard play. The crowd was ecstatic with energy and the bleachers were vibrating with the echoes of cowbells.

"The Bearcats are now on the Tigers 13-yard line approaching touchdown territory!" the commentator announced.

The Bearcats lined up in their offensive formation. Rob motioned to his right and pointed out a linebacker who was showing signs of blitzing. The ball snapped and Rob dropped back throwing a lob pass to the same tight end in the back of the end zone.

"Touchdown Bearcats! Robert Pounds with the thirteen-yard touchdown completion to his tight end Lee Whitfield!" the game commentator said with high energy.

Coach Joe turned to Big Rob. "That was a nice lob pass Rob just threw. Those lob passes not that easy to throw."

"It really was. We've been working on his lob passes and short passes whenever we could this past offseason. I told him if he wants to play on the next level he got to be accurate and able to read the field," Big Rob responded.

Halftime was quickly approaching and the Bearcats were in the lead 21 to 7. Rob had two touchdowns and fifty rushing yards. Even though their focus was on the game J.B., T.C. and Malachi couldn't help but notice two men at the bottom left bleachers. The two black men both randomly kept looking up in the section they were sitting in. One man was light skin with a thick mustache and stocky build. The other man was brown skin, skinny with no facial hair. Both men had on all black fitted hats.

"Who the hell is them randoms down there?" T.C. asked observing the two men.

"I don't know but they definitely suspect. Niggas sitting in the front row but keep on looking up in the bleachers," J.B. explained.

"Alright, it's halftime folks. Go to our concession stands for some delicious refreshments before we begin the third quarter," the announcer voiced.

"Y'all hungry? Get me a hot dog and a large ice water from the concession stand." Coach Joe pulled a wrinkled 20-dollar bill out of his pocket and handed it to his son.

"Large ice water?" What you on a diet coach?" J.B. asked.

Coach Joe and Big Rob started to laugh. "Na negro, I'm not on no diet. I'm getting older, I got to keep these fluids circulating in my body," Coach Joe said answering his question.

"We got you daddy," Malachi spoke.

A lot of the student body had already evacuated the bleachers to walk the stadium during halftime. Exiting the bleachers, they walked past the two suspicious men who had been watching them. One of them was on the phone talking and the light skin man looked at them awkwardly as they strolled past.

"Yeah, them dudes look super skept," Malachi said in a state of caution.

"Watup baby, why haven't you called me?" the waitress Kandi, T.C. had met at LaRosa's in the summer asked him.

"My bad boo I ain't still think you was feeling me," he replied.

Kandi wrapped her arms T.C. and hugged him. Whispering in his ear she spoke, "Really Thomas. We just had sex last week!" Kandi pushed T.C. off of him after she got done completing her sentence.

T.C. grabbed Kandi by the waist bringing her back in close. "You know I was just playing Kandi."

"Yeah, whatever!" she said rolling her eyes. "What up with y'all?" she asked turning her attention to Malachi and J.B.

"We good. I see you got my bro wrapped around your finger," J.B. commented sarcastically.

"You know it! He ain't going nowhere!" Kandi looked back at T.C. nudging him in his dreads.

"He a sucker for love," J.B. joked laughing. He was laughing but behind his laughter J.B. secretly had a strong crush on Kandi. He knew he could never admit that to anybody though. Malachi had ordered the food and came back with two hot dogs, an order of cheese nachos and two large cups of water.

"Damn fat ass! You got enough food?" Kandi asked being funny.

Malachi mean mugged her. "Shut up Kandi. You know you want some of these nachos." Malachi must have been reading her mind because not a second later Kandi was dipping one of the nachos into the thick nacho cheese. "Why you want some of my nachos though?

Your breath already smell like the relish I'm about to put on this hotdog!" Malachi said opening the condiment package.

Kandi's brown skin complexion started to blush as she laughed. "Aww, Malachi shut your Bill Bellamy looking ass up!" Everyone busted out in laughter as she fired back.

"Yeah bro, don't be capping on my boo, she can cap," T.C. mentioned kissing Kandi on the cheek.

Malachi paused from his laughter. "Nigga don't' try to get in your feelings now!" he yelled raising his voice.

The game announcer came back on the intercom notifying every one of the start of the third quarter.

J.B. and Malachi made their way back to the bleachers while T.C. stayed back occupied with Kandi. J.B. saw them kissing and started to envy T.C. He once again blocked out the weak thought and shifted his attention towards the field. Journeying back to their seats they passed the same two men. This time though the light skin man gave them a head nod as if he knew them. Malachi mean mugged while J.B. looked at the man with a stale face.

"What took y'all so long?" Big Rob asked as he grabbed the nachos from Malachi.

"That line was super long down there plus T.C. was all wrapped up with his girl down there," Malachi answered.

"What I tell y'all about letting them young girls get the best of y'all!" Big Rob commented with humor.

"Rob, you know they not gone learn until they get our age and these women take all they money!" Coach Joe spoke adding more humor. An older lady sitting below them had overheard him and turned around shaking her head. "It's the truth isn't it!" Coach Joe shouted as if he was responding to the ladies head gesture.

T.C. walked back up the bleachers rejoining the crew. "Coach Joe, Big Rob, aye y'all know who them two randoms are down there that keep looking up here?" T.C. stretched his arm out pointing out the two men with the fitted hats.

"I don't know who the hell they are. You got any clue who they are Rob?"

Big Rob stared down on the two men from the top of the bleachers with an eagle's eye view. The look on his face almost resembled that he knew exactly who they were. "I don't know who they are," he responded.

"Oh, well don't worry about them unless they say something to y'all," Coach Joe spoke focusing back on the game. The last two quarters of the game flew as the Princeton football team ran the score up 42 to 21. Rob had put up all-star numbers throwing two passing touchdowns and one rushing td.

"Rob definitely got it in tonight. He looked like a senior out there," J.B. said.

Big Rob nodded his head in agreeance. "That's how he gotta ball if he want them scouts to be out here recruiting him," Big Rob stated.

The game analyst came back over the speaker for the last time announcing the end of the game.

Coach Joe stood up. "Come on. Let's get out of here so we can try to beat traffic."

Big Rob stood up with him. "I'ma head out with y'all. I'm just gone wait for little Rob at my truck.

"I think we parked right next to you," T.C. said fixing the headband around his dreads.

-

The crowd was thick but was moving swiftly as they exited the stadium. The five of them walked in their own steady pace as they walked upon the dark parking lot across the street from the football field.

"Rob, Rob, Big Rob" were the yells coming from behind them in the parking lot.

Turning around they laid eyes on the suspect men from the game. The skinny brown skin man extended his hand speaking, "What's good Rob?"

Big Rob stood solid not accepting the man's handshake. "Do I know y'all?" Big Rob asked in a demanding tone.

"Na, we don't know you personally but we know you the man in the city. We wanted to know if you could hook us up with that good stuff."

"Good stuff! What's that?" Big Rob asked in an agitated voice.

The man replied in a hesitant voice, "You know that good stuff. We just trying have a good time with a couple of our lady friends tonight."

"Na men, I don't got no good stuff or whatever the hell you talking about. Now get the fuck out of me and my family's presence."

"My bad, Rob we don't want no drama," the man said as him and his partner retreated in the opposite direction.

The five of them remained silent until the two strangers were well out of hearing distance. "You sure you haven't seen them before?" Coach Joe asked now on edge.

"Na, I never seen them. Just some under covers or fake jack boys trying to catch me slipping." Big Rob opened his truck door and got into the driver's seat.

"I was about to hit em with two quick jabs for you!" T.C. mentioned with his fists balled.

"Yup, and I was gone follow up," Malachi added.

"Yall youngins cool. It wasn't no need for all that." Big Rob lit up a black and mild but hit it robustly like it was a weed blunt.

"I'm about to take them home. You good Rob?" Coach Joe asked.

He took another hit from the black and mild before he answered. "Yeah, I'm good."

"Alright now, we about to get on outta here," Coach Joe spoke. They all shook Big Rob's hand before they hopped into Coach Joe's Durango.

-

"I knew it wasn't something right with them dudes," Malachi voiced rolling down the front window.

Coach Joe started to cough from the breeze of the outside air. "I kind of figured they were some type of under covers or funny guys. I definitely didn't expect them to approach us. Them dudes is crazy!"

"Coach, you think them dudes were trying to set Big Rob up?" T.C. questioned.

"When you in that type of life it's always somebody trying to set you up. It just comes with the territory."

"Real talk, Big Rob need to wash that money and go legit. I know he sitting on a couple hundred thousand but I don't want to see him get locked up," J.B. stated in a worried monotone.

"Me either," Malachi added.

Pulling up to T.C.'s house Grandpa Gus was sitting on the porch smoking his pipe. T.C. got out of the car and slammed the door. "Got damn T.C. What I tell you about slamming my damn door!" Coach Joe commented in a fury. Coach Joe waived at Grandpa Gus before pulling off. Riding through the Rolling Heights neighborhood it was still massive amounts of people out as if it was daytime.

"Man, I hope don't none of us ever get caught up in the dope game. It's good money but it's too crazy," J.B. spoke from the backseat.

"It's only good money if you hustling right. It's an easy trap to fall through, especially for a black man."

"Yeah daddy, you know Heavy already trapping. We was down at the Dungeon last week and he was on the block cranking weed."

Coach Joe looked at his son surprised at his statement. "Damn for real?" he asked.

"He want to be like his big brother Tank," Jerome iterated.

Coach Joe waited a second before he began to talk again. "Well, all y'all young men now and can choose what direction in life that you want to go. Just know it's plenty of ways to accumulate money other than selling dope. You just have to use your mind."

"You right coach. I'm starting to design internet sites for people. I took a couple courses on it in the summer and I'm starting to get good at it now."

Coach Joe's mood seemed to change instantly. "That's what I'm talking about J! Now you got that Blue Magic!"

"What you talking bout coach?" J.B. questioned.

"Remember on the movie American gangster, Frank Lucas called his product Blue Magic. He stood by it and endorsed it to the fullest. Do the same thing with your brand. Enforce the Blue Magic mentality with your brand also," Coach Joe advised J.B.

"That's definitely the plan. I'll hit you up tomorrow Mal," J.B. said as he got out of the car.

"Tell your mama we said hello J," Coach Joe remarked.

-

J.B. opened the house door to the sight of his mama in a tight burnt orange dress revealing her curves. "Where you going ma?"

"I got a date J. I'll be back later on tonight."

"Date with who? Do I know him?"

Mama J grabbed her purse as she walked out the door. "Boy bye! I got this. I'll be back later."

-

Malachi and Coach Joe entered their home and were greeted by the snores of Mama Kelley. "I should record your mama snoring like that. That's a damn shame." Coach Joe took his Flyers hat putting it on the hat rack by the door.

"Yeah, that's some serious snoring. Daddy I gotta feeling these next couple years might get crazy for the gang."

Malachi's father glanced at him as if he was onto something. "Well, son the four of you are on the brink of manhood. The transition from boyhood to manhood for any man is never an easy one. You guys are at the point in your life where you have started to really form an identity for yourselves."

"I know we'll be good though. Even though sometimes I worry about Rob and T getting caught up in the dope game."

Coach Joe nodded his head in agreeance. "I don't really worry too much about Rob. I think he's seen a lot of the battles his daddy has to face and I think he wants to take his life a different route. I will say though, that he is just as tough as his daddy."

"What about T though?"

"Now, I do worry about him, only because his grandparents are older and really can't keep up with him. T.C. also has a big money fetish but hell, I guess we all do! It hurt me earlier when you told me Heavy had stepped out on the block. Lord knows I tried my best to be a positive influence but I can't hold you all hands as y'all get older."

"You right, you really can't," Malachi added.

"And as for my son, you bet not think about pushing no dope or else you gone have to see these!" Coach Joe balled up his George Foreman sized fists and threw two swift punches that landed in Malachi's chest. Malachi felt the full velocity of the punches but tried to play it off like he was all right. He ran up the stairs to his room and threw on a sleeveless white t shirt and black hoop shorts. He ran back down the steps with his basketball in hand.

"I'm about to go to the park pops."

"Alright, love you son." Malachi loved going to the court late at night because he knew that he would have the court to himself.

Arriving at the court he instantly started shooting shot after shot. He worked on his ball handling, post moves and pump fakes. He had got an extreme amount of motivation by Rob's spectacular performance earlier that night. He wanted to be sure he shined on the court the way his brother had just shined on the field. He ended up practicing so hard on the court that night that he hardly had any energy to walk home. Leaving the court, he saw an old man sitting across the street sitting on his front porch. The old man lifted his hand and flicked his wrist like he was shooting a basketball. Malachi paused in his tracks and repeated the shooting motion. Both him and the elderly man smiled at each other but spoke no words.

-

"You see class, the melanin you have in your body is what allows your skin to have its dark pigmentation. It also gives black people's eye's iris a brown color and the dark color to our hair. The melanin we possess is activated and nourished by the sun. This is the reason why people of color do not have to apply sunscreen to our skin because our god given melanin protects us from the sun's harmful UV rays. Are you guys keeping up with me?" Mr. Smith asked.

Some of the students were taking notes but most of them were just listening to him in awe as he taught them on another topic they had never received knowledge about.

"You see class, melanin can be found in space, plants and also water. With that said remember the same element that makes up the key components of the universe also helps to make up you." The bell rung as the African American studies teacher finished his sentence.

"Mr. Smith gotta be one of the best teachers we ever had," Rob commented as him, T.C. and Malachi walked into the hallway.

"He definitely is. I didn't know nothing about any melanin but I do gotta chick named Melanie who lookout for me," T.C. said jokingly.

"You silly bro," Malachi laughed as J.B. started to walk up.

"What up y'all."

"We cooling. What's up with you?" Rob asked.

"I'm cooling myself. I just had to flex on somebody trying bully somebody out they pocket money. Niggas stay thinking they hard!" J.B. exclaimed.

"Nigga, you not hard either!" T.C. iterated challenging J.B.

"I'm too fly to be out here fighting every day. It's only the ugly and broke niggas that be wanting to bang all the time," J.B. remarked gliding his brush across his head.

Malachi pulled his phone out to check the time. "Men, what we about to do since we getting out of school early?" he asked.

"I'ma probably go and chill with Kandi since I know her mama not off work yet," T.C. stated counting some change in his hand.

"I don't even feel like going to practice. I probably won't even go," Rob spoke looking sluggish.

"You mines will go bro, ain't nothing else popping today," Malachi suggested.

"I know I'm about to shoot to the crib. I'm super tired. Ima just chill until practice time later," J.B. stated.

"Yeah, me too," Malachi added.

-

Jerome heard the common tones of R&B music ringing through the cracked window in the front of the house as he took his keys out of his pocket. He took his time walking in the house thinking nothing was out of the ordinary until he seen a tall bald-headed man standing in the kitchen. The brown skin man was standing in his boxers and a white beater drinking a glass of lemonade.

"Who the hell is you bro?"

Before the man could get an answer out J.B. was rushing in on him. He threw a wild right punch that landed on the left side of the man's jaw. J.B. followed up with a left punch but the man blocked it with his right forearm. The man wrapped his hands around J.B.'s chest pushing him back into the refrigerator which made the entire kitchen shake. He hit J.B. with two body punches which slightly stunned him. J.B. tried to push himself off the refrigerator but his opponent put his thick forearm to J.B.'s neck keeping him pinned.

"What the hell is going on?" Mama J asked frantically as she ran in the kitchen. She had on cheerleader shorts and a white t shirt. J.B. tried to throw another right punch but he hit nothing but air because the man had already moved out of the way.

"Mama who the hell is this in our kitchen?"

"First off, this ain't your damn kitchen and why the hell were y'all down here fighting in my damn house?"

"I swung on dude because I ain't know who the hell he was!" Jerome spoke just now starting to catch his breath.

"Jade, you know the last thing I would want to be doing is fighting your son but I couldn't just let the boy beat me up!"

"Who you calling a boy nigga? I'ma grown man!" J.B. yelled still fired up.

"Shut up Jerome!" Mama Jade hollered still containing her son. "I am extremely sorry you all met this way. Paul this is my son Jerome.

44

J.B. this is my friend Paul. Paul go upstairs please. I will be up there shortly."

"I'ma just go head and get ready to leave Jade," Paul voiced.

"No, keep your ass here! I will be up there to talk to you shortly."

Paul followed her commands walking out the kitchen up the steps. Mama J's hair wasn't done which was unusual for her at this time of day. This indicated to her son that she must have been laying up with that man Paul all day.

"J, why are you home early? I thought you had practice?" she asked in a confused state.

"Mama we got out of school early today. We had an early release." J.B. walked into the living room and grabbed his keys off of the coffee table. "I'm going up to Mal spot. I'll be back later after practice." J.B. left the house feeling angry and awkward off of the fact that he had just seen a half-naked man in the house. Mama J felt extremely guilty that J.B. had to walk into the house seeing a random man that he had never met before.

-

Mama Kelley pulled up in the driveway as J.B. was knocking on her house door. He was livid but he still showed Mama K respect as she got out of her navy-blue Acura.

"How you doing J?"

"I'm good Mrs. Summers."

It was obvious to her that something major was bothering him but she decided not to interrogate the matter until a later time.

"Mal, J.B. here for you," she yelled walking through the door.

"Mrs. Summers, I'ma just wait outside."

"Okay baby, that's fine. Have a good practice."

J.B. waited on the porch in the crisp fall air. Even though he was at Malachi's house seeing Mama Kelley stand in her kitchen reminded him of the incident that had just took place.

"Bro you trying to leave for practice already?" Malachi asked leaning out of the door.

J.B. looked at Malachi with a hard look of hostility. "Damn nigga, you just looked at me like you seen a stranger in your house."

His statement nearly made J.B.'s eyes pop out of his head. "Oh, you got jokes. See that's the problem y'all be taking shit too lightly!"

Malachi adjusted his posture standing straight up. "Ay, you know what bro, I'm bout to grab my practice bag and be out here," Malachi replied in a stern voice. Malachi came back through the door wearing his black swishy pants and black Nike practice bag. "Now what's up?" Malachi asked keeping his same stern monotone.

They began to walk but J.B. said nothing.

"Bro you gone talk or walk around on some sad shit all day?" Malachi's statement sparked J.B. to elaborate on what was bothering him.

"Man, I seen the foulest scene earlier! When I walked into the crib earlier," J.B. paused.

Malachi's eyebrows raised up giving off a curious expression. "What you see?"

"I walked into the house and you know usually it's not nobody there or my mama just be chilling."

"Right, right," Malachi replied still waiting for the rest of the story.

"Mannnn, I open the damn door and see some bald head nigga in the kitchen drinking lemonade. On top of that dude was in his beaters and boxers!"

Malachi hardly cussed but the first words out his mouth were, "What the fuck!"

"That was my same reaction! As soon as I seen dude we started banging. I slipped a right in on his jaw and damn near landed my left but he blocked it. I think he got salty when I slipped that right in on him though because he tried to ball me up against the refrigerator. He rocked me with two body shots before my mama came running in the kitchen."

Malachi was speechless. "What your mama was saying? What she do?"

"Bro, the crazy part about it all is that she tried to go off on me like it was all my fault. Well at least that's how I took it."

"Honestly dog, that was some bs you walked into. Anybody would have been tripping walking in the spot seeing that."

"Exactly! It might have been different if I would have met dude before all this. I didn't have a damn clue who he was."

"Then you said dude was in his boxers? That's even more messed up!" Malachi spoke frowning his face up.

"Honestly, I don't know what I'm more salty about. The fact that I didn't know dude or that I seen that nigga in his draws! I mean common sense would let anybody know that they just got done getting it in. My mama hair was all wild!"

"Yeah, that's a messed up situation. Don't nobody wanna see they mama after she just got done doing it." Malachi could see that the situation was really messing with his brother so he tried to change the subject. "Just ball out at practice and get that negative energy off of you. Where your practice gear at?"

"I left the house so fast I forgot my bag. I got some shorts on under here though and some extra shoes in my locker."

-

Malachi and J.B. walked into the school gym seeing most of their teammates already shooting around. Big Sean was catching alley oops from one of the team's point guards.

"You don't want none of this work Mal!" Big Sean yelled out.

Malachi yelled back at him, "You might be right but save that for our comp big bro."

Shortly after they walked in T.C. and Rob followed. They both walked in the gym as if they had no cares in the world. "I thought you had football practice bro?" Malachi questioned Rob.

"Na, they cancelled it. I wasn't going anyway," Rob said picking his afro out.

"I tried to tell him they gone trip on you practicing with us and football season still going," T.C. commented.

47

Rob frowned his face up at Malachi and T.C. "Look at my face. Do y'all think I'm tripping? They not benching they star qb."

"Where y'all coming from anyway?" Malachi inquired again.

"We just got off that ho train," T.C. elaborated with a grin on his face.

J.B. and Malachi both knew what that meant. "What y'all got some act? Y'all ain't even hit us up," J.B. voiced finally joining the conversation.

Rob was on one knee strapping up his all black mid tops but looked up to comment. "We was going to T grandma house and ended up running into Felicia from the hood. I was talking to her when we got off the bus and she ended up letting us come chill at her spot."

"Felicia who?" J.B. asked.

"You know Felicia who say right there on Taylor street. Powerball thick, dark skin Felicia!" Rob stated

"Oh, I know who you talking about," Malachi stated.

"She snuck us in through her basement door and went hard for the team," T.C. spoke in a laidback voice. A loud whistle echoed throughout the gym before T.C. and Rob could discuss the details of their story.

"Lineup on the baseline!" It was the voice of Coach Phillips Princeton's varsity basketball coach. Coach P was about 6'7 in height with a husky build. The big framed glasses he wore on his face stood out against his light skin complexion."

"Welcome to the start of another season. I look forward to leading my team to another state title. I have two under my belt already in my eight-year tenure here at Princeton. I'm confident that with this year's roster we can achieve the ultimate pinnacle of greatness in high school basketball."

Coach Phillips was an all-American whose roots were from Princeton. He played at the collegiate level for the University of Louisville. He also had a seven-year career in the NBA. His basketball resume positioned him to be looked at as a basketball god in the state of Ohio.

"This man standing to the right of me is Coach Lane. All of you know him as the junior varsity head coach from years previous. Respect him how you respect me. Coach P's voice was extremely deep and commanding as he spoke towards the young men. "Let's start this season off right. Suicide drills for the first ten minutes of practice." He blew his whistle and the teams started running the suicides drills full throttle. They ran from the free throw line back to the baseline, to the three-point line back to the baseline and so on.

"Mr. Crawford!" Coach P yelled out. T.C. slowed down his pace as he turned in his coach's direction. "Now son, you know you got them damn locks bouncing around on your head. Why don't you tie them up?"

He wiped some of the sweat off of his forehead before he responded. "I forgot a rubber band at the house. That's my fault coach."

Coach P sighed. "How the hell you gone run point if you can't see the floor?" Coach P reached in his pocket and pulled out a rubber band throwing it to T.C.

"Five more minutes, let's get it!" Coach P yelled out sounding like an older version of Young Jeezy.

The five minutes faded away but seemed like twenty minutes to the players. Coach P blew the whistle and half of the team leaned over on their knees trying to catch their breath.

"Lineup squad, back on the baseline," Coach P directed.

The Bearcat squad assembled themselves in a straight line as if they were in the military. Both of the coaches took a brief scan over the team observing that they were fatigue from the suicides.

"Tell me men, what do you want out of the game of basketball?" The players looked at their head coach in a bewildered state, unsure of what he was getting at. "Why y'all looking at me like that? Just let me know briefly what you intend to achieve from playing the game of basketball. Sean since you the captain of the team, you can start it off."

The 6'10 player thought for a quick second before he answered. "Coach I want to go pro and be known as one of the greatest to come out of Ohio like you." Big Sean's statement caused his coach to crack a smile. As they went down the line a lot of the player's responses were to go pro or at least play at the next level.

"So, what about you Mr. Brown?" he asked looking at Jerome. "I just want my mama to be proud of me. So, whether it's basketball or using my mind, if she proud of me then I know I succeeded."

"Good answer Jerome." "Mr. Pounds what about you?" Rob stroked the short patch of his chin hair with his index finger and thumb before he answered.

"Coach you know football my main sport but I feel the same way as J. As long as my daddy proud of me I know I did something right."

"Good answer also. Now what about you Thomas?"

"I'm not gone lie coach, I want the money and the lifestyle it can bring. I see it as the best way that I can get me and my family out the hood and into a better situation."

"T.C. your bluntness shows your maturity level but I must ask you what if the game of basketball doesn't bring you the money and an extravagant lifestyle?" Coach P eyes penetrated T.C. as he asked him the question. T.C. took the words his coach spoke to heart which made him ponder on what he asked him.

"So, what about you Mr. Summers?

Malachi was the last player in the line. "Well, Ima say for me personally I want everything I put into this game to come back to me double fold. Every practice, every ounce of sweat, all the late-night sessions with just me and the hoop court, the videos I watched studying the greats, the passion I have for this game. I want the game to give it all back to me double."

"Good response Malachi," Coach P insinuated.

Coach Phillips knew after hearing his team's answers that they had the formula to have a special season. "I asked you guy's right after we ran suicides for a distinct reason. The reason being is because whatever you want from not only basketball but life in general." The husky built coach slightly paused in the middle of his sentence. "If you can clearly identify what you want when your body and mind is fatigue then you can truly achieve it. In this life your present circumstances may not always be the best. The key to success is keeping your focus and staying persistent even when times get hard." The varsity coach was giving the young men a life lesson he hoped that they would carry with them throughout their lives.

Coach Lane rolled the ball rack over. "Alright, lineup for shooting drills. Guards at the north hoop and big men at the south hoop." The team ran a series of drills and basic foundation plays which made practice go fast.

-

"Real talk, for a first practice that went in," Rob commented changing back into his street attire.

"You should already be in shape bro. You already been playing football," T.C. said.

"Nigga you know that basketball conditioning and football conditioning almost completely different. I take that back though. I forgot you never strapped up and put them pads on," Rob confirmed aggressively.

"Man, don't say it like I'm scared to step out on that field! Is you staying at my grandmas or is daddy coming to get you?" T.C. asked Rob.

"Ima just post at your grandmas. I think my pops running the streets. Where J at? Did he leave already?"

"Na, I think he outside waiting on my mama," Malachi answered.

"Oh okay, he been tripping all practice," Rob mentioned.

"Yeah, some other shit popped off with him earlier. I'll let bro tell y'all himself."

As they walked outside J.B. was already getting into Mrs. Summers parked Acura.

"Ima holla at y'all tomorrow," Malachi yelled out back to T.C. and Rob.

"Alright Mal," T.C. and Rob yelled out to him.

-

"How was practice y'all?" Mama Kelley asked as she turned the Jill Scott song on her satellite radio.

"It was cool. I'm just ready for the first game ma."

"I already know son. How was practice for you Jerome?" J.B. was staring out the window zoned out.

"It was cool," he answered giving a delayed response.

Mama Kelley turned her satellite radio volume back up instead of trying to converse with them. Pulling into J.B.'s driveway all of the lights were off. J.B. figured that his mama had already left for work.

"Thanks for the ride Mama K."

"You welcome J," she replied.

"See you tomorrow bro," Malachi said out of the car window.

"Is everything okay with Jerome? He was acting real different today."

"I don't know. I guess he just tired from practice," he answered.

Malachi got out of the car as his mama put her Acura into the park gear. Mama Kelley stayed in her car as her son walked into the house. Not being content with her son's answer she put her phone on her car charger and dialed Mama J's number.

Mama K- Hey Jade. How you doing?

Mama J- I'm good girl. I'm about to clock into work now. Were you able to get Jerome and Malachi from practice?

Mama K- Yeah, I just dropped J off. I guess it's time for us to get back into the swing of things since basketball season here already again.

Mama J- Girl, it seem like basketball is year-round for us. I'm trying to switch to 1st shift so I can make more games this year.

Mama K- Yeah, I'm going to try to makes as many as I can. Hey Jade, is everything ok with Jerome? He gave off the vibe that something was bothering him when he got into my car earlier."

Mama J and her had become extremely close over the years through the relationship of their sons. They often confided in one another especially when it came to their sons.

Mama J- Girllll, some shit happened earlier I'm so mad and embarrassed about. I can't believe I got caught slipping like that!

Mama K- What happened Jade?

Mama J- Paul had came over earlier. You know Paul who went to school with us, who own that car wash over their on Vine St.

Mama K- I remember Paul. He was a couple of years older than us.

Mama J- Me and him have been kicking it pretty hard since the beginning of September. I usually have him come over to the house in the mornings when J leaves for school. He usually doesn't go to check on the car wash until later on in the afternoon. Kelley, I forgot all about the boys having a damn early release today.

Mama K- Shut, I would have forgot myself if Mal wouldn't have reminded me last night. Did J and Paul run into each other?

Mama J- Yes, but that's not even the worst part. We had just got done doing it! So when J walked in, he saw Paul in the kitchen fixing us some lemonade in his boxers.

Mama K- So he saw Paul in draws? Oh lawd!

Mama J- Yeah, his damn boxers! We both got caught slipping hard thinking nothing of it. I'm upstairs and all of a sudden, I feel THE HOUSE SHAKING AND HEAR ALL THIS RUMBLING DOWNSTAIRS. I run downstairs and Paul and J down there fighting!

Mama K- That is crazy as hell!

Mama J- Right! I was so damn embarrassed. I had to jump in between the two of them to break them up. I've been single since J was three years old and never have I got busted like that!

Mama K- Did J throw the first punch at Paul? How did they start fighting?

Mama J- Yes, he threw it. He said he didn't know who he was. I guess he was just reacting off of instinct.

Mama K- That is understandable. He is so used to only seeing you and him there that it probably scared the hell out of him!" Have you talked to him about it yet?

Mama J- No, not yet. He was so mad at the moment. He left right after it happened.

Mama K- Okay, which explains why he came over my house so early today. You know he probably is going to be mad about this for a minute, right?"

Mama J- I know. I don't even know where to start at with trying to talk to him about it.

Mama K- Give him a couple days to cool off, maybe even a week. It was a bizarre predicament that happened but you still a damn good mother. At the same time none of us are perfect either.

Mama J- I will definitely talk to him soon.

Mama K- Okay Jade. Ima let you go. I know you have to go into work.

Mama J- Okay Kelley. I will call you soon. Love you.

Mama K- Love you too.

Mama Kelley got her keys out to open her house door but Malachi ended up opening the door for her with his basketball in his arm.

"Where you headed?" she asked him. "I'm about to go the court and shoot."

"Okay, don't be there too long. You still have to eat and get ready for school tomorrow."

"Okay ma."

Malachi walked to the court dribbling the ball between his legs the whole way. He only stopped for a slight second to waive to his dad who was cruising home from work in his Dodge Durango. When he got to the court he mainly focused on his dribbling. He did crossover drills, behind the back drills, one hand dribbling and spin move drills. He finished his practice session shooting a hundred jump shots. Leaving the court, he saw the same old man who usually sat on the porch. The old man flicked his wrist in the shooting motion and smiled. On the short travel home, he thought about the words that Coach P had spoken at practice earlier.

"Even when you're tired and not in the best position, you have to focus in and go achieve your goal no matter what!"

-

The month of October went quickly and the first varsity game of the basketball season was now at hand. The whole school had crowded themselves in the gymnasium for the pep rally.

"B-E-A-R-C-A-T-S, go Bearcats, go Bearcats," the cheerleaders chanted full of energy in their red and black uniforms.

The students were overly hype shouting out the year they graduated repping their classes. Surprisingly, the freshman class was the rowdiest, probably because they were new to the pep rally scene.

"Alright students calm down," Mr. Plusky the school's superintendent said as he stood in the middle of the gymnasium. The students continued to stay rowdy though. The teachers had to come and threaten to kick them out of the pep rally if they didn't settle down.

"Welcome to the first pep rally for the 2018 varsity basketball season. I'm highly anticipating a strong and successful season from our basketball team this year. I don't want to talk long so without further due, I'll hand the mic over to Coach Phillips."

Coach Phillips walked onto the bearcat logo. The two men shook hands before swapping the microphone.

"Thank you, Mr. Plusky. It's good to see all of you students here today and to have the opportunity to coach talented young men for another season. The students were shouting out Coach P's name. The warm greeting Coach Phillips caused him to pause and smile. "I'm looking to forward to big things this year from my team and they have the same expectation of themselves. All I ask from the student body is that you guys manifest the same exuberance at tonight's game. I'm not going to talk long though. I know y'all ready for the team to come out."

The cheerleaders lined up right across from each other forming a tunnel line near the rear entrance of the gym. The edited version of Future's song "Layup" came on blasting through the speakers. The varsity basketball team ran through the tunnel line as the students got up and started to the dance to the song. The team ran to the Bearcat logo forming a circle. Taking turns, they all got in the middle of the circle dancing. The captain Sean was the first to initiate the dancing followed by some of the other upperclassmen. T.C. got in the middle shaking his dreads like he was a mad man along with J.B. who was doing the dab dance. Rob and Malachi jumped in doing all types of dances mixed in together. Big Sean grabbed the mic and they turned the music down slowly.

"All I gotta say is y'all know what it is and y'all know what to do. So turn up, turn up, turn it!"

The instrumental from the song "Cut it" started to play after he got done talking. The school security guards had to stand in front of the student crowd to stop them from impeding onto the court. Mr. Plusky ran onto the court and told the team to return the team back to the locker room. He knew he had to act immediately before complete mayhem broke out.

-

"Mannn, that pep rally just went in that one way!" T.C. expressed in a loud voice as they went back to the locker room.

"Yup, it went in that one way little bro. It's really gone be poppin when we hit that court tonight," Big Sean spoke dapping up T.C.

Coach P walked in the middle of the locker room directly where the bearcat emblem laid. "That pep rally was so rowdy, I think my blood pressure shot up!" Coach P said laughing. "With that same energy and focus we should have no problem achieving victory tonight. Coach Lane you have anything to say?"

Coach Lane replied, "No sir."

"Alright squad, let's bring it in. Remember to stay on the school's premises. I'll go get the team something to eat. We'll start warming up for the game about 6 o'clock. Go head Sean and take us out." Sean stepped up into the middle of the circle.

"1, 2, 3, Bearcats!" the whole team shouted.

-

"Yo, where y'all bout to post up at?" Rob walked over asking the F.M.B. crew.

J.B. grabbed his gym bag and threw it over his shoulder. "We should all prolly just post up in the players' lounge since we can't leave."

"Yeah, you right cause that's where the food gone be at," Rob agreed.

The players' lounge was on the backside of the main gym so the players could hear all of the ongoing action occurring on the court. The lounge was furnished with four sofas, three single beds and two forty-inch flat screens plastered on the wall.

"Ay wake me up when it's time to change." Malachi spoke. He threw his gym bag down on the ground and laid straight out resting his head on his gym bag. Meek Mill's lyrics played through his all black Bose headphones as he faded off to sleep. A couple hours later his sleep was interrupted by his teammates clowning.

Coach P came into the locker room and told the team to start changing into their uniforms. Coach P started to draw up the team's offensive and defensive schemes on the large white eraser board. The time was about six thirty, an hour before the varsity game.

"You ready to ball bro?" T.C. asked Malachi.

Malachi looked at his brother like he was half crazy. "Man am I ready to ball? T, you know we been waiting on this for a minute now. Sophomores starting varsity, this our time right here."

T.C. grabbed a rubber band out of a plastic bag twisting his locks back. "Yeah, we ready. On the real I'm lightweight nervous. I heard it's mas scouts here because of all the attention Big Sean getting."

"It is a lot of scouts out there but me and you been ranked in the state. We built for this bro," Malachi commented motivating his brother.

Most of the team was stretching out and doing their own personal pre-game rituals. Malachi threw on his red and black Bearcat jersey that bared the number 24 like Kobe Bryant. He turned on some Lil Boosie and B.G. on his Ipad before Coach P and Coach Lane walked back in the locker room about 6:55 pm. Both coaches were dressed in black slacks and collared bearcat shirts.

"Alright y'all, huddle around the play board," Coach P said as Coach Lane threw him an eraser marker. Yall already know our offensive scheme for tonight. Let's feed it to our big men and when they double down they can find the open shooters or cutter. On defense were running our 3-2 zone all night. If necessary we'll run our diamond press also. Let's go out here and stick to what we know. Coach Lane rally us out."

Coach Lane's charcoal face was gleaming under the bright room light. "Bring it in Bearcats. I only got one thing to say. Let's get it!"

The team walked out into the hallway that led to the gym organizing themselves in two lines. The big men were in one line and the guards in the other line. The Bearcat team ran into the gym into the atmosphere of a noisy crowd and band playing a lively song selection. Princeton's opponents were already on the court running routine drills. J.B. spotted his mama and Mama Kelley while he was in the layup line. They waved at him as he caught the ball for the layup. He ended up dunking the ball to show off for the massive audience. J.B. ran to the rebound line after the dunk. He glanced at the crowd and spotted Heavy their former teammate shouting out something to him. J.B. yelled, "Watup" in the crowd and continued to partake in the shooting drills. The teams ran warm up drills for about ten minutes until the final warning buzzer rang.

The five starters from each team walked to the scores table to check in. The gym lights had the court intensely illuminated for the primetime Friday night game. Malachi, T.C., and J.B. were the underclassmen starting for the Bearcats. Big Sean and Big Gerald were seniors which completed the starting lineup.

"Let's get it!" J.B. shouted out as they lined up for the opening tip off.

Their opponents, the Fairfield Vikings roster consisted mostly of stocky white boys along with three or four blacks. Big Sean and the Vikings center lined up for the tip off as the ref threw the ball in the air. Big Sean tipped the ball directly to Malachi who caught the ball and dribbled hastily to the rim. He spun off of a defender and threw a slick no look pass to T.C. to the left of him. T.C. laid the ball in for an easy layup.

"Good dish," T.C. shouted out as they ran back on defense.

Coach P yelled out, "3-2" from his chair as the Vikings dribbled up the floor.

The Vikings guard blew by T.C. and Malachi only to be met by J.B. who was anticipating the shot. The Vikings guard pulled up for the jump shot but J.B. took flight in the air fully blocking the shot with his right hand. The ball almost flew out of bounds but T.C. saved it throwing it in to Malachi. Malachi took off for the fast break crossing his defender over to the left. He scoped Big Sean running the court on the opposite side. He threw him the ball up to Big Sean who slammed in the two-handed alley oop. The crowd went crazy. The Bearcats ended up dominating the 1st half with the score being 35 to 17 in favor of them. With a brief review of the game plan the team conducted shooting drills for the last ten minutes of halftime before third quarter.

Malachi and T.C. ran over to the Gatorade barrel on the sideline.

"We running them for real," T.C. commented taking a gulp of the orange drink.

"Yeah, we is. The only one doing something is dude who I'm guarding. I'll shut him down 2nd half though," Malachi said.

"Good game guys," two men spoke as they walked past them.

Before T.C. could respond Malachi answered for them saying, "Thanks" as the men walked off.

"Where the hell we know them dudes from bro?" Malachi asked.

T.C. was quiet for a short second before he spoke. "Bro! That's the two niggas who was at the first football game that night we played Winton Woods. The ones who was acting like they wanted to cop some soft (cocaine) that night."

"Oh yeah, that's gotta be the boys. I don't know why they be at the games like they gone catch Big Rob slipping here."

"I don't know either but every time I see they face I get pissed off," T.C. spoke drinking the last gulp from his Gatorade.

They ran back onto the court. Malachi scanned the crowd searching for Big Rob and his daddy. He seen Big Rob, his daddy and Grandpa Gus all conversing at the top of the bleachers. Malachi and T.C. knew Big Rob wouldn't be caught slipping easy but it was a sense of eeriness that crept over them knowing that the feds were investigating someone so close to them.

-

The halftime buzzer went off signaling the start of the third quarter. The same starters took the floor for the Bearcats except J.B. who was replaced by Rob. The Fairfield Viking team had tried to come out more aggressive but it was to no avail. The Bearcats size was too overpowering for them plus Malachi, T.C. and the senior guard Ryan were trading off three-point shots all night. Rob, Big Gerald, J.B. and Big Sean caught a series of alley oops throughout the night which kept the team's momentum at a steady high. The final score of the game was 72 to 43 in favor of Princeton. The crowd cheered as their home team shook the opposing team's hands and ran into the locker room.

"Good game tonight men. We stuck to our game plan executing it well." Coach Phillips glasses had a tint of fog on them from his facial perspiration. "We have a long season ahead of us but that's a hell of a way to start it off! Now bring it in!"

"1, 2, 3...let's get it," the whole team shouted. Most of the team changed into their black hoodies with red letters that read "Bearcat basketball".

-

"That game was easy work. No type of comp at all!" J.B. said walking over towards T.C. and Rob.

"It really was but that's how we about to be wrecking on teams the whole year. Y'all know me and Mal seen them wanna be undercover cops here at the game tonight," T.C. reported.

Rob lifted his head up as he was tying up his Air Max. "For real?" Rob inquired.

"Yeah bro, shi wild. They walked up to me and Mal at halftime trying to talk to us."

"That's crazy. My damn daddy can't even come watch his son play in peace!" Rob voiced shaking his head.

"I was so in the game into the game I didn't even notice em," J.B. commented as they walked back into the gymnasium.

Big Sean and Malachi were conducting separate interviews. "So, Mr. Summers what do you think of tonight's game?" the reporter asked as the camera light shined brightly in their face.

"I feel like it was a solid game for us. We displayed a solid effort on the court and got the job done."

The short reporter held the microphone closely to Malachi's mouth. "I know it's early in the season but what have you learned from playing with the all-American Sean Mays? I know you must look up to him."

Malachi paused before he returned with an answer. "For sure! That's big bro so I do look up to him. Not only is he the captain of our team but he's the hardest worker on the team."

"I agree. Thank you for your time Mr. Summers. This is Carol Swift reporting live for Channel 4 news at our Friday night live game where the Princeton Bearcats have defeated the Fairfield Vikings."

"I ain't even know they was interviewing you," J.B. commented as they walked up.

With a surprised look on his face Malachi responded, "I didn't either."

"That's what's up though bro. Everybody want a postgame interview," T.C. iterated.

Underneath his compliment T.C. was envying his brother because he had gotten the spotlight. Nevertheless, he kept his cool because he didn't want to come across as a hater. Coach Joe, Big Rob, Grandpa Gus, Mama J and Mama Kelley all came up to the teens and congratulated them on their victory as they exited the gym.

-

Right before Malachi got into the Durango with his parents they ran into Big Sean. "I seen you over there getting that interview in," Big Sean said.

"It caught me by surprise big bro. I didn't even have a standout game."

Big Sean looked down to send a text off on his phone but was sure to look back up before he started talking again. "It's all politics Mal. You might not have had a standout game but they know this is my last year and that you are the next superstar in line. By next year all of the attention will be on you."

Malachi took in what Big Sean was saying wholeheartedly. "That's all cool but on the real T just as good as me, if not better."

"You know what, you right. If it was up to me I would make sure that both of y'all shine in the spotlight. When it come down to it though, you got the cleaner image. T.C. is a known hood nigga so they instantly gone knock him because of that."

"Damn that's crazy," Malachi expressed sounding dismayed.

"That's just how it go and for real they look at Rob as a hood nigga too. By next year though, they not gone have no choice but to give him his proper accolades for the work that he put in on that football field."

"You definitely right," Mal replied.

"I'm just giving you the game and some jewels that nobody else at the school gonna give you, not even Coach P."

"I appreciate that big bro," Malachi said as they fist bumped each other.

The following week at school the varsity hoop squad received a multitude of praise for their victory. The team went on to win their next two games the same week. They were in first place in the GMC conference.

Third quarter Sophomore year

"**A**y, hurry up bro it's cold as hell out here," J.B. shouted out. J.B., T.C. and Malachi stood outside of Big Rob's house in their skullies & hoodies. Rob came and opened the door with his hair in a fro and half braids.

"Bout time you opened the door!" J.B. shouted mean mugging Rob.

"Man shut up. It can't be cold as hell out there because hell is hot," Rob replied.

It was a slight silence in the room after Rob's comment. "Nigga shut your politically correct ass up. My damn locks was about to turn into icesicles out there," T.C. dramatized rubbing his hands together.

"All y'all acting soft! Who trying get whooped in this 2k though!" Rob said turning on his Xbox 1.

Malachi picked up one of the joysticks to the Xbox. "I ain't catch the bus out here to get busted. Give me the Rockets."

Rob stayed with his dad inside the city boundaries of Cincinnati in a neighborhood called Avondale. Avondale was considered to be the hood. Although, Big Rob's house was located on a ducked off street and actually was pretty nice.

"What's good with this pizza Rob? I'm bout to warm me up a couple of slices," J.B. spoke from the kitchen.

"I don't care J. Just take that red skully off in my kitchen. Ain't no telling how many chicks then rode your face while you then had that skully on!"

Malachi paused the game. "Man, he ain't just say that man get his face rode with that red skully on. Rob you silly!"

T.C. got up from the couch and started to walk to the bathroom. "Man, I'm about to piss on myself, I'm laughing so hard."

"It's all good. I get the most action out the clique anyway," J.B. replied stuffing pizza in his mouth.

"Yeah right. Yall already know I get the most act," Rob talked as if he was willing to put money on it.

"Bro, Bro!" T.C. shouted from the bathroom. "Why the hell your toilet not flushing?"

"Did you flush nigga?" Rob asked answering a question with a question.

"Yeah, I tried to flush a couple of times. I don't know what's wrong with it."

Rob got up to go check on the toilet but was interrupted by loud knocks at the door. "Bang, bang, bang!" the knocks continued to come. Rob looked through the peephole on the door.

"Man, I don't know who."

Rob was cut off midway in his sentence. The man on the outside of the door yelled "Police" and bombarded through the door. Rob flew back onto the ground and was nearly knocked unconscious. In a matter of seconds twelve men had stampeded the two-story house. Each man had on navy blue shirts that had the letters DEA on them in yellow. Their bottom attire was black pants and black boots. All twelve of the men had nine-millimeter guns drawn ready to fire off with any resistance from their opposition. J.B. hardly getting a chance to react dropped his pizza before three of the DEA officers violently took him to the ground. Malachi was seized by two officers pinning him down on the couch.

"Ay what we do? What the fuck going on?" Malachi shouted in an angered voice.

"Shut the hell up, you thug!" one of the officers yelled at him.

Two of the officers monitored the front door entrance while the other five officers searched both levels of the house. Five minutes later two of the officers were escorting T.C. down the stairs in handcuffs.

"This the reason I couldn't flush the toilets. These pigs thought we was in here bagging dope. These pigs dang near ripped the toilet off thinking I had flushed drugs down it!"

"Shut up, before we shut you up!" The officer who made the threat grabbed a handful of T.C. dreads as he shoved him out the door.

"This some bullshit!" T.C. yelled refusing to be quiet.

Rob, T.C., J.B. and Malachi were all taken out the house in handcuffs on the gloomy Saturday November morning. The police had blocked the street off and wouldn't let any of the surrounding neighbors enter their house until the drug raid was completed. Ironically, there weren't any regular police cars on the scene. There were only undercover black Denali trucks with black tinted windows. Approaching the truck, T.C. and Malachi noticed the two African-American men who they had been suspecting were undercover agents.

"Well we meet again," one of the suspicious men boasted with a menacing smile on his face.

T.C. and Malachi gave the men a grimacing look that could knock a man's soul out. The DEA isolated the four of them putting them in separate vehicles. After they put Rob in the SUV the captain over the unit went around shaking his partner's hands.

"Good work men. We've seized him and will soon be apprehending his dad in the same day."

Rob glanced out the window shaking his head at the bizarre event that had just taken place. The ride downtown to the precinct was a long one. All types of thoughts drifted through their heads. What was really going on? How long were they going to be locked up? Where was Big Rob at? When could they contact their parents? Could they be charged as drug dealers even though they had never touched drugs in their life? All of their thoughts were like grey clouds caught up in a whirlwind.

The young teens were every bit of confused. Pulling up at the precinct, the agents pulled their trucks into the back of the station. The fact that they were going through the back of the station made them a little more nervous. They were only accustomed to seeing the front of the police stations. All four of them received brutal treatment from the officers.

"Come on boy," the agent said gripping J.B.'s arm.

Two officers walked on both sides of them buzzing them through a large steel door. Walking them down a long hallway they saw small jail cells lined up side by side to each other. Even though it seemed like they were caught up in a matrix, reality set in when they seen the jail cells. The cops placed them in four individual rooms continuing to keep them isolated. Hoping they could make the young men panic the detectives stalled about a half hour before they interrogated them.

-

A stocky man with a red mustache and a bald head entered the tiny room where Rob was sitting. The man had on a white collared shirt and black pants with black dress shoes.

"How are you doing Mr. Pounds?"

The detective un cuffed Rob's hands after he questioned him. Rob gave the man nothing but a blank stare. Between Rob's massive frame and hair being half afro and half braids, he could intimidate anybody.

"It's unfortunate we had to meet under these conditions but first let me say I am a major fan of your football career."

Rob was looking at the man still with the same blank stare. The bald detective sat in a chair right across from Rob.

"I'm going to cut straight to the chase Robert. Your dad is responsible for distributing major shipments of cocaine throughout the tri state. We have a secret indictment specifying him primarily for his drug activity in Cincinnati. Do you know about any of the drug activity that involves your father Robert Pounds Sr.?"

The man stared at Rob anxiously anticipating an answer. It amazed Rob that this random man expected him to snitch on his own father. Instead of paying the man any attention, Rob's mind drifted back to when he was a little kid. Images of him and Big Rob throwing the football in the street flashed in his mind. Distant memories of his mama's yellow face also popped in his head. He wondered where she was at. He wondered what was going to happen to his daddy. The thought of Big Rob going to prison was too overwhelming at the moment. Examining that Rob would not talk the detective switched rooms and shifted his attention to J.B.

The detective walked in the room where Jerome was at. Jerome still had his red skully on top of his head. The detective lit a Marlboro cigarette before he began to talk. J.B. beat him to the punch.

"Excuse me sir, can you put that cigarette out. I'm allergic to secondhand smoke."

"Sure, I can," the man said burying his cigarette into the clear ashtray. "Let's cut straight to the chase Jerome. We both know you and your friends are in some deep shit right now. Tell me how you are affiliated with your friends? More importantly how are you affiliated with Big Rob?"

J.B. frowned his face up at the Caucasian man.

"You want me to answer your questions, really? How you expect me to supply you with any sufficient answers after y'all bombarded our house and drug us down to this hellhole against my will?"

Noticing J.B. was being resistant the detective decided to take another avenue to question him.

"Well, let me start over again. I think I jumped the gun. I know all four of you young men are excellent student athletes and none of you are under arrest. To keep you out of trouble though, we just need you to answer some."

"Answer what?" Jerome asked cutting the detective short. "Answer what? You already told me we not under arrest which I already knew in the first place. Second off, I'm under the age of eighteen. Has my mama been notified that I'm being detained for questioning? Oh yeah, where is my legal counsel at? I want legal counsel for me and the rest of my brothers. We not giving any statements but we want legal representation just to make sure our situation a hundred."

J.B.'s knowledge and slick mouth had angered the detective. The man got up out his chair gripping J.B.'s shirt by his collarbone. "Listen, you fuckin teenage thug. You're going to tell me what the hell I want to know!"

The detective's harassment was interrupted by a knock on the door. Another detective walked into the room.

"Lay off the kid Burt. Their parents are here now, gotta let em loose."

This made detective's Burton's face redder than it already was. J.B. got up from the chair with a smirk on his face. Walking down the hallway Jerome could hear his mama going off on the police in the front of the station.

"Why the hell is my son down here at this damn station? He never touched a drug in his sixteen years of life, so why the hell y'all think it's okay to arrest my child? Not your child, but my child!" Mama J spoke full of fury.

Turning the corner, J.B. seen the short stature of his mama looking up at the taller officer. Coach Joe and Grandpa Gus were trying their best to tame Mama J and Mama Kelley. Malachi, T.C. and Rob were already out of custody.

"You good bro?" Malachi inquired as he seen J.B. walk out from the back. They were all relieved to see their last brother walk out.

"I'm good. I'm just ready to get out of here!" Mama J and Mama K slowly ceased their wrath seeing that J.B. was okay.

"Let's get outta here," Coach Joe instructed. Walking outside Coach Joe turned his attention towards Mama J and Mama K. "I understand we all are mad but it's a certain way we have to handle this situation."

"A certain way my ass Joe! They had our kids locked up like they were savages!" Mama Kelley said flaring up with anger.

"I agree with Kelley, Joe. What you want us to be peaceful when they just run up in our houses and take our kids away?" Mama J's ponytail blew in the wind as she waited on Coach Joe's response.

"I'm just as angry as y'all are. It's just a certain way we got to go about getting justice. All that yelling not gone get us anywhere."

"Joe is right. These white folk on the police force ain't ever played fair when it comes to us. It's a game of chess and we have to be strategic about how we go about anything we gone do," Grandpa Gus spoke.

"Is everyone still coming over the house? I'm going to cook breakfast for everyone," Mama K said.

"Yeah, I'll be over," Mama J replied.

"I will too," Grandpa Gus added.

Rob, Malachi, Coach Joe and Mama K all got into his car to ride home. Mama Kelley reached into her purse and pulled out a pack of Virginia Slim cigarettes. Malachi knew she was truly stressed when he seen his mama light the cigarette because she rarely smoked. Pulling up at the house Mama Kelley went to the kitchen and started to cook breakfast. She fixed cinnamon rolls, turkey bacon, turkey sausage and grits. The cold bottles of orange juice in the refrigerator complimented the meal. Everyone posted up in the living room of the Summer's house.

-

"They didn't let you all get your jackets or hoodies?" Mama J asked them.

"Na, they didn't let any of us take anything with us. Everything happened so quick," Rob responded.

"Right! So, I need y'all to tell me y'all versions of the story from start to finish of how everything went down." Mama J sat down in the single sofa seat anxious to hear the story.

Grandpa Gus pulled up a chair anxious to hear the story as well. T.C. and J.B. started off reiterating of how they remembered the intense action scene. Their stories were interrupted by a couple of knocks on the door. The F.M.B. crew all looked over at the door now paranoid from the events earlier. Coach Joe walked to the door and opened without looking through the peephole as if he already knew who it was. Coach Phillips stepped in the door with his large glasses and Princeton fitted on the top of his head.

"I'm glad to see you all are safe," Coach P said shaking everyone's hands in the room.

"Do you want anything to eat?" Mama Kelley shouted from the kitchen.

"No, I'm not hungry. Thanks for the offer Kelley."

Not only was Coach P the young teens coach but he was also a close friend to the F.M.B. family. He had grown up in the community of Woodland a couple years ahead of Coach Joe and a handful of years behind Grandpa Gus.

"They were just telling me the story of what happened, Vince," Mama J said crossing her legs in the sofa seat. Coach P flipped his hat to the back as if he were young.

"Well I pretty much know the basis of what happened. My main concern is the hereafter."

Joining the dialogue Coach Joe said, "I talked to Big Rob today on the phone and he's going to turn himself in today. Rob you're going to stay over here until he bails himself out, which shouldn't take long."

"That's cool. I just don't have any clothes." Rob was cool and laidback like the day had been ordinary thus far.

"Don't worry about clothes. We will buy you some if need be. I don't know how soon were going to be able to get back into you the house," Coach Joe elaborated.

Grandpa Gus cleared his throat before he started to speak. "Now, will this whole situation affect the boy's season in any way?" he asked Coach P.

"No, I give you my word, it won't Gus. I will talk to the athletic director and the superintendent to ensure them that they were just in the wrong place at the wrong time." Grandpa Gus nodded his head silently liking what Coach Phillips was saying. "With that said, Malachi, T.C., J.B. and especially you Rob. You all have to stay on the straight and narrow. This incident is going to cause people to look at you with a magnifying lens. It doesn't help either that you guys are on one of the best teams in the state. A lot of people are waiting on the day you guys fall off from the top."

"And you definitely know them white folk don't want y'all to succeed. They asses been racist way back since I came through school!" Grandpa Gus spoke as if he was having a flashback.

"You right Mr. Gus. They had our sons down at that station like they was all felons!" Mama J vented uncrossing her legs.

Mama K joined the conversation. "I want to get our attorneys in on this. It has to be some illegal procedures they did in that whole raid operation. Something like that can traumatize people, especially teenagers!"

"Baby we can't waste our time and energy on investigating police operations. Our focus still has to remain on getting these boys through the school year, in spite of the obstacles."

"I agree with you Joe," Coach P stated starting to speak again. "As I was saying before because of this situation all four of them will have a bigger spotlight on them now. They all will be offered athletic scholarships and some academic scholarships. Our job as coaches and parents is to guide them to help them remain eligible for the free money. They can handle the court and the field without us but we have to be a powerful force to assist them in the game off of the court. The game of politics that is."

Everyone in the room agreed with Coach P a hundred percent.

"Is the food ready ma? We hungry that one way," Malachi remarked.

"Yeah, it's ready," she responded. They all went in the kitchen to eat the food she had prepared.

-

Later on that night, Malachi and Rob were posted in Malachi's room. T.C. and J.B. had went to their houses for the night. Rob still hadn't heard from Big Rob but his body language was still mellow and cool as a fan.

"You trying run a game of 2k bro?" Malachi asked. He was hoping that would take their minds off of all the controversy.

"Bro, I'm so zoned out right now I really can't do anything but chill."

"I feel it. All this shit crazy. I just hope your daddy good."

"I'm not worried. I know he all right. What's so crazy in the back of my head I knew this day could eventually happen. It's just suck that it actually happened."

"I know bro. Big Rob been balling and doing his thing for so long it felt like he was never gone get knocked." Malachi aimed the remote at his forty-inch TV harnessed on his wall. He turned it to channel five news. The news reporter appeared on the screen.

"In our top story for the day. Suspected tri state drug lord Robert Pounds Sr has turned himself into police custody. This morning police performed a raid on his home in Avondale recovering narcotics and drug paraphernalia. Mr. Pounds has yet to receive a court date but his bail is estimated to be set at a million dollars."

A mugshot of Big Rob's stocky yellow frame appeared on the TV screen as the reporter talked.

"If anyone has information on Mr. Pounds and his affiliates please call the crime stoppers number at the bottom of the screen," the reporter spoke wrapping up the story.

"Man, that story some straight bs. They know damn well they ain't find no type of work in the house. Pops ain't never keep none of his work there or do any transactions there." Rob's face had turned a chimney red. The news report had angered him. This was the first time Malachi had seen Rob display any emotion since the drug raid.

"Man, you know what I say all the time. Fuck the media! You know they never portray us in a positive light unless they can benefit from it," Malachi replied.

"I already know bro. They not for the right. I was gone have your mama twist my hair up tonight but Ima just lay it down. The more I think about it the more pissed I get."

"Yeah, me too it's been a long day," Malachi spoke.

Malachi and Rob went to sleep that night knowing that life was about to be different for them. The words of Coach P echoed through their head when he said, "More spotlight would be on them."

-

Monday morning came and the four members of the F.M.B. crew were gathered in a ducked off hallway away from the student body.

"Real talk, I don't even wanna be here this morning," T.C. commented stuffing a honeybun in his mouth.

"You already know I'm not trying to be here. I still haven't even heard from my daddy yet," Rob voiced.

Rob was leaned up against the locker with one foot up on it. His braids were freshly done and his poise was back to being cool. J.B. was brushing his hair and making sure his shoe game was on point.

"Bro I know things crazy but at least you got your daddy. I haven't heard from my daddy in years. It's been just me and my mama rocking for some years now," J.B. said trying to console Rob.

"Yeah, that's how it's been with me and my daddy. I don't know where my mama at right now," Rob replied back to J.B.

Malachi had on a fresh white tee and some old school Bo Jacksons on his feet. "To keep it a hundred none our families perfect but all of us together right here is la familia."

They all agreed with Malachi as they walked into the main hallway. The young squad didn't know what type of response they were going to receive from the students about the weekend's events. All they knew is that they were on edge and ready to pop off at any sight of drama.

"What up! Yall good?" Ben a teammate from their summer league AAU team asked.

"We good Ben," J.B. responded knowing nobody else wanted to talk.

"How it pop off though? I know yall had to be tripping!" Ben questioned wanting a play by play scenario.

Feeling that Ben was being too pushy, T.C. remarked, "We good bro. It ain't nothing to discuss it just is what it is."

"I feel it. If yall need anything just let me know," Ben said walking in the opposite direction.

-

Continuing to travel through the hallway they felt the glances and stares from the students and teacher staff. Kandi walked up to T.C. and gave him a big hug. Her soft body and feminine presence comforted Thomas temporarily.

"Hey baby," she spoke to him. "Yall good?" she asked directing her attention to all of them.

"We cool," Rob answered. He also felt comforted by Kandi's aura.

Kandi reached in her small purse and pulled out her lip gloss applying it to her lips. "I know everything will be alright. Your daddy got a lot of love in the city Rob."

"Kandi, Kandi." Kandi's best friend Tisha was calling her name. "What up y'all. Come on girl I need to get something out of your locker before class start."

Kandi gave T.C. a quick hug before she and her best friend walked off. J.B. and Tisha, the short redbone with black hair and grey eyes had a history of messing around, although they never got serious. Ironically, J.B. still had strong feelings for his brother's girl Kandi even though he had messed with her best friend. The bell rang for first period. J.B. and T.C. went their own ways while Malachi and Rob stayed together.

Stopping at Rob's locker, they couldn't help but notice a teacher by the name of Mr. Tate who had been creeping along the side of them down the hallway. Malachi knew Mr. Tate had a reputation of being an asshole so he decided to try to kill him with kindness.

"How you doing Mr. Tate?" Malachi asked him.

"I'm doing good. I should be asking you all that seeing you guys have a street reputation now."

Mr. Tate was about 5'9 in height with a dark skin complexion. He had a devious smirk on his face as he looked at the two students. Rob felt Mr. Tate's energy and knew his inquiry about their welfare wasn't genuine. The smirk Mr. Tate had on his face made Rob want to slam his small body against the lockers.

"We good Mr. Tate," Malachi answered.

"I heard about you guys run in with the law. It's a shame that you young men don't have any real role models to look up to outside of these school walls. Hopefully you young men can do something positive with your lives but as the saying goes, "The fruit don't fall too far from the tree."

Mr. Tate looked Rob squarely in the eye as he finished his sentence.

Mr. Tate's words made Rob more livid then he already was! Rob balled his fists preparing to hit the teacher with the fury of a Mike Tyson punch. Fortunately, Malachi stepped in with lightning speed to restrain Rob. He had to use all his strength to keep Rob to keep Rob from doing severe physical damage to the teacher.

"I'll beat your ass! Don't you ever try to play my daddy! You can get bodied in these streets too. These school walls can't protect you twenty-four seven bra!"

Rob's voice filled the hallway but he didn't care about who heard him or any of the consequences. Mr. Tate walked off after he seen how serious Rob was about assaulting him. Walking to math class Malachi was glad he stopped from Rob messing his school year up over somebody as petty as Mr. Tate.

-

Later that day Mr. Smith was wrapping up his African American study class. The bell rang and most of the students exited early as usual. Thomas, Rob and Malachi stayed behind to converse with Mr. Smith.

"Look at this Malachi." Mr. Smith handed him a picture of an ancient Egyptian carved in stone. T.C. looked at the picture also.

"Dayg Mr. Smith, it look like dude got waves!" T.C. exclaimed.

Malachi looked at the picture like he was trying figure out where he knew the ancient Egyptian man from. "That's crazy he got waves just like me and J," Malachi commented.

"Yes, you observed the photo correctly. I showed you all this photo to clearly show you all how deep our roots trace back to greatness."

Mr. Smith walked to his door and closed it. His demeanor seemed to change after he shut the door. "So, how are you young men coping with the chaotic situation from this weekend?" The three of them were silent for a long second.

"I guess we coping as best as we can Mr. Smith," T.C. answered.

"And how are you Mr. Pounds?"

"I'm staying strong Mr. Smith. You know rolling with the punches."

"Yeah, that's all we can do is stay strong in this uncertain life of ours. Stay strong, stay intelligent and stay true to self," Mr. Smith commented adding to Rob's statement.

"We had a run in with Mr. Tate earlier and he came at us crazy. It almost escalated into something else," Malachi spoke rejoining the conversation.

Mr. Smith took a seat down behind his desk. "You talking about the freshman gym teacher? What happened?"

"Rob and me was walking to first bell this morning and Mr. Tate was on some creep stuff trailing us the whole hallway. He caught up with us when we got to our lockers."

"What happened then?" Mr. Smith asked even more curious now.

"He started talkin crazy. Saying stuff like we don't got any real role models and the fruit don't fall too far from the tree. Rob and I took it as that he was trying to throw shots at his daddy."

Mr. Smith loosened his black tie and rolled up his cuff links. "It most definitely sound like he was trying to throw low blows. It's sad when an older man tries to knock a young man's confidence because of his own insecurities within himself."

"He was about to get bodied. He think shit sweet because we inside this school!" Rob commented harshly.

"I'm glad I wasn't there because I ain't never liked dude anyway. Mal would of had to hold both of us back off of him!" T.C. replied with flare.

Mr. Smith analyzed his thoughts before he started to talk to the young men again. "I truly understand that these past couple of days has been hectic for all of you, Jerome included. Being an older man with some wisdom I have to plead to all of you not to get caught up in the irrelevant drama. Now Rob, if you would have whooped up on Mr. Tate you would have won the battle but loss the war. You would have got expelled from school and any major scholarship offers from big schools would have been forfeited. All over what? An insecure man who's envious of your superstar potential and bitter about his past."

Rob, T.C. and Malachi tuned in on everything Mr. Smith said because he wasn't talking to them from a teacher's perspective but more of a mentor who truly cared.

"Yeah, you right. He had just pissed me off talking that weak stuff," Rob elaborated.

"Just think Robert, even though your daddy is caught up right now, he still needs you to succeed. Your daddy is here and still living. He just unfortunately might have to serve some penitentiary time. I'm not trying to water down the severity of the situation but I'm just telling you not to focus solely on the negative."

"I agree Mr. Smith," T.C. implied.

"I see where you coming from. You made me look at the bigger picture," Rob added in.

"I just want to see you all prosper and I will do everything in my power to make sure that happens. Mr. Smith walked over to the door and opened it." I'm not gonna hold you all up. I know you all have to get to practice." The three of them grabbed their books and shook their teacher's hand as they walked out of the room.

Malachi pulled out his phone and read a text from his mama. The text read "Be strong and of good courage son. I love you. See you after practice."

Arriving at practice Coach P and Coach Lane made the team go through a rigorous practice. The coaches knew it was mid-November and that the season was not going to get any easier. The team was exhausted after the practice session ended. Coach Joe and Mama Jade were waiting on their cars to take them home. T.C. and Jerome rode home with Mama J. Rob and Malachi rode with Coach Joe.

"Y'all gone get sick if y'all don start wearing coats after practice. It's mid- November, not August!"

"I hear you Pops," Malachi replied swiftly not wanting to argue about the subject.

-

Walking into the Summer's house the aroma of meatloaf, mash potatoes, green beans and homemade peach cobbler filled the air. "Smell good baby," Coach Joe said giving his wife a kiss.

Rob's Galaxy phone started to ring but it was unfamiliar number he didn't recognize.

Rob- Hello

Big Rob- (Operator's voice) This is a call from Hamilton County jail. Press one to accept. Press two to decline. Press zero to further decline calls from this facility.

-

Big Rob- What up son, you good?

Rob- Yeah daddy, I'm good. I'm glad you called tonight. I been waiting to hear from you.

Big Rob- I called as soon as I could. Let me start by telling I'm sorry for this messed up predicament I put us in.

Rob- It's all good. It's a crazy situation, I'm just glad everybody alright.

Big Rob- I can't say too much over this phone but you know they been watching us for a minute now. They tried to blindside me and catch the god slippin.

Rob- What Jerry talking about? Have you spoken to him yet? (Rob was referring to his dad's lawyer)

Big Rob- I'll be contacting him soon enough. This is the exact reason I pay him the type of dough that I give him every month.

Rob- I already know.

Big Rob- Do me a favor son.

Rob- What you need? (Rob took a seat on the sofa tired from the school day)

Big Rob- I already know you do this anyway but stay low key and stay close to your family. Don't put no new shit in your routine or new people in your circle. It's a lot of haters out here and I need to make sure you good until this case pass.

Rob- (Rob thought of the recent conversation he had with Mr.

Smith earlier) I am pops. Ima hold it down for us out here. It's still a lot to accomplish out here.

Big Rob- You got a lot to accomplish in life in general not just in sports. All of y'all do that's why I always told y'all to stay loyal and stay close to each other. You and your squad is the winner's circle.

Rob- Yeah, we are. We definitely get it in.

Big Rob- Everything is going to be all right son. I want you to stay at Joe's until we get everything figured out.

Rob- I am. You know this home away from home anyway.

Big Rob- Yeah, it is. Gina (Big Rob's girlfriend) is supposed to be putting some money on my books tomorrow but if she can't I need you to put it on there for me. You know where I keep it at. (Big Rob was referring to the stash of money he kept in a discreet place.

Rob- Okay, I can do that.

Big Rob- Thanks son. I love you and will be calling you before the end of the week. Tell Joe I'm going to call him tomorrow morning.

Rob- Love you too.

Big Rob- Everything gone be one hundred Rob. I'ma make bail soon.

Rob- I already know you are.

The operator interrupted the conversation notifying the two of them that their was a minute remaining on the call. Rob said his final goodbye to his father and hung up the phone. Rob walked in the kitchen and sat down at the dinner table.

"How is he?" Mama Kelley asked.

"He good. He told me to tell you that he gone call tomorrow morning Coach Joe."

Coach Joe was stuffing his mouth with the mash potatoes Mama Kelley had cooked. "Okay, that's cool. Go head and fix your plate Rob. I know you hungry."

"You know it. I'm starving!" Rob got up and started to fix his plate. He now felt content and gratified on the inside. Hearing from Big Rob calmed his nerves and helped clear his head.

-

Two weeks later the Princeton Bearcats had the Friday night live game of the week against the Woodward Thundercats. The game had sold out of tickets. People from all over the city were present. Big Rob was in attendance also. He had bailed out a week earlier paying the bail price of a of million dollars. Snoop their rival from the AAU summer league was the leading scorer for Woodward. He averaged twenty-six points and seven rebounds a game. The game was being hosted at Woodward and the city crowd was a little bit more rowdy than Princeton was accustomed too. The crowd makeup varied from students from different schools, dope boys, hot girls, parents of the players and people who just wanted to see a good game. The only white people were the refs and the scouts who came out to recruit talent.

"Alright men, let's apply the pressure to them straight out the gate. We're at their house so we need to get our momentum going early," Coach P hollered out over the crowd.

He drew up a couple of plays and they broke the huddle. Rob was starting this game in place of J.B.. T.C., Malachi, Big Sean and Big Gerald started alongside of him. It was going to be Malachi's duty to match up with Snoop. Snoop still had a skinny frame but his broad shoulders and muscular arms let Malachi know that he had gotten stronger. The two teams exchanged fist bumps at mid court before the tip off.

"You know I'm bout to give you this work right!" Snoop spoke confidently as he fixed his headband around his braids.

Malachi mean mugged Snoop then smiled. "Na, nigga I'm about to give you this work on ya homecourt. The respect the two of them had for each other was mutual but their winning mentality made them compete fiercely.

Big Sean and Big Gerald started off the game controlling the offensive and defensive rebounds. Malachi's matchup with Snoop was a tough one. Woodward was setting multiple screens leaving him fighting to catch up to Snoop. Snoop made about five jumpers in the first quarter alone frustrating Malachi. T.C. also faced a tough matchup against Woodward point guard who was playing air tight defense against him. He wasn't allowing T.C. to penetrate to the hole which was the main part of his skill arsenal. At the end of the first quarter the score was 18 to 14 in favor of Woodward. Malachi and Rob came out and dominated on both sides of the ball in the second quarter. The crowd was naturally biased towards the Thundercats but that changed after Rob made a spectacular play. T.C. was dribbling at the top of the key crossing over to his left gaining a step on his defender. Snoop shifted off of Malachi and ripped the ball from Thomas as soon as he started to drive to the hole.

Snoop yelled out the phrase, "Got em" after he stole the ball and began pushing it up the court.

Even though he was a big man, Rob ran with swift speed. Snoop led the fast break unaware that Rob was behind him. Instead of dunking he laid the ball up softly for the layup. Rob went airborne pinning the ball to the backboard.

The crowd went crazy as Rob yelled out the phrase, "Got em".

He threw the ball up to Malachi who pulled up to hit an open three pointer. Big Rob and Coach Joe were at the top of the bleachers. So everyone heard them when they yelled out, "Good play Rob".

The second quarter was just as intense as the first. Woodward's big men began to get more physical with Big Sean and Big Gerald which turned the paint into a warzone. The score at the end of the first half was 40 to 36. Woodward still had the lead. Big Rob and Coach Joe decided to walk to the concession stand to get something to eat at halftime.

"Nice watch Big Rob," a young teenager from the neighborhood of Avondale said he passed them.

"Thanks youngin," he replied.

Big Rob had on an iced-out watch, red button-down polo with the blue horse, blue jeans and a pair of all wheat Timberland boots. Both of them greeted several people as they walked to get their food. Big Rob's popularity drew a high level of magnitude from the people since they were in the city. His infamous drug dealer status made him a revered as a superstar in the city.

"Stay up Rob", "What up OG" and "I'm here if you need me"

were some of the various compliments he received from young to old people in the hallway.

"Shut, I feel like I'm walking with Jordan! Let me get a picture in while I can," Coach Joe said laughing.

"Na, that's you Joe. Remember you the sports legend not me," Big Rob said returning the compliment.

Finishing their ketchup hot dogs, they walked back to the bleachers. Big Rob tried to scope the scene for under covers because he knew they were keeping twenty-four seven surveillance on him. He decided not to worry about it but rather just enjoy watching his young mentees play.

The start of the third quarter was rough for both teams. They were playing extremely aggressive with each other. The refs had to monitor the game closely as altercations started to erupt between the players.

"Come on baby let's go!" J.B. yelled out as he threw ball up the court to T.C..

T.C. pulled up making the jump shot avoiding the drama in the paint area. The next possession Snoop dribbled up the court. Malachi was waiting for him at half court in his defensive position. The Thundercats power forward set a hard pick on Malachi staggering him long enough for Snoop to pass him. Snoop drove directly to the hole. Big Sean assumed that he was going to pull up for the easy jumper but Snoop did the opposite. Snoop sprung into the air off of a hard jump step. Big Sean tried to jump in the air at the last second but it was too late. Snoop had already elevated over him and had cocked the ball back with one hand. He slammed the ball in right on the head and shoulders of Big Sean. The crowd went crazy as the refs blew the whistle to call a foul. The whole Bearcats team stood in a state of awe and shock. It was the first time that any of them had seen anybody dunk on Big Sean.

"They not seeing me! They not seeing me!" Snoop shouted beating his chest with his fist. Snoop hit his free throw to close out the third quarter. The score was 56 to 55. Woodward still maintained the lead.

"Listen here, we gotta stay focused. Forget the crowd and that damn dunk. Let's finish these last eight minutes out strong and win this game!" Coach P hollered in the middle of the huddle.

The Princeton team walked back out onto the court refocused. Malachi and T.C. had average games but they both dominated the fourth quarter. Malachi scored twelve of his eighteen points in the last quarter along with four rebounds. T.C. had five assists in the fourth quarter alone. He ended up completing the game with sixteen points and nine assists. Pulling out the win the Bearcats got the victory with the score being 78 to 73.

"Good game bro. You showed out tonight. Nobody on this earth has ever gotten a dunk off on me like you did tonight!" Big Sean said to Snoop as they shook hands.

"Thanks bro. Man I was scared as hell when I was in the air. I thought you was going to lay my ass out on the floor!" Snoop responded. They both laughed.

"Yeah, your quick ass caught me slipping. See you on the next level little bro."

"Oh yeah, most definitely," Snoop replied.

On the other side of the court the F.M.B. family was assembled together.

"Good game. Y'all pulled a tough one out tonight," Big Rob spoke congratulating the squad.

"I agree yall looked good out there but how did Snoop get that dunk off on Sean? Uhh weee that wasn't even right!" Coach Joe said making a crazy facial expression.

"I don't know I was on the bench looking like geesh!" J.B. said.

"Yeah, we ain't never seen anybody boom on Sean like that and we been watching him since he was a freshman. I ain't see it coming either because him and Gerald was in the paint getting it in tonight," Rob spoke.

"You was in there banging too son. By the end of the season I wanna see you grabbing at least ten boards a game though," Big Rob demanded to his son.

"I can do that now for real," Rob replied. It was a bittersweet moment for Rob. He fully appreciated the support he received from his father but he knew in his heart that was probably one of the last high school games his dad would get to see him play.

-

Three weeks later Mama Jade was standing outside of the downtown courthouse smoking a cigarette in the frigid December air briefly before the start of Big Rob's verdict hearing. Big Rob entered the courtroom in a two-piece black suit and white collared shirt. The look he wore on his face revealed that he was ready for whatever verdict came his way. Him and his Jewish lawyer sat down and conversed briefly before the judge came in. It was nine thirty on Tuesday morning and the courthouse was filled with sheriffs, lawyers, convicts and people their supporting their family members. The F.M.B. family and plenty of other people were there to support Big Rob. Big Rob's girlfriend Gina was there also.

"Will all rise for the judge," the bailiff spoke. The short white female judge walked in with a stern look. Judge Maggie had a reputation of not showing any mercy to those who appeared before her.

"Case number 1480AD23 Robert Pounds Sr vs. the state of Ohio. The charges pending against Mr. Pounds are conspiracy to distribute cocaine, possessing a firearm and operations of a criminal enterprise." "Are all of these charges accurate?" the judge asked the prosecutor.

"Yes, all of these charges are correct your honor," the female prosecutor with blonde hair replied.

"What do you recommend the defendant receives for these charges?" the judge asked.

"Your honor, I recommend that the defendant receives the maximum sentences for the charges pending against him. Mr. Pounds is a well-known drug dealer in the city of Cincinnati and his criminal enterprise has wreaked much havoc throughout our communities. Our law enforcement has hours of surveillance video on him and has been building a secret indictment on him for the past three years. Your honor Mr. Pounds is not getting charged with any violent charges but I can assure you that he is a violent criminal. I recommend that he gets sentenced with the maximum penalty."

"This bitch is the devil!" Malachi heard Mama J murmur under her breath. T.C. and Malachi nodded their head silently in agreeance.

"Mr. Nathan do you have a rebuttal for the defense of your client?" the judge asked Big Rob's lawyer.

The Jewish lawyer stood up. "Yes, your honor. I first want to start off by saying that my client Mr. Pounds is in no way violent or a threat to society. He is also very active in the community with helping the elderly. He also coached youth football and basketball for his son's teams when he was younger." Judge Maggie had a look on her face that she wasn't being persuaded by anything that Jerry was saying.

"Your honor, I'm not trying to portray my client as the perfect citizen. He has made some bad choices but he in no way deserves to be punished to the maximum sentences for any of the charges he is accused for. That is all I have to say at the present moment your honor, thank you."

Big Rob's lawyer sat down next to him. There was an awkward silence in the courtroom as the judge read over some document papers.

She lifted up her head and said, "Mr. Pounds would like to say anything on your behalf before I issue out the verdict?"

Big Rob stood up in his black suit and began to talk. "Your honor, first let me say that I take full responsibility for any decision that I've made in my life. My main obligation in this life has been to provide for my son and to give him a better life than I ever had. I'm a good-hearted man and have a lot of love for this city and in return receive a lot of love. I'm not a perfect man but I try to please God in every aspect of my life. I pray that he guides your heart in delivering me a fair verdict."

He sat down in the brown wood chair after he got done with his short speech. The energy was dense in the courtroom as everyone waited anxiously for the verdict to be delivered. Judge Maggie began to scan over some documents again. Jerry and Big Rob started to quietly converse.

"May the defendant party arise. I have reached my verdict," the judge confirmed in a calm voice. Big Rob towered over the small Jewish lawyer by at least a foot in height. "After carefully reviewing the evidence presented in the case, the state of Ohio hereby finds the defendant Robert Pounds Sr guilty on the charges of conspiracy to distribute cocaine and possession of a firearm. You will serve a sentence of eight years in the Lebanon Correctional Institution. You have one week from today to report in."

Big Rob's girlfriend Gina started to cry as soon as she heard the verdict. Mama K and Mama J also shedded tears messing up their makeup. The young men in the F.M.B. crew showed no emotion on the outside but all were crying on the inside. Big Rob walked out of the courtroom behind his lawyer Jerry.

"Come on y'all, let's get out of here," Coach Joe said directing everyone.

Exiting the court doors, they spotted Jerry and Big Rob talking in a corner avoiding the news cameras there to cover the case. Big Rob and his son gave each other a passionate hug. Rob started to release some tears as the pain was too immense for him to hold in.

"It's gonna be alright son." Big Rob wrapped his arms around him strongly comforting his son. The pain was massive for all four of the brothers because they were having to accept the reality that one of their father figures was going to the penitentiary for almost a decade.

"Let's pray to the lord. He can make this all right," Grandma Lois said. She grabbed her grandson's T.C. hand and Mama Kelley's to the left of her. Grandpa Gus and Grandma Lois were the only religious ones in the circle but they respected the elders request and bowed their heads.

"Lord we just first want to thank you. We thank you for protecting us and being a strong light in the midst of our darkness. Even though the judge delivered a verdict, lord we know that you have the final verdict. Be a shelter of refuge for him as he takes this journey. Keep him in the palm of your hands. Not only him Lord but prosper and protect the whole family. I pray these four young men grow up and strong and highly successful. Keep them on the right path in this evil world." Grandma's Lois voice got stronger as she ended the prayer. "All these things we ask in Christ name, Amen." Her prayer released a lot of the burden that was weighing heavily on everyone's heart.

Big Rob felt better after the prayer and despite of the verdict, he was still grateful. He had paid the judge an extensive amount of money to the judge three days before she delivered the verdict. He knew if he hadn't done that then she would have added ten more years to his sentence.

Summer going to Junior Year

"You gone put on a condom? I'm not trying to get pregnant," Kandi said worried as she sat on her bed half naked.

"I thought you had one baby. I used my last one the other day with you."

"No, T.C. I don't have one! We can't do it if you don't got a condom."

T.C. frowned his face up at her. T.C. couldn't resist Kandi's body. Every time he went inside of her it felt like a piece of heaven to him.

"Come on baby, I'm already on hard! Don't leave me hanging boo." T.C. begged Kandi hoping that she would give in.

"Come on but you bet not cum in me! I can't afford to be getting pregnant Thomas."

"I'm not baby," he replied.

He started to kiss on her neck as he laid her on her back. He lifted her legs into the air as he went into her. Kandi grabbed T.C. by his dreads as he stroked powerfully inside of her body. They both started to sweat as the sex session went on.

"Get that shit baby," Kandi whispered in T.C.'s ear.

T.C. lasted for about five minutes before he climaxed. He pulled out shooting his semen on Kandi's stomach. T.C. didn't last long but they both were tired from the activity. Kandi wiped herself off with a hot rag.

"You got to get dressed baby. My mama is going to be here soon."

T.C. admired her naked brown skin body before he responded, "I'm about to now. The squad waiting for me outside right now."

-

"Men it's the summertime. You can't let Kandi keep you whipped!" J.B. exclaimed as T.C. got into Rob's Ford Explorer.

"Nigga shut up and keep brushing your hair. I'ma always be able to get that ass," T.C. replied sharply.

Big Rob had made sure he left Rob a starter car once he got his license. He also left him a big lump sum of money that Rob could live on while he did his eight-year bid.

"Where y'all trying roll out to?" Rob asked pulling out of Kandi's driveway.

Throughout the midst of the chaos the four of them had managed to make it through the school year successfully. They all ranked in the top two hundred students in their class academically. J.B. had earned the honor of being ranked in the top ten class with a 3.9 GPA.

"Let's hit up the court in the hood. I know it's thick out there," Malachi commented. He had had the ball in his hand sitting behind Rob.

"Nigga! It's too hot to be hooping right now. My damn waves gone sweat out," J.B. insisted.

"Shut your pretty boy ass up. Ball is life, you know this J!" Malachi hit the ball with his hand as he finished his sentence.

"Real talk, it is hot as hell out here but we can hit the hood though," Rob said stopping at the red light.

It was a hot June day in Cincinnati. The sun was beaming down through the naked blue sky. "Ay, J throw in that blank cd over there. It should be that Future cd. J.B. grabbed a blank cd and held it up. "You talking about this one bro?"

"Yeah put that in for me." J.B. inserted the cd in and an old school beat with trumpets came on blasting through the speakers.

A voice came on singing the lyrics "Do you remember dancing in September, do you remember dancing in September".

"What the hell is this bro. You got us listening to some Earth, Wind and Fire! For real bro?" J.B. asked looking at Rob.

"Rob you on some real live bullshit. Take this shit out J!" Malachi yelled out from the back.

Rob was laughing hysterically. "Y'all know this live. Y'all act like this not no classic," Rob talked still laughing.

"Nigga, you trippin. Throw in that Future J," T.C. implied hitting J.B. on the shoulder.

Driving into the Rolling Heights neighborhood everybody was outside enjoying the hot weather. Rob rode down Colt Street where T.C.'s grandma stayed.

"What up. What y'all doing out here?" Tisha Kandi's best friend asked.

"Question is, what you doing out here? This our part of town not yours," J.B. responded swiftly.

Tisha started smiling. "I came out here to see you boo," Tisha explained rubbing Jerome's arm outside the window.

"Yeah right. We just left your friend house picking T up." "Oh, I know I'm texting her right now. You better make sure you treating my bestie right Mr. Thomas."

"That's my baby. She good with me," T.C. responded.

"You seeing me later Tisha?" J.B. asked staring at her thighs in her shorts.

"I might, just hit my phone up," she said as she walked away from the car.

"Damn Tisha a bad ass redbone! She looking good today!" Rob spoke pulling off.

J.B. agreed, "Yeah, she bad but she be scheming like just us. Ain't no telling who gone end up scooping her up today out here."

"You right," Rob replied.

Pulling up to the Dungeon the court was thick as they had expected. The usual dice games and drug dealing was in motion on the outside of the court.

"What up Heavy. You hopping on that court today with us?" Malachi yelled out the window.

Heavy was looking like a giant on the corner standing at 6'6.

"Na, Mal you know I'm not out here hooping no more. I'ma full time trapper now," Heavy spoke walking closer to Rob's four door.

"Your big ass need to get on the field with me and hit something!" Rob offered trying to recruit Heavy.

"Only thing I'm hitting is these licks! I'm running a full time jug a thon over here."

"Throw us a bag of that green though," T.C. said with a serious face.

Heavy started to laugh at T.C.'s request. "Nigga y'all don't smoke no loud, no Reggie, no drough, no Newport's, no mild's, no nothing. What the hell you talking about T?"

"I just wanted to see what you was gon say. You know we got them basketball conditioned lungs over here."

"Right, I already know! Real talk y'all be cool driving around here today. The boys been lurking all day. They been thirsty to pull somebody over," Heavy spoke.

"Good lookin out bro," Rob said. Heavy walked back over to his post spot noticing that activity was starting to pick back up on the block.

"Ride back up to Colt street bro. I got to grab some money out the crib," T.C. said.

"Yeah, we can do that. We gone have to fill up the tank soon anyway."

-

Pulling off from Memphis street a black Rolling Heights police cruiser started to trail them.

Malachi looked in the rear-view mirror. "Is that the boys behind us?"

Yeah, it's them. I'm not worried about them," Rob expressed driving as careful as he could.

"I ain't worried about em either. We not doing nothing wrong," T.C. commented as he text on his phone.

"We wasn't doing nothing our last encounter with them but fuck em!" J.B. added.

Rob made a left onto Harp Street. Harp Street was a street over from Colt street. Immediately after Rob made the left turn the police cruiser lights came flashing on. The policeman was waiving his hand out the window signaling them to pull over. Rob pulled over to the side of the road putting the car in park.

Malachi had a flashback of the police kicking the door in at big Rob's house. He said a quick prayer hoping things would go better this time. Two officers got out of the cruiser. One was a tall, slender white officer who had a skin head haircut. His name was Officer Dankey. He was notorious in the hood for being an asshole. His sidekick, ironically was a short stocky black officer. His name was Officer Littles. Everyone from the Rolling Heights and Woodland neighborhood knew him because he was a local native. Officer Dankey walked up on the driver's side and his partner walked on the other side.

"Where exactly you boys headed?" Officer Dankey asked bending his head down.

"We headed over to Colt street to my brother grandma house," Rob answered.

Rob was conscious enough to keep his hands planted on top of the steering wheel. He knew the officers were thirsty to draw their pistols for any random reason.

"Oh yeah, Colt street huh? So, you guys brought a bag of dope down there on Memphis street. Now you're going back to the house to get lifted!"

"Men we ain't bought no bag of dope on no street!" T.C. shouted from the back.

"Hey, who the hell you think you talking to?" Officer Littles yelled at him. T.C. knew it was a rhetorical question so he didn't say anything back.

"We didn't buy any drugs. We all are superior athletes and take care of our bodies," Rob commented.

Officer Dankey scanned over the car front to back before he

talked again. "Superior athletes huh? We seen that thug walk over to your car and start talking to you guys. It's only a matter of time until we arrest that lowlife. Littles what's that boy's name?"

"I forgot his name. I do now that he has an older brother that's likes to sell narcotics on that same corner also though," Officer Littles reported. The F.M.B. crew knew that they were obviously referring to Heavy and his brother Tank.

"Well I could give a damn about their names. What I do know is that it's dope in this car. If you all tell us where it is at now we won't take you all to jail."

Rob let out a short sigh. "It's not no weed, no coke, no dog (heroin) in this car. Shut it's not even a cigarette in this car," Rob explained getting fed up with the harassing police officers.

"Okay, but of course we have to search the car to make sure that you're telling us the truth." Officer Dankey had a deceitful smirk on his face.

"No search warrant then y'all can't search this car," J.B. stated also tired of the harassment.

"We have probable cause and that's all we need!" Officer Littles said flexing up at J.B..

"Us being young and black is not considered probable cause!" J.B. spoke with an attitude.

"Listen kid, either you get out the car and let us search it, or we can force you out!" Officer Littles pulled out his gun pointing it at J.B. and Malachi.

"Man, what the fuck!" Malachi said in response to the drawn pistol.

Officer Dankey also pulled out his gun. "Evacuate the vehicle slowly with your hands up!" Officer Dankey yelled in a commanding voice.

The four of them exited the car as slowly as they could. The officers made them walk around to the front of the car and put their hands on the car hood. "Spread your damn legs smart ass. Spread em, I said spread em!" Officer Littles kicked J.B.'s and T.C.'s ankles causing their legs to spread further.

"Damn house nigga," T.C. murmured under his breath.

"Where is the damn dope at? I know it's in here somewhere." Officer Dankey's white hands searched through Malachi's pockets frantically. He even went as far as searching up under Malachi's scrotum sack. He repeated the same frisking procedure with T.C., Rob and J.B. violating their manhood.

"I'm not finding shit in their pockets. Search the damn car!" Officer Dankey shouted to his partner.

The officers had them pulled over for about ten minutes now and had an attracted a scene. Traffic slowed down to see exactly what was going on. Some people even came out of their house to record it on their phones. Officer Littles searched the car like he was trying to locate a hundred thousand dollars. He lifted up the car mats and emptied papers out the glove compartment. He even went as far to check the inside of the rims on the car tires.

"I don't see a damn thing in here," the officer yelled out. The two policemen walked back to their cruiser for a brief talk.

"Let them niggas go!" somebody yelled out walking by.

The two officers walked back over to the four teens now with a different disposition. "We are going to let you boys go but don't give us any reason to suspect foul play from you all. We'll have a close watch on all four of you all," Officer Dankey told them. The two cops took their time pulling off.

Finally, out of sight they all got back into the SUV. "They ain't even ask to see your license did they bro?" J.B. questioned.

"Na, men they aint ask for nothing. They just wanted to fuck with us," Rob mentioned.

J.B. shook his head in disgust at the officer's pettiness. Rob put in the throwback album "All Eyez On Me" by 2Pac as he pulled off.

"Ay, is that Ziggy?" Rob asked setting his sight set on the dark-skinned man walking down the street in a white beater and jeans.

"Yeah, it's gotta be. He the only person with locks that long out here," Malachi answered.

Ziggy's dreads hung down nearly to the bottom of his back. "Zig, Ziggy," J.B. yelled out the window.

Ziggy turned around squinting his eyes trying to decipher who was calling his name from the car. Seeing who it was he started to walk toward the car.

"What up my souljas," Ziggy spoke getting into the backseat.

"We chilling Zig, what's good," J.B. commented.

"I hear you souljas in here bumping this Pac. I won't deny it/ Ima straight rider/you don't wanna fuck wit me!" Ziggy sang along with the song. His Jamaican accent made him sound funny but made you believe that he would follow through on the lyrics he was rapping. He stopped rapping abruptly and began conversing again. "Just chilling huh? I saw you souljas over there on Harp Street. Those pigs had y'all pulled over."

"They ain't want nothing. You know how petty they are," Malachi spoke.

"Yeah, very petty. That's why they will never be gods like us," Ziggy confirmed pulling some weed out of his pocket. The odor from the weed was stronger than skunk spray.

"Uhh wee what you got back there Ziggy? What's that some loud?" T.C. inquired.

Ziggy laughed. "What you know about loud T.C.? This ganja right here will put you down after one hit!"

"Yeah right! I can blow a whole joint of that and be good." Malachi, Rob and Jerome were looking at T.C. crazy knowing he had never smoked anything in his life.

"Oh yeah, well let's see about that. I have more than enough to share with you rookies," Ziggy voiced wrapping the weed back up.

"I'm down. What about y'all?" T.C. asked. He was hoping that his brothers wouldn't leave him hanging solo.

Malachi looked at Rob and Jerome. "Y'all down?" Rob and J.B. both agreed with a head nod.

"Okay, let's roll down to my house. I show you young souljas a new way of life! Jerome don't say a damn word to your mama about this. Heaven knows I don't need to hear her mouth!"

"Ziggy you already know I'm not. She would kill me and you both!"

Ziggy smiled. "Oh, trust me I know all too well what your mother is capable of." Ziggy referred to the experiences of when he used to date Mama J when J.B. was a toddler.

Rob drove down Colt Street to Ziggy's house. Ziggy had an average house but had immaculate cars in the driveway. He had an all red Corvette with black rims and all black tinted windows. The next car was an all-black Chevy Tahoe sitting on twenty-two-inch chrome rims. Ziggy was the definition of an all-around hustler. He had apartment buildings around the city and used to own a local corner store in Woodland. Alot of people often said that he turned the money he got from selling pounds of weed into the money he used to invest in his apartment buildings. Walking into his house it was extremely clean and neat. It gave off the vibe that he knew exactly where everything was at.

-

"Let's go down here in my basement. This is where I conduct all my herb sessions at."

Ziggy's basement gave off a much more artistic atmosphere then upstairs. He had a wood grain bar stand with an assortment of different alcohol bottles behind it. On the wall were posters of Bob Marley, Malcolm X, Biggie, Mike Tyson, Marcus Garvey and random black beauty vixens.

"You boys like them women you see over there. I took them photos myself. Them women are from the islands of Jamaica and Trinidad."

T.C. and J.B. were staring at the women like they wanted to marry them. Ziggy walked into the back corner of his basement and pulled three different bags of weed out of a drawer. "Let me teach you youngins sumin about this ganja." The five of them sat next to the card table he had next to his bar. He picked up the first bag that had dark green buds in it. "Smell that and pass it around," he instructed to Rob.

"That's some strong shit right there!" Rob said as he passed the bag to Malachi.

Malachi frowned his face up passing it along to his other brothers. They shared the same reaction frowning their face up also.

"That's good weed right there but this next bag is some loud. You youngins notice how most of the buds are light green," Ziggy spoke teaching them. "Now smell this bag."

Rob sniffed the opened plastic bag and leaned his head back quickly. "Gad damn, I see why they call this loud! It's gone have the whole basement reeking."

"You don't even gotta pass that around bro. We smell that shit already," J.B. said examining the bags.

"Now this last bag is what I call fruity pebbles. Notice all those red, orange, purple and white hairs in them buds!" Ziggy got more excited as he talked about the marijuana. "I don't even have to pass this around either cause the odor reeks through the bag." Ziggy briefly went on teaching the basics of the measurements and different prices for the weed.

Finally, he asked, "You souljas ready to light this ganja up and go into the higher realm?"

"Light it up!" T.C. replied like he was ready.

Ziggy pulled a pre-rolled blunt out of his cigar box lighting it up. The stench was extremely aggressive and made the basement air foggy. Ziggy hit the blunt four times before he passed it to T.C.. T.C. grabbed the blunt with his left hand and instantly hit the blunt blowing a little smoke out.

"Ziggy this ain't nothing!" T.C. boasted.

That cause your ass ain't hit the ganja right! A little baby hit you take." T.C. looked at Ziggy confused. "This time when you hit my weed inhale it and breath it out slowly through your nose."

T.C. did exactly what Ziggy instructed. He inhaled the smoke and tried to hold it in but started coughing roughly.

"You see soulja I told you. This ganja lay your young ass out!" Ziggy was laughing loudly. T.C. wanted to reply but couldn't because he hadn't caught his breath yet. J.B. and Malachi were laughing at T.C. but Rob wasn't.

"Nigga you only hit the joint once and you passing it already?" Rob questioned looking at T.C..

T.C. still didn't respond but just held the blunt out for Rob to grab. Rob gripped the blunt and hit it strongly like he was trying to prove something. He too started coughing heavily. He coughed so hard his face turned bloodshot red just like his eyes did.

"You boys talk all that stuff and pass my weed after one hit!" The more trash talk Ziggy spoke the stronger his accent got. Ziggy's trash talk provoked Rob to find the strength to take another hit before passing it to Malachi. After seeing the trauma that his two brothers had went through Malachi honestly didn't want any of the hemp. Nevertheless, he still put the blunt to his lips not wanting to punk out. Malachi hit the joint strongly and let out a couple of mini coughs.

"Ay Zig, why they coughing so hard?" Malachi asked feeling confident. Ziggy leaned back and smiled.

"Hit the blunt again Mal." Malachi hit the blunt again boldly and started coughing worse than Rob and T.C.. His eyes turned ketchup red after a couple of blinks.

"Take this bullshit J!"

J.B. took the herb from Malachi nervous as hell on the inside. He also tried to get away with taking baby hits but Ziggy put him on blast.

"Hell na, soulja take a gangster hit of that ganja. No baby puff puff pass over here!"

J.B. hit it the second time the correct way. He froze up not being to feel anything except the smoke come out of his nostrils.

The now halfway recovered T.C. asked, "You cool bro?"

"Na, bro. I can't feel my damn face!" J.B. exclaimed.

Ziggy took the blunt from J.B. taking another large hit. "You boys still want to hit this?"

"Yeah keep passing it," Malachi answered.

The four of them hit the blunt still continuing to cough while the Bob Marley music was playing in the background. Malachi was zoned out but he tuned into the lyrics that Bob was singing. He had never listened to reggae so deeply. He figured it was the weed having an effect on him. Everything was moving in slow motion to T.C.. He began imagining himself with a ton of money. He didn't know how exactly he was going to get it but he knew one day he would have it. He figured maybe if he kept getting high maybe he would come up with the perfect idea to get rich.

Rob was in his zone reminiscing about his father. His conscious seemed to be talking to him clearer than he ever heard it. He knew he had to excel in sports and hold it down while Big Rob was doing his bid. His thoughts drifted into questions of where his mama was at but he snapped out of it because it started to sadden him.

J.B.'s world was in slow motion like everyone else's but his mind was accelerating. In his head he was breaking down mathematical equations and trying to come up with new inventions on the computer. It became clear to him at that present moment that his heart was in sports but he would use his mental capabilities to get ahead in life.

"Pass the damn blunt J!" Rob yelled with his eyes half closed.

"My bad, I'm over here zoned out," J.B. replied.

Malachi looked around the room and focused on the Allen Iverson poster. Even though Kobe was his favorite player, he revered Iverson because he was fearless on the court. He felt the motivation more than ever to get drafted into the league. All four brothers had different dreams and aspirations but the common factor was that they all wanted to achieve greatness.

"Zig is that a studio you got over there?" T.C. asked. T.C. pointed his hand over to the far corner in the basement.

"Yeah, Thomas that's my studio. From time to time I go in there and drop some of my Rasta fire!" Ziggy's studio was a small cubicle. On the inside of it he had a mic hanging down from the ceiling and a pair of headphones.

"I should go in there and drop some hot shit," T.C. said looking at the studio.

"Go head soulja. I'll turn a beat on for you."

Malachi looked at T.C. saying, "Nigga you can't rap!"

"Watch how I'm bout to drop these bars bro, just watch."

T.C. walked into the booth closing the door behind him. Fitting the headphones on over his dreads he heard the instrumental by Future "Blow a bag" start playing. He bobbed his head trying to catch the rhythm of the beat. " Ay yo/ Ay yo/yeah first time I blew a bag today/ sum loud, sum red and a little bit of that haze/ trying to make this money a 1,000 different ways/ I give a damn what a hater gotta say long as I get paid/ if it's beef best believe we got them k's/ ice cold nigga but I spit that flame/juggin 4 girls at once with this pimp tight game/ I been the man I ain't never changed/ Ain't never been no lame/ young trill niggga stayin knee deep in the game/ yeah,yeah,yeah." T.C. ran out bars and decided to let the beat play out.

"That was hot bro," Jerome said as T.C. walked out the booth.

"Oh yeah, shit it's your turn now," he said looking at J.B.

J.B. stepped into the booth and threw on the headphones. Ziggy turned on Young Jeezy's "Soul Survivor" instrumental. "Oh yeah this the one right here Zig. I'm feeling this. Yeah, yeah, let's go. Slavery, crack cocaine and poverty/ and they wonder why niggas committing robberies/ They look at my black skin and the police think they can bother me/ Turning into a revolutionary I think I oughta be/ But they sayin J you too smart and political/ But I be like na I'm just spiritual/ showing you the world through an intelligent niggas mirror view/ So I'm telling you now you can run from the devil but what you gon do when the Lord get at you. Yeah, yeah, yeah." J.B. took the headphones off and stepped out the booth.

"Hot shit soulja!" Ziggy exclaimed scrolling through more instrumentals on his computer. He looked at Malachi and asked, "You stepping in soulja?"

"Men yall know I'm not no rappin nigga," Malachi said.

"Nigga none of us are. You mines will though. We just clowning anyway," J.B. talked using persuasion.

"Fuck it I will." Malachi got up from the card table and stepped into the booth.

"This a throwback beat, you might not know anything bout this youngin." Ziggy turned on the instrumental "Cash money is army" by the rapper BG.

Malachi threw his hand up in the air bouncing to the beat when it came on. "Na, I know exactly what this is. Big Rob used to play BG all the time in his car. In fact, start the beat over for me Zig." Ziggy ran the beat back for Malachi. "Yeah,yeah, uh huh, FMB nigga, FMB/ FMB is an army/better yet a navy/Don't try to play me or it ain't gone be gravy/ smooth player guy who just might take ya lady/ Just a couple months ago/Feds kicked down our door/With pistols out asking where the dope/Our reply ain't no dope, it's just us foe/ Learned the game from Big Rob and my daddy Joe/Running shit from the Nati down to the NO/ I show love to everybody but don't play cuz Malachi aint no hoe. FMB nigga, yall know what's up."

Malachi stepped out the booth receiving dap from J.B. "Thought you wasn't no rapping nigga. Them seemed like some bars to me."

"Y'all know Mal be trying downplay everything," T.C. added in.

"I still ain't no rappin nigga! You steppin in Rob?"

"Yeah, Ima drop a couple bars real quick."

Rob walked into the booth occupying most of the space in the tiny cubicle. The classic beat "We gone make it" by Jadakiss and Styles P came on. "Yeah watup this Rob. All Ima say is FMB nigga. Best believe we gone make it. Put money on it, put your house on it. We here to stay nigga. Yeah we gone make it!" Rob stepped out the booth still letting the beat play on.

"I thought you was dropping bars bro?" Malachi asked.

Rob laughed. "Now I really ain't no rappin nigga. I just wanted to get my high ass in the booth and talk shit!"

"I feel it!" Malachi replied.

"Man, we ain't even hooped or nothing and I'm hungry as a mu," T.C. spoke gripping his stomach.

"Yeah, we need to get something to eat sap!" J.B. added in.

"You souljas getting ready to leave out?" Ziggy got up from the computer chair lighting another joint.

"Yeah we bout to bounce Zig," Malachi answered.

"Okay, it was my honor initiating you young souljas into the different realm of life. I would be wrong if I didn't warn you all that this ganja is very powerful and can have both positive and negative effects on you. The key is to use it to bring out the positivity and creativity in you. Don't let it control you." The four of them took the words that the OG Ziggy spoke to heart.

"Lock the bottom lock on the front door when y'all leave out," Ziggy said as they walked up the basement steps.

Rob turned on his personalized YouTube mix as they rode to Wendy's to get something to eat. They devoured their food like they hadn't ate in two days. They drove back to Woodland and ran four games of two on two basketball. Playing the quick pickup games helped slowly bring them down to a level of mediocre sobriety. Other than Rob attending football camp and their AAU league their summer consisted of three things. Playing pickup games of basketball every day, getting high with Ziggy and chasing the teenage girls that they ran into. They enjoyed a summer of fun but they still tried to be careful not to do anything too foolish.

-

"Malachi can you hand me the sugar please?"

"Yeah mama, what you making?

"I'm making a sweet potato pie. I haven't made one in a while."

"Na, you haven't," Malachi said handing her the sugar.

"It looked like you grew an inch or two baby."

"I think I have ma. I'm just trying to stay up on my workout routine so I can make sure I'm getting stronger."

"Yeah, baby that's the right mindset to have. It seems like the four of you grow every year. Are you ready to start your junior year tomorrow?" Mama Kelley began to mix the ingredients for her pie as she spoke to her son.

"I'm ready. I know I really gotta ball out this year since Sean and Gerald gone now."

Mama Kelley paused from her baking to be more attentive to her son. "You know the school work is going to get tougher in your junior year. It's imperative you keep your grades up so you can remain eligible for these scholarships." Her eyes were directly on her son's face as she spoke to him.

"I'm staying focused mama. In fact, the whole squad is."

"How you going to answer for them Mal? I know we're all a family but at the end of the day you can only ensure that you stay focused, not anyone else."

"Mama, you know we all do our thing on and off the court. We got this."

"Listen son, I know all four of you have a very bright future and will do anything for each other. Speaking from experience though son, I am just telling you that you can only guarantee your own success. As you all get older you will most likely stay tight but will choose your own paths in life."

"Yeah, I hear you mama."

"Trust me usually around your junior year is when everybody start feeling themselves and thinking they're grown."

Malachi smiled and replied, "We already think we grown now." They both shared laughter together at Malachi's statement.

Mama Kelley regathered herself and switched back to a serious monotone. "I know you are always going to keep an unwavering loyalty to your brothers but at the same time make sure you keep an unwavering loyalty to yourself. The older you get; the more complex things get." Mama Kelley got up and kissed her son on the forehead and went back to fixing her sweet potato pie. Malachi listened to his mother but knew his clique was ready for whatever their junior year brung their way.

Eleventh grade Junior year

"Wake up, wake up Jerome!" Mama J yelled into J.B.'s room. "Your ass bet not be late to school on the first day!"

J.B. rolled out the bed opening his eyes. "What time is it mama?"

"You got twenty minutes to get to school. Malachi is already in the driveway waiting for you."

"It won't take me long to get ready ma. I took my shower last night."

Mama J was fixing the wrap on her head scarf. "Okay J. Have a good day at school," she said turning around walking down the stairs.

J.B. put on an all-black tee, blue jeans and some all black air max. He made sure he grabbed his brush and ran down the steps. Mama J was in the kitchen fixing herself a cup of coffee.

"Love you ma," J.B. said giving her a kiss on the cheek.

"Love you too J."

-

"Damn nigga, what took you so long?" Malachi asked starting the car. Coach Joe had purchased a new car and gave Malachi the Durango to drive.

"I ain't even feel like waking up bro," J.B. replied.

"I feel you on that. The first day of school don't even be live no more."

"Right we been waking up for this shit like twelve years now," J.B. elaborated brushing his hair.

"We meeting Rob and T at school?"

"Yeah, Rob just called me and said he gone pick T up." Malachi turned the morning radio up as they rode to school.

"What up though," Rob shouted out. T.C. and him were posted up against the lockers in the main hallway.

"I can't call it," Malachi responded.

"Men is we seniors yet?" T.C. asked with a serious tone.

"I was just asking myself the same thing when I woke up this morning. Another year of this school shit," Rob said as he wiped some lint off of his white tee.

"I guess we all feeling the same way. My mama tried to take me school shopping a couple weeks ago like I was a young boy!" Malachi commented laughing.

"Hell nah that's crazy. Ima pretty boy and I don't even feel the need to get fly for school anymore. Why should we? We been seeing the same chicks for years now!" J.B. spoke with a dry expression.

"Right! I think that's Mr. Smith right there," T.C. stated staring down the hallway.

Mr. Smith had on an all-black suit that his short, stocky frame filled all the way out. His jet-black beard stood out boldly against his yellow skin tone. "How are you young gods doing?" he asked the four gentlemen.

"We good," the four of them replied at different times.

"Mr. Smith I always hear people call other people gods. How do other people call other people god? I thought it was only one God?" J.B. asked seeking the knowledge.

"I'm glad you asked that Mr. Brown. You see no matter what your religion is we all are children of God. All of us descend from the Creator. We all possess the "Christ conscious" or god like characteristics. When we manifest our naturally inherited god traits, we operate in our higher consciousness." The hallway was filled with students but Mr. Smith spoke deeply as if no one was nearby. "The flipside to that though is when we function in our lower consciousness. We all are human so it is impossible to function in our higher conscious twenty-four seven but we should strive too. The second reason why I refer to us as gods is because we all have sole control over our life. No, we can't control everything that happens to us but we can control how we react to our circumstances and position ourselves. We all are gods descended from God to do complete our destiny. When we die we shall ascend back to God. This is why I call you god, god."

The four young men were speechless at the knowledge that he dropped on the in the early hours. They respected the fact that he would drop jewels on them anytime, anywhere. Mr. Smith never held back.

-

That Friday the Princeton Bearcats stadium was at capacity attendance for the high school football game. T.C., J.B., Malachi and Heavy were on the backside of the locker room behind a huge cement wall where they couldn't be spotted.

"Pass the blunt Heavy!" T.C. yelled at Heavy. Heavy's large dark hands almost made the blunt disappear when he held it.

"You know I'ma big nigga. I need to hit the blunt at least five times when I get it. This my weed anyway!" Heavy replied.

"We would've just bought a bag from you if we knew you was gone booth the whole thing!" J.B. exclaimed thirsty to hit the weed also.

Heavy passed the blunt to Malachi whose eyes had a crimson tint from the first rotation. "Ay, light the mild up so we can camouflage this smell," Malachi said with a deep voice. The brother's voices had gotten deeper over the summer along with their chin hair starting to grow in fuller.

"You still gone front me a pack Heavy?" T.C. voiced referring to selling weed.

"Anytime bro. Just let me know when. This loud sell itself. All you gotta do is let people know you got it in."

"I already know that loud do numbers. You still got that 258 number?" T.C. questioned scrolling through his phone contacts.

"Yeah, just hit me up. We can tag team shit and run this money up together!" Heavy spoke persuading T.C..

The voice of the game announcer overwhelmed the stadium welcoming everyone for the introduction of the game. The roars of the football players shook the stadium as they ran out onto the field.

"So y'all wasn't gone let us partake in the smoke session?" Kandi and her friend came questioning them as they creeped around the backside of the wall.

"How y'all even know we was back here though?" Malachi asked wondering.

"My boo text me and let me know where y'all was at," Kandi replied running her fingers through T.C.'s dreads. T.C. kissed Kandi light brown forehead in return.

"Y'all gone make us hot coming over here all random and loud." It seemed like as soon as Heavy finished his sentence the school security guard came walking around the cement wall with his flashlight in his hand.

"What you kids over here doing?" the chubby security guard asked in a husky voice. Everyone was silent as he looked at them waiting on an answer. "I smell the marijuana in the air so somebody better say something!" Mr. Summers, Mr. Crawford, and Mr. Brown I would hate for your basketball season to be ruined for something as petty as this." The security guard spoke in a grave tone to let them know he wasn't playing any games.

"What do you girls know? Who was over here smoking weed?" Kandi was silent but Tisha's yellow face turned pink as she mumbled some unclear words out. The chubby guard focused his eyes in on Heavy. "Young man what's that bag in your pocket?" The security seen the plastic tip of the weed bag hanging out of Heavy's pocket.

"What bag you talking about?" Heavy acted like he was clueless.

The security guard shined his flashlight towards Heavy pocket. "That bag right there young man!" the security guard said aggressively

"I don't got no bag on me!" Heavy slid his hands into his pocket which made it obvious that he was trying to conceal something.

The security guard reached into his back pocket grabbing his walkie talkie. "Alright, since you won't hand the bag over, I'll just call for the police to come and search you. Matter fact, they can come and search all of you." The girls looked like they were on the verge of tears while the boys just had blank stares on their faces hoping that they wouldn't get caught up. The security guard held the walkie talkie up to call for backup but was interrupted by Heavy.

"Alright man, you can have the damn bag," Heavy stated pissed off. Heavy pulled the bag out of his pocket and tossed it to the guard.

Catching the bag, the guard pulled one of the money green buds out of the bag and held it up to his nose. "Geesh! This is some strong stuff you kids over here smoking! What kind of weed is this?"

"That weed is called these nuts," Heavy replied sarcastically.

The chubby man dropped the bud back into the plastic. "Yeah right, kid. I think I'll keep this for my own recreational purposes. You kids make y'all way into the game and get from back behind this wall." The guard tied the bag up stuffing it in his pocket and vanished back around the wall.

"That's some bullshit bro. I want my pack back sap!" Heavy said balling his fists up. T.C. held him back.

"It's not worth it bro. It's just a pack. You can get that back," T.C. told him.

"T right. You gone make that money right back before the end of the week. Let's just get in this game," Malachi commented.

J.B. took a small bottle of clear eyes out of his pocket and passed it around to everybody as they walked around the wall. The security guard trailed them to make sure they went into the game. Walking in the fan section it was different not seeing Big Rob at the top of the bleachers. The Bearcats ended up winning the game. Rob passed for two hundred yards and scored two touchdowns. He ended up being ranked the number three quarterback in the state of Ohio at the end of the season.

Second quarter Junior year

"Lineup, three-man weave. I want to see execution and nice crisp passes. We have to do the simple drills before we can run a complex offense," Coach P instructed. It was the last practice before the first game of the year. Coach P and Coach Lane were both wearing their Bearcat fitted caps and were in a militant state as they prepared their team for the game.

"Thomas, what part of execute don't you understand? You know how I like my offense ran!"

"Yes sir, I know," T.C. confirmed responding to his coach.

T.C. setup the motion offense working the ball around to all five players. Coach P wanted to see all the players touch the ball at least twice before a shot went up. The offense worked the ball around smoothly resembling a young San Antonio Spurs team.

Coach P blew the whistle. "Good ball movement. I still want to make sure our big men are a main focal point of our offense this year."

Ryan Mats a junior transfer from Cleveland had replaced Big Sean as the new center on the team. The whole F.M.B. crew would be starting consistently this this year on the varsity squad making for good chemistry amongst the five of them.

"Run it again. I want to see second string run it." Coach P blew his whistle.

Both strings ran the drill flawlessly impressing both coaches. Coach Lane blew the whistle and gave the team a brief talk while Coach Phillips gathered some paperwork. Coach P came walking back over to the team with a stack of papers.

"Alright guys, your parents have been asking me about team pictures. This is the paperwork displaying all the info for the individual pictures packages. Make sure I get these papers back by the start of next week. I think we take the pictures next Wednesday. Also remember to wear your collared shirts tomorrow for game day."

The team rallied in the huddle ending practice after their coach got done talking.

-

"Can you shoot me to the spot bro? I ain't even drive to school today. Ashley came and got me today and we was posted at her house all day today while her peoples was gone," Rob mentioned to Malachi.

"Yeah, I got you bro," Malachi replied.

Rob was always on the move staying different places. He would still spend a lot of nights alone in his house in Avondale. Occasionally, Big Rob's girlfriend Gina would stop by bringing him plates of food.

"Who y'all riding with J?" Malachi asked J.B. as they walked out of the gym.

J.B. grabbed a blue Gatorade out of his Nike sports bag. "I think T bout to have Kandi come get us."

"Alright bro. Ima come swoop you in the morning," Malachi told J.B.

Walking out to his car Rob was already waiting on Malachi.

"We good daddy," Rob said holding his phone up to his ear.

"That's Big Rob. Tell him I said what up," Malachi spoke.

Rob pressed the speaker mode button on his phone. "You on speaker phone now daddy. We both can hear you."

Big Rob- What up Mal. How you doing young king?

Mal- I'm good Unc. Maintaining out here. You feel me?

Big Rob- I feel it. How you been doing in school?

Mal- Mainly A's and B's. I been trying to stay on it because I know these schools looking at us.

Big Rob- You right keep them grades up and everything else will fall in place. How your mama and daddy been doing?

Mal- They good just chilling. You know everybody just holding everybody down.

Big Rob- That's one hundred. You boys got to come see me next time Rob come up here.

Operator- (Malachi was about to respond but he was interrupted by the operator.) You have sixty seconds remaining on this call.

Mal- Yeah, we definitely will have to do that. Love you Unc.

Big Rob- Love you too Mal.

Rob- Love you daddy. Call me Saturday so I can fill you in on the game.

Big Rob- Okay son, I'll call you Saturday. Love you.

The call ended shortly after Big Rob said his final goodbye.

"Even though he locked up, it be good to talk to him," Malachi said.

"Hell yeah, it do. Sometimes that be the only thing getting me through. I'm just trying to learn how to count my blessings out here bro," Rob spoke humbly.

"Same here bro," Malachi said driving onto the highway entrance.

Malachi reached into his side console and grabbed a Black Ice car freshener. He tore it open and placed it around his rear-view mirror. Jim Jones song "Prayers" came on through the speakers. They got off the highway early coasting through the city neighborhoods. The nighttime air was thin with a crisp chill and the streets were filled with people making moves. The vibe in the air was evident that everybody outside had the same mentality of trying to make ends meet before sunrise.

They pulled up to Rob's house about fifteen minutes later. The houses in the city were built close together with narrow driveways.

"Alright bro, I'll see you at school tomorrow," Rob spoke.

"Alright, dog."

Driving back home Malachi took the expressway route the whole way back home. Zoning out he went into deep thought about how him and his brothers had bonded closer ever since Big Rob went off to serve his bid. His next thoughts were how he wanted to ball the hell out at tomorrow night's game. Big Sean's words still resonated in his head when he told he them it was going to be his team when he left. Big Sean was gone now and he was now ready to take on the obligation of being the general of the team.

-

J.B. woke up the next morning to the smell of French toast, grits, eggs, and turkey bacon in the kitchen. He figured his mama must have been in the kitchen cooking up a marvelous breakfast meal. J.B. hopped in the shower getting dressed quickly to make sure he ate before he went to school. He put on his black Dockers, black long sleeve dress shirt and black dress shoes. He completed his wardrobe with a black and white striped tie.

"You look so handsome baby. That all black look good on you."

"Thank you, mama. You gone be able to make the game tonight?"

"Yeah, I'll be there. You know I can't miss your first game. Paul will be with me, we can't wait to see you play," Mama J said handing him his plate. "We most definitely gone play good tonight. All four of us starting this year so you know we gone run the score up ma."

"Oh, I already know. How are you coming along with your web development?"

"I'm doing good. I already have a couple people who want me to build their websites for them." Jerome stuffed a piece of turkey bacon in his mouth. "I have a question though ma. How much you think I should charge per web design?"

Mama J's orangish black hair bounced as she turned around from the fridge to see her son's face. "Start off low baby. When your demand for your service increases then you can increase your prices. That's business etiquette 101."

"Right, so build my clientele up first and then I can consider increasing my prices."

Mama J pointed her index finger at her son. "Exactly J, you got the concept."

J.B. finished his orange juice and the rest of his food. "Alright mama, Ima see yall at the game tonight. He gave his mama a kiss and a hug then headed out the front door where Malachi was waiting. Brushing his hair on the way out he ran into Paul who was walking up to the porch.

"What up Paul," J.B. spoke walking out the door.

"Hey J.B. How you doing this morning?" Paul asked taking a sip from his McDonald's coffee.

"I'm good, ready for game day."

"Me too, I'll be there tonight watching the squad get it in!"

"Okay then Paul, I'll see you there."

J.B. ended the conversation getting into Malachi's whip (car). J.B.'s and Paul's relationship had gotten a lot better ever since their initial toe to toe brawl. They both respected each other and didn't overstep their boundaries with one another.

-

The Princeton Bearcat gymnasium was filled with people from wall to wall for the Friday night game. The Princeton team had on all- black and red accessories complimenting their jerseys.

"Y'all ready to work?" T.C. shouted as the game buzzer rang.

Coach P stood up out of his coach's chair. "Bring it in," he yelled. The team huddled around Coach P who was in the middle of the circle. "Let's go out here set the tone early. The theme for this season is domination. I want to come out here and let everybody know that our team hasn't lost a step since last year!" The game hadn't even started yet and you could already see the sweat from under the brim of Coach P's hat. "Alright now bring it in. Victory on three. 1,2,3."

"Victory!" the whole team shouted.

The F.M.B. squad plus Ryan walked on the court facing off against their opponents the Colerain Turpins. Malachi and T.C. gave each other a head nod letting each other know that they were both ready to put in work. The ref threw the ball in the air and Rob won the tip off tipping it to T.C.. Malachi instantly ran towards the hoop and T.C. was aware of it. T.C. pushed the ball up the court and threw an alley oop to Malachi from the three-point line. Malachi soared in the air like Jordan in his prime. He caught the ball with two hands slamming it in for the dunk. The crowd went crazy.

"They gone get this work. I promise they is!" Malachi hollered as he got back on defense. The Turpins tried to throw the ball to their big man in the post who ended up throwing up a weak shot. J.B. came out of nowhere blocking the shot out of bounds.

"Good block Jerome," Coach Lane shouted out from the bench.

The Turpins inbounded the ball missing their next shot attempt. T.C. once again wasted no time getting the ball up the court. He found Rob in the paint for the easy layup. The first quarter consisted of complete defensive annihilation by the Bearcat team led by Ryan and J.B.. T.C. and Malachi both had a pair of threes in the first half but Malachi led all scorers in the first half with fifteen points. The score at the end of the first half was thirty-one to eleven in favor of Princeton. Coach Phillips team ran into the locker room full of confidence.

"That was good ball out there. Keep playing with that high intensity and let's be smart about our shot selection. Coach Lane you got anything to add?" Coach Lane shook his head. "Okay, let's go back out on this floor and handle our business then!"

Entering back into the gym Malachi took a scan of the crowd. He observed some of the familiar recruiter faces from different colleges.

"These scouts out here heavy," he mentioned to J.B. and T.C..

J.B. finished drinking his Gatorade before he responded, "Yeah, I seen the one from Michigan and the other one from O State here."

"Yup, that only mean we gotta ball out more," Malachi confirmed.

"You right, we do. Ain't no choice but to let them pay for our schooling. We the elite with this hoop shit," T.C. boasted.

The buzzer signaled and the same starting five took the court for the Princeton. The Bearcats setup in a two-three zone defense as the Turpins point guard dribbled up the court. Malachi guarded him closely. Their point guard dribbled to the left side of the court and attempted to pass the ball to the other side of the court. The pass was intercepted by T.C. who stuck his hand into the passing lane. T.C. got control of the ball and dashed down the court with the Turpins guard trailing right behind him. T.C. took a drop step attempting to go up for the dunk but was fouled hard by the trailing defender. He flew in the air landing on his back. He held his hands out in midair trying to brace his fall but that might have made it worse. The crowd stood up along with the players from both benches. The impact from T.C.'s fall had echoed throughout the gymnasium. Coach P and Coach Lane ran out onto the floor after the ref stopped the play.

"You okay Thomas?" Coach P asked as he kneeled over T.C.. He was sure not to touch him, not knowing necessarily what was wrong.

"I don't know coach. I really can't move my right arm," T.C. responded as he laid out on the floor.

The team trainer ran out onto the court in a rush. Rob, J.B., Malachi and Ryan gathered around their teammate trying to see exactly what was wrong. The trainer asked T.C. a series of questions. Rob overheard him say that it felt like somebody had hit his elbow with a hammer.

"Damn, I'm salty T took that fall. That look like it might be a serious injury," Rob spoke with a worried look on his face. Malachi and J.B. had the same expressions on their faces.

"I'm salty too. I just hope he can bounce back sap!" J.B. replied.

The team trainer and Coach Lane slowly helped T.C. up of the floor. They had T.C.'s arms propped up around their shoulders as he walked in between the two of them. Coach P threw a towel over T.C.'s face so the crowd couldn't see the pain in his face. Both teams and the crowd gave him a loud applause as he limped off the court. Coach Joe and Grandpa Gus also followed the trainer to the locker room.

The Bearcats went on to win the game 70 to 37. Malachi led all scorers finishing the game with twenty-eight points. The team felt like they had won the battle of the game but felt like they had lost a soldier in war when T.C. got injured.

-

"Yes, Thomas Crawford is in room 215. Take the elevator to the second floor and it will be to your right," the young receptionist said to Grandpa Gus. Grandpa Gus, Coach Joe, Mama J, Mama Kelley and the other three members of F.M.B. were all in attendance at the hospital. T.C. was laid halfway propped up in the hospital bed watching Sportscenter. His right arm was elevated and elbow was wrapped up.

"How you doing son?" Grandpa Gus asked in a husky voice.

"I'm cool grandpa. The doctor said I broke my arm. My back been hurting too."

Coach Joe pulled up two chairs for his wife and Mama J. "How long they say you gone be out?"

"Doc said he don't got a recovery date for me yet but worst-case scenario is two months. This shit fucked up. I'm salty!" T.C. usually didn't curse in front of his elders but the injury had thrown his mental off.

Mama Kelley grabbed T.C.'s left hand. "Well hopefully you can come back before then baby." Mama Kelley was hoping that they could all encourage T.C. before they left.

"Yeah bro, we hope you can get back in there sap. We need you out there if we gone be running the score up on these bustas this year," J.B. added in.

"I already know. All we got is Ryan because that young boy Larry not ready to run the point! He ain't developed court vision yet because he only a freshman," T.C. elaborated in a loud voice.

"Ima prolly have to help the point until you get back. Coach P only trust me, you and Ryan running the point this year," Malachi spoke.

Mama J interrupted the conversation. "Listen here baby, the team will be alright. I'm just glad that Thomas is okay. We were worried the whole drive over here. It scared the hell out of me to see you flying in the air like that!" Mama J exclaimed to Thomas like it was her firstborn son J.B..

"Jade is right. Basketball will always be here but the main concern right now is your health. We want you at a hundred percent before you come back," Coach Joe spoke bringing clarity into the room.

"Joe is right. As soon as I told your Grandma Lois what happened to you, she started praying over the phone. She was on the phone praying for about ten minutes. I had to tell her Lois, it's not me who needs prayer. It's our grandson, shit!" Grandpa Gus made everyone in the hospital room laugh at his short rant.

"We mines will stay the night out here with you bro. We don't want you out here dolo all night," Rob said turning his attention away from Sportscenter.

"I appreciate that bro but y'all don't have to stay out here bro," T.C. spoke humbly.

"Nigga, you know we staying with you rain, sleet or whatever," Rob responded sincerely.

"Speak for yourself but I'm too old to be staying in a hospital overnight. My ass won't even stay here if I'm sick!" Grandpa Gus fixed his overalls after he finished his sentence.

Mama J rolled her eyes at him. "Now you know if you got too sick Mrs. Lois would have you check into a hospital."

Grandpa Gus looked at Mama J with a straight face. "Or she might let my ass sit and the house and die!" Grandpa Gus replied with humor. He made everyone in the room laugh once again.

"I'm with Mr. Gus. We gone head out for the night," Coach Joe said pulling out his car keys.

"Jerome, you know we have to go to Columbus tomorrow to see your uncle. I'm not going to feel like coming back up here to get you in the morning," Mama J explained looking at J.B..

"Go ahead with mom dukes bro. You can just holler at me on Sunday," T.C. iterated making the decision for J.B.

J.B. commented, "Yeah, I'll be out here Sunday bro for sure."

Mama Kelley and Mama J gave T.C. a kiss on the forehead before they all left the room.

"Shut, they don't got no covers in here for a king?" Malachi asked.

"Right, it's cold as ice in here right now!" Rob replied.

"We gotta call a couple of the nurses and have them bring us some. Better yet we can game some of em up and have them keep us warm themselves," T.C. said scheming.

"Yeah, let's get that second option popping," Malachi said stroking his short chin hair.

Rob was laughing. "Yeah call that nurse asap. In fact, call a couple of them!"

They all let out a hard laugh. They were just talking stuff though because they were all sleep thirty minutes later. An old nurse ended up bringing them all blankets. It was about eleven forty-five when they drifted off to sleep.

The next morning, they were wakened by a loud knock on the door. Rob got up and opened the door. Heavy came through the door in a black hoody. His hoody carried the usual aroma of a weed scent.

"Nigga what you doing here?" T.C. asked opening his eyes. Malachi and Rob were wondering the same thing but they didn't speak on it.

"You know y'all my woes. I was at the game last night and seen that crazy fall you took. I knew had to come out here. How you feeling bro?"

"I'm good. I gotta broken arm and some back pain. Ima bounce back though," T.C. answered.

Heavy glanced up at the new morning episode of Sportscenter that was being aired. "Yeah, you'll be back in a month or so most likely," he said.

"Heavy you one of the only niggas I know coming to the hospital smelling like a pound of weed," Rob commented folding up his cover.

"Right! You stay smelling like some loud. You must have rolled up as soon as you woke up," Malachi added.

Heavy was silent for a long second. "Na, y'all got it wrong. What y'all fail to realize is that I rarely smoke this shit. I'm too busy trying to sell it. Ima fuckin h-u-s-t-l-e-r.!"

"Let me hold something then hustler," Rob stated in a commanding voice.

"I can put you on. That's way better than letting you hold something." Heavy pulled a wad of twenties out of his pocket and started counting it. He counted about six hundred dollars. "This is what I made this past four days," he portrayed putting the money back in his pocket.

"We not messing with the dope game. You know Rob daddy just got banked for that shit," Malachi spoke. He didn't want any himself or his brothers getting persuaded into distributing narcotics.

Heavy took the wad of money back out of his pocket gripping it with one hand like it was a hamburger. "What seventeen-year old's you know making this in a week Mal? No disrespect but Big Rob got banked for that soft (cocaine). Where the money a lot better but the consequences more severe. The weed game is a lot easier."

T.C. was laying on the bed soaking in all of the dialogue before he finally spoke. "Heavy you know the game is the game. The only decision we got to make is whether we gone play or not. You right about one thing though. Nobody our age is making money like that in a week."

Heavy looked at T.C. sensing that he was vibing with him. "You said a couple months ago that you wanted me to front you. This the perfect time for you to hop in the game. You can just sit back and make money while you recuperate. This weed gone sell itself. I promise you that!" Heavy sounded like a salesman as he spoke with confidence.

T.C. turned and looked at Rob and Malachi as if he was waiting on them to express their opinions.

"Don't look at us. If you wanna push weight, that's all on you T," Rob commented leaning back in the chair.

Malachi didn't follow up on Rob's statement. He remained quiet.

"Shit, for real Heavy I'm not going to say yes or no to you fronting me. I definitely don't want my grandparents having to pay this hospital bill by they self though. They already struggling to make ends meet as is."

"Moving these sacks will help pay for way more than this bill. You gone be able to help your peoples out on a daily basis bro." Heavy got up and shook everyone's hand as his phone started to ring. "Look bro, all I'm saying is that the money there for the taking. The same way we ran the courts is how we can run the streets."

T.C. nodded his head and said "I'll let you know bro."

"Yeah, let me know," Heavy said exiting the room.

"Mal you ready to roll out? I need to lay in my bed," Rob said checking the time.

"Yeah, we can bounce. We gone hit you up later T."

"Make sure y'all close the door all the way," T.C. said drifting back off to sleep.

-

Malachi and Rob walked out of the hospital in their Princeton two-piece jumpsuits they had on from the night before. Getting into Rob's car, Rob drove slow still feeling fatigue.

"Even though Heavy cool as hell with us, he on one trying get T into the game."

"Gotta say he is. I don't think neither one of them see all the bullshit that come along with selling that shit," Rob added.

"Right! Let me call this nigga J so I can tell him what just went down. I know he bout to be tripping too." Malachi pulled his IPhone out dialing J.B.'s number.

J.B.- Hello

Mal- What's Good king

J.B.- Nothing about to get fresh and roll out to Columbus with mom dukes. Y'all left the hospital yet?

Mal- Yeah, we on our way home now. That nigga Heavy came up to the hospital this morning on some random shit.

J.B.- Heavy? What he want? Knowing him he had another motive other than just checking up on T.

Mal- You right. He came up there talking about hustling and getting in the game.

J.B.- Yeah, they been talking about that for a minute now. Besides his cousin Snake, I think T is the only dude our age Heavy feel like he can somewhat trust.

Mal- Yeah, I guess you right. You know T the most money hungry out the squad. Every time somebody start talking big money his head swell up.

J.B.- That nigga know not to start flipping them packs. The temptation always there but I'm cool on it.

Mal- Right, you would think after seeing Big Rob get popped he would be cool but that's on bro if he wanna get down like that.

J.B.- You a hundred percent correct. Ring my line later bro.

Mal- Okay bro. (hangs up phone)

About a week later Malachi was at the court down the street from his house shooting jump shots by himself. It was about ten am in the morning and no one was outside. He had scored thirty-four points and nine rebounds the night before in Friday's night game. Despite his good game the Bearcats lost 62 to 55. It was hard for the team to adjust without T.C. facilitating the offense. The loss made Malachi reevaluate how he would approach the upcoming games while T.C. was on the sideline.

-

"You rolling with us or not?" Rob shouted from the car window. Malachi snapped out of his short trance and seen Rob and J.B. waiting for him to get into the Ford Explorer.

Malachi took his twenty-four-ounce blue Gatorade to the head as he walked over to the car. Closing the door, he seen the same elderly man flicking his wrist in the shooting motion.

"Bro don't be throwing that bottle down in my car. I stay having to clean up after y'all negros!" Rob said sounding annoyed.

"Nigga I stay cleaning up y'all stuff in my whip. You ain't saying nothing," Malachi responded hastily.

J.B. jumping in the conversation said, "Real talk y'all niggas be dirtying up the cars yall self. Especially when we be high."

Rob focused his energy in on J.B.. "Man J, I ain't trying hear that shit until you get your own whip. You gone be saying the same thing."

"I don't need no whip anyway. Right now, y'all niggas is my Uber," J.B. said laughing.

"Fuck outta here!" Rob said in retaliation.

"We headed to the hood?" Malachi asked changing the subject.

Rob was driving the railroad tracks as he replied, "Yeah, we meeting T down there on Memphis street.

It was the second week of November and the temperature was about forty degrees outside. Thick Carhartt jackets, skullies and Timberland boots became a common sight as they rolled through the streets of Rolling Heights. Pulling up to the block Heavy and T.C. were posted up along with about ten other dudes scattered out in the street.

"Bout time yall pulled up," T.C. stated walking up to the Explorer. T.C. had on a beige overall Carhartt with two black thermals up under it. His right arm was in a sling from the injury he had suffered the previous week.

"I had to go get them. What's good though nigga? I see you out here on the block like you running it," Rob observed.

T.C. didn't respond instantly but rather looked down the street scoping it out. "Na, I'm not doing nothing too much. Ima make this quick money until I can hop back on the court."

"Hop in the whip bro. You letting all my heat out," Rob insisted.

After T.C. got into the backseat Rob pulled down the street away from traffic.

"Damn nigga, how much of the weed you got on you? It smell like you got on weed cologne," Malachi commented sarcastically.

T.C. pulled out a plastic bag of lime marijuana from one of the pockets inside his Carhartt. He reached in the bag and pulled out one of the large buds. "Smell this god. This that super loud!" he said handing it to Malachi.

Malachi sniffed the bud holding it up to his nose. "You right. That shit is official. Call that stankonia."

"Yeah, that's reeking that one way," J.B. added in.

"So Heavy put you on?" Rob asked making eye contact with T.C..

"He looked out for me. Keep this info in this car but Heavy got all Tank's connects now."

J.B. handed the weed back to T.C. and questioned him. "Damn Tank let Heavy get all his plugs? How that happen?"

T.C. looked around outside to make sure nobody was walking up on the car. "Shit, y'all know the boys(police) just indicted Tank for the murder of Officer Dankey," T.C. spoke in a low voice.

Rob looked in his rear-view mirror again. "Damn for real? I ain't even surprised by how he was acting when he pulled us over this summer. It was only a matter of time before somebody put it to him."

T.C. nodded his head in agreeance. "That's the same thing I was saying. Everybody saying that they traced the scene of the crime down there on Memphis street through some deep forensics investigation."

"That forensics investigation pinpoint out the smallest details. Somebody probably snitched on him though real talk," J.B. commented.

"That's crazy man. I guess that's karma for all the foul stuff Dankey was doing out here. I'm salty for Tank though hopefully he can beat the case," Malachi spoke from the front seat.

T.C. nodded once again in agreeance. "Yeah, you know Tank solid. He don't care who you is he not gone take nobody shit. Heavy about to be one of the main plugs out here now. I only then had this pack for a couple days and about to make a profit."

"Here come that nigga Heavy now," J.B. reported looking in the right-side mirror.

Heavy walked up on the passenger side of the car. "What it do?"

"I don't know, you tell us boss," J.B. spoke.

"Shit, J you know the motto. Money talk, bullshit walk. Speaking of money, T you then missed out on two licks since you been over here."

"I ain't tripping. I'ma make it back," T.C. commented from the back seat.

"Ay, Heavy how many times a week you re-up?" Malachi asked.

"I re-up probably twice a week now. The only people who ask that question is people who trying to get in the game or jack boys. I take it you trying to hop in the game because I know your love for me wouldn't let you rob me," Heavy said in a serious tone.

Malachi started to talk before Heavy could finish his sentence. "You know damn well the only game I'm playing is on that court. You right though my love for you and my principles would never let me do anything ill to you. I'm too trill for all the bullshit."

Heavy replied, "That's a hundred bro."

"I keep on trying tell y'all niggas we got a better chance of getting paid playing these sports than selling dope," Malachi iterated.

Heavy took a step back from the car lighting his black and mild cigar. He blew the smoke out into the frigid air. "I then chose my path bro and I'm in it to win it."

"You gotta respect that," J.B. said.

"Yeah you do. I'm about to the roll to the store. You rolling with us T?" Rob questioned.

"Yeah, Ima go. I'll be back in a little bit bro," T.C. told Heavy.

Heavy took steps back towards the car grabbing the door handle. "I'm about to hop in here too. I need to grab a couple of relos from the store."

Rob looked at Heavy arching his eyebrows. "Hell na! Ya big ass not getting in my whip nigga. You gone mess and around and throw my shocks and suspension off!" Rob shouted.

"Nigga you just as big as me. You just a yellow boy! Grab me a couple of relos from the store." Heavy pulled out a couple of singles out of his pocket and handed it to T.C..

-

Mr. Smith took a sip from his bottled water. "With a show of hands how many of you all listen to rap music?" The whole class raised their hands. "How many of you all listen to R&B music or technically speaking rhythm and blues?" The majority of the class raised their hands again as Mr. Smith took the quick census. "Okay, now how many of you all listen to rock?" he asked curiously. A couple of the students hesitated raising their hands looking around at their other classmates. "Hmmm very interesting. Stay with me class. I'm going somewhere with this. Now how many of my fellow students listen to classical music?" None of the students raised their hands. Instead they looked at their teacher with puzzled faces and like he was half crazy. "Really, none of my students listen to classical music? I'm astounded.

T.C. raised his left hand due to the fact that his right arm was in the sling. "Not trying to be funny Mr. Smith but what does classical music have to with anything?"

Another student shouted out, "Right!" in reaction to T.C.'s question.

"I am glad you asked that question Mr. Crawford. I observed that predominantly all of you listen to Rap and R&B. Which makes sense because most of these genres of music have African American musicians. So, the obvious conclusion is that you students do not listen to these other genres of music because they contain few black artists or messages that aren't relevant to you guys life."

Mr. Smith began to write on the board.

"Class your homework for this week is to look up influential African American artists in all these genres of music." Mr. Smith had written a list of Rap, R&B, Rock, Classical, Blues and famous violinists on the board. He turned around giving his full attention back to his class. "It's good to have your favorite genres of music but individuals should also study and explore other areas of music. This helps you to expand your mind and better understand different cultures."

"Mr. Smith what you know about rap? You old school ain't you?" another student from the class asked.

Mr. Smith took another gulp from his water bottle. "I'm old school but I know what's up young buck! I know about Future, Drake, Kendrick Lamar, J Cole, Nipsey Hussle, Dave East, Young Dolph and a lot more. Y'all forget I have a daughter around your age."

"Dayg, Mr. Smith you do know something!" Malachi exclaimed.

"More than you know Mr. Summers. I'm old school though so I grew up off Rakim, LL Cool J, Hot Boys, No Limit, Big Daddy Kane, 2Pac, Biggie, Nas, Outkast, Jay-Z, UGK, 8ball&MJG the LOX and many more. That's when rap artists actually took pride in their lyrics. The songs might not have all been positive but their content and delivery was always on point!"

Mr. Smith looked at the time on his wrist watch. "Class is almost over but I expect that you guys will all enjoy your project," Mr. Smith spoke as the bell rang.

-

The class broke for the hallway only to be met by the other packs of students in the hallway. Rob, T.C. and Malachi spotted J.B. at the end of the hallway conversing with Kandi. Kandi was explaining to J.B. how she needed his help designing her website to display her modeling photos.

"When is a good time for you?" J.B. asked Kandi. Kandi put on her p coat and gloves preparing for the cold weather outside.

"T.C. is coming over my house later. Just come over with him when he comes through."

"Okay cool. I can do that," J.B. replied.

"I'm for real J, don't spin me. I want to get this site up and running as quick as I can."

"I won't spin you. We don't got practice today so I'll be able to help you for sure."

"What y'all over here talking about?" T.C. asked giving Kandi a hug.

"Talking bout getting her modeling site up and runnin," J.B. voiced.

"Modeling site for what? Just get your Instagram popping," Rob commented.

"No, Rob! That's what's wrong with these females now. These damn social sites got these females thinking they models! In reality they not though. I'm trying to be official with mine!" It was evident that Kandi was passionate about her modeling career by the flare in her voice.

"Yeah, J the man if you want to get your website on point. He gone get you right," Malachi said joining the conversation.

Kandi turned to T.C.. "What time you gone be over babe?"

"Probably about five or six boo. Ima go home for a little bit first. Ima call you when we on the way," T.C. responded hugging Kandi with his left arm.

"You want me to shoot you to the house T?" Malachi asked.

"Man, hell yeah I need a ride! It's too cold to be on that bus!"

"Yeah T right, it is cold as hell. Ima need a ride too," J.B. stated.

-

T.C. walked in his grandma's house as quick as he could after he got out of Malachi's car to escape the freezing air. Grandma Lois was sitting in her living room gazing out the window. Thomas walked over and gave her a kiss on the cheek.

"How you doing grandma?"

"I'm good baby. Just sitting here enjoying the scenery," she answered.

T.C. looked at his grandma confused as if she was speaking in a foreign language. "Why you looking like that son?" she inquired.

"Because granny this neighborhood is not anything pleasant to look at. It looks like a warzone out there."

"Come here baby and look out this window with me," she said waving her hand in the fetching motion. T.C. started began to gaze out the window with his grandma.

"You see baby in reality it does look rough outside these doors but beauty is in the eye of the beholder. I remember this neighborhood when I was a little girl. That's when people actually took pride in it. Whenever I look at this community I reminisce on the beauty that it once had and could very well return with a joint community effort."

"You right grandma. I talk about it so harshly because I've always seen it in this condition," he explained with meekness.

"Yes, I know baby. Just remember in this life no matter how ugly your circumstance may be, always paint a beautiful portrait in your mind. To be victorious in a negative atmosphere, positivity first has to be triumphant in your heart and mind."

"You exactly right grandma." Thomas loved his grandma because she would always say the things he needed to hear to get his mind right.

He walked in his room throwing his Carhartt and skully onto the ground. Flopping on his pillows he dozed off to sleep. Shortly after, he was interrupted from his phone vibrating. Opening his eyes, he looked at his phone trying to figure out the random number that was calling him. He assumed it was somebody trying to buy a bag of weed so he answered.

T.C.- Hello

Tisha- What you doing?

T.C.- Who this though?

Tisha- This Tisha. (Kandi best friend)

T.C.- Oh, what's up with you?

Tisha- Nothing. I need some loud. You got some you can sell me?

T.C.- I got it in. How much you need?

Tisha- Just a blunt. You charge twenty a g, don't you?

T.C.- Yeah, twenty a g for loud.

Tisha- Okay, that's cool. Can you walk down my house and bring it to me?

T.C.- I can. Give me about twenty minutes.

Tisha- Okay, call my phone when you outside.

T.C.- Alright.

T.C. was tired but he wasn't going to let the twenty-dollar lick pass him by. He grabbed his Carhartt jacket and walked out the door. Tisha's family had recently moved out to the neighborhood at the beginning of the school year. The cold weather caused him to power walk to her house a couple of streets over. He called her phone as soon as he laid eyes on her front porch.

T.C.- Aye, I'm outside.

Tisha- Okay come around to the back door.

T.C. walked through the thin grass to the back where Tisha was waiting for him with the door open.

"Aye, Tisha it's freezer cold out here. You better be glad you cool or else I wouldn't have made that trip."

"I agree, it is cold. You can come in." She extended the screen door open. T.C. pulled his bag of weed out as soon as he stepped in her house but Tisha stopped him. "Don't pull that out yet. My little brother in the other room watching Sponge Bob. Follow me to my room."

"Alright," he responded. In the back of his head T.C. felt like Tisha was dragging the process out but he followed her anyway. He knew Kandi would be pissed if she found out that he was going into Tisha's bedroom but he was focused on the money. Trey Songz was playing through the radio speakers as they walked in.

"You got a relo on you?" she asked shutting her room door.

T.C. checked his jacket trying to find a cigar. He pulled one out and threw it on her bed. "You want a lot Tisha, damn! In fact, I'ma have to tax you two extra two dollars for that!"

"They only cost a dollar at the store," Tisha responded counting a handful of singles.

"I know how much they cost. It's a dollar for me buying it and a dollar for that cold ass walk down here!"

He pulled out a pocket size digital scale weighing out a gram of the herb.

Tisha squinted her face up at the overwhelming odor. "Geesh, that's strong!"

"Yeah, this that real loud right here Tisha. Just call it that stankonia!"

"Right! That's the best name for it. Tisha handed him twenty-two dollars after he took the weed off the scale. "You want to smoke with me?"

"Right now?" T.C. asked curiously.

"Yeah, right now goofy," she replied letting out some giggles.

T.C. hesitated briefly then replied, "Roll up."

He knew he had already overstepped his boundaries by being in his girl's best friend bedroom. On top of that he was starting to examine Tisha sexually as she sat on her bed. Tisha had a small frame but her curvy thighs in the purple leggings she was wearing caught his attention. Staring at her he could tell her small but plump booty was pillow soft.

"Where we gone smoke at?" he asked.

"I smoke right here in my room all the time. My mama don't get home until late night."

"Okay, but what about the smell? How you get rid of it?"

"I put a wet towel at the bottom of the door and crack open my window. Sometimes I light an incense but most of the time I spray a bottle of this stuff called "Weed be Gone.""

T.C. started to laugh. "Where you get a bottle of that at? Do it work?"

"I got it off of Amazon's website. Yeah, it work super good. My mama never said nothing about smelling anything."

"That's what's up. I need a bottle of that pronto," he insisted.

"Let me go get the towel and check on my brother. Can you start rolling up?"

"Yeah, I will."

T.C. observed Tisha's black hair with highlights of red in it. He admired how good it looked against her yellow skin tone as she walked out the room. His mind was telling him to evacuate the scene but his body didn't move.

He split open the cigarillo with his thumb nail and emptied out the tobacco. As he began to break down the ganja his phone started to ring. J.B.'s name appeared on the screen. T.C. chose not to answer already knowing that him and J.B. were supposed to be going to Kandi's house. Coincidentally a text message from Kandi came immediately after J.B.'s missed call. The text read, "What time y'all gone get here baby?" Kandi had put four of the kissy face emojis at the end of the message. He chose not to respond back to her message either.

Tisha came back in the room about five minutes later. "You rolled that up quick?" she asked as she bent over to place the towel at the bottom of the door. "Kandi told me that you and J.B. supposed to be going over her house so we can hurry up and smoke this."

T.C. felt Tisha's vibrant body heat as she sat next to him on her bed. Lighting the blunt, he handed her the lighter so she could spark the incense. He hit the joint four times and passed it to her. Tisha inhaled the weed smoke and blew it out through her nose coughing a little.

"How long you been smoking Tisha?"

"I started smoking a couple of summers ago. How long you been hustling?" she asked in return.

"I just started not too long ago. You know my main focus is hoop but then again living out here money don't come along too easy." T.C. took a strong hit of the weed after he finished his sentence.

"Na, it don't. So, let me ask you, have you been staying faithful to my friend?"

It was complete silence in the room as he looked at her with his bloodshot eyes. "Why you ask that?"

"I'm just asking because I know a lot of chicks be jocking you and your clique heavy. What y'all call y'all selves, F.M.B. right?"

"Yeah, it stand for forever my brother." Passing the blunt back to Tisha he decided to change the subject as Trey Songz "Slow motion" song played in the background. "Purple your favorite color?" he asked pointing at her walls.

"Yes, purple it is. I painted them the week before we moved in here. Anything with purple I like. You see I got on these purple leggings."

Tisha's comment caused Thomas to look down at her thighs once again. "Yeah, it is a nice color," he said. The longer he sat on the bed with her the more enticed he got by her.

"This might sound lame but a lot of times when I get high, I just sit back and stare at the stars on my ceiling. I like to imagine that I'm somewhere other than here. You know just put myself in a whole different life."

Tisha flopped her head back on her pillow. T.C. followed suit flopping back on the other pillow right next to her. Tisha's dark lampshade made the lighting in the room dim.

"I wonder if it's life on other planets. Like other people we don't know about." The THC from the marijuana was now starting to have its effects because his thoughts began to drift all over the place.

"I wonder too. I just want to get rich and live like a black Kardashian."

T.C. laughed as he put the blunt out in the ashtray. "What's a black Kardashian?"

Tisha turned her head on the pillow so she could see his face. "You know what I mean. I want to ball out like the Kardashians do. You see how Kim and Khloe splurge like its nothing. Well if I had money I'd do the same thing except I would be the black version."

"I feel you. I want to ball out too. That's why I'm bout to be hustling hard so I can be a young rich nigga or better yet a young rich king."

"I definitely feel you on that. To be honest I wish I could just get rich, smoke weed, go shopping and have sex all day."

Tisha's statement enticed T.C. even more. "Sex the shit now, so I can only imagine when we get paid. We gone be busting million-dollar nuts!" They both laughed hysterically at T.C.'s comical remark.

"Shit, we might not be rich but we can still fuck our boos like we are," Tisha said.

"Oh yeah?" T.C. asked as he slid his left hand onto her thigh starting to rub it.

He couldn't contain himself any longer. The temptation from lying in the same bed as Tisha had overtaken him. Tisha had put up no resistance as he started to rub on her. He smoothly slid his hand inside her leggings and in between her legs. Tisha let out a slow moan as he started to rub on her g spot. The climate in between her legs was full of warmth and moisture. He slid his hand around to her backside gripping a handful of booty. He was making the most of only using his left hand since his right arm was still in the sling. Kissing slowly on her neck they eventually ended up locking lips. The intensity of the moment made them forget about everything and only focus on pleasing each other. Tisha assisted T.C. with taking his shirt off then quickly took off her leggings. Admiring Tisha's yellow skin T.C. propped Tisha's legs into the air holding them stable with his left forearm. He had a full erection as he stroked her insides powerfully for which seemed like an eternity but in reality, was only six minutes. Switching positions, he flipped her over and began stroking her with strong back shots. Tisha buried her face in pillow to muzzle her intense moaning. By this time, he had missed two calls from Kandi and two from J.B..

-

Kandi- Hey, have you talked to my bae?

J.B.- Nope, I was gone ask you the same thing.

Kandi- I don't know what his ass doing!

J.B.- I don't know either. He probably fell asleep.

Kandi- He tripping! I'm salty because I really wanted to start working on my website asap!

J.B.- I feel you on that.

Kandi- Well, can you still come over here? We don't have to be long but I at least wanted to get it started.

J.B.- Yeah, I will. Give me about twenty minutes.

J.B. was at the house lounging. He put on his black sweats, white thermal and polo coat. He stopped in the mirror brushing his hair about fifty times. He threw on his hat and left out into rugged evening chill. Kandi stayed about ten minutes down the street. J.B. knew in the back of his head that he had a crush on her for a long time now, so he felt a little awkward going over her house. He didn't want to play her though so he kept walking, making it to her house in about seven minutes.

Walking up the driveway he noticed her mama's car was absent. He figured she must have made a store run. J.B. knocked on the door and Kandi opened it about fifteen seconds later. She came to the door in some grey sweats and loose-fitting Bengals shirt. Her hair was tied back in a ponytail. J.B. could tell that she was in a relaxed mood.

"What up J," she said as he walked in the house.

"Nothing at all. It's cold as hell out there!"

"I see, your nose red. Got you out here looking like Rudolph!" she expressed jokingly.

"I see you got jokes," J.B. replied.

Kandi grinned at him. "You know it. Come on, my computer in the basement."

He followed her to the basement observing the elegance and immaculateness of the house. "From the looks of the crib I can see y'all balling over here."

"My mama do interior decorating as her side hustle. She went to my little brother parent teacher conference so she'll be gone for a couple of hours. Kandi turned on her grey Mac pc that was in the corner of her basement. J.B. flopped down on the all-black sofa that sat in front of a forty-two-inch TV.

"I'm glad Patrice (Kandi's mama) didn't see you flop down on her furniture like that. She would have had a fit!"

"My bad, did you ever talk to T?"

Kandi turned hastily from the computer replying, "Nope! I don't know what his butt doing. I'ma let him have it when I finally do talk to him."

Kandi opened a file she had saved on her pc. "These are all my modeling pics J."

J.B. scanned her pictures closely as she scrolled with the mouse. Kandi had on an assortment of outfits and different hairstyles. Her caramel skin tone seemed to compliment every picture in the perfect way.

"Yeah, these hot. You look about twenty-two in these pics, not seventeen."

"I know I do. When I apply makeup, it gives me a mature look. What website do you want to go to get started?"

"You can go to sitebuilder.com," he insisted.

Kandi moved to the side letting J.B. take over the computer. He spent the next hour showing her the basics and laying the foundation for her website.

"Does T.C. cheat on me?" she asked randomly. J.B. didn't respond logging out of the internet session on the pc.

"Hello! I asked you a question!" Kandi had an ice grill on her face as she waited for an answer.

"Na, Thomas Crawford has never cheated on you. You know that man love your ass."

Kandi rolled her eyes. "You wouldn't tell me anyway because that's your bro!"

J.B. got up from the chair brushing his hair trying to avoid any further interrogation from Kandi.

"Your ass been brushing your hair faithfully since we been in the fifth grade. OMG, we juniors now! Your butt ain't changed one bit!"

J.B. grabbed his Polo coat putting it on. "You haven't changed either. I remember in the fifth grade you used to like me though."

Kandi let out a big smile. "Na, nigga you had a big crush on me but you was too scared to say something!"

"I wasn't scared. I just knew your ass was crazy! That's why you and bro perfect for each other!"

"Ha whatever!" Kandi exclaimed as they walked up the basement stairs.

"You know I'm just playing with you."

"Whatever J! Thank you for starting my website though. I appreciate it."

Kandi reached up to give Jerome a hug. He hugged her back with a firm grip and they suddenly ended up locking lips as they were about to let each other go. It was a sudden intense rush between both of them as they engaged in the intimate act for about five seconds. Letting go of each other they silently stared at each other. Being drawn in by Kandi's eyes and her luscious lips J.B. grabbed Kandi and began kissing on her neck. His conscious got the best of him though, when an image of T.C. popped up in his head clear as day. J.B. stopped himself abruptly taking a step back from Kandi.

"Shit man!" he yelled out shaking his head.

Kandi opened her front door. "I know we messed up. Thank you again J," Kandi said as he walked out.

"Yeah, you welcome."

"Jerome?"

J.B. turned around. "What's up?" he asked.

"Let's make sure we keep this strictly between me and you please!" Kandi had a tense urgency in her eyes as she made the request.

"Of course. This never happened!" He turned back around starting his journey down the street.

-

This was the first time in his life he could ever recall committing a treacherous act against somebody he loved, especially one of his brothers. It was weighing heavy on his mental and Jerome knew he had to tell somebody. He knew he couldn't tell Rob because he knew Rob might slip up and tell T.C.. He knew he couldn't tell T.C. because he knew that would put their brotherhood bond in jeopardy. On top of that he knew that he would probably want to fight him if he found out. He decided to call Malachi whom he was probably closest with in the squad. The temperature had dropped ten degrees but J.B. was sweating on the inside of his Polo coat.

Malachi- What up J.

J.B.- (slight pause) what up bro.

Malachi- Chilling at the spot. What you on?

J.B.- Nothing walking back to the crib.

Malachi- Word, where you coming from?

J.B.- Kandi spot.

Malachi- Oh yeah, you and T was supposed to be helping her with that website. Y'all get it started?

J.B.- (long pause) Yeah, we did.

Malachi- What the hell wrong with you bra? You over here talking like somebody then stole your money or something.

J.B.- Na, bro. Some bullshit just happened though.

Mal- (Malachi sat up from his slumped position on his bed) What popped off?

J.B.- Shit, men I was at Kandi house and before I left I hugged her.

Mal- Alright nigga. Is that it? (Malachi asked now anxious to hear what J.B. was going to say)

J.B.- Man, we ended up kissing.

Malachi- (J.B.'s statement made Malachi jump up from his bed.) Men hold the fuck up. You and Kandi kissed? Like a friend kiss on the cheek or we about to get it in kiss?

J.B.- Like we about to get it in kiss.

Malachi- Where the hell was T at men?

J.B.- Bro never came through. We was blowing his phone up but he ain't never hit us back up. She damn near begged me to come over there, so I just went.

Mal- Your first mistake was going over there solo. Still at that you was off one pushing up on that ass. You know damn well that's been bro main chick for a minute.

J.B.- I know bro I fucked up going over there solo. I thought her peoples was gone be there though.

Mal- On some real shit, that was ill on both of y'all part. She just a chick though. T your brother.

J.B.- (No response)

Malachi- How y'all end up kissing anyway?

J.B.- Man, honestly, I don't even know. That shit just happened right after we hugged each other when I was about to leave.

Malachi- Stuff like that just don't happen bro. Y'all probably been liking each other. It just hit the surface today.

J.B.- I mean we used to like each other back in elementary but you know that don't count for nothing.

Malachi- Apparently yall still feeling each other though. If T find out you already know he gone wanna bang with you.

J.B.- Mal, don't tell nobody bro. Only reason I told you is because I had to get this shit off my conscious.

Malachi- You putting me in a fucked-up position bro. I feel like I'm not being loyal to T by keeping it from him. On the other hand, I know a scenario like this could put a black cloud over the squad.

J.B.- I already know bro.

Malachi- You know we was taught not to let a dollar bill or broad come in between the squad.

J.B.- I know bro I messed up. Keep this shit between me and you though.

Malachi- This convo not gone go past this phone. You know we built on loyalty. You violated that J.

J.B.- I already know bro. I swear to God some shit like this will never happen again.

Malachi- I hope it won't bro. Evaluate your actions my nigga!

Malachi hung up the phone pissed that his brother would violate the principles of brotherhood over a female. He remembered vividly the words of Big Rob from a couple years back when he told them not to let women separate them. Malachi's phone started to ring again and he assumed that it was J.B.. He was wrong though as he looked at T.C.'s name appear on his screen. It was ironic that he was getting a phone call from T.C. immediately after he had given Jerome his word that he wouldn't let him know about the foul scenario that took place.

Malachi- What up T.

T.C.- Nothing I'm at the crib chillin on some high shit.

Malachi- You tripping smoking bro. You gone be out of shape when you get back on the court.

T.C.- I'll be cool bro, I don't smoke every day. Something crazy popped off earlier though.

Malachi- (In the back of his head he thought that Kandi had already told him what happened with her and J.B.) What happened?

T.C.- Mann (Dragging his voice out) Tisha had hit me up earlier wanting me to sell her a sack of some loud. I wasn't bout to do it but I knew I couldn't let that money pass me up.

Malachi- I feel it.

T.C.- I went down her house about five something. I was supposed to be meeting up with J and Kandi but I got caught up with Tisha.

Malachi- So what happened?

T.C.- I went down there her spot and ended up smoking a blunt with her. I wasn't even trying to smoke but we both ended up posting up in her room. Her mama was gone so she ain't even care about us smoking in there.

Malachi- Damn y'all smoked in her room. Tisha look good bro. I would have been wanting to smash that.

T.C.- Nigga!

Malachi- Holdup king, did you smash Tisha?

T.C.- Man, I got caught up. I smashed her and wasn't even trying too.

Malachi- Damn bro. You smashed Tisha? What her sex game was like? How it pop off?

T.C.- Real talk we was just having a good conversation while we was partaking in the smoke session. We was both laying on the bed and her thighs kept rubbing up against me. I started playing with her g spot and kissing on her neck. It was a wrap after that.

Mal- I guess this smash a friend day. (Malachi said before he could stop himself). Did you put a rubber on? You know Tisha be going hard for real.

T.C.- Smash a friend day? What you talking bout bro? Real talk, I ain't even put one on. I was trying to get in that ass as quick as I could on some thirsty shit.

Malachi- (Lets our laughs) You pulled out in time, right?

T.C.- Barely! I was super faded and the way that ass was wobbling, she damn near had my kids inside of her!

Malachi- Boy, you bet not let Kandi find out! (He spoke not wanting either of them to find out about their mishaps).

T.C.- You best believe she not. That was some good sex but I do feel bad for smashing her best friend.

Malachi- Nigga your ass don't feel bad. From now on don't sell no more loud to Tisha! (he said sarcastically)

T.C.- Men what! I'm drug free as far as Tisha is concerned. Wait til I tell J and Rob. They gone be tripping off this story how you was.

Malachi- Right. Holler at me tomorrow bro.

T.C.- Okay king.

-

Malachi turned on his TV to watch Sportscenter but was interrupted by a knock on his door. It was his mama.

"I heard your conversation," Mama Kelley said standing in his doorway.

"For real though mama? You just gone be that nosey though?"

Mama Kelley frowned her face up as she wrapped her night scarf on her head. "Boy, this my house so whatever conversation happen in this house is my business! Ima just say this though, remember what two biggest things that men fall out over."

Malachi figured that he knew what she was going to say but he still asked, "What's that?"

"Women and money. No matter how close a group of men are those two variables can always destroy the bond. I know your daddy and Big Rob already told you that but now you hearing it from your mama herself. Take heed!" Mama Kelley looked sternly at her son. "Another thing, your ass bet not be bringing no little girls up in my house either!" Mama Kelley ended the conversation swinging the door shut.

Malachi fell asleep watching Sportscenter.

-

At the end of the same week the Princeton Bearcat team were preparing for their night game against Snoop and the Woodward Thundercats.

"Bro you think you can run me over to Evanston tonight after the game?" T.C. asked.

Rob finished drinking his cup of Gatorade before he responded. "Evanston? What you trying go out there for?"

"I got this plug out there. He gone let me cop a pound for about half price. I gotta make it out there by tonight though."

Rob looked at T.C. with a crooked expression on his face. "So, you trying go to Evanston late night and cop from some random nigga?"

"Na, he ain't random. I already copped from him a couple times. He a hundred."

"On some real shit I don't know about that move T. My daddy ain't even like moving weight through that hood. They real territorial out there."

"Bro I already know that. Ima be super up if I can hit this lick tonight though. Super UP!!" T.C. pointed his right index finger in the air symbolizing the up signal.

Rob looked at T.C. as if he was deliberating whether to take him or not. "I can take you tomorrow. Ima chill with this shorty on the west side after the game tonight. I can't spin her no more because I then already spinned her twice. Ask Mal."

"Ask me what?" Malachi asked stepping into the conversation.

"I got fifty for you bro, if you can take me to go get this pack tonight," Thomas negotiated.

"Pack tonight? Where at?" Malachi inquired again setting his game bag down in the locker room.

"Out in Evanston. We gone be in and out bro," T.C. spoke trying to persuade Malachi.

"Evanston? Shut, I don't know bro. How much you say you was gone give me?"

"I got you with fifty god."

"Alright, I'll take you but if the scene look skep, we getting ghost sap!" Malachi spoke with a serious manner as he looked at his brother.

"See if J trying to roll with y'all," Rob added in.

J.B. was entering the locker room in the midst of Rob's statement. "What up kings," J.B. said.

"Nothing, T and Malachi trying to go out in Evanston and jug tonight."

J.B. was brushing his hair as usual. "Why Evanston though?"

"That's where the plug at. You trying to jug with us?" T.C. questioned.

"I want to because honestly it just don't need to be y'all two going out there tonight. Only thing is me and mom dukes going to Indiana tonight so we can check out this campus in the morning."

"That's what's up," Rob replied.

"Yeah, they offering me a full ride academic scholarship," J.B. mentioned.

Malachi threw his arms around J.B.'s shoulders saying, "I'm proud of you son!"

"Men na, y'all my sons," J.B. said laughing.

"Real talk, that's what's up though. Me and Mal gone be good tonight." We all making moves tonight after the game. The main thing is that we all stay safe," T.C. spoke ending the conversation.

When game time arrived, the gymnasium was filled to capacity as expected for the rival game. It was a tough, physical game. Malachi and Snoop were going back and forth scoring buckets on each other all game. Snoop's braids easily hung down his back and people would often call him "young Iverson." The name fit him perfectly because Snoop was the leading scorer in the state. Malachi was the 3rd ranked scorer in the state. The Bearcats team knew that if T.C. was playing, then the game probably wouldn't have to been as close. T.C.'s absence on the court took away at least eighteen points that the team had to make up for. Nevertheless, the Bearcats managed to pull out the win 77 to 74. The game came down to the last possession. J.B. made a crucial steal on a pass that was intended for Snoop at the three-point line. When he made the steal, he avoided the Woodward defenders letting the last seven seconds in the game expire. A lot of the Woodward players were bitter after their loss choosing not to shake the Bearcats hands.

"Good win guys," Coach P spoke in the middle of the locker room. "Our defense got stronger as the game went along and that's the type of defensive mentality we need to embrace as we get closer to tournament time." Coach P wiped his forehead with a white towel. "Now we won't have practice this Monday but be ready to practice hard in Tuesday so we can be ready for Thursday's game. Alright now, bring it in. Victory on three. One, two, three, victory!" The team broke the huddle and the players went their separate ways.

"Y'all still going out there?" Rob asked changing in his street gear.

"I guess so. We still going T?" Malachi asked.

"Yeah, we are. For real, we need to be there in about an hour."

"What time is it now?" Malachi asked.

T.C. replied, "It's going on ten now. You still going to see ol girl in Colerain Rob?"

"Yeah, I am. Ima hit y'all up as soon as I leave her spot."

"Okay bro. You bout to leave out with mom dukes J?"

"Yeah, we gone start our expedition soon as we leave here," J.B. spoke to T.C..

"Alright cool. I guess it's just me and you then Mal," T.C. stated.

Malachi was reading a text message from Coach Joe as they exited the locker room. "Solid game son. See you at home. Love you," the text message read.

-

"Turn on that GPS so we know where the hell we going," Malachi directed Thomas as he drove onto the expressway.

"I know the way bro. We'll be there in about fifteen minutes," T.C. mentioned from the passenger seat.

Malachi had the heat on full blast to fight off the chill of the night air. T.C. lit up a small blunt after he told Malachi, "Get off at the Mitchell exit bro." Getting off the exit it took them about ten minutes to drive into the neighborhood. The streets were dark as the only illumination came from the tall street lights with the orange light bulbs. They rode by a block in the backstreets that was occupied by a gang of young men from Evanston.

"Where we supposed to be meeting dude at?" Malachi asked now on edge.

"A couple streets over by that corner store on Woodburn."

Malachi made two right turns onto the street that T.C. was talking about. It was more illuminated than the eerie back streets but was also filled with more young men posted in Carhartt jackets and skullies.

"Pull around to the side of the store bro. You see dude right there in the black skully and red Carhartt?" T.C. asked as they rode directly by the store. "That's the plug I was talking about. Everybody be calling him Pacman out here."

143

Malachi tried to get a good view of who his brother was talking about but he could only see a husky dark skin figure. He didn't get a clear view of his face but did see the gold grill in the bottom of Pacman's mouth. Malachi parked the Durango truck on the side of the store where he still had a decent view of the activity on the block. T.C. pulled a wad out of money out of his pocket. He dropped the fifty dollars he owed Malachi into his middle console.

"It ain't gone take long bro," T.C. said as he dialed Pacman's number.

T.C.- I'm here bro.

Pacman- Come around to the front of the store. Ima have my manz give you what you need.

T.C.- (hesitates) Alright, Ima be around there.

Pacman- Alright.

"Walk around where?" Malachi asked eagerly.

"I gotta go meet him in front of the store."

"Na, fuck that dude need to come to the whip. That shit don't sound right at all!"

"We out here now and I need to hit this jug bro. These niggas wild but they not gone do anything on a main street where the cops ride heavy," T.C. explained.

"Alright bro. Just hurry up," Malachi told him.

T.C. got out the car putting a black skully over his dreads. Malachi knew T.C. was rolling the dice trying to succeed on his money mission.

Neither one of them had a gun plus T.C.'s elbow was still in recuperation so he wasn't a hundred percent.

The dark tint on Malachi's windows gave him a slight sense of security as he checked his mirrors and tried to monitor the block at the same time. T.C. was visible for a moment but eventually faded out of sight. This worried Malachi a little bit. Two minutes later his phone started to ring. It was T.C..

Mal- Yeah nigga?

T.C.- Bro that fifty I dropped in the console, I need you to bring that to me real quick.

Mal- You need the fifty? What for?

T.C.- I'm bout to cop a half on top of what I was already getting. Run that to me sap bro!

T.C. hung up the phone before Malachi could talk again. Malachi was pissed that T.C. had put them in this vulnerable situation but he knew they were in too deep to turn back now. He grabbed the money and opened the door into the freezing air. Every time he breathed he could see the white vapor from his breath. Approaching the block, he walked past a couple of dudes who were standing on it like they were statues.

"What up though," one of the dudes spoke as Malachi walked by.

Not making any eye contact with the men Malachi replied, "What up."

Malachi spotted T.C. down by the end of the store talking to two dudes. One of them was Pacman. "Here this shit bro." Malachi handed T.C. the balled up fifty-dollar bill out of his jean pocket.

Instantly after he handed T.C. the money he felt a cold piece of steel being pointed to the side of his neck. "Give up everything nigga!" a voice from behind him shouted fiercely.

Malachi foolishly tried to turn around but the robber pointed the gun harder into his neck. "Don't fucking move!" the voice yelled. Malachi looked to his left and seen another man with a gun pointed at T.C.'s head.

"We don't got no more money than what we came here with. I already gave all my dough to Pac," T.C. elaborated with his hands in the surrender position.

Malachi noticed that Pacman and his boy had vanished out of sight in the midst of all the chaos. The two robbers searched through their pockets emptying everything out.

"These niggas don't got no dough man!" one of the robbers yelled. Malachi and T.C. were both praying that the two robbers wouldn't end up shooting them.

"Fuck it! We just gone have to take these niggaz to the alley and strip em down. We can at least take they whip," the other robber spoke anxiously.

"Ay, ay, ay cuz don't rob them!" a third voice spoke from behind them.

Malachi felt the barrel of the gun slightly change angles as the jack boy turned to see who it was. It was Snoop, surprisingly but yet calming Malachi and T.C. at the same time.

"Cuz what the fuck you mean don't rob these niggas? We about to take em up top!"

"Little cuz, I know you family but these is my niggas. They not from here but they a hundred. Trust me when I tell you that," Snoop confirmed.

The jack boys both got quiet briefly. "Alright fam, Ima let them go but you owe me!" the robber said.

"I got you!" Snoop replied confidently.

Removing the guns from T.C. and Malachi's heads the hooded jack boys ran off in the opposite direction.

"Pick y'all shit up. Ima walk y'all back to y'all car," Snoop spoke in a calm but demanding voice.

T.C. moved so quickly he picked up his belongings and Malachi's all in one swoop. Walking back past the store the block was vacant other than a couple of dope fiends standing on the other side of the store.

"Ay bro, we owe you our lives Snoop, real talk," Malachi commented opening his front door.

Snoop shook his head in disagreement with Malachi. "Na, bro y'all don't owe me nothing. I'm just glad I was out here when that shit went down. It was bout to get even uglier real quick! Why y'all was out this way trying to cop a pack anyway?"

Malachi turned his head and looked at T.C. pissed off.

"It's all on me. I had Mal drive me out here trying to hit a lick on a pack. That shit damn near got us bodied though!"

Snoop eyed T.C. with a twisted look on his face. "I didn't even know you was in the game T! All Ima say is the game on the court and the game on the streets is two different games. If you lose out here my nigga, it's not no game to play the next week after that."

"I know Snoop. I just needed this fast money right now though," Thomas replied.

"I feel you we all want that fast money but you gotta do your homework and know who you dealing with my nigga. That plug you had was my cousin. He a well-known jack boy out here."

"You right, I was slipping. Best believe it won't happen again though. I thank God you came out there though. We owe you gold my nigga!" T.C. exclaimed.

Snoop extended his hand to give Malachi and T.C. dap. "Like I said it's nothing. We rivals on the court but out here y'all official with me. Make it home safe my niggas," Snoop spoke before he left their presence.

The two brothers got into their car both thanking God that they were going home in one peace. They know they could have easily have been statistics on the nightly news.

-

"What up Ziggy," Malachi yelled out from his car window. Ziggy looked over with his filter tip cigarette in his mouth. "Get in Zig," Malachi shouted. Ziggy got into the car with his long locks sinking into the passenger seat reeking of incense.

"How ya doing Mal? Ya boys haven't been by the house in a minute," Ziggy spoke with his strong Jamaican accent.

"We just been busy with hoop season Zig. Where was you headed to?"

Ziggy pulled a ten-dollar bill out of his coat pocket. "You can take me to the store. I heard what happened to you boys the other week in out there Evanston. You souljas need to be more careful."

Malachi was quiet trying to figure out how Ziggy had found out about the incident. "Yeah, that happened about a week ago. We good now."

"Are you good? It's by the grace of God and the universal energy that you're not in the cemetery right now!"

Malachi pulled up to the corner store and parked his car. Ziggy reached in his all black coat and randomly pulled out a small hand-held compass.

"I know you and your brothers are close. Take heed though, to your own life compass. No man can follow another man's compass because it will be inevitable for him to arrive at his own God appointed destination."

Ziggy handed Malachi the compass as he got out the car. Malachi archived Ziggy's words in his heart. They would be something he would carry into old age. He checked a message on his phone before he got out of the car.

Rob- Where you at?

Malachi- Store down the hill. Bout to link up with T and J.

Rob- Alright, I'm bout to be through. Stay down that way.

Malachi- Alright.

-

The corner store block was thick for no particular reason that Malachi could pinpoint as he walked up in his black Levi boots, sweatpants and hoody. He shook a couple of hands making his way over to talk to J.B. and T.C..

"What the hell took you so long nigga?" J.B. asked fiercely. He had his hands to his mouth trying to warm them up.

"I got here as soon as I could. Stop crying ugly dude!" Malachi spoke.

"It's cold as hell out here. Especially for a Saturday morning," T.C. said.

Malachi looked at both of them like they had six eyes. "Ain't nobody tell y'all asses to leave the crib and post in front of the store. Y'all on one for real!"

"Damn, T.C. you ready to hop back on that court? It look like you moving that right arm pretty easy now. Is it all the way healed up?" A teenager who went by the name Pier questioned him.

"I'm about ninety five percent healed now. Thanks for asking bro."

"I forgot the doc supposed to clear you this week. You coming just on time for tourney time," J.B. mentioned.

"Yeah, something like that," T.C. replied in a dry voice.

Both J.B. and Malachi were puzzled at their brother's answer. J.B. asked, "What you mean something like that bro?"

T.C. took a glance down the block as if he was trying to spot somebody from a long distance. "I'm not hooping no more. I'm about to be hustling full time now."

"Men stop playing nigga," J.B. remarked cracking a smile.

"I'm serious. I ain't bout to halfway hustle no more. I need to be getting to this money twenty-four seven!"

"Nigga get off that bullshit and tell me you playing," Malachi declared in a serious tone.

T.C. didn't laugh or smile any. He had a stone-cold face on. "I'm serious as can be. I don't need to be hooping if I'm trying to get this money." T.C.'s words instantly got up under Malachi's skin making him irate.

"Man, what the fuck you talking bout! My fucking life was on the line last week because of this bullshit and now you talking bout not hopping for this bullshit!" Malachi was so loud he had the attention of everyone outside.

"Like I said bra, I'm not hooping no more. I'm out here getting to this money!" T.C. lit up a mild as he was talking.

"Na, fuck this trapping and the dough that come with it!" Malachi yelled.

T.C. blew the mild cigarette smoke out of his nostrils. "Na bro, fuck anybody who ain't with me getting to my money."

T.C.'s statement pissed Malachi off so much he smacked the mild out of his mouth. T.C. was shocked but instinctively swung on Malachi, throwing a left hook. T.C.'s quick punch gazed Malachi's jaw as he leaned back to avoid the punch.

Malachi followed up landing an overhand right that caused his brother to take a slight step back. He retaliated rushing back at Malachi scooping him on the ground. T.C. lunged on top of Malachi and threw a wild right punch that landed in Malachi's jaw. T.C.

added a left punch but Malachi blocked it with his forearm. Malachi leveraged himself enough to throw an elbow into T.C.'s mouth causing his bottom lip to leak blood. The elbow strike gave Malachi enough momentum to wrestle T.C. off of him and hop back onto his feet. He hastily began to rush T.C. but was gorilla tackled by Rob. Rob's car was parked in the middle of the street with his driver door still open.

"What the fuck wrong with y'all?" Rob yelled as he contained Malachi. J.B. had managed to semi contain T.C. for the time being.

"Man, fuck dude!" T.C. shouted spitting blood out his mouth.

"Na, fuck you weak ass nigga. You on some other shit!" Malachi shouted back.

Rob was bloodshot red in the face. "Both of y'all on some other shit! All this fighting shit is shut down as of now!"

Rob let Malachi get up from the concrete but still kept a close watch on him.

"J why the hell you let our brothers start banging? I know these other niggas don't care but you was here when it popped off. You should have put an end to this shit sap!"

Everyone on the block was surveying the scene closely as the F.M.B. team was in disarray.

Before J.B. could respond to Rob's question, T.C. interrupted. "This dude think he can run my life. Ima grown man. He better worry about his own fucking self!"

"Ay, Rob you better move your whip. The boys about to swoop down on the block," a spectator on the block yelled out.

Rob ran over to his car quickly parking it in a legal spot. He hopped back out with lightning speed in his wheat Levi boots, black Carhartt overalls and his braids to the back.

"The only way to settle this is on the court," J.B. spoke trying to resolve the problem.

T.C. side shifted his eyes mean mugging J.B.. "I told y'all niggas I'm not hooping no more. What part of that shit don't y'all understand!"

"Man shut up T. You know you a hooper at heart and that's where y'all gone settle it at. J.B. punk ass got the right solution cause y'all damn sure not bangin no more!" Rob looked at Malachi to see if he was going to contest J.B.'s idea.

Malachi looked at T.C. from the distance that was separating them. "It is what it is. We can go to war with these hands or on the court. Either way I'm winning!" It was cold outside but Malachi's delivery was even colder as he finished his statement.

"Win or lose I'm hustling nigga. Ima bust ya ass on this the court though to end all this shit though!" T.C. spoke boldly.

"Nobody stopping you from that T but it's more of the principle y'all playing for now. You know any beef we ever had we always settled it out on the court," J.B. added in.

"Right, so let's hit this court!" Rob demanded.

-

Everyone on the block cleared out. T.C. got into Rob's car and J.B. rode with Malachi. The drive to the Dungeon court was short. Everybody from the block plus more were already there when they pulled up. Both T.C. and Malachi got out of the cars displaying the wrath of God in their eyes. T.C. tightened up his sweatpants. He threw off his hoody and skully letting his dreads breathe. Malachi changed into his shorts and a white thermal.

The environment at the court was filled with hostility and mixed emotions. Sideline bets were being made on the game from some of the hood dudes that were watching. The money that was being bet off the game angered J.B. and Rob. They played it cool though because the anger wasn't stronger than the pain they felt from seeing their brother's feud.

"Ball up," T.C. said as he checked the ball up to start the game.

Malachi squatted into his defensive position and put his hand directly into his opponents face. T.C. drove the ball hard to his right blatantly pushing Malachi off with his left arm. Managing to get some separation T.C. drove to the hole making a fade away jumper. The next possession he missed a contested jumper he shot. Malachi rebounded the ball and instantly posted T.C. up. They were both using full strength and, in all actuality, fouling the hell out of each other. Malachi determined to score, hooked his left elbow to the side of T.C.'s neck throwing the shot up with his right hand. The ball rolled into the rim tying up the game.

"Lucky shot nigga. That's the only point you scoring lil nigga!" T.C. boasted talking shit.

"You a hooper at heart nigga. I'm bout to bust your ass on this court though. You better pray to God they don't bust ya ass out in the streets!"

Malachi shot a three pointer in T.C.'s face. The shot went in and out of the hoop. T.C. rebounded the ball and dribbled back to the hoop in a haste. He went up for the dunk like he was Lebron James but Malachi turned into a middle linebacker knocking him out the air. T.C. hit the pavement hard but got up quickly balling his fists up preparing to swing on Malachi once again. Luckily, Rob and J.B. were already on the court to end the fight before it started.

Rob elevated his voice as he stood in between them. "I told y'all ain't gone be none of that banging shit! Y'all settling this on the court or not at all!" Rob took on the role of officiating the game as he stared at both his brothers in their eyes daring them to try him.

"Let them niggas bang if they want to Rob," somebody yelled from the sideline.

"I got this bra!" Rob shouted back.

J.B. threw the ball back to T.C. at the top of the key starting the game back up. T.C. and Malachi stared each other down on the verge of hating one another in the present moment. T.C. was sizing Malachi up and Malachi anticipated T.C. to be aggressive.

"Do something bum!" Malachi yelled swiping for the ball.

T.C. rose up for the shot elevating over Malachi scoring the three-point shot.

"Nice shot T," Heavy who was now at the court yelled out. Rob shifted his focus mean mugging Heavy but not saying anything.

T.C. missed his next shot. Malachi rebounded the ball and shot a Jordan like fade away jump shot avoiding contact with his defender. The shot fell in smoothly boosting Malachi's confidence. The two of them exchanged buckets back and forth. They also traded numerous elbows, contested jump shots, brutal fouls and even some bloodshed. The game was so rough that even the old school gentleman watching the game saluted the young bucks. The score by the end of the game was 11 to 10. Malachi was up by one and had the ball in his hands ready to score the game winning point.

"End it right now Mal. Don't waste no time," one man shouted from the sideline.

J.B. and Rob figured the man probably had bet a large amount of on money on Malachi to get the win. Both Malachi and T.C. were exhausted and drenched in sweat. Malachi gripped the ball with one hand analyzing his next move. In his heart he hated that it had come to this between him and the brother he was closest too. The last thing he wanted to do was defeat his brother publicly but his desire to achieve victory had to be appeased.

Malachi dribbled the ball slowly in his left hand while T.C. was in a solid defensive position. He accelerated to the left side of the court going towards the rim. He paused and crossed the ball behind his back to the middle of the paint. He seen T.C.'s body mass shift far right when he crossed over so he countered T.C.'s momentum making a quick spin move back to the left side of the hoop. The smooth spin move made the crowd have a loud reaction as they watched in awe. Malachi glid in the air putting up the shot after the spin move. T.C., desperate not to lose the game knew he had no choice but to deliver a hard foul to Malachi's body. He jumped in the air clashing chest to chest with Malachi. It was too little too late though. Malachi's lay in shot went through the bottom of the net. T.C.'s contact caused Malachi to hit the pavement back first. Malachi was motionless on the ground and a handful of people ran onto the court to check on his welfare. Rob stood over Malachi.

"You good Mal?" Rob questioned.

"Yeah, I'm good. Did that shot go in?" Malachi asked still on the ground.

"It did. You won nigga," Rob replied.

"Let's help bro up," J.B. said. The two of them grabbed Malachi's hands slowly helping him up.

T.C. approached Malachi with his hand out to shake his hand. T.C. looked Malachi squarely in his eye saying, "Good game bro. We gone agree to disagree. You do you and Ima do me."

Malachi responded, "I can rock with that."

"What you about to do bro?" J.B. asked Thomas.

The look on T.C.'s face was faint. "I don't know, just hit my line later," he said.

Malachi was also physically and mentally drained from the game. He walked to the sideline grabbing his clothes and then walked straight to his car. After the short convo with T.C., he didn't speak to anyone else. Although, he did over hear some people talking about how they had won money off of the game. Both Malachi and T.C. left the court feeling ill on the inside because they had just went to war with each other. It was the first time in the history of the squad that a major fallout of this magnitude had happened between any of them.

Pulling up to his house Malachi parked his car and entered the garage code. When the garage door lifted fully he saw Coach Joe changing the oil on his car.

"What up son."

"What up daddy."

Coach Joe examined his son as he walked through the two-car garage. "What happened to you? It look like you been in a battle."

"I have. Me and T fought today."

"Oh, for real? What happened and who won?" Coach Joe wiped his hands pausing from working on his car.

Malachi spent the next ten minutes relaying the chaotic episodes that had happened earlier that day and the previous weeks. Malachi never minded being an open book with his dad because he knew he wasn't biased and would always be real with him.

"Families fight and go clash also. Y'all brothers though and just aren't seeing eye to eye. Nevertheless, it's the love y'all got for each other and the bond of brotherhood that's gone always override everything else," Coach Joe told his son.

"Yeah, that's always gone be bro but he off right now daddy. You gone turn this heater off man? Its super hot in here."

"Hell na, I ain't turning it off. Its freezing outside!" Coach Joe exclaimed.

Malachi laughed as he walked into the house.

Third quarter Junior year

The next two months the F.M.B. squad wasn't as tight as they usually were. All of them felt some type of way about Malachi and T.C.'s violent encounter. Rob was still pissed at J.B. for even letting the situation evolve into a brawl. T.C. and Malachi hadn't hung with each other since they went head to head on the court. The Princeton Bearcats ended the season winning the conference title but lost in the third round of the state tournament. T.C. stuck to his decision and never returned to the team. He kept hustling and started hanging with Heavy a lot more.

Rob- Hello

Mama J- About time you answered this damn phone boy. I been calling you all day!

Rob- My bad mama J. What's good though. How you?

Mama J- I'm living and keeping my head up. How you been Robbie?

Rob- I'm good, just trying to push through this year.

Mama J- I feel that. How Big Rob doing?

Rob- He cool. I just got off the phone with him not too long ago.

Mama J- That's good I been praying for him. Robbie you think you can do a favor for me?

Rob- What's that mama?

Mama J- I'm having dinner at my house tomorrow and I need all of the family to be in attendance.

Rob- Okay, I'll be there. What time?

Mama J- Okay good and it's tomorrow at seven.

-

"J.B., can you get that door for me? I'm about to take this chicken out of the oven," Mama J shouted from her kitchen.

J.B. stroked his hair with his brush before he greeted who was at the door. "How you doing J.B.?" Mama Kelley asked walking through the door. Coach Joe and Malachi walked through the door also.

"I'm good ready to eat!" J.B. replied.

"Me too, that baked chicken smelling that one way good," Malachi added in.

Mama J walked out from the kitchen with her apron on. "Hey y'all, go head and get comfortable. Dinner should be ready in about ten minutes." Mama J went quickly back into the kitchen where Mama Kelley followed her.

Coach Joe walked into the dining room where him and Paul started talking.

"Ay, why your Mama call everybody over here?" Malachi inquired curiously.

J.B. stroked the patch full of his chin hairs he had replying, "I don't even know Mal. We still waiting on Rob, T.C. and his grandparents. The doorbell rang twice shortly after J.B. finished his sentence. J.B. proceeded to the door.

"What up bro," J.B. said as Rob walked through the door on the phone.

Rob said, "What up," in return ending his phone conversation. He gave Malachi and J dap. "What the hell is smelling so good?" he asked.

"Come on bro, you already know how my mama get down in the kitchen," J.B. voiced.

"Yeah, I know she throw down. I got the munchies too. Is my eyes still red?"

Malachi looked at Rob's eyes. "Na, they not red but they got that Asian squint right now."

"That's cool. I got some fresh braids and tried to look halfway decent coming over here since I ain't seen none of our parents in a minute," Rob elaborated.

Mama J walked out of the kitchen to see who had just walked in her house. "Hey Rob!" she yelled as she wiped her hands.

"What up Mama J."

"I'm good. Y'all can get ready to sit at the dinner table. I'm about to make plates right now."

All of them walked into the dining room and sat at long dark brown wood table. The table was decorated with orange place mats and fancy silver plates that sat on top of them. Mama Kelley assisted Mama J bringing out the large salad bowl and freshly made bread rolls. Mama J loaded all the plates with two pieces of her famous baked chicken and rice.

"We were expecting T.C. and his grandparents also. I called Grandpa Gus but he didn't answer," Mama J said as she brought the last plate out. "Paul can you go ahead and say grace?" she asked.

Before Paul could start the prayer, the doorbell rang. Paul got up to answer the door. "Hey Mr. Gus, how you doing?"

"I'm god Paul. Finally made it over here." Paul and Grandpa Gus shook hands. T.C. walked in the door directly after his grandpa also shaking Paul's hand. Mama's J face lit up as she seen the two of them walk through the door.

"Hey y'all. We been waiting on you all. Wash ya hands so we all can eat."

"I had to make sure Lois was alright before we got here. She told me to tell everyone hello and sorry she couldn't make it," Grandpa Gus said facing everybody.

"Aww, tell her we love her and it's okay she couldn't make it. Let me hurry up and fix y'all plates," Mama Jade said.

"How y'all doing?" T.C. spoke as he sat at the table next to his grandpa.

"Hey Mr. Crawford, I been missing you! Your locks then got long," Mama Kelley spoke trying to spark conversation.

"Yeah, they starting to grow faster now. I been making sure I take care of them," T.C. replied.

Mama Kelley smiled, "They look good."

"Don't hype his head Mama Kelley. He over here looking like a brown skin Waka Flaka," Rob joked humorously. The joke made J.B. and Coach Joe laugh but Malachi kept a straight face.

Mama J came back in the dining room setting the last two dinner plates on the table. "Okay Paul, now you can say grace."

"Everybody bow your heads please. Lord we thank you for this food. Let it be well in all of us. Amen." They began to rotate the salad bowls and rolls as soon as Paul got finished.

"I want to thank all of you for joining us tonight. I'm so happy to see all my sons back together." Mama J was smiling but Mama Kelley felt great vibes of pain coming from Mama J's spirit. Mama Kelley stayed quiet about it until she knew exactly what was wrong. T.C. and Malachi were sitting directly across from each other but made little eye contact with each other.

"Jade this baked chicken is hitting!" Coach Joe said as he was the first to finish both of his pieces.

"Thanks Joe. I just want tell you guys that I'm proud of all four of you for maintaining an honor roll GPA all year. This has been a rough year for all of us but we have been pushing through and making it. I thank God for that." Mama J was speaking as if she was leading up to something. It was obvious that she had some sort of burden to get off of her chest.

J.B. tired of waiting asked, "Ma what up. What's the real reason you wanted us to link up tonight? You know whatever it is we gone back you a hundred percent on it."

Paul grabbed Mama J's hand to comfort her as she began to talk. Mama J exhaled a deep breath as a fast tear rolled down her last cheek. She quickly wiped it off. "I went to my doctor last Thursday." She paused for about ten seconds leaving everyone on edge to see what she was going to say. Paul gripped her hand a little bit tighter trying to strengthen her through his physical affection. Mama J exhaled another deep breath. "I went to the doctor last Thursday and they have diagnosed me with breast cancer. Luckily they have said it is still in the first stage."

J.B.'s face dropped in reaction to what his mother said. "Cancer? That can't be it mama. They must have read the wrong report or something. Na, not my mama man."

"Baby they have the report right. They ran test on me several times and they are for certain I have it."

Any hostility that resided in the air between the brothers had now vanished and turned into sadness.

"As a cancer survivor myself I can attest that it is hard but you can beat it Jade. You are going to beat it." Grandpa Gus spoke his words with sternness to assure her that she would come out victorious.

Mama Kelley wiped some tears from her face before she talked. "Anything you need Jade, you know we are all here for you. You are not alone. When one of us is in a tribulation, we all are. Are you going to do chemo?"

"I don't know yet. I'm still unsure on everything honestly," Jade iterated depressed.

"I know survivors who have went chemo free. They say the radiation you receive from the treatment kills the cancer but at the same time takes away life from the rest of your immune system," Coach Joe spoke.

"What did they use to fight off the illness, if not chemo?" Paul asked curiously.

"Paul that is definitely something I will have to find out. I do know they were taking an assortment of herbs but I will find out the specifics." Coach Joe was hurt about Mama J's condition but tried to maintain a certain look of calmness on his face.

T.C. had been reserved to himself and tried to remain that way. Nevertheless, the intensity and high emotional volume of the moment was too heavy on his heart. He started to shed tears and his eyes turned bloodshot.

"Mama, I promise you whatever we gotta do to help you push through we gone do! We got you!" T.C. moved his hair away from his eyes as he wiped them. He turned his attention towards Rob, Malachi and J.B..

"Ay y'all, my bad for all the bs I been on. I take all the responsibility for why we ain't been as tight these last couple of months. I love y'all kings and will go to hell and back for any one of y'all!"

"We love you too T," Rob said first.

J.B. responded in the same way.

Malachi didn't say anything but instead got up and walked to the other side of the table where T.C. sat.

Malachi held his hand out and said, "Love you too god."

T.C. got up and hugged Malachi with a heart full of brotherly love. Coach Joe and Grandpa Gus smiled knowing that the young men were starting to mature. Mama J and Mama Kelley felt a sense of joy also. They both knew their sons were starting to comprehend the sweet science of turning a negative into a positive. The negative news revolving around Mama J had helped the adolescent crew see the bigger picture and cherish the true bond of brotherhood.

-

"This shit crazy men, I swear!" J.B. commented hitting the blunt in the back seat of Malachi's car. "Why my mama though? Like why God have to let this cancer shit exist on the planet?" J.B. hit the blunt again with major velocity hoping it would take some of the pain away.

"I know God don't want no cancer on this earth bro. That shit is man-made," Malachi explained pulling into Ziggy's driveway.

Rob grabbed the blunt from J.B. in the backseat. "Man, if we gotta find the cure ourselves then that's what we gone do!" Rob said.

"Damn sure will!" T.C. added.

Ziggy came out of the door tying his dreads up. He was walking to the car in a slow pace like he was already high himself.

"Watup Zig," Malachi stated.

"Nothing much. How you shottas doing?"

"Blazing up Zig, trying get through the bullshit," T.C. commented.

"I feel ya on that. You souljas hold your head up especially you Jerome. I heard the unfortunate news about Jade. Ya mama has a lot of people that love her though and I know Ra (God) will help her push through."

"I know God got her but we need cures Zig," J.B. mentioned.

Ziggy hit the blunt trying to brainstorm some remedies he could name off the top of his head. "Of course, an all-natural diet is mandatory. Herbs such as butcher's broom, cats claw, bloodroot, astragalus, turmeric and ganja are some of the best to use for that condition. I'm going to check with some health gurus to find out what else will be best." The four of them looked at Ziggy not knowing any of the herbs he had named off but they trusted his judgment.

"Zig, I need a pack of that fire ganja so I can flood the streets with it," T.C. said.

"No way Jose soulja, my ganja is not to be distributed through these streets. I get my fire from an out of state connect to be sure that I'm not smoking the dirt these fools out here are rolling up."

T.C. countered Ziggy's statement with a stale face. "Come on Zig. You know I get it in out here. I would be putting double the money back in your pocket."

Ziggy nodded his head in agreeance. "I'm not doubting your hustle young soulja. I just want to keep my fire exclusive. I will tell you this though; your name is starting to get a buzz in the neighborhood. Be careful and strategic in everything you do because it's a lot of hating fools out here. Remember it's not bout the man who has the most dollars but the man who exercises the most intelligence." Ziggy was talking to T.C. but made sure he made direct eye contact will of them.

Malachi passed the joint to Ziggy, who hit it twice blowing the smoke out through his nostrils.

"I'm about to head back in this house. You souljas hold ya head and make it back home safe."

"Alright Ziggy," they all said at different times.

"Mann Zig always be dropping jewels whenever we be getting high with him," T.C. remarked.

Rob turned his head around from the seat to respond what T.C. said. "He definitely do. I wonder what all he meant by exercising intelligence?"

"I don't exactly know but I think whatever we do we got to stick to our principles of loyalty, respect and love for each other. At the same time though finding out the best way to be successful and get to this money," J.B. spoke wisely.

"Hell yeah J. I think you just hit that shit straight on. I know my daddy a smart nigga but I think he would have did a couple things different if he had the chance to," Rob spoke.

"You right, because all the money your daddy made was crazy but now his freedom gone," Malachi affirmed hitting the last of the blunt.

"I ask myself everyday was the money he made worth his freedom for eight years," Rob spoke in a calm voice.

"Ay Mal, hit the store so I can get some Grippos bro," J.B. instructed as they rode down the street.

Since the squad was on their knowledge tip Malachi turned on a mixture of Nas and Styles P songs to keep the knowledge circulating.

-

After basketball season ended the rest of the year flew by. Everyone in the F.M.B. clique still managed to finish out the year on honor roll despite their tribulations. Even T.C. was able to still perform well academically even though he missed gaps of school due to hustling in the streets. The summer going to their senior year had now begun and they were all were accelerating in their own personal endeavors. Malachi attended the Nike basketball camp which most of the McDonald All Americans for the upcoming school year attended. Snoop also was present at the camp. Rob invested his time in a highly rated quarterback camp and other high school combines. Rob was deliberating on whether to attend Ohio State or Michigan State, who both had offered him full rides scholarships. J.B. spent a great portion of his time taking care of his mama and researching cures for her illness himself. He also continued to design websites for new clientele he acquired. A couple of small division three colleges had offered J.B. scholarships to come play basketball for them. T.C. decided to expand his drug hustle to other neighborhoods throughout Cincinnati. To increase his profits, he started selling cocaine. He made enough money to put a decent down payment down on a 2013 Camaro he found at a small car lot. Heavy and him would often go in half on the weight of cocaine that they got fronted from their connect.

Summer before Senior year

"Aye, what time is it bro?" T.C. asked Heavy. Both of them stood on Memphis Street by the Dungeon court along with a couple of other hustlers on the humid July night.

"It's going on eleven. I'm about to go over my peoples spot on Taylor Street," Heavy told T.C..

"Alright bro, Ima hit you up in the am." T.C. checked his pocket and seen that he still had another eight ball of white to sell. He was going to put it off until tomorrow until he seen an all-black Chevy Malibu pull up.

"Got soft?" a voice spoke from the other side of the cracked tinted window. The tinted windows and dim street lighting made it hard to see who was driving the car.

"I got it. Pull over here inside the parking lot." T.C. walked over to the parking lot complex to perform the transaction.

"Unlock the door," T.C. yelled out to the driver of the Malibu. Hearing the locks click T.C. opened the door. The sight of the driver took him by surprise. "Coach Lane? What you trying cop white for?" T.C. asked confused.

"Thomas don't tell nobody about this. I'm just getting it for my girlfriend."

"Coach Lane it's not a good look with you being out here on the block like this buying work. Too many people know you."

"I know Thomas but it's for my girlfriend. She needs her fix."

T.C. looked closely at Coach Lane's charcoal face and the glow that his eyes had. T.C. had learned to observe the dope fiends he served and he knew Coach Lane was lying.

"Coach Lane you ain't on this shit, are you? Don't tell me you are, too many people look up to you."

Coach Lane turned the volume down on his radio as his ex player waited on an answer. "Look Thomas, the years you have known me you have always known me to be honest. The truth is I have been on and off of cocaine for the past twenty years. As far as Coach Phillip knows he doesn't know that I'm using again. I would hope this conversation between me and you stays in this car."

"It will coach. I don't even feel right selling you this shit real talk," T.C. mentioned feeling guilty.

"I'm not gonna tell you to and I'm not gone tell you not too. You got in the dope game for a reason and that's to make money. What I will tell you is that I then seen a lot of cats with great potential get killed, go to jail and even to turn into dope fiends themselves selling this stuff. The same way I'm trying to find the road to recovery I hope you find it to Thomas."

Coach Lane's words took a toll on T.C.'s mental but he still ended up serving him the cocaine. "Stay up Coach Lane," T.C. said as he got out of the car.

It blew his mind that he had just served dope to his old coach. It was evident to him at that point he had to put his personal feelings to the side when it came to the game.

-

Make it from half court nigga!" Rob shouted out to Malachi.

Malachi was at the court up the street from his house working on his jumper. "If I make this shot you owe me a dub king."

"It's on bro," Rob agreed vehemently.

Malachi backed up numerous steps from the free throw line focusing on the rim the whole time. The weather was perfect outside so no outside elements could affect Malachi's money shot. He took a short dribble to the right and elevated in the air with a perfect shooting motion letting the ball go. It was the closest impersonation that you were going to get to Steph Curry in street ball. The ball fell through the top of the net smoothly. Malachi held his shooting form up frozen as he seen his shot go in."

"Give me a new twenty too nigga. I don't want none of that crumpled up shit!"

Rob slapped twenty in Malachi's hand. "Good shot bro. You ready to go see pops?"

"Yeah, I am. I gotta change of clothes in my bag." Walking off the court they seen the same old man out who always sat on his porch.

-

"You got your Id bro? I meant to ask you that before we left out," Rob said as they drove down a long driveway that led to the entrance of the penitentiary.

"Yeah, I got it. Men this shit look like a plantation. It's in the middle of nowhere with a big ass field around it!" Malachi spoke describing the scenery.

"They holding people captive and making em work for basically nothing. It basically is slavery," Rob mentioned as they started to walk through the entrance.

Malachi and Rob checked in with the prison guard at the front desk. They gave him their identification card and walked through the metal detectors emptying their pockets.

Completing the entry process the guard yelled, "Open door 782Bbc." A loud buzzing sound went off and the large steel door in front of them opened slowly.

"You good Mal?" Rob asked.

"I'm good bro."

Rob had a grin on his face as he spoke. "I know you ain't built soft but this your first time walking through the joint. I ain't gone let nobody run up on you!"

"Yeah, okay nigga. You know I'm the hardest out the squad!" Malachi replied. He wasn't laughing though.

Walking into the visiting room one of the guards assigned them to a certain table to sit at. Malachi noticed all of the prison staff had on the same attire wearing tan collared shirts, black pants and black shoes.

"You ain't seen daddy since the trial, have you?" Rob asked.

"Na, I haven't. It's been a minute. That's why I made sure I came with you this time."

They both sat down at the small round table that was surrounded by three chairs. Rob pulled out a white pay card. "I'm bout to hit this vending machine up and get us something to eat."

"Okay bro," Malachi commented.

Looking around the room he noticed families of whites, blacks and Hispanics. About ten minutes later Rob came back to the table with microwaved hamburgers, Ruffle chips bags and twenty-four-ounce pops. They both started to indulge in the food waiting for Big Rob.

"There he go right there," Rob pointed out.

Big Rob came walking through the door in the corner of the visiting room. He spotted his son and Malachi walking over to them. Locking arms, Big Rob and his son gave each other a passionate hug. Big Rob turned to Malachi giving him a strong hug also.

"How y'all young men doing?" Big Rob asked them.

"We Good. Glad we made it up here to see you," his son replied.

"You been hitting them weights Big Rob? You looking like you cut up," Malachi commented.

Big Rob's body was still stocky but had a great mass of muscle definition that was visible. He had on a baby blue collared shirt and dark blue denim pants which was the custom inmate uniform.

"I don't even hit the weights. I just hit the dip and the pull up bar every other day," Big Rob said taking a bite out of his hamburger.

"What made you cut ya hair though pops? You rocking the baldie now," Rob asked eager to know.

Big Rob rubbed the top of his bald head with his hand. "I just wanted to turn a new leaf. A lot of these young cats in here look up to me. Starting new, my braids was the first thing to go. What's been happening out there on the streets though?"

The three of them spent the couple of hours discussing sports, the F.M.B. family, women and the next moves they were planning to make.

"O state Mal, that's where you and Rob both need to go. Y'all both gone get scouted heavy by pro scouts there. The other benefit is that y'all can look out for each other being on the same campus," Big Rob elaborated as they got up from their seats to end the visit.

"Yeah, that might be the move. Big Sean already there right now too," Malachi said.

The two of them exchanged handshakes with Big Rob. "Y'all stay up and remember make your next move your best move. I'll call you tomorrow night son."

"Alright pops," Rob said just before they exited the visiting room.

Walking out of the prison the weather was extremely humid outside.

"It was clutch seeing Big Rob today bro," Malachi said.

"Yeah, it's always good seeing him. These visits and phone calls help me push through week to week." Rob drove out down the long driveway that led back to the street.

"Even though he locked up, he still a legend on these streets," Malachi affirmed.

Rob lit a black and mild as he turned onto the road. "Real talk bro, I wish my daddy was just a regular guy so he could be here for me every day. The streets could of kept the legendary reputation for somebody else."

"I feel you on that king," Malachi replied.

-

"Pull up then!" T.C. shouted from the driver's side of his yellow Camaro.

Rob and Malachi had just got off at the Woodland exit on the seventy-five-south highway. "We just did nigga. Ay J, I thought you was out of state?" Rob yelled over while they were at the stop light.

J.B. pulled out an all-black pair of shades and put them on his face before he responded. "I leave out tomorrow morning bro. Me and T been bagging these hos all day. You niggas need to catch up!"

Malachi made a funny face as he turned towards Rob. "Aye, who they think they stunting on?"

"I don't even know bro. What y'all trying to do though?" Rob asked.

T.C. took off his Cincy fitted and instead just put on a pair of black shades also. "Let's hit the city and get some chicks. Y'all already know its thick out!" Thomas said.

"We following y'all," Malachi commented.

When the light turned green, T.C. accelerated and made a U turn in the middle of the street and got back onto the expressway. Rob did the exact same thing, knowing that they were fortunate that no cops were in the vicinity. T.C. was accelerating up to a hundred miles per hour shifting lanes like he didn't have a conscious. Rob managed to keep up though. T.C. was going so fast that his dreads were blowing in the wind due to the fact of him having his car top dropped.

"I ain't gone lie, T shiting on everybody our age with that Maro," Malachi commented.

"Yeah, he is. I salute him for going all in on his hustle. That shit can be here today and gone tomorrow though!"

"Yeah, you right." An image of Big Rob in his prison uniform popped up in Malachi's head.

T.C. got off at the Paddock exit and rode through the backstreets of Roselawn. The backstreets were quiet but when they drove onto Leading road the atmosphere completely changed. The street was flooded with traffic and pedestrians. The pedestrians were doing everything from catching the city bus to selling bootleg DVDs. T.C. could hardly drive straight because him and J.B. were trying to holler at every decent woman they seen on the street. The eighty-two-degree weather was humid, so most women had on sundresses, skirts or thigh high shorts on.

Continuing down the road it led them into the neighborhoods of Brown Hill and Avondale. The scenery was a little bit rougher but the women were still appealing. Malachi looked over at the park he always used as a landmark to get to Rob's house. He saw little kids playing football, families grilling out and people playing spades. It brought a smile to his face. It was good to see black people relaxing with no drama.

"It look like T not the only one trying to stunt today," Rob spoke. Two Benz trucks drove past them. One was pearl white and the other was candy painted red with tinted windows. Rob started to envision himself in the driver's seat of the truck.

"Yeah, they fucking the city up with them. What the hell T.C. trying go through Evanston for?" Rob asked.

Malachi didn't respond but just shook his head.

"Bro, why you rolling through this hood? Ain't this where they tried to rob y'all at?" J.B. asked on edge.

"Yup, but that was in the winter. This the summer now and I got my game up, so fuck em!" T.C. noticed that J.B. was a little bit uncomfortable. "Look bro if you worried, just know I keep that banger on me at all times now!" T.C. reached up under his seat showing J.B. his all-black Glock forty pistol. "It's a thirty-eight special right up under your seat too if you feel like you need to pop off too."

T.C. pulled up to the block him and Malachi got held at gunpoint at. The environment on the block was active and it was evident that it was a danger zone. Pulling up to the stop sign by the corner store they could feel the ice cold mean mugs through the summer heat. T.C. looked in his rear-view mirror and seen that Rob and Malachi were still behind them. T.C. didn't see any familiar faces on the block but Malachi did.

"There go two of the niggas that was out there the night that bullshit went down!" Malachi noticed taking a glimpse over the block.

"You sure it's them?" Rob asked.

"Hell yeah, I'm sure. I remember that shit like it was yesterday," Malachi confirmed reminiscing on the situation. They drove down another long street and finally left the hostile neighborhood heading downtown.

-

Downtown Cincy had went through major construction and was now considered tourist friendly. Although, a vast section of it was still populated with all black people which was considered the hood. Once you past twelfth street the buildings started to look brand new. This was the part of town that Caucasian people didn't mind walking around in. T.C. pulled into a Shell gas station on the busy Liberty street. A group of little kids came running up to his car as he parked it.

"Can we drive it?" one of the kids asked.

T.C. laughed," Na you can't drive it little man but y'all can have this." T.C. pulled out a wad of money and gave the group of kids five dollars each.

"You better save your money bro. You know gone need some money to trick off on ya hos later," Rob commented sarcastically.

"Yeah, ok nigga. Don't be asking me for no dough later," T.C. responded.

"Hey boys, what are y'all doing in this part of town?" a feminine voice behind them spoke.

Turning around they laid eyes on a caramel brown skin lady with long black hair and video vixen curves. Malachi, Rob and T.C. mesmerized by her sex appeal couldn't even reply.

"What up Miss Regina. How you doing?" J.B. replied. He seemed like he was the only one with some type of conscious out the four.

"I'm good Jerome. Malachi, T.C., Rob are you alright?" Miss Regina asked jokingly. She already knew the young men's sexual imaginations were running rampant as they stared at her in her orange sun dress.

Snapping back to consciousness Rob replied, "We good just out here enjoying this weather. What you doing out this way?"

"I have a condo down here. I stay about five minutes from here."

"That's what's up Miss Regina. You got that big money," Malachi said jumping in the conversation.

Miss Regina let out a gorgeous smile as she laughed a little bit. "Not on this salary baby. You think my salary from the school district is providing my means for my condo?" Miss Regina didn't give Malachi a chance to answer. "No sweetheart, I have a second job. I only teach because that is one of my passions."

"Speaking of teaching, we need to be making sure we enrolled in your class this year," T.C. spoke. T.C. had pulled his roll of money out of his pocket trying to flex in front of Miss Regina.

Miss Regina looked at T.C. and rolled her eyes. "Don't enroll in my class if you not gone attend regularly Thomas. I heard about you!" she stated referring to his absenteeism.

"I promise I won't miss a day Miss Regina!" T.C. confirmed with surety.

She replied, "I hear you," as she walked inside of the store.

The F.M.B. squad looked at her ass cheeks rotate from side to side as she walked away in the sundress.

"I swear to God as soon as we graduate Ima marry her!" J.B. exclaimed.

"You can marry her as long as she cheat on you with me. I don't mind ever being her side piece, ya hear me!" Rob exclaimed with passion. Rob made everybody laugh with his remarks.

"Forget graduation, I guarantee I can bag her before the end of the year," Malachi boasted with confidence.

Freaking his black and mild cigarette, T.C. commented, "If any of us ever got her then they got the title from me personally as head honcho. Getting Miss Regina is a hell of an accomplishment!"

"I agree," Rob said vouching to T.C.'s statement.

Miss Regina came walking out of the store as if she was in a runway for a fashion show. Her face was flawless and her plump booty made heads turn.

"I'll pump your gas for you," J.B. offered as she walked back over.

"Thanks Jerome." Miss Regina got into her all red Cadillac CTS with tinted windows.

"You all filled up," J.B. yelled as the gas meter stopped at forty dollars.

"Thanks Jerome. Y'all be safe out here. I'll see you guys when school starts." Miss Regina started her Cadillac and rode off eloquently in style.

"We been stuck on Miss Regina so hard, we missed all the other bad chicks walking in the store," T.C. commented looking around.

"We damn sure have!" Malachi agreed.

The rest of the day consisted of them cruising the city and clowning with no worries. They hit up a couple of parties later on that night.

-

It was midday afternoon and Mama J had furnished up enough strength to make one last errand run to Chase bank. She was wearing a short brownish orange wig that resembled her original hair. It had been three months since she told everyone about her illness and the radiation from the chemo was starting to take a toll on her body.

"Yes, I want to make a deposit of a thousand dollars into my account."

"Okay, no problem mam. How is your day going?" the young female teller asked.

Mama J's self-esteem was low in result of the emotional trauma she was going through because of the breast cancer. Nevertheless, to mask any pain she told the young clerk that she was great. After she made the deposit she knew she had to go straight home because her energy was becoming faint.

"The Lord told me I was gone see an angel today," a voice spoke as she walked out of the bank doors. Mama J looked to her left setting her eyes on the sight of Grandma Lois.

Grandma Lois and Mama J instantly locked arms hugging each other. Their bonding affection came natural as Mama J started to weep on Grandma Lois shoulder.

"I feel your pain baby. Trust in God & know that you are going to get through this," Grandma Lois assured her.

It was Grandma Lois first time seeing Mama J since the announcement because she herself had been sick. Through her river of tears Mama J managed to utter out the words, "I'm scared. I'm scared I might not make it."

Grandma Lois stepped back so she could have a clear view of Mama J. "Wipe your tears child." Grandma Lois tone got stronger but was still consoling. Mama J wiped the tears off her face. "I don't want to hear no talk like that nomo. This is just an obstacle that will turn into your testimony. You hear me?" Grandma Lois had a strong look of faith on her face.

"Yes mam, I hear you," Mama Jade replied.

A couple of people walked past them as they stood in the parking lot but they paid them no attention. They were completely engulfed in making sure they captured the essence of the moment. Grandma Lois small brown hands grabbed Jade's. She stared deeply into her eyes like she was trying to look into the eyes of her soul.

"Repeat after me Jade. I will not be defeated. I will be victorious!"

Mama J received strength and increased motivation from the elder ladies grip and words. "I will not be defeated. I will be victorious. I will not be defeated!"

"Say it again sweetie," Grandma Lois said encouraging her.

"I will not be defeated. I am victorious!" Mama J shouted twice in firm belief.

Grandma Lois stepped back and smiled as she felt the burden being lifted off of Jade's spirit.

Mama J lifted her hands and shouted once again, "I am victorious. I have already won!" Tears started to run down her face once again. The difference was her tears now resembled tears of hope and confidence instead of sorrow. Still on the pinnacle of her spiritual epiphany, Mama J hugged Grandma Lois and whispered the words "Thank you" in her ear.

The short elderly lady replied back, "Stay strong child. Some days will be high for you and some days will be low. Nevertheless, always stay strong and remember that you are already victorious. Claim your victory and walk in it! Life and death resides in the power of the tongue."

Grandma Lois gave Mama J a kiss on her cheek. Jade knew that the universe had used Grandma Lois to minister to her, which she greatly needed at the time.

-

"Alright bro, Ima holla at you tomorrow," Malachi said as he dropped Jerome off.

"Okay bro. Be on time bro, don't be up all night talking to them hos!"

Malachi laughed "Na that's you bro. I'll see you tomorrow."

Malachi pulled out of J.B.'s driveway at about eleven forty-five pm. It was the last night of summer and the young men of F.M.B. would be entering their senior year starting tomorrow. Malachi walked into the house and noticed that his mama was cleaning up the kitchen.

"You good mama?" Mama Kelley turned around and her eyes were a light red. Malachi could instantly tell that she had been crying.

"I'm okay son," she said wiping down the kitchen table.

Malachi stood motionless not persuaded by his mother's reply. "Ma, what's wrong for real? Be honest," he said hoping he could get something out of her.

Mama Kelley threw the dish rag back in the sink and held her head down with a hopeless expression on her face. "Nothing is wrong baby. I guess your best just ain't always good enough." Mama Kelley wrapped her loose black hair into a ponytail walking to her room.

Malachi knew his mama well and knew she only shut him out like this when she got into bad arguments with his dad. It wasn't sitting well with him that his mama was upset so he decided to go to holler at his dad about it. His daddy Joe was easy to find because he was bumping some old school Al Green songs loudly in the basement. He walked down the wooden steps turning to the left where the big screen TV was. He looked on the black leather sofa where his daddy usually sat but he wasn't there. He walked back past the steps where the pool table and bar was at. Coach Joe was sitting on the stool slumped over on the wood grain bar stand. A host of empty Bud Light cans and a half empty Hennessy bottle surrounded him.

"Pops, pops," Malachi spoke nudging his shoulder. "Pops wake up."

Startled by Malachi's force, Coach Joe rose up randomly talking shit. "This shit just ain't worth it. You give somebody everything you got and they still don't appreciate it! What the hell more can I do?" Coach Joe was staggering over his words with his eyes barely open.

Even though he was pissy drunk Malachi still tried to converse with his father. "What got you down here drinking like it ain't no tomorrow pops?" Malachi decided to take a shot of Hennessey himself while he waited for his dad's response.

Coach Joe turned his black Flyers cap from forwards to backwards for no apparent reason. "Listen Mal, I know I fucked up more than a couple of times but I'm only a man. Your mama and I got married young as hell. Did I run the streets a lot? Yeah, I did."

Coach Joe paused to take a swig from one of the Bud Light cans he had been consuming. "Did my family ever miss a meal? Hell no, my family never been in the streets. I gave ya mama the world but shit I can't give her the sun, moon and stars too!"

Malachi knew he had walked into an argument between his parents that was much bigger than he could even try to tame. His dad was now hanging halfway off the bar stool again and a half stumble from being on the floor. Malachi bent down putting one of his dad's arms around his shoulder. He slowly helped him back to the couch where he usually sat. He threw a cover over him and walked up the steps.

He checked on his mama who was sound asleep in her bedroom. He didn't take any of the issues his mama and dad had to heart because he knew all married couples had fallouts. Their life wasn't perfect but he was thankful for the sacrifices his parents made. Walking in his room he turned Dave East song "Talk to Big" on his computer. As usual Malachi fell asleep envisioning himself in the NBA.

First quarter Senior year

"**A**ye, if we late, we just gon be late!" T.C. exclaimed before he took another hit from the blunt. It was six forty-five in the morning on the first day of their senior year.

"Nigga, just make sure they put my order of French toast in the bag. You know they be messing the orders up early morning," Malachi stated.

"We at Burger King so have it your way bro," T.C. spoke mimicking the company slogan.

T.C. had the top down in his Chevy Camaro. Him and Malachi had no cares at the present moment smoking weed like it was legal in Ohio. Receiving their food, they cruised to school.

"Slow down bro, there go the boys over there," Malachi dialogued.

T.C. hit the blunt checking his left side mirror to monitor the police. "You know I ain't worried bout no weed charge. I can pay that case off. That's petty money."

Malachi replied, "I hear you. Pass that blunt though."

T.C. turned into the school parking lot at 7:05 am, ten minutes before school started. "It's some Weed be Gone spray and some clear eyes in the glove compartment," T.C. spoke seeing that Malachi was hitting the last of the herb. Malachi used an excessive amount of the spray and about twenty drops of clear eyes into his pupils.

"Got damn king. You gone use all my shit up!"

Malachi laughed saying, "My bad bro. I'm over here faded."

T.C. cracked a smile as he side eyed Malachi. "Yeah, okay bro. You faded but we both know you got an image to protect. You know it's a bunch of haters in here anyway!"

"You a hundred percent right. Fuck around and blow my high thinking about all the hating that be popping off!" Malachi mentioned with aggression.

T.C. counted his money and put his top up before they got out the car.

"Y'all niggaz late," a voice yelled out from the other side of the parking lot. Looking to their left they seen Rob and J.B. walking up both sporting Black Owned shirts.

"That power loud we just blew got us on some late shit," Malachi said as they all got within talking distance.

"Mannn, if you just blew some power then the shit we just smoked must have fell out of heaven. I swear, I'm so high it feel like at anytime right now I'm about to meet the Lord," J.B. spoke in a lackadaisical tone.

T.C. pulled out the mini bottle of clear eyes tossing it to J.B.. "You silly J. Take that nigga. You just like Malachi. You gotta image to uphold too."

J.B. replicated what Malachi did overdosing his eyes with the drops. T.C. took the bottle back handing it to Rob also.

"You too king. You gotta image to uphold too gangsta. They want you to fall the most out of everybody," T.C. spoke looking directly to Rob.

Rob looking back at him expressed, "I know this nigga."

The three of them found it ironic that T.C. cared more for their reputation then he did for his own.

-

Walking into school all eyes were on them. Not only were the four young men seniors but by a landslide were the most popular in the school. Several of the underclassmen gave them dap to show respect and to give off the impersonation that they were cool also. A handful of teachers greeted them but some mean mugged. They spotted Mr.

Smith at the end of the hallway who waved and pointed to his temple with his index finger copying the Malcolm X pose.

Malachi, J.B. and T.C. all had Miss Regina's class for the last class of the day. She taught JCG (Jobs for Cincinnati Graduates). The class was a program setup by the school district to empower and help advance students for life post- graduation.

"Welcome class to JCG. I see a lot of familiar faces and some faces I still have to get acquainted with. Nevertheless, before this year is out we all will become very close."

Miss Regina had on a cinnamon blouse top complimenting her skin tone and beige skirt. Her silky black hair was hanging halfway down her back. Even though it was the end of the day Miss Regina still had a full cup of coffee. Taking a sip, she asked, "Do you all have any questions?"

"I do Miss Regina. After we graduate do all the women look as good as you?" T.C. asked. His question made the class laugh but he was serious. Miss Regina blushed ignoring the young man's bizarre inquiry.

"Nigga, don't be shooting no shots at my chick," Malachi leaned over saying.

T.C. tilted his head over towards Malachi saying, "It ain't your chick bro."

J.B. pulled his brush out stroking his waves. "Y'all know that's all me. Stop playing like y'all don't know," he commented.

"Remember what we said last time we seen her. If any one of us can get that, then they head honcho out the squad!" Malachi exclaimed staring at Miss Regina's ass.

Leaving the class, they met up with Rob in the hallway. "What's the word?" Rob asked.

"We can't call it," T.C. responded putting some books in his locker.

"Man, you putting them books in your locker like you ain't bout to miss mas school this year," J.B. spoke to T.C..

T.C. stabilized a pencil in between his ear and locks before he responded. "Bro, Ima be here this year. Just observe how I make the trap jump and still knock this school shit out."

"We gone see how you manage that for the whole year. Don't get caught slipping!" Malachi added in.

Two freshmen approached them giving them fist daps. "Can't wait to see what y'all do on that court this year. Rob we already know you bout to put in work on that field!" one of the slender freshman said energetically.

"We gone get it in. Y'all been watching us over the years?" Rob asked wanting to know.

The two freshman's faces lit up. "Man what! We been watching y'all since y'all sophomore year."

"That's what's up. It's gone be y'all time to shine after we leave," Rob said encouraging the underclassmen.

"Thanks, big bro. T.C. you hooping this year? You a beast too on that court?" The two-freshmen stared at T.C. while they waited on his reply.

T.C. was showing no emotions on his face so it was hard to read him. "Ima be back out there this year." The two freshmen walked away believing T.C. but his brothers knew he was lying.

-

The first game of the football season was sold out and Rob was the main attraction. People from all over the state had come to watch Rob in action. The Princeton Bearcats took the field wearing their red and black jerseys facing off against the Lakota Hawks. J.B., T.C. and Malachi sat of the top of the bleachers in the student section having a good aerial view of the game. Coach Joe and Grandpa Gus were sitting a section over.

"I thought Rob decided to go to Ohio state?" Grandpa Gus asked scanning the crowd spotting scouts.

"He only verbally committed so there are still other schools pursuing him. I think he should go to O State though," Coach Joe spoke.

Grandpa Gus nodded his head agreeing. "I do too. Urban Meyer has built a solid program there."

When the game started Rob took control of the game immediately. He was scrambling out of the pocket like a young Michael Vick and passing like Brett Favre in his prime.

"Rob out there in his zone. I never seen him ball like this!" T.C. spoke astounded.

"Yeah, he untouchable out there. It damn near seem like he was born to throw that ball," J.B. added astounded as well.

Rob finished the game throwing for two hundred and twelve yards. He rushed for seventy yards scoring three touchdowns.

-

"That was a hell of a game tonight Rob!" Coach Joe commented as they walked out the stadium.

Rob was carrying his helmet underneath the opening in his shoulder pads but he still had on his football pants and cleats.

"Yeah, you looked good out there. You almost looked better than me in my heyday," Grandpa Gus spoke reminiscing on his youth.

Rob replied, "You know I got the game from y'all. Y'all the OG's."

Before Rob could ask where his brothers were at a middle aged white man intervened in their conversation.

"How are you doing Mr. Pounds?" the man asked being sure to shake Rob's hand. He also shook Grandpa Gus and Coach Joe's hand. "Hey, I'm Jake Foyer, a recruiter from the University of Virginia. I just want to say that was one hell of a game out there."

Rob replied, "I know who you are and thank you."

"You know with the addition of your talent it wouldn't be anything that could hold our team back from making the bowl games the next four years. I know you've verbally committed to Ohio State but I still think you should consider talking to our head coach before you make anything final."

"Thank you, sir, but my mind is made up. Ohio State will be my school of choice."

The recruiter grinned with a devilish look on his face. "I have to say O State is a solid school but a lot of their star players often end up in trouble. I would hate to see you end up in an ill predicament such as your father's."

Coach Joe and Grandpa Gus knew the recruiter had crossed the line but they stayed in retreat mode to see how Rob would handle the situation. Rob knew the recruiter was trying to get under his skin but he kept his composure.

"Look here man, I told you already I got my mind made up. Don't you ever try to defame me or anybody I'm close too ever again!" Rob spoke firmly.

The recruiter stood frozen trying to brainstorm a crafty comeback response.

"Get your punk ass out of my grandson face before I whoop ya ass all the way back to Virginia!" Grandpa Gus said balling his fists up. The recruiter's eyes got big as he seen Grandpa Gus's massive fists. He made a wise move and chose to vanish quickly.

"I'm proud of how you handled that situation Rob. You didn't let that recruiter shake you," Coach Joe commented.

"Yeah, if it had been a couple of years ago he prolly would have got to me but dude wasn't even worth it," Rob expounded.

Grandpa Gus shook his head. "Na, he wasn't worth it but I still wanted to whoop him! You handled it the right way though."

Coach Joe and Grandpa Gus walked with Rob to the parking lot proud of his growth and maturity. Rob finished his senior year football season being ranked the second ranked quarterback in the state of Ohio. He also broke a couple of records in the city of Cincinnati that year.

Second quarter Senior year

With football season ending the first game of basketball season approached quickly. The Princeton Bearcats were a top ranked team with Malachi, Rob and J.B. leading them.

"Miss Regina, you coming to our game tomorrow night?" J.B. asked as he walked into her classroom.

"I will try my best to make it Jerome," Miss Regina stated as she passed out some papers. "Okay class, the papers I'm passing out are asking you two questions. The first question is asking you to list your first two career choices post-graduation. The second question is asking you what college you want to attend, if any after high school." Miss Regina toured the class calling on students to answer the questions and elaborate on their answers. She noticed that the bulk of females in the classroom had some type of plan for themselves after they graduated.

"Mr. Summers what about you? What are your plans?" Miss Regina questioned him. Malachi was laid back in his seat not expecting to get called on. He adjusted himself to an upward posture before he answered.

"Miss Regina you know ball is life. I'm hooping until you see me in a NBA jersey," Malachi answered without hesitation.

"Okay Malachi, what else? Surely you have to have something else in mind that you want to do." Miss Regina was trying to pick Malachi's mind.

"Nothing else Miss Regina. Its ball or nothing, feel me bro," Malachi said reaching over and fist bumping Rob.

"That's interesting Malachi. I expected more from you," she said with a look of disappointment on her face.

Malachi honestly wanted to be a sound engineer later on in life but all the hype for the upcoming hoop season had went to his head.

"What about you Jerome?" Miss Regina asked moving on.

Jerome rubbed his chin hair like he was trying to improvise a crafty answer. "Other than my web design, I plan to attend Indiana University. My choice careers are to work for Google or become a neurologist."

"What's a neurologist?" a student in the class asked randomly. Miss Regina didn't answer but rather looked at J.B. so he could.

"A neurologist is a doctor who specializes in dealing with the nervous system," J.B. explained.

"Oh, okay then," the girl replied still unsure.

"Class your assignment for tonight is to write all the steps and process that it will take for you to become certified in your choice career. I asked you all to do the same thing in the beginning of the year but a little reassurance won't hurt anything," Miss Regina spoke passing out more paperwork. The JCG students worked on the assignment for the next thirty minutes until the bell rang.

"Malachi can I talk to you for a minute?" Miss Regina asked as the class cleared out. Malachi stopped in his tracks.

"What's up Miss Regina?"

"Sit down so I can talk to you." She pulled up a chair as they both sat down. "So, explain to me why you gave me that shallow answer earlier. You and I both know that you have more ambitions than to just play basketball."

Malachi's eyes shifted to the side and then back to Miss Regina. "Honestly, Miss Regina it's so much attention on me and the team this year I feel like I'm being consumed in it. I mean I always been all about hoop but now it seem like all eyes on me literally."

Miss Regina appreciated the young man's honesty as she gazed at him through her brown eyes. "I understand where you're coming from. You are in the spotlight because of your talent on the court. Best believe me that's not the only thing people see when they see you.

Not only do people admire your athleticism but also your intellect. It's actually your intellect and the way you carry yourself that's more appealing than your basketball skills. Promise me you won't let any arrogance get the best of you this year?" Miss Regina grabbed Malachi's hand to be sure she had his undivided awareness.

Malachi was thrown off by her warm touch feeling his dick get hard. "I promise you, I won't Miss Regina." Miss Regina smiled at him as they both got up from the desks.

"Thank you, Mal."

"What Miss Regina was talking about?" Rob questioned.

Malachi opened his locker replying, "Nothing for real. She ain't want shit for real."

Rob looked at Malachi dubiously saying, "Yeah, okay bro."

"Hit me up when y'all get out of practice," T.C. said throwing his hoodie on.

"We is bro. Be careful out there, it's a lot of hating going on right now," J.B. commented.

"I already know it is. Ima hundred though," T.C. iterated giving them dap before he walked off.

T.C. didn't even try out for the hoop team that year. It was a hard pill for Rob, J.B. and Malachi to swallow, knowing that they wouldn't have their brother on the court with them for another season.

-

The next night at the game the expectations were high for the Bearcats team to perform well. The gym was filled to capacity. Malachi was on pace to break the record for the most points scored by a Princeton varsity basketball player. He needed three hundred twenty-six points to claim the record. He was sure to waste no time scoring thirty-four points their first game. Rob added twenty points along with J.B.'s seventeen points. The Bearcats recorded their first victory winning the game 87 to 62.

-

The next day Rob pulled up in Jerome's driveway. It was about nine in the morning. He blew the horn a couple times to notify J.B. to come outside. J.B. came walking outside with a homemade sausage biscuit in his hand.

"Where my sandwich at bro?" Rob asked as J.B. got into the car.

"Come on bro, you know my motto. Mi casa su casa. You can go in my house and make your own damn sandwich negro."

Laughing Rob replied, "Nigga I know this. How mom dukes doing?"

J.B. took another bite of his sandwich. "She good, still being the soldier that she is. She not doing chemo no more though. She said it was killing too many of her good cells and draining her energy."

"I feel that. I can only imagine. Ima slide by the bootleg man spot in the hood before we head to my crib." "Okay, that's cool," J.B. stated.

J.B. thought Rob was talking about the bootleg man in Rolling Heights but he knew he meant Avondale when he got straight on the highway. Rob turned the Kendrick Lamar album up as they began to coast through the Avondale streets. It was a chilly and gloomy day outside but the streets were filled with people on the move.

"There go the bootleg man right there bro." J.B. pointed to the Shell gas station parking lot.

"Get some good bootlegs king. Don't be getting no bullshit. I'm bout to run in the store to grab something to smoke and a Faygo."

Rob gave J.B. the money and walked into the store. J.B. had hardly heard anything Rob said. All of his attention was focused on a chocolate woman searching for movies at the bootleg movie table. J.B. brushed his hair and got out of the car ready to exercise his mouthpiece to get what he wanted from the indigo skin toned woman.

"This a good movie right here," J.B. said pointing down at the table.

"Oh really? You seen it before?" the woman asked looking up.

J.B. made sure he made direct eye contact with her. "Yeah, I seen it last night. It's too bad I didn't meet you a couple days ago. You could have seen it with me."

The older woman smiled and replied, "Now why would I want to watch a movie with you mister?"

J.B. smiled back at her as he thought of his next line. "Because baby, I make good company. I know how to show you a good time."

"Is that right? What's your name mister and how old are you?"

"I'm eighteen and my name is Jerome. Everybody call me J.B.. What's your name and where you stay at?"

"Damn, you a youngin baby but my name is Lexus. I stay out this way."

He pulled his phone out preparing to get Lexus number. "What's your number boo? So, we can check out that movie together."

"Un un boo, first you gotta take me out before you can get in house movie privileges!" Lexus declared checking him.

"I was gone do that regardless!" J.B. replied confidently.

Lexus paid the African man for her movies and then put her number in his phone. J.B. made sure he saved the number as she handed the phone back to him.

"Ima hit you up boo."

"You do that," Lexus said as she walked away.

J.B. stared at her booty and thick thighs in her blue jeans as she walked away. Through his peripheral, Jerome noticed two dudes in a Buick Century mean mugging him but he paid them no attention.

"You get digits! You get digits?" the African bootleg man asked.

"You know it!" J.B. responded.

"My niggaaa! She was thick as fuck!" the bootleg man shouted. His African accent was strong making his word pronunciation aggressive.

Rob walked over drinking an orange Faygo. "Who you get on with bro?"

"Some ol thick chocolate chick named Lexus. That's why I like coming out here to the city, cause I be seeing chicks I ain't never seen before."

"You not gone smash though," Rob challenged his brother.

"Yeah alright bro. You already know what it is," he spoke glancing over the movies.

"Ya name Rob ain't it?" a voice from behind them spoke.

Both Rob and J.B. turned around simultaneously. It was the two dudes that were inside the Buick Century who J.B. spotted mean mugging.

"Who wanna know?" Rob asked firmly.

"I wanna know," one of the young men replied.

The two young men were both wearing pullover hoodies, jeans and black boots. One of the men in the red hoody had braids with a gold grill in his mouth. The other young man had an even-Steven haircut that looked like it hadn't been cut in weeks. He was wearing a black hoodie and had a gold grill also.

"I'm Rob. What you asking for?" The guy in the black hoody looked to his left right before he began to speak.

"I don't got no issue with you. I know you rock with T.C. and Heavy hard though. Tell them niggas until they pay us for them packs we fronted them, they bet not show they face in the city."

"Man, tell you truth that's my bro, so if you got an issue with T than you gotta issue with the whole squad. Honestly though, I don't even know what you talkin bout right now, so I really don't give a fuck!"

Both of the men continued to mean mug J.B. and Rob. The energy was extremely hostile between the four of them.

"Like I said bro, let them niggaz know they bet not bring they ass out to the city no more trying hustle. If they don't pay us our dough by the end of next week we riding out to they hood!"

Rob started to turn red as he listened to the man in the black hoody speak.

"You got me fucked up! I ain't no damn messenger. You got something to say to them, go say it yourself nigga!"

Both of the men's faces froze up after Rob's statement. "Look here bro, the man in the black hoody started to say.

"Fuck you and whatever you got to say bra!" J.B. yelled interrupting the stranger. The two men balled their fists up as if they wanted to fight.

"What's up!" J.B. shouted stepping up next to Rob.

Rob dropped the bag in his hand ready to get it in also.

"You niggas take that bullshit somewhere else, you crazy motherfuckas!" the African bootleg man yelled harshly.

"We Good. We ain't even gone buss no heads right now," the other guy in the red hoody said finally speaking.

"Fuck outta here! You niggaz ain't bouta bust shit over here!" Rob spoke furiously.

The two hooded men retreated back to their Buick Century car still looking like they were plotting. J.B. and Rob still ended up buying some movies and got back into Rob's car.

"Man, who the fuck was that?" J.B. asked Rob furiously. He figured Rob might know since he lived in the city.

Rob lit up a black and mild as he started the car. "Man, them niggas from Avondale. Everybody know them as the Pratt brothers. I ain't remember who they was at first but when I kept looking at them I remember I used to play little league football with them!" Rob blew the mild smoke out the driver side window.

"Them niggas was bouta get offed out here approaching us on that bullshit!" J.B. exclaimed. J.B. rarely got mad but had a bad temper just like the rest of his brothers.

"They knew who the fuck I was the whole time. Them niggas just wanted to see what we was gone be on," Rob explained.

J.B. dialed T.C.'s number on his smart phone.

"I'm bout to call T sap. We need to figure out what the fuck going on!" J.B. dialed T.C.'s number five times but got no answer, only his voicemail.

"That nigga not answering. I don't know where the hell he at!" J.B. said redialing the number again.

Rob had pulled up in front of his house but decided not to park. "Fuck it then! We bout to roll back out to the hood. He gone most likely be out there somewhere. Call that nigga Mal phone and see if he know where he at," Rob commented.

J.B. dialed Malachi's number but he didn't answer either. Rob hit eighty miles per hour all the way up the expressway, livid from the recent encounter.

-

"Just hit the block, we gone see one of these niggaz out here," J.B. stated as they entered Rolling Heights.

Jerome was right. Heavy was standing on the block across the street from the Dungeon in a tan thermal, jeans and Cincinnati hat. Rob parked the car and they both hopped out immediately.

"Heavy, ay Heavy," Rob yelled out. Heavy and the other pod of hustlers looked at Rob wondering why he was yelling his name like he was crazy.

"What up Rob. What up J." Heavy observed Rob's and J.B.'s disposition. He observed that they were full of hostility so he didn't bother to shake their hands.

"Some niggaz in the city ran up on us talking some bullshit, talking bout y'all can't hustle out there no more cause y'all owe them paper. That shit wasn't cool. Y'all need to check that shit sap!" Rob said looking Heavy square in his eye.

"Some city niggas? You talking bout the Pratt brothers? I ain't worried bout them niggas but you need to be hollerin at T.C. with this bullshit! Not me!" Heavy said angered by Rob's approach.

"We don't know where T at but we was gone pull up on you regardless nigga!" Rob said with flare.

"No need of pulling up on me. I'm good everywhere I hustle at bra. Like I said you need to holler at T. He the one that be doing rookie shit out here!" Heavy mentioned fiercely.

Rob looked at Heavy distraught at his response.

Everyone on the corner was scoping the scene feeling the animosity building up.

Trying to reason with Heavy, Rob voiced, "Look bro, I ain't bout to make no bullshit up. Niggas coming at us with your name in they mouth. That shit need to be checked sap!"

"No bullshit Heavy. Y'all niggas got smoke out there in the city. It is what it is," J.B. added in.

Heavy started to turn his back the other way. "Like I said, that's y'all problem, not mine. I don't owe nobody shit. That's on T if he owe them niggas paper!"

Rob started to turn fire truck red again in the face. "Who the fuck you think you is bro! You ain't ya brother Tank. You don't run the hood nigga!"

"What you say about my cousin nigga?" Heavy's cousin Snake questioned. Snake was short with a small box fade and a gold grill. He was known in Rolling Heights for his boxing skills. Snake and Heavy now stood side by side facing Rob and J.B..

"Fuck y'all F.M.B. niggas!" Snake shouted.

"Y'all niggas heard what the fuck I said. If y'all got an issue do something about it!" Rob yelled sending the challenge out.

Instantly, Heavy pulled his jeans up and squared up with Rob. Heavy and Rob were both heavyweights standing at 6'5 but Heavy outweighed Rob by twenty pounds. J.B. kept a close scope on Snake, who he knew would try to jump in the fight at any time. Heavy threw the first punch which was a right jab. Rob dipped the punch hitting Heavy on the left side of his jaw with a straight right hand. Heavy hit Rob back quickly with a left jab and tried to grab him. They scuffled for a brief second but Rob threw a body punch that Heavy ate up. Heavy countered with two hard body shots that didn't shake Rob either. Rob followed up throwing a thunderous uppercut that connected on Heavy's chin.

A couple people yelled out "Oh shit," as the punch landed.

Heavy stumbled back from the uppercut and Rob was anxious to continue his assault but Snake jumped in rocking him with a ferocious left hook. J.B. was on it though and hit Snake with the quickest right hand he could throw, being fully aware of Snake's boxing skills. Snake dipped his head weaving J.B.'s next punch aimed at him. Snake retaliated throwing a series of punches at him backing him up five feet. The punches were coming so fast all J.B. could do was back pedal to avoid them.

"Get the strap, grab the strap Snake!" Heavy yelled out.

Rob had pushed Heavy against the cage fence of the basketball court gaining the momentum. He now had a platform to throw his punches how he wanted to but he still had to be careful that Heavy didn't counter.

Snake and J.B. were now going head to head fighting by Rob's car.

Snake penetrated his punches to the body of J.B. since he was clearly shorter than him. J.B. managed to get off a left jab that Snake wasn't able to dodge. Slightly pausing Snake, J.B. shocked everyone by side stepping swiftly to his right. Instantly after the side step he threw a quick right jab which made Snake stumble to the ground.

"Geesh!" someone surrounding them yelled out.

At this point in the brawl J.B. had lost all form of sanity. Knowing his opponents had ill intentions for him & Rob, he moved swiftly to the driver's seat of Rob's car grabbing his pistol. J.B. firmly gripped the three-eighty caliber handgun and cocked it. Everything and everybody froze as he pointed the pointed the chrome down at Snake's body who was still trying to recover.

J.B. was one squeeze on the trigger away from having a body up under his name. Snake and him locked eyes as J.B. himself stood motionless for about five seconds. All types of thoughts raced through his head in the short time span that seemed like an eternity.

"Ya gone shoot his ass or not soulja?" a voice from behind him said loudly. The voice caught Jerome's attention but he was too focused on Snake to see who it was. "If you not gonna shoot him then put the gun down," the voice urged getting closer.

Slightly glancing over his shoulder J.B. seen a man with locks. Doing a double take, J.B. identified that the mysterious man was Ziggy.

Ziggy asked him again, "What you gonna do soulja? If ya not gone shoot, put down the gun."

J.B. looked down at the block and seen that all eyes were still on him. He bought his attention back to Snake, who was still at his mercy.

"Do you want to spend the next fifteen years of your life in prison for murder of this man?" Ziggy asked earnestly with his strong Jamaican accent. Ziggy's question made Jerome think logically as he continued to hold a firm grip on the weapon.

He really didn't want to catch a body plus he also knew that it was too many witnesses present to get away with the crime.

J.B. started to lower the pistol as he said, "Na, I don't."

"Smart choice youngin. Now hand me the gun." J.B. placed the three-eighty in Ziggy's hand who walked past Snake into the nucleus of everybody. "This shit is over. None of y'all young negroes shooting each other today. I suggest you all get off this block because the cops will be here soon enough trying to arrest niggas!"

Everybody started to disperse in their separate directions. Nobody contested Ziggy because he was revered as an OG in Rolling Heights. Snake got up off the ground with an ice-cold grill staring down J.B. but he didn't say anything. Heavy and Snake got into their car vacating the scene.

Rob walked over to where J.B. was. It was apparent by looking at both of them that they had been in a serious brawl. "Shit crazy man!" Rob said shaking his head. Ziggy made his way back towards Rob's car. He handed J.B. the gun staring directly into his eyes.

"Next time you point a gun at a man, you better make sure you use it!" Ziggy's short sentence made J.B. take into account the bizarre event that had just transpired. "I squashed this beef for now but in the hood, retaliation is a must!"

Ziggy walked off saying no more. Rob and J.B. got into the vehicle knowing that drama could pop off at any time now.

-

"Malachi you trending baby!" Mama Kelley said sitting on the couch.

Malachi was in the kitchen pouring a glass of Hawaiian Punch. "What you talking bout ma?"

"Come here, Ima show you."

Malachi walked into the living room where his mama was at.

"Read that article on Facebook they got about you and a couple of others."

She handed him her IPhone. Malachi read the article naming the top high school basketball players in the country. Both him and Snoop were mentioned in the brief article. Malachi scrolled through the comments section and read comments from people all over the country. It made him feel good that he was receiving national recognition.

"This what's up ma. You see all the love they showing your son," Malachi spoke handing her IPhone back.

Mama Kelley smiled. "You deserve all the notoriety you are getting. You worked hard for it. I remember when you were young. Your daddy and I bought you a mini hoop and basketball. Lord knows you played on that thing every day, all day." Mama Kelley let out another smile as she reminisced. "I'm proud of you baby."

"Thank you, mama." Malachi walked up to her and gave a kiss on her forehead.

Malachi's phone started ringing. Noticing he left it in the kitchen he speed walked to see who it was. T.C.'s name was on the screen. He took another gulp of his juice and answered.

Mal- What up.

T.C.- Ay Rob and J.B. got into some bullshit just now on the block! (Frantic voice)

Mal- What the fuck popped off? They called me but I was sleep.

T.C.- I just now got off the phone with em and everybody in the hood talking about it. These niggas fought Heavy and his cousin Snake right in front of the Dungeon.

Malachi- I knew that nigga Heavy was on some bullshit now and that nigga Snake stay on some other. What they was banging for?

T.C.- Rob talking bout some niggas in the city ran up on him and J.B. talking bout me and Heavy owe them money. I guess Rob approached Heavy about it and that's when shit escalated.

Malachi- Men holdup. So, Rob and J was banging over some shit you and Heavy fucked up on? That shit don't add up!

T.C.- Me and Heavy got fronted some weight from some niggas in Avondale. I had my half to pay em back but Heavy spinned em and never gave em the dough we owed em.

Malachi- Who fronted y'all? (Curious voice)

T.C.- The Pratt brothers. They had low ball prices on soft, so me and Heavy copped from em.

Malachi- But y'all shouldna spinned em. That's where y'all went wrong.

T.C.- I know. That ain't even our main issue though. Erybody saying J pulled the burner out on Snake pointing it at his dome.

Malachi- Damn J pulled the strap out? That ain't even like bro. This shit crazy!

T.C.- I know it is but everybody saying he ain't have no choice. They said Heavy was yelling at Snake telling him to get the strap.

Malachi- We at war now. Its prolly gon be on sight once we see em.

T.C.- It might be but I'm bout to holla at Heavy and dead the situation. Heavy go back go little league hoop with us. He know it's all love at the end of the day.

Malachi- Na T, that love shit out the door. J pulled a pistol out on his peoples, so it is what it is now. Everybody wanna be respected at the end of the day.

T.C.- I'm bout to dead this shit bro trust me. I'm on it.

Malachi- Yeah bro. (Hangs up phone)

Malachi took another gulp of his Hawaiian Punch. He was livid at the news he had just received from T.C..

"Everything cool?" Mama Kelley asked.

"Yeah mama, everything cool."

-

Malachi threw on his coat and headed out the door to see if J.B. was at home. He knew that his mama knew he was lying. It's not until he got outside that he realized how much he had cursed on the phone in the hearing range of his mama. Malachi decided to jog over to J.B. house to blow off some steam. Turning the corner, he laid eyes on Rob's and T.C.'s car in the driveway. As he got closer to the house he heard Rob's voice escalating through the windows.

Malachi pounded on the door anxious to see what drama was popping off now.

"It's open!" J.B. yelled.

Malachi opened the door and was met by his three brothers in the living room politicking the recent chaotic events.

"You gotta handle that shit T. Random motherfuckers in the city approaching me and J talking money. I'm looking at these niggas like who the fuck is y'all!" Rob shouted in T.C.'s direction.

"And you and Heavy had to be duckin these niggas for a minute. Them niggas came out of left field approaching me and Rob!" J.B. added. J.B. wasn't as loud as Rob but it was obvious he was just as pissed off.

Malachi trying to get full clarity in the situation jumped in the dialogue. "So, you and Heavy got fronted some work and basically ran off on the plug?"

T.C. was leaned against the wall in his all wheat Carhartt overall with half of his dreads covering his face. "Yeah, them niggas fronted us some work. Heavy and I both been flipped our money to pay em back. Heavy said fuck paying em back though, so I did too. Shit it was his plug anyway."

"Them niggas the Pratt brothers. I remember playing little league football with them for Avondale," Rob commented.

"Yeah, that's them. Me and Heavy fell out about him not trying to pay them back. I was trying to tell him we would of been that one way up if we would have kept getting work from em," T.C. mentioned.

"You should of took your half to them niggas and told em what the situation was. Cause now this shit then got ugly," J.B. said putting some peroxide on a scar he had from the fight.

T.C. sighed, "Shit I was thinking bout doing that but shit this the dope game. Niggas want all they money plus that was Heavy's plug, not mine."

"You right. How y'all wanna handle these niggas Heavy & Snake? Cause that beef is right around the corner from us," Malachi said.

"Fuck em, they ain't bout shit! I never was too fond of Snake and Heavy ain't start thinking he was the shit until he started hustling. I know we gone have to hit with them niggas again!" J.B. commented amped up.

"Man, what made you up the banger on that nigga Snake?" Thomas asked.

Jerome didn't hesitate to respond. "I didn't have no choice but too! Heavy kept yelling out telling Snake to get the strap cause Rob had started bustin him up against the fence."

Malachi and T.C. listened to J.B. fully comprehending the severity of the situation. They all knew J.B. kept a level head but would make the necessary accommodations for survival at anytime.

"Not gone lie, it did feel like kill or be killed out there," Rob stated finally sitting down on the couch.

"So how y'all wanna handle this shit?" Malachi asked once again.

"It's really my beef. Ima go holler at Heavy and see if we can come to some type of resolution," T.C. spoke.

His brothers respected him for taking responsibility of the scenario.

Wanting to be sure T.C. was stern in his decision to rectify the problem Malachi asked, "You sure you wanna handle it dolo T?"

"Yeah, I'm sure. It's all on me." T.C. responded.

The sound of a key turning in the doorknob diverted their attention from the discussion at hand. Mama J came walking through the door with a couple of grocery bags in her hand. She was wearing a Cincinnati Reds fitted on top of her head. The symptoms from the cancer had caused her to shed some weight but she looked healthy in the face, no longer partaking in chemo.

"So what y'all gangsters now!" she asked aggressively.

"What you talking about mama?"

Mama J looked at her son with a stale expression on her face. "Y'all know damn well what I'm talking bout. What y'all think cause I'm older that I don't keep my ear in the streets. Now y'all got five seconds to explain to me what the hell happened!"

The four of them knew that she wasn't naive to what happened earlier. They all knew she had dated her fair share of street guys and was young at heart. J.B. figured that Ziggy had called his mama and told her that he had stopped him from putting a bullet into Snake.

"Me and J was banging with Heavy and Snake. Things escalated real quick and got out of hand," Rob elaborated speaking up.

"But why was y'all fighting? I know y'all not as close with Heavy anymore but y'all played on the same team for years!" Mama J commented trying to get to the nucleus of the plot.

T.C. decided to join the conversation knowing that he was the culprit of the situation. "It's my fault Mama J. Me and Heavy owe some dudes in the city some money. The dudes we owe ended up running into them and confronting Rob and J, trying to get to me. Rob and J ended up coming back to the hood and pulled up on Heavy about the whole situation."

Mama J looked around the room getting a good read on all of them. "So why didn't y'all holler at T.C. first? And sit y'all asses down! I'm tired of looking up talking to y'all!"

Malachi, T.C. and J.B. sat down next to Rob on the new black sofa set.

"T wasn't picking up his phone. Heavy was on the block so we hollered at him," J.B. responded.

"So how did all this escalate into a fight?" she asked setting the grocery bags down.

"When we hollered at him, he act like he ain't have nothing to do with anything. That nigga was talking sideways. Me and J was already lit. After words exchanged, we squared up cause it really wasn't nothing else to talk about," Rob spoke explaining the event.

Mama Jade was quiet for a long pause as she processed the events in her mind.

"Heavy shouldn't have flipped out like that. He know we owe them dudes in the city money. I swear he been off one ever since he started hustling!" T.C. exclaimed.

Mama J turned her body fully in T.C.'s vicinity stepping into his face. "Negro, you have too! I don't know why you wanna degrade yourself to being another statistic out here! You got way too much talent on the court and too damn smart to be resorting to this shit! All the work your grandparents put in to raise your ass and this is how you repay them?" Mama J spoke with a fire that T.C. dared not to challenge. T.C. sat motionless with a blank stare having nothing to say.

Mama J continued to speak. "Since y'all can't handle this issue, I'm going to resolve it myself."

"Na, ma we got it. I don't want my own mama getting involved in this bs," J.B. said urgently.

"Boy shut the hell up! I'm already in this. What the hell you doing pulling guns out on people anyway!?"

J.B. mumbled over his words at first. Finally, he was able to clearly say, "I didn't have no choice but too."

Mama J shifted her body now stepping into her son's face "No choice my ass! Were you ready to face a murder charge? Were you ready to go to the joint for the next twenty years? I thank God Ziggy was there! Were you really ready to throw away your future?"

Her son didn't respond.

"Answer me J!"

J.B. looked his mama in her eyes and said, "No ma, I wasn't ready for that."

The emotional side of Mama J made her want to hug her son and hold him but she stood firm. "Listen y'all I know this fight was intense and you all did what you felt was necessary. The part y'all went wrong at was not consulting T.C. before y'all spoke to Heavy. You always holler at family first so everybody can be on the same page."

"Yeah, you right," J.B. and Rob both replied.

"And since I feel like this is something that's going to keep elevating, I'm going to step in. I'm calling Heavy's mama later to come to some type of even terms. Between the two of us we'll put an end to all this controversy."

Mama J was still tight with Heavy's mama whom she had known since childhood. She knew that it would hurt her just as much to know her son's were feuding with each other.

"Malachi what's your outlook on all this? You been quiet over there," she inquired seeking his opinion.

"The whole thing wild. I'm salty we got smoke with Heavy. Real talk we looked at him like a brother too. It is what is though. Either we gone squash the beef or end up hitting again."

-

About a month had passed since the incident with Heavy and Snake had went down. Mama J was correct when she said that she would put an end to all of the chaos getting any more intense. Heavy and Snake never said anything when they saw the squad but they always mean mugged.

The four brothers were on edge more than they had ever been before though. The hectic events that had taken place in their high school tenure had taken a toll on them. In their sophomore year they had to deal with the drug raid and Big Rob getting locked up. Junior year brought along the pressures of choosing their choice colleges, Mama J's cancer battle and T.C.'s injury. His initiation into the dope game was the monkey wrench that threw them all for a loop. Now finally in their senior year they were having to deal with the turmoil of beefing with Heavy, Snake and the Pratt brothers. The situation was dead for the moment but was still the trending topic amongst a lot of people. Nevertheless, they tried their best to focus on keeping their grades up and graduating successfully.

-

"What up big bro. You breaking that record tonight?" a young freshman asked.

"Ima try my best too little bro," Malachi responded.

The young freshman's eyes lit up. "You only need thirty-six points. You minds will drop fifty on em!" the freshman said with excitement.

"He will. We gone make sure he break that record tonight," Rob confirmed. "I already know Rob. I'll be watching y'all put in work at the game tonight," the young man spoke.

"Okay, little bro," Malachi commented.

Rob and Malachi gave the freshman some dap before he walked off in the opposite direction.

Rob poured some Grippo's into his mouth before stating, "Damn man its crazy how these young boys look up to us. It just seem like yesterday we was freshman running up and down these hallways.

"Bro who you telling! We been through a lot. These youngsters don't even know the half," Malachi replied in a modest tone.

"You right, they don't. But hey what don't break you, make you."

Looking down the hallway they spotted Mr. Smith and Miss Regina walking down the hallway together. "We see you Mr. Smith," Rob shouted insinuating that he was flirting.

"It ain't even like that young king. This is my good friend and colleague," Mr. Smith spoke as they got closer.

"Yes, I have been knowing Frank for years. Besides don't you young men need to be focused on winning the game tonight? And Mr. Summers you have a big record you're going for tonight, also don't you?" Miss Regina was dressed down in a Princeton Bearcats shirt and blue jeans, but she was still gorgeous.

"Yeah, I'm going for the record tonight. Hopefully I can break the record here on our home court. Y'all gone be there right?"

"I'll be there watching you guys in action," Mr. Smith commented.

"I'm going to try my best to make it. I have to work my other job tonight," Miss Regina said putting her hair into a ponytail.

"Come on Miss Regina everybody gone be there, you gotta show up!" Malachi pushed urging her. Both Rob and Malachi know they would play twice as hard by having women as pretty as her in attendance.

Miss Regina smiled, "I'm going to try my best. Just make sure we bring home the win tonight."

"We definitely will," Rob replied. Malachi and Rob followed them towards the gymnasium as they prepared to meet up with the team.

-

Walking into the player's lounge room most of the team was

already there conducting their own personal rituals before game time.

"What you over here drawing up bro?" Rob asked J.B..

"Nothing much. I'm just trying to figure out some new designs for a new website I'm about to construct." J.B. had a page full of numbers and abstract designs unorthodox to the eye.

Rob started to laugh. "Men, you the only nigga I know working his mind right before game time."

J.B. delayed from his drawing looking up at Rob. "Come on bro, you already know how I rock. You know this web designing shit brings me peace."

"Yup, I already know bro." Rob put on his all red beats headphones turning on some NBA Youngboy music to transcend into his zone. Looking around he noticed that Malachi was already in his as he laid stretched out on the sofa with his headphones on also.

Game time couldn't come quicker as the team heard the game buzzer go off notifying the end of the junior varsity game. The crowd noise echoed from the gymnasium to the locker room. It was evident that it was close to being a capacity crowd in attendance already.

"Alright team, let's go out here and have some fun. I want you guys to start off with some suicides to get our blood pumping. After that you guys can run shooting drips until tip off," Coach P told his team. Coach P and Coach Lane's auras were laid back, but the players knew that they wanted nothing less than a victory as a result from the game.

The Bearcats organized themselves into two separate lines evenly, preparing to make their entrance into the arena. Malachi and Rob were the head of both lines with J.B. trailing directly behind Malachi. Malachi said a quick prayer before the doors opened.

Rob looked over his shoulder, "Y'all ready?"

"Let's get it!" teammates shouted back randomly.

The team's ball boys opened the doors and the two separate lines ran in down opposite sides of the court. They were met with an abundance of applause from the fans while the band played in the bleachers. The two separate lines eventually assembled back into one meeting up under their home team basket. Preparing to run the suicide sprints Malachi took a full glance around the gymnasium. He noticed channel 5 news media there to cover the game. He also seen big poster signs students were holding up that read "Break the record Mal" and "You can do it Malachi." The reality sunk in that he was literally only thirty-six points away from being the all-time scoring leader at Princeton. Another reality set in that he would most likely go down as the best player to wear a Princeton Bearcat jersey thus far. The team ran shooting drills until the buzzer went off signaling the start of the game. Coach P decided not to give his team a pep talk.

The starters went onto the court understanding the expectations that Coach P had of them. The whole team had on head bands but Rob, Malachi and J.B. wore armbands also. Robs black armband had the word "Elite" wrote on it in red stitching. J.B.'s black armband had the word "Gifted" on it in red stitching. Malachi wore two armbands putting one on each arm. His right arm band read "Greatness" and the other had the word "King" stitched in it.

Lining up for the tip off they were facing off against a Milford Cougars team that was the second to last ranked team in the conference. Ironically, the Cougar team came out with a chip on their shoulder playing a persistent three-two zone defense. They paid special attention to Malachi doubling down in him with assertive defense. The Cougars goal was to take Malachi out of the game mentally and they succeeded. Malachi became frustrated not being able to get the shot attempts he wanted. At the end of the first quarter the score was 20 to 14 in favor of the Cougars. Rob had seven points to go along with J.B.'s four and Malachi's three.

When the second quarter began the Cougars applied a vicious full court defense that forced the Bearcats to turn the ball over.

"Take care of the damn ball!" Grandpa Gus yelled out. His voice echoed throughout the gym. Coach Joe and Mama Kelley accompanied Grandpa Gus at the top of the bleachers.

"T.C. could have easily broke that press if he was out there playing. Him and Malachi together were both too quick for em," Coach Joe explained.

"'Yeah I know. That's why teams hardly pressed them. Rob, Heavy and J.B. used to stay getting easy dunks because they used to break them presses so easy," Mama Kelley spoke monitoring the game play by play.

Coach Joe and Mama Kelley both spotted T.C. sitting in the student section. They could see the passion he still had for the game still burning in him as his eyes were glued to the game.

Midway through the second quarter Coach P took his starters out the game disappointed at their lousy performance.

"I guess y'all wanna take a loss at home tonight! Sit yall asses down!" he yelled to his starters.

The cool manner he had before the game had left him. He kept his starters out for the rest of the quarter. The score at halftime was 38 to 27 still in favor of the Cougars. Malachi had eleven points. Judging from his stats in the first half it looked like he probably would have to wait until their next game to break the record. Coach P spent the majority of the halftime interval revising the team's game plan on the drawing board.

Exiting the locker room T.C. was standing in the short hallway that led back to the gym. T.C. and Coach P made direct eye contact, but Coach P didn't say anything to him walking straight past him. Coming out the locker room Rob, J.B. and Malachi were talking about the game.

"Y'all gon run this score up or not. I know y'all ain't gon let these scrubs run y'all on our home court! What's up!" T.C. said challenging them.

"Nigga be quiet. Your ass not even out on the court!" Rob stated.

"Y'all already know if I was out there, we ah be running these bums!" T.C. exclaimed.

"T right though. We ain't never loss to this team," J.B. stated agreeing with him.

"Shut up nigga, cuz you not out there with us now!" Rob affirmed strongly.

Rob walked back into the gymnasium not trying to hear anymore of T.C.'s shit talking. J.B. followed behind knowing the game was soon to start back up. With the absence of J.B. and Rob, T.C. could now focus all of his energy into Malachi.

"Come on Mal, why you out there bull shiting? Do you want the win? Do you want this record king?" T.C. questioned in a serious tone.

Malachi had a nonchalant disposition. "I ain't trippin bro. I know we bout to come back second half. As far as that record go I still got the rest of the season to break it."

"Oh yeah? How you know you got the rest of the season? I pray to God it don't happen but you might go out there and get injured the second play of the game bro. You need to take full advantage of the opportunity God giving you to shine bro. All these people here ready to see you make history king. Go head and take care of ya business bro."

Malachi knew T.C. was telling the truth. "That's why you bro. You know I needed to hear that real talk. Thanks T."

Malachi gave T.C. a fist bump and ran back inside to the court. Both of them left the convo appreciating the bond they shared. They both never hesitated to criticize and motivate each other when necessary. They knew that was a vital element of true brotherhood.

The second half started off with a quick jumper from the Bearcats guard Ryan. The Bearcats fell back into a two three zone defense. The Cougars tried passing the ball around with a fast pace to tire down the zone defense. Malachi read the offense and stepped into the passing lane intercepting the ball. The crowd stood on their feet anticipating a big dunk. Malachi soared in the air putting together a two-handed windmill dunk. The crowd went crazy and the school band started playing to keep the crowd energy rushing. The Bearcats kept up the intense defense leading to a steal by J.B. on the next play. J.B. passed the ball up to Ryan who threw a mid-court alley oop to Malachi who caught it and dunked it with one hand. The home crowd went haywire again causing the Cougars coach to call a timeout. The time out was to no avail though.

The Bearcats finished the quarter taking the lead making the score 54 to 47. Before the start of the fourth quarter Rob called a player's huddle on the court.

"Let's go head and close this shit out and make sure my bro break this record!" he shouted.

The Bearcats managed to extend their lead to twenty points with two minutes left in the fourth quarter Malachi now had thirty-five points. With the crowd yelling for Malachi to get the ball, Ryan passed the ball to Malachi in the corner who caught it behind the three-point line. He crossed over to his left and back to his right driving down the baseline. Limited on what he could do, Malachi palmed the ball in his right hand leaving his feet. He glided in mid-air as his right hand took the ball to the other side of the rim dunking it in.

"That's my baby!" Mama Kelley yelled.

Her, Grandpa Gus and Coach Joe cheered in excitement along with the rest of the crowd. The game ended with the Bearcats winning 85 to 62. Malachi's teammate's paraded around him congratulating him. They were interrupted by the channel five newscast that wanted to interview Mr. Summers. The short Caucasian blond hair reporter smiled as she began to talk to him.

Reporter- So Malachi, how does it feel to become the all-time leading scorer in Princeton basketball?

Malachi- (Has both hands on his hips trying to catch his breath leaning down towards mic) I just first want to thank God, my parents, my coach and teammates. Without them none of this would be possible. To answer your question though, the feeling is unexplainable. It's an honor to achieve this record.

Reporter- I have to ask you, that last move you did in the baseline to make your last shot. Did you plan that out?

Malachi- (Malachi smiles) Na, I didn't plan it, but I had to improvise because I had ran outta room.

Reporter- Improvise you did! So, what's the next move for you Mr. Summers?

Malachi- Right now, I just want to finish the season out strong with my team. After that sky's the limit!

Reporter- I couldn't have said it better myself! Thank you for your time Mr. Summers.

Malachi- Thanks for the interview.

"I'm so proud of you!" Mama Kelley said walking out onto the court. Coach Joe and Grandpa Gus weren't too far behind her.

Malachi hugged his mother saying, "Thank you mama."

Malachi rested his chin on top of her head as his mama gave him a strong teddy bear hug. Finally letting go, Grandpa Gus and Coach Joe shook his hand congratulating him.

"Good game out there tonight son. Way too keep your head in the game," Coach Joe complimented.

"Thanks pops. You know they can't hold your son down forever. He wiped some sweat off his forehead with the Gatorade towel somebody had thrown around his shoulder.

"You right about that son. Your old man can still get out here and bust your ass on the court on my good days!" Coach Joe joked humorously. Grandpa Gus and Malachi had no choice but to laugh at Coach Joe's comedy.

"Anytime you ready to get this work pops, lace up your sneaks," Malachi commented.

Coach Joe grinned, "Okay son, see you when you get home tonight."

Making his way towards the locker room Malachi ran into T.C. and Mr. Smith who were already conversing. "Good game young king. You will be forever honored at this school as far as sports is concerned," Mr. Smith said.

Mr. Smith had on all black outfit. A black fleece, black jeans and black dress shoes. He topped it off with an all-white Kango hat with the black emblem to top it off.

"Thanks Mr. Smith. I'm glad to see you made it out," Malachi replied.

"Your welcome. I gave you my word I was going to be here so by all means I wasn't going to let anything stop me from being here. I was just sitting here telling T.C. he doesn't have to receive a scholarship to play ball after school. With his talent he still possesses he can easily be a walk on at a majority of these colleges."

Mr. Smith and Malachi both looked at T.C. but he had his head buried in his phone sending off a text.

Eventually lifting his head, he spoke, "I hear y'all. We still meeting up at Ziggy house, so we can step out?"

"I'll be over there as soon as I leave here," Malachi replied.

"All right now you young bloods stay safe. I'll see you all Monday," Mr. Smith spoke as he started to walk away.

"Ring my line when y'all get close to Zig's spot. Ima already be there."

"Okay bro," Malachi responded.

-

Pulling up at Ziggy's house, Malachi trailed J.B. who was riding with Rob.

"You get them relos bro?" J.B. asked Rob.

"Yeah, I got em." Checking his pockets Rob asked, "You got my lighter bro? You know y'all stay taking my lighters."

Malachi butting in the conversation, "Nigga, don't nobody got them cheap ass lighters you be buying!"

J.B. knocked on Ziggy's door. Ziggy's opened the door instantly passing J.B. a joint of sour diesel. J.B. took a strong hit of the joint letting out a couple of coughs.

The three of them walked into the house hearing the vocals of Bob Marley playing through the speakers. They walked down to the basement where T.C. was already posted smoking a blunt of purple haze.

"Y'all niggas don't know nothing bout this haze," Thomas said blowing O's out of his mouth.

"Men you ain't said nothing! That blunt of diesel got me feeling like I can crip walk," J.B. commented. He started to crip walk on the carpet in Ziggy's basement. Rob, T.C. and Malachi broke out in hysterical laughter.

"You ugly J!" Rob yelled capping on J.B..

"Holdup, y'all ain't seen shit yet!" J.B. shouted.

J.B. paused and took his brush out of his pocket. He started to crip walk and brush his hair at the same time. T.C., Malachi and Rob were still laughing hard as Ziggy walked down his basement steps.

"What the hell you doing soulja?" Ziggy asked with a weird look on his face.

"This my get money dance Zig".

T.C. squinted his face up and spoke "Na, that's that I'm not getting no ass tonight dance!"

Ziggy went behind the wooden bar pulling out a pint of Hennessy. "You souljas riding with me to the martini bar tonight downtown?" he asked.

"I'm with it. I ain't get fresh just to sit and look around at y'all." Malachi had changed into a red polo fleece, blue jeans, and some navy-blue Sperry's. He wore a red Polo cap to compliment his outfit.

"I'm riding out. Shit I'm trying to bag me something older. I heard them cougars is where it's at!" J.B. exclaimed passing the blunt to Rob. "Y'all rolling?" J.B. asked Rob and T.C..

Rob took his time responding blowing the smoke out of his nostrils. "I want to but I'm bout to slide over this shorty house in Westwood. After I pop her I'll prolly slide down there."

Malachi frowned his face up at Rob. "Man, you ain't coming through. That ass gone have you on lock for the night!"

Rob tried to reply quickly but began to cough from the pressure of the haze joint. He finally managed to respond with the short comment, "Shut up nigga."

"You rolling T or you gone be pussy whipped for the night too?" Malachi asked aggressively.

"I don't know bro. I think I got some act setup for tonight too," T.C. said.

"Damn J both these niggas whipped tonight. T know he ain't smashing nobody but Kandi," Malachi spoke loudly. He could tell he was faded from the weed and liquor because he was starting to talk more shit.

"This dude act like he ain't never left the squad to get some act. Let's set the record straight too bro, I ain't smashed Kandi in like three months. I been on a drought though, shit I need some act!" T.C. said intensely.

"Well whatever we gone do we need to get goin. Prices go up on drinks after one at Martinis," Ziggy told them throwing his black leather jacket on.

Before they left Ziggy's basement the four of them checked themselves a couple of times to make sure they had everything from their phones, wallets and keys. They knew they had been drinking and smoking heavily and didn't want to forget anything. Stepping outside onto Ziggy's porch, all five of them exhaled, feeling relieved to get out of the thick clouds of smoke that consumed Ziggy's basement.

"Y'all riding with me?" Malachi asked J and Ziggy.

"Yeah soulja, we'll ride with you. I would drive but them pigs got a warrant out on me. You okay to drive?" Ziggy asked inquiring of Malachi's sobriety.

Malachi responded, "I'm good. I just need a mild to mellow my high out."

T.C. hit the auto start to his Camaro starting his engine up.

"Alright, I'ma holler at y'all kings later on. Y'all gods be safe out here tonight," T.C. stated. He shook everybody's hand and migrated to his whip. He hit the gas a couple times and sped off into the night air.

Rob searched through his pockets again. "I know I better get my damn lighters y'all niggas been stealing from me!" he said in a sluggish voice.

"Men get your high ass outta here and make it to ol chick house safe!" J.B. spoke instructing Rob.

Rob opened up his driver door and got in. "I better get my damn lighters or it's y'all ass. I got money on y'all heads for my lighters," Rob commented continuing on with his rant.

"I think that Hennessey got the best of you soulja. Make sure you drive safe out there. Shoot us a message when you make it to her house."

"Okay Zig, Ima do that." Rob pointed his arm out the car at J.B. and Malachi eyeing them down.

"Get your drunk ass outta here bra!" J.B. demanded.

Rob finally pulled off swerving down the street but steadily started driving straight by the time he got to the end of the street.

"Let's roll out y'all," Malachi said opening his car door.

Even though J.B. and Malachi knew they were tipsy and high they felt more secure knowing Ziggy was with them. The four brothers had grown extremely close to Ziggy in the past two years. They now looked to him as their personal OG and held him in the same regard as Big Rob, Coach Joe, Grandpa Gus and Coach P.

They arrived at the martini bar about twenty minutes later. A valet guy ran up to the car in a yellow shirt staring at Malachi. Malachi rolled his window down.

"Yeah how much y'all charging?"

The valet employee responded, "Twelve dollars sir."

"We good," Malachi said rolling his window back up.

"Twelve dollars just to park a car? They fooling!" J.B. mentioned from the backseat.

"Yeah, they tripping. We'll find somewhere to park, even if we got to walk a little distance," Malachi told them making a right turn.

Ziggy was in the passenger seat throwing on some of his smell good cologne. "What you young gods fail to realize is that we're in the nice part of downtown. Twelve dollars is merely pocket change to the people we bout to be around."

Malachi looked at the cars they passed as he looked for a parking spot. He noticed a couple BMW's, Lexus's, Cadillac trucks and different model Hybrid cars. Parking the car, Ziggy, Malachi and J.B. walked down street and turned the corner. There was a host of clubs on the street but the establishment they were entering stood out. The club was displaying a neon blue logo that read "Martinis" on top of the building. The December wind chill mixed with the night air made the temperature cold outside. Fortunately, Ziggy knew the bouncer at the door, so they were able to walk straight in.

-

Walking in the club the atmosphere was dark. The club was only illuminated by color strobe lights and the necessary lights the bartenders needed. It was apparent that Ziggy's popularity reached far beyond the streets of Rolling Heights. He shook hands and hugged people varying from younger black women to older white men. He even talked in a different language to a couple of women from Ghana.

"It's so many women in here, I don't even know where to start! Shit!" J.B. shouted over the music.

"Yeah, it's a little bit of everything in here," Malachi added. Him and J.B. stood in awe looking at the assortment of females that occupied the club. Black women, white women, Asians and Latin women were running rapid throughout the club.

"We gotta come with our A game if we gone bag something in here tonight," Malachi stated still observing the eye candy.

Ziggy spoke up before J.B. could respond. "You damn right soulja! These are some good ass women. Most in here prolly have some type of career. Gotta shoot ya best shot!"

J.B. held up his gold watch that shined brighter in the club. "Ima work my mouthpiece but hopefully this gold thang help me out."

J.B.'s comment made Ziggy grin. "Ima catch up with you souljas later on." Ziggy disappeared somewhere off into the back of the club.

Malachi and J.B. migrated towards the bar. The bar was flooded with people and the four female bartenders were moving with a swift pace. "Damn who the hell is that? That ass damn near bout to bust out the bottom of that skirt," Malachi spoke in a gaze.

J.B. looked at the bartender also being hypnotized by her booty. "I don't know who that is but I'm damn near ready to jump over this bar to holler at her!"

The bartender was turned around fixing a drink but from the back they saw perfection. She had on a short black skirt with a short sleeve black cut off top that showed a portion of her flat belly. Her jet-black hair hung down her back complimenting her caramel skin. The two brothers were both shocked at the sight they seen when she turned around.

"Miss Regina?" Malachi and J.B. said at the same time. She had a huge smile on her face, but she was astonished as well.

"Malachi, Jerome. What the hell are you guys doing in here?"

"Come on now Miss Regina you know we be everywhere it's popping at in the city," Jerome stated. He wasn't trying to be too obvious that he was looking at Miss Regina's cleavage hanging out her shirt.

"How did y'all get in here? That's what I really want to know."

"We with one of our OG's, Ziggy from Rolling Heights," Malachi answered.

Fixing her cleavage in her black shirt she responded, "Yeah, I know Ziggy. He went to school with my older sister."

"If I would have known you worked here, we would have been hitting this spot up. You my teacher and bartender at the same damn time!" The three of them laughed at J.B.'s humor.

"Okay well y'all be safe in here tonight. I need to get back to fixing these drinks."

"Okay then, Miss Regina," Malachi replied.

Miss Regina walked down to the other end of the bar and served a couple of customers.

"Damn Miss Regina looking good as shit!" Jerome said passionately.

"Hell yeah, she is. I'm on hard just looking at her! Her ass look pillow soft," Malachi commented lustfully.

"It's too many other chicks in here to be stuck on her though. It ain't like we gone be able to smash that anyway," J.B. assured. He had his eyes on a curvy Latino woman who was on the dance floor. "I'm about to go get her bro."

"Go head bro. I'll be right here posted at the bar," Malachi told him. J.B. started to walk off but paused in his tracks turning back around.

"Ay, nigga don't be getting too drunk. We still gotta get home!" J.B. shouted.

"Man gone head on king!" Malachi yelled back.

About thirty minutes had passed and J.B. still hadn't returned. Malachi figured that he still was scheming. Meanwhile, Malachi had gotten a couple numbers while he was at the bar. His laidback persona attracted older women. Nevertheless, he still had his sights on Miss Regina. He didn't know if it was the liquor or not, but he felt like he had the confidence to at least get her number before he left.

"Miss Regina can you make me a shot of Henny?" he asked as she walked over to him.

Frowning her face up at him she replied, "Now Mal, you know I can't do that. I have the knowledge that you're underage." She was bent slightly over the bar, so she wouldn't have to yell.

"I got in here, so I'm good to drink. You the only one that know I'm underage."

She took a step back looking at him. "I'll see what I can do. By the way, congrats on your success tonight. How does it feel have the scoring record?"

"It feel good. I'm just not trying to score on the court though. I'm trying to score other places too," Malachi spoke confidently.

"Oh yeah, well where are you trying to score at?" Miss Regina knew that Malachi was intoxicated and flirting but she wanted to see how far he would take it.

Malachi responded, "Anywhere I see opportunity at."

"Okay then, I hear you," she said walking back to other end of the bar.

About ten minutes later a Caucasian bartender with short red hair walked over setting a shot of Hennessy in front of Malachi. "Here you go baby," she said.

Malachi didn't ask any questions about where the drink came from. He seen Miss Regina at the end of the bar winking at him.

"Bro you still at this bar posted? You need to be out getting these chicks like me," J.B said.

"What you think I been doing. I been getting em right here at the bar."

"That's what's up. That thick Latina chick I got earlier talking about she want me to go home with her. I been gaming her all night. She waiting for me by the door right now," J.B. said checking his phone.

"Oh yeah? Where Ziggy at?" Malachi's speech was a little bit more slurred as the liquor started to have more of an effect.

"He over there in VIP posted. I just spoke to him. He said he bout to come over here and holler at you. You sure you good bro?" Jerome asked concerned.

"Yeah, Ima hundred. Hit my line soon as you make it to her spot."

"I will. She stay in Newport so she not too far." They exchanged handshakes and J.B. walked to the front of the club.

Malachi signaled for the same bartender to bring him another shot of Hennessey. Bringing him the next shot Malachi gave her twenty dollars and told her to keep the change.

"How many rounds is that for you soulja?" Ziggy asked walking up.

"My third, I'm good."

"Oh, alright then. I know you going to talk shit but I'm bout to leave out with one of my girls too. I ain't popped that ass in a minute."

Malachi shook his head. "All y'all just gone be whipped all in the same night. It's cool though, I was about to leave out anyway." Malachi started to frisk his pockets for his keys but noticed they weren't there. He stood up looking on the ground but didn't see them there either.

"What you looking for Mal?"

"My keys, I thought I had them in my pocket." Both him and Ziggy searched the ground trying to locate his keys. Miss Regina walked over to the spot they were searching at.

"What y'all looking for?" she asked.

"Young soulja lost his keys," Ziggy spoke pushing his dreads out his face.

"I can check with the club owner to make sure no one turned them in," she iterated.

"Yeah, can you do that for me please?" Malachi asked.

"I sure will give me about five minutes."

As she walked away both Ziggy and Malachi stared at her in the black skirt.

"Damn, after all these years Regina still look good. You know what I just thought bout soulja? I think J.B. has ya keys. Remember he had to run back and get something out the car."

Malachi thought about it for a second. "You right Zig! I had forgot to get em back from him. Let me call bro."

J.B.- I was just about to ring ya line. I just made it to ol girl spot.

Malachi- Bro, you still got my keys? I forgot to get them back from you.

J.B.- Damn, you right. I forgot I had em. They right here in my pocket.

Malachi- I'm big salty. Ima have to leave my whip down here.

J.B.- My bad bro. I forgot to give em back on some tipsy shit.

Malachi- Its cool. Ima just call an Uber or leave out with Zig.

J.B.- Yeah, if you can't find a ride hit me back up. I'll have her drive me back over there.

Malachi- It's cool bro. Ima just grab em from you tomorrow. Be safe bro.

J.B.- Alright bro, you too.

Miss Regina walked back over to them. "I spoke to the owner and he said nobody turned keys in."

"It's all right Regina. We found out J has the keys," Ziggy told her.

Wearing a face of relief, she commented, "That's good to hear."

"You think you can take Mal home? I'm bout to leave out with my girl and I don't want him talking an Uber because he's a little bit too drunk," Ziggy sought.

"I ain't drunk Zig!" Malachi said hastily. It was obvious that Malachi wasn't in a sober mind though.

Miss Regina hesitated before she replied to Ziggy. "Yeah, I guess I can take him home. Somebody needs to make sure he gets home safely."

"Okay cool. Well I'm bout to leave up outta here. My girl waiting for me outside."

"Alright Zig, I'll hit you up tomorrow, Malachi mentioned."

"Alright soulja. Drink some coconut water in the morning to shake that hangover," Ziggy advised before he walked off.

"Give me about ten minutes and I'll be ready Mal," Miss Regina stated.

"Okay, that's cool," he responded.

Malachi looked at his phone and seen that it was almost dead. It was about two in the morning. When she came back she was wearing a gray pea coat that stopped right at her waist sitting comfortably on her booty.

"Okay, I'm ready Mal."

"Thanks for the ride Miss Regina. I know you didn't have to do this."

"Don't say that. I'm not just going to leave you stranded out here."

As they exited the club she pulled a yellow ticket out her purse to give to the valet. About three minutes later the valet attendant was pulling up in her red Cadillac CTS. She gave the valet man a ten-dollar tip.

Malachi got into her car that was laced with black leather interior and tinted windows. The song "Put your phone down" by Erykah Badu was playing via Bluetooth from her phone. The aroma of a smell good car freshener had her car smelling marvelous. Malachi knew he had to be drunk because he couldn't figure out how he ended up in Miss Regina's car.

"How are you going to get in the house if you don't have your keys?" she questioned stopping at a red light.

Malachi was in the midst of side eyeing her thick thighs as she questioned him. "I don't even know. I really don't want to wake my peoples up since it's so late, you know?"

Miss Regina accelerated on the gas and said, "I understand that plus you're drunk, so that's not a good look."

Malachi added, "Right, not at all."

There was an awkward silence between them for a long minute.

Suddenly she asked, "Do you want to stay at my house for the night? I know I'm your teacher, but I feel responsible for you tonight. You can just sleep on my couch."

Malachi almost peed on himself in reaction to Miss Regina's last statement. He almost lost his mind at the thought of staying the night with her. "Yeah, I'll stay with you. That's prolly the best thing for me to do," he replied trying to play it cool.

"Okay, that works for me as well. I don't have to drive all the way back down here so late at night."

"You got a condo down here don't you?"

"Yeah, were only about five minutes away from it now," she said.

Malachi was so hype on the inside he wanted to text his brothers, but he didn't.

Pulling up at the complex they passed a big sign that read "Deluxe Condominiums". Malachi could tell that you had to be making good money to live there.

Miss Regina parked her car in her assigned garage. "You got everything?" she asked before they got out the car.

"Yeah, I do, he replied."

Walking up the steps outside he couldn't help but be mesmerized by the sight of Miss Regina's booty. It took all his power not to grip a handful of it. Arriving on the third floor they walked into her condo which was vibrant with color. Her furniture was very eloquent, with everything in its proper place.

"Take your shoes off and place them by the front door Mal," she instructed as she walked to her bedroom. Walking back out her room barefoot Miss Regina asked, "You want any lemonade? Don't worry it's non-alcoholic!"

"Yeah, I'll take a glass."

Handing him the glass, Malachi noticed her red toenail polish that matched her fingernails.

"I didn't put too much sugar in it did I? I just made it this morning."

Malachi took a couple gulps of the lemonade. "Na, it's perfect," he answered.

"Okay good. I'll bring you bring you some pillows, so you can sleep out here for the night."

About ten minutes passed and she still hadn't bought any pillows out. Malachi had already stretched himself out on her couch starting to doze off.

"Malachi can you come here for a second please?" Miss Regina yelled from her room.

Malachi woke up. "You say something Miss Regina?"

"Yes, come here please."

Malachi was pissy drunk, so his movements were staggered but he moved as quick as he could.

Entering her room, she was sitting on the edge of the right side of her king size bed.

"Mal you can take your Polo hat off," she said giggling. "I didn't even know I still had it on."

He took his hat off and set it on her black wood frame dresser.

"Can you take my necklace off for me please?" she asked lifting it up.

He walked over to the other side of the bed sitting next to her. Her perfume smelled so good he wanted to lick it off of her.

"Do you see the little latch back there?"

"Yeah, I see it," Malachi said even though the lighting in the room was dim.

Trying to unlatch her necklace Malachi's intoxicated thoughts overtook him. His lust caused him to start to kiss and slowly suck on the right side of Miss Regina's neck. Ironically, to his surprise she didn't stop him. Instead, she started to move her hand up and down the side of his leg. As Malachi kissed on her neck, he steadily moved down, beginning to caress her chest until her breasts were in his mouth. He sucked and licked on them like they were made from honey and sugar. Malachi slid his left hand down her back until he gripped her ass. Miss Regina backed away putting a pause on their intimacy.

"You sure you know what you doing?" Malachi tried to improvise an answer as he stared at her admiring her goddess figure as she sat half naked on the bed.

"I never had a woman on your level, but I promise whatever we do is gone stay between me and you."

"You promise me?" she asked seeking more assurance.

"I promise," he confirmed

"Lay back on the bed baby," she spoke instructing him.

Malachi removed his Polo shirt and laid back against the headboard. Miss Regina got closer to him. She began to rub his chest with her hands and kiss on it also. She unzipped his jeans and pulled his dick out from under his briefs. She stroked it up and down with her left hand like it was her own personal toy.

"Reach in the drawer next to you and get a condom, she told him."

Opening the small drawer that was next to the bed Malachi grabbed the condom with the gold wrapper. He handed it to her. She opened it and placed it on him herself. Immediately after she put it on Miss Regina slid off her black lace panties. She sat on top of Malachi inserting his dick into her. She started to ride him with an intense rhythm as she stared into his eyes. Malachi felt like he was experiencing heaven as he watched her breasts jiggle and feel her ass bounce up and down. Even though Malachi wanted to last all night he only was able to last about three minutes before exploding inside the condom. Getting up off of him she gave him a kiss as she laid next to him.

"Sorry for coming so quick," Malachi said disappointed.

"It's okay baby. I know this is your first time with a real woman."

She curled up next to him putting her booty into his stomach. Malachi wrapped his arms around her holding her throughout the night. It was about three-thirty am.

Five hours later, Malachi woke up with Miss Regina laying next to him looking picture perfect. He got back on hard and started to kiss on her neck waking her up. He kissed on her back and moved down to her booty kissing it. Miss Regina positioned herself on her knees as he was kissing. Malachi got onto his knees lining himself to penetrate her insides once again. This time though, neither one of them attempted to get a condom. As he went into her this time it was even more pleasurable than the first time. He steadily stroked inside of her as she started to throw her ass back. As they kept going, the pace increased, and Malachi tried to think about anything other than coming inside of her. He felt like God was favoring him to give him a chance to see the sight of her ass cheeks jiggle together naked.

"Smack it baby!" she yelled out.

Malachi started to smack her booty as she commanded him too. Malachi slowed his strokes to try to hinder himself from climaxing. It was too no avail though. He exited her vagina ejecting his semen onto her booty. He fell out on the pillows exhausted from the sexual cardio.

Miss Regina smiled, "I'll get you a washcloth." He watched her as she walked to the bathroom resembling a video vixen. A couple minutes later she came back with a warm washcloth handing it to Malachi. He cleaned himself as she put on her sweatpants and a tee shirt.

"Go ahead and get dressed Mal. I have to be somewhere in a couple of hours."

"Okay, I am."

Before he threw on his clothes he grabbed his phone sending a message to his brothers. "Meet me at Ziggy house sap!" the message read.

Slightly prior to getting on the highway Miss Regina stopped at White castle getting them both breakfast sandwiches and herself a coffee. It was about nine thirty am when they pulled up in front of Ziggy's spot.

"Thanks for the food and letting me stay the night," Malachi said grabbing the sandwich bag.

"You welcome Mal. Remember keep your mouth quiet about what we shared together."

"I will. I promise." Before he got out the car Malachi gave her a short kiss on the lips. Getting out of her Cadillac he felt like the man of the year! Ziggy and T.C. were on the porch, anxious to see who was in the Cadillac car.

-

"Damn bro, who is that?" T.C. asked curiously.

"Stay out of grown folk's business. Ya hear me!" Malachi commented.

T.C. made a stale face at Malachi in return to his comment. Ziggy waived at the Cadillac car as it pulled off.

"Just know I'm on some real live player pimp shit out here, ya heard me," Malachi boasted in a New Orleans accent.

"Yeah, okay bro. What the hell you call us over here for anyway?" T.C. asked.

"Ima tell you king. Where J and Rob at? They here yet?" Malachi questioned.

"You so geeked up soulja you walked right past Rob car." Ziggy pointed at Rob's SUV in his driveway as he finished his statement. "Them two negroes down there in my basement right now rolling up that fire!"

The three of them made their way down to Ziggy's basement.

"Dayg bro just come down here with White Castle though. Where ours at?" J.B. inquired.

"Man, I ain't trying hear that shit. All y'all niggas bounced on me last night for some ass! Where my keys at nigga?" Malachi said sitting on Ziggy's pool table.

J.B. threw Malachi his keys as he responded, "My bad bro but that damn Latino chick put it on my ass last night!"

"Damn, you smashed a Latino? Was she talking in Spanish?" Rob asked.

"Yeah, a Latino broad that stay right there in Newport. Men we was both talking Spanish. I was making up words and shit talking that espanol right with her!" J.B. said comically.

"Men you silly J," Rob commented.

"I'm serious bro. I would have laid up with her today, but I knew I had bro car keys. What you call us over here for anyway Mal? Jerome told them."

"That's what I'm trying to figure out. Somebody dropped bro off in a Caddy CTS just now," T.C. reported.

"Oh, bro prolly popped one of them established chicks that was in the club last night," J.B. stated trying to figure it out.

"Yeah, something like that," Malachi said.

"Nigga is you gone tell us or keep stalling us out?" Rob asked impatiently.

"Just put it like this y'all bro a legend just like that man on the wall." Malachi pointed at the Bob Marley poster.

Ziggy laughed, "Na, you not there yet soulja but you will be!"

Malachi finished off the last of his White Castle sandwich. Ima tell y'all this but y'all gotta swear for God that it won't leave past this room."

"Come on king, you know the crew ain't telling shit!" T.C. affirmed.

With his squad confirming their confidentiality, Malachi finally said, "That was Miss Regina. I smashed her last night!"

"Get the fuck outta here bro!" T.C. yelled with a face of astonishment.

"Swear to God bro! I know she was there last night but Miss Regina!! How the fuck you end up smashin her?" J.B. asked full of intrigue.

"That shit was crazy last night man! I don't even know where to start," Malachi spoke. He pulled out a red Bic lighter putting the flame to the black and mild in his hand.

Rob was coughing like crazy from the weed he had lit up, but he managed to get a sentence out. "Bro I know you don't be on no lying shit, but you need to explain how the fuck you smashed Miss Regina! What the hell! You just said some shit!" Rob exclaimed.

"Pass the god that blunt so I can elaborate on this pimpin to y'all," Malachi boasted.

Rob took another tote of the reefer before he passed it. Malachi took two strong hits and blew the smoke out before he started narrating his adventure. "First off, I gotta thank you J for leaving out Martini's with my keys. And Zig, I owe you for life for choosing her as my designated driver."

"Man, what exactly is you saying? You still not telling us how you ended up in that pussy," T.C. said sitting on the bar stool.

"I'm getting there bro, let me finish. I let J see my keys last night, but he forgot to give em back to me. When he left with that Latino broad last night he ain't have no way of getting em back to me. Ziggy was leaving with one of his chicks and it was his idea to have Miss Regina take me home."

"What was Miss Regina doing down there? She was at the club?" T.C. asked trying to piece the story together.

Ziggy answered T.C.'s question. "Ya forgot that was an older club soulja. She work the bar down there on the weekends," Ziggy told him in his strong Jamaican accent.

"Yeah, gotta say she was down there looking good as hell! " J.B. added.

"Right! She was spotting me on drinks all night last night. That's the reason I was so wasted. Zig asked her could she take me home and she didn't turn it down."

Rob interrupted Malachi, "How you end up popping her though? Where was y'all at?"

"I was just about to get to that. Since I was wasted and didn't have no keys to get in the spot, we just ended up going to her condo downtown. I was so fucked up as soon as we got there I started falling asleep on the couch. She called me in her room to take her necklace off though. We was both on her bed when I started taking her necklace off and her titties was busting out the black top she had on. To keep it a hundred, if I wasn't gone off that Henny I prolly wouldn't have made a move on her! Soon as I know it though I was kissing on her neck and suckin on her titties."

All of them were fully tuned into the story he was telling play by play.

"Them titties tasted like cinnamon in my mouth! I swear to God they did! If I'm remembering right she told me to lay back on the bed. We took our clothes off and she started kissing on my chest.

Then she start stroking my meat with her hand. After that I put on a condom and she got on top and start riding me! Titties, ass bouncing everywhere! Malachi described."

"Man what! On everything?" T.C. shouted out.

"On God bro!" Malachi swore holding his right hand up.

J.B. and Rob's were faces were in a state of shock. "What her sex game was like bro?" J.B. asked anxious to know.

Malachi took a hit from the blunt blowing the smoke out. "Live as hell. Felt like I was in heaven bro. Real talk I came quick as hell though," he said laughing.

"Shit her sexy ass prolly make dudes bust fast all the time. Fact is you smashed!" Rob spoke.

"Yeah, you right. And I hit that ass from the back when we woke up! She gotta video vixen body," Malachi said reminiscing on her frame.

T.C. was looking at his brother in amazement. "Real talk bro, we all kings but that shit you just did was legendary. Niggas our age just don't go around smashing chicks like Miss Regina," T.C. acknowledged congratulating his brother. T.C. got up and fist bumped Malachi.

"Yeah bro, you a legend for smashing that. You the head honcho," Rob added on. J.B. and him got up and both gave Malachi a fist bump.

"Good shot again Zig for setting that up," Malachi spoke.

Ziggy was on the computer by his studio playing around with some instrumentals. "No problem young king. I been knowing Regina a long time. You not the first person to tell me some freaky shit about her."

"Y'all heard about that party they having down on Vine street next Friday?" J.B. asked looking at his phone.

"Yeah, somebody just tagged me in the flyer on a Facebook post. That's right up the road from here for real," Rob spoke.

"Yup, that's senior night too. That whole night gone be lit!" Malachi commented.

-

"Y'all think y'all so live! Y'all get on my nerves," Kandi spoke.

"We is live Kandi. You already know this," Rob said grabbing some books from his locker.

"T.C. can you give us a ride home after school?" Tisha asked.

"I got y'all. Just be by my car after school," he responded.

"Kandi you know y'all don't gotta ask for a ride. That's your old boo, he gone look out for you anytime!" Rob stated trying to get a reaction out of her.

"Negative! I don't need Thomas to do anything for me!" she replied aggressively.

Kandi and T.C. had broken up because of his infidelity issues. Although, she had never found out that T.C. and Tisha had slept together in their junior year.

"What's good y'all!" Jerome yelled out. Malachi and J.B. had walked up on them from the opposite end of the hallway.

"I'm hungry. We should leave school and go get some waffle house," Tisha suggested.

"Damn you always hungry. Do ya mama ever feed you at home?" J.B. asked sarcastically.

Tisha's eyebrows raised up on her forehead as she replied, "Shut up J.

"Me and J was trying figure out some senior pranks we could do before we came over here," Malachi said.

"Oh yeah? What y'all come up with?" Kandi asked.

"We think we found a way to rig the school intercom for about ten minutes. Rig it and say anything we want too on that muthafucka!" Malachi told them.

Kandi smiled saying, "Omg, y'all is too much but I know I'm with it!"

"Hell yeah, me too! Every teacher I don't like getting they shit roasted!" T.C. commented making the crew laugh.

"Yeah, we definitely gotta get that poppin. Y'all going to the party down in Hartwell Friday?" Tisha asked.

Rob froze his face up at her. "I don't even know why you asked that! Is y'all going though? I know y'all might be scared since the party out in the city."

"Whatever Rob, we out here! When you see us, speak!" Kandi commented as the school bell rang.

The six of them diversed walking to their classes.

The school week went fast with Friday's eve quickly coming. Malachi had been nervous every time he walked into Miss Regina's class, but she put on the perfect teacher act. She conducted herself in a professional manner, not giving off the slightest inclination that her and Malachi had been intimate. Every time Malachi laid eyes on Miss Regina his mind relapsed to the sexual experience they shared together. He often wondered if he would get the chance to indulge in her again.

-

"Jerome, what should I wear tomorrow to senior night?" Mama J said walking down the hallway. She had a black dress and black boots in her hands walking into Jerome's room. "Do you think this looks good or am I doing too much?"

J.B. was in his room watching old episodes of the Fresh Prince of Bel Air. "Ma, you know you look good in whatever you wear." J.B.'s compliment made her feel a lot better.

"I know baby. You know I just be so self-conscious now because of my battle with this cancer. It's taken a toll on me mentally, physically and spiritually."

Mama J hadn't lost all her hair, but she did lose a majority of it. To avoid the dilemma of figuring out different hairstyles, she just sported a low even-Steven haircut and wore wigs.

"Cancer or not mama, you beautiful."

"Thank you, J. I'm so proud of you and all your accomplishments."

"Thanks ma. I'm proud of you too. We both have came a long way," J.B. stated turning down the TV volume.

Mama J sighed heavily. "Yes, we have. I remember having you at the UC hospital in Clifton eighteen years ago. Your dad and I were so happy. Lord knows I had no clue that he was going to run off, start another family and never look back on us."

J.B. noticed his mama was getting sentimental and on the verge of crying. He got up out his bed and hugged her looking over her head.

"Lord knows I tried my damnest to raise you to be the best man you could be J." Mama J hugged her son as if she knew it was her last time hugging him.

"I know mama. I appreciate everything you've done for me. What's our motto mama?"

J.B.'s mama wiped her tears and leaned back so she could see her son's face. "Educate, accelerate, elevate!" they both said together in harmony.

-

Across town Rob was driving to Steak & Lemonade, a local Cincinnati restaurant to get something to eat. He was listening to Young Dolph's album until the music was interrupted by a phone call.

Rob- Hello

Automated system- Hello. This is an call from a Ohio Correctional Facility Inmate. To accept this call press zero. To deny this call press 1.

Big Rob- Watup son. How you doing?

Rob- I'm Good bout to get something to eat.

Big Rob- I hear that. What's happening out there?

Rob- Nothing too much. It's senior night tomorrow for our hoop team.

Big Rob- I figured it would be this week or the next. I'm sorry I can't be there for that son.

Rob- Its cool pops. I know you got every intent to be. (Rob said that but was still hurt his dad couldn't be present)

Big Rob- It sound like you in the car. Where you going?

Rob- Bout to hit up Steak and Lemonade.

Big Rob- Damn that sound good! They cheesesteaks and lemonades be hitting!

Rob- Yup and that's exactly what I'm bouta get.

Big Rob- How you been managing your paper?

Rob- I been cool for real. Not spending too much and paying the basic bills.

Big Rob- Okay, let me know if you run into a jam. I'm still trying set things up, so we can rent that house out to other people once you graduate. You been running them hos through the spot?

Rob- Yeah, we minds will make some dough off it since neither one of us gone be here. And Daddy you know I keep something on deck, but I been chilling for real.

Big Rob- Okay then. Make sure you strap up. Did anything else ever happen with that Heavy situation?

Rob- Na, ain't nothing happened since the fight. Mama J basically tried to take over the conflict and dead the beef.

Big Rob- I heard. Some little young cats from Rolling Heights came up to me trying give me the scoop after I had talked to you about it.

Rob- Yeah, it's crazy cause we for real looked at Heavy like family. I guess money change niggas though.

Big Rob- I wouldn't even say change. It just bring the best and worst out of people.

Rob- You right about that.

Big Rob- I want y'all to stick close to each other and move smart. Me being in the streets so long I know that beef not over yet. J.B. pulled a gun on that boy so that instantly took it to another level.

Rob- I don't think it's over yet either. I know we bound to collide with em again sooner or later.

Big Rob- I just want y'all to graduate so y'all can get outta here and move on with y'all lives.

Rob- I do too. We gone be good though.

Big Rob- Ima save some money on this phone. Ima call you back Saturday. Love u son

Rob- Okay pops. Love you too.

Rob continued to drive hanging up the phone. The convo with his father helped to confirm the underlying thought that had been on his conscious. He knew that the beef wasn't over between his brothers and Heavy. He just prayed everybody he loved would be one hundred if the situation escalated again.

-

The next night the gymnasium was packed once again for the senior night basketball game. Coach P stood in the middle of the locker room with his clipboard in hand.

"Alright fellas, let's go out here execute and play hard and get this win. To all my seniors, you guys already know I've enjoyed coaching you for the time we've been together. I pray God prosper all of your endeavors in whatever you do. Bring it in team."

The team broke the huddle after yelling out their victory chant. Running into the gym the crowd cheered and the band played. Coach P started all five of his seniors on the team. From the start of the game the Bearcats came out playing with full force intensity. At halftime the score was 42 to 13. It was obvious that the game was going to turn into a blowout in favor of Princeton.

During halftime Mr. Plusky the school's superintendent stood at half court with a microphone.

"Welcome to the 2018 Princeton Bearcats senior night basketball game. First, let me say I am extremely proud of all our seniors. They are the prime example of extraordinary student athletes. Let me introduce our five seniors. First up is Malachi Summers."

Coach Joe and Mrs. Summers walked out on opposite sides of Malachi to mid court. His parents were dressed in their Princeton Bearcats attire being known as proud ambassadors for the school.

"Next up we have Jerome Brown," Mr. Plusky said in a high-pitched voice.

Mama J and J.B. walked down to midcourt arm in arm. Mama J had a glamorous smile on her face. She had on her black dress, black boots and extravagant earrings on. They handed her roses and a plaque as they did with Malachi's parents.

"Next up we have Mr. Robert Pounds Jr."

Mama Kelley handed her roses and plaque to Coach Joe to hold.

She decided to escort Rob to midcourt along with Grandpa Gus. Grandpa Gus and Rob waited for Mama Kelley before they began to walk onto the court. T.C. smiled as he watched from the bleachers. The short ceremony was bittersweet for him. While he was proud of his brothers he knew that he should been right alongside of them getting acknowledged as well.

Mr. Plusky introduced the last two seniors and asked the crowd to give them all a round of applause. The crowd stood up giving them a loud ovation for their years of dedication being student athletes. The Bearcats ran the score up on the opposing squad and Coach Joe rested his seniors for most of the fourth quarter. The seniors reminisced and joked around on the bench. They knew this would be the last time they would be able to share their comradery in their home arena. The final score of the game was 72 to 34. Before entering the locker room, they were stopped by Coach P. Instead of shaking their hands he saluted them and gave them hugs. The respect was mutual between him and his players.

"Ay who car we gone roll in tonight to this party? I know I don't feel like driving," Rob stated.

"Shit, we in the maro with T," J.B. commented.

"Hell yeah, we minds will stunt on em tonight," Rob replied.

"Yeah, T definitely gone have to drive. All I feel like doing is sipping that bottle of Remy I got in the whip," Malachi said taking his jersey off.

J.B. threw his gym bag around his shoulder saying, "Yeah, it's warm enough to take the top off even though it's January. I swear this Cincinnati weather bipolar.

"Let's step out here and see what this nigga T talking bout," Rob commented.

Walking back into the gym they were greeted by the F.M.B. family and remnants of the leftover crowd.

"We so proud of y'all," Mama Kelley said laying her eyes on them. Her and mama J started to hug on their sons.

"Ma no more hugs!" "Shut up boy we can hug on y'all if we want too!" she replied sharply.

"Y'all played a good game tonight. I expect y'all to go far in the tournament," Coach Joe spoke.

Smelling her bouquets Mama Kelley asked, "What are young men about to do?"

"Go to the spot and hit up this party in T whip," Malachi answered.

Looking up from his phone screen, T.C. sarcastically said, "I like how you just gone hop in my whip without even hollering at me first."

"Men you act like you ain't trying stunt tonight! We in your whip tonight!" Rob commanded.

"Well whatever y'all do make sure you all stay safe. I'll be home later J.

"Okay ma," J.B. replied.

"Yes, make sure y'all stay safe tonight!" Mama Kelley reiterated.

-

On the way to J.B. house T.C. followed Rob and Malachi there.

"Who got loud?" T.C. asked as they walked into the house.

"You the dope boy king. You spose to have that shit on deck," Malachi stated looking at T.C..

"Come on now, you know I don't move green no more. I'm only fuckin with soft now. We just gone to hit the hood before we hit the party," T.C. responded.

"I got a bottle of Hennessey in the car and I know Mal still got that Remy," Rob mentioned.

"Yeah, we bout to be fucked up hitting the scene tonight. I'm on everything bad I see tonight" Malachi stated.

"Me and you both.!" T.C. said.

J.B. walked in the living room with two washcloths handing them to Rob and Malachi. It didn't take them long to freshen up and throw on their fits they were sporting for the night. Rob was wearing a fresh all black tee, black jeans, with some clean all black Airmax. He had on his all black shades and wearing one of Big Rob's flamboyant watches on his wrist.

J.B. was fresh as well. He had on his all-black Akoo shirt. On the shirt were the words "Akoo is what I do." Wearing some red and black air max on his feet he rocked an all-black Cincy fitted cocked to side, so you could still see his waves.

Malachi had on a navy-blue Polo, blue jeans and his navy-blue Air Max. Of course, he wore his navy-blue Polo hat with the white polo man to complete his attire.

T.C. had on a crispy white tee with the words "Trap God" on it and black bold letters. He had on all black jeans and black Airmax for his footwork. His locks that hung down his back and six-piece gold grill would make him easy to see amongst the masses.

"Gotta say we fly as fuck tonight! Swag on a million!" J.B. professed tilting his fitted a little bit more.

"Oh yeah, royalty at its finest," Malachi stated in accordance.

T.C. grabbed his keys making his way towards the door. "Let's roll to the hood and cop so we can get to this party. Grab that bottle of Henn out ya car," he said.

"I'm glad you said something, cause I damn sure was about to forget it," Rob replied.

Rob grabbed the bottle of Hennessey out of his car while Malachi got the bottle of Remy out of his.

T.C. decided to drop the top on his yellow sports car for the night.

Rob passed the bottle of Hennessy to J.B. commenting, "Yeah we bout to shit on em tonight."

"Hell yeah, we are. Let me run in the crib and grab us some plastic cups for this liquor," J.B. said.

"Hurry up nigga," T.C. spoke pressing on his gas pedal making the engine roar.

About two minutes later J.B. came back out with the cups.

"Shotgun!" Malachi yelled out before Rob or J.B. got a chance too.

Rob just stared at Malachi with a mean mug. "Come on king, you know my big ass too big to be in the backseat."

"He do gotta point bro, he is big as hell," T.C. added.

"Na, I ain't trying hear that. Y'all stay calling that shotgun shit out before me. It's my turn now."

Malachi usually wouldn't have cared but the liquor intake made him more defiant. Since T.C. had taken his top off, J.B. and Rob still sat in the back comfortably.

T.C. backed out of the driveway turning his music up full blast.

Rob hit Malachi on the shoulder. "Pass that Remy bro," he shouted over the music.

Malachi poured another cup and passed the bottle back to Rob. It was careless of them to be drinking the liquor so freely, but they had no worries that night. Crossing the tracks into Rolling Heights the traffic in the hood was thick. The environment was turnt up due to the parties and spontaneous warm weather. T.C. drove through the neighborhood speeding down every street, showing out.

-

"Slow down bro. I'm bout to hop out and cop from Meek," Malachi said. Meek was a young boy from the Rolling Heights neighborhood who Malachi had watched grow up over the years. Meek was on the corner across the street from "Dungeon". It was the same spot Rob and J.B. fought Heavy and Snake at.

"What's good bro!" Meek yelled out from a distance.

"What up little bro. You good out here?" Malachi asked.

"You know it and I got that fire in big bro!" Meek stood about 5'6, dark skin and skinny. People rarely messed with him because he was a young hot head who would pop off his pistol at the slightest sign of beef.

"Let me get a quarter of that shit," Malachi stated.

Meek reached deep in his pockets and pulled out a bag of reefer that was light green. Meek took out a couple of buds and gave Malachi the rest of the bag.

"Its prolly like three extra buds in there for you big bro.

Malachi took a sniff of one of the buds before putting it in his pocket. "Damn this some fire!"

"I told you bro, Meek iterated."

Malachi gave Meek fifty dollars for the reefer. "Don't be out here all night juggin young king," he said bumping fists with Meek.

"No sleep for me big bro. I'm grindin until I pull up in something like T.C. in."

Malachi got back to the car only to see Rob sitting in the front seat. "You ain't call shotgun when you got out bro," Rob stated.

"Yeah, alright bro. Who got the relos? So, we can roll this fire up."

J.B. pulled two relo cigars out his pocket. "I got em. Let me roll em up real quick." Malachi gave J.B. the weed as he climbed into the back.

-

Driving off, T.C. found the nearest e way entrance to get to the party. He rolled up his tinted windows to block majority of the wind. J.B. already had one of the blunts rolled by the time they got onto the expressway. Between the liquor and the weed they were as far from sober as they could be. Getting off the exit, traffic was bumper to bumper.

"Damn! Man, all these cars can't be going to the same party. That center ain't gone hold all these people," T.C. expressed trying to switch the lanes.

"Shit, I don't know bro. They been promoting this party for a minute," J.B. spoke from the backseat.

Looking out the window Rob said, "This gone be a wild ass night. It look like it's a little bit of everybody out here.

"Right look at these hos twerking on top of the car!" T.C. shouted accelerating slowly.

"Ay, get it get it," the two girls yelled out to each other as they danced.

J.B. stood up from the backseat with the big bottle of Remy in his hand yelling out, "What's good!"

"Shit, you tell us," one of the girls yelled back.

"We trying hit this party then chill with y'all after," J.B. spoke taking a sip of the bottle.

"Oh really? Y'all got another bottle in there for us?" the young girl asked.

"Yup, what's your number. Ima hit you up a little later." J.B. was lying, they had already finished the bottle of Hennessey and were already halfway through the bottle of Remy.

"652-9540. Hit me up later on," she yelled out continuing to dance. J.B. sat down in the car making sure he locked the number in his phone.

"Look like the party gone be out here tonight too," Malachi said.

"Yup, we finally bout to turn on Vine now but it's still gone be a minute before we actually hit the real party," Rob added. He emptied the guts out of the cigarillo beginning to roll up the second joint.

By the time Rob had finished rolling up T.C. was in the process of making the left turn onto Vine street near the Hartwell rec center. The street was flooded with twice as more traffic than the previous. People were jaywalking in the street recklessly in front of their cars. Cop cars were scattered throughout the street with their lights flashing but they weren't patrolling too much of anything.

A couple of cars ahead of them, a couple of dudes were hanging out the window of a black Caprice flashing their pistols. "Who want smoke? Who want it?" one of the dudes spoke loudly out the window.

Rob took his three-eighty handgun off safety and cocked it. "You got ya banger T?" Rob asked.

T.C. reached up under his seat and pulled out his black Glock setting it on his jeans. "You know I ride with mine. I'm not playing no games with these niggas tonight," he replied.

J.B. poured the last of the Remy bottle into his cup. "I already know some shit gone pop off tonight," he stated.

Not even seconds after he had made the remark a loud gun blast echoed throughout the atmosphere. A lot of people ran in different directions while some girls nearby screamed. Nobody got hit with any bullets. The young boys in the black Caprice had let off a shot in the air trying to showboat in front of everybody.

"See that's that bullshit. Niggas always trying to stunt like they hard until shit get real," Malachi stated.

Creeping steadily down the street they were still passing various mounds of people. It seemed like every hood in Cincinnati was there. Westwood, Linton Terrace, Avondale, Brown Hill, North side, College hill, Rolling Heights, Roselawn, Walnut Hills and the infamous "down the way" neighborhood all stood on the street establishing their position. Even people from the suburbs were running the streets like they were from the city.

Looking at the masses Malachi stated, "I swear it feel like we in a movie."

"Damn sure do," Rob replied.

"There go my F.M.B. niggas," a loud voice projected from behind the car. It was Snoop walking up on the car.

"What up bro," T.C. said shaking his hand.

"You almost got a shot in ya direction yelling out the squad name like that bro," Rob joked.

Snoop held his hands up in the surrender position. "I don't want no smoke bro. It's crazy out here though, muthafuckas out here off one, literally!" he exclaimed.

Malachi passed Snoop the freshly rolled blunt that he had just sparked saying, "Yeah, they is. You out here dolo like you ain't tripping off nothing."

Snoop took a robust hit of the ganja blowing the smoke out through his nostrils. "Shit, y'all know Ima true Nati nigga born and raised. I'm good anywhere out this bitch."

The F.M.B. gang knew he was telling the truth. Malachi's mind flashed back for a moment to when Snoop had stopped them from getting robbed and stripped in Evanston the previous year.

"I see y'all flexing in the drop Maro. T.C. then got his game all the way up!" Snoop spoke with excitement.

T.C. nodded speaking, "You know I'm staying on my grizzy nonstop."

"I hear you bro. Your ass should of stayed on that court though. You trippin," Snoop replied.

"Tried to tell him bro," J.B. added in.

"Snoop, Snoop," somebody from down the street yelled. Snoop turned his head squinting his eyes to see who it was.

Finally recognizing who it was, he yelled back, "Stay right there bro. I'm bout to come holler at you." Snoop turned his head back toward the four of them. "Ima link up with y'all kings later. Make sure y'all stay safe out here," Snoop spoke starting to walk in the opposite direction.

J.B. and Malachi sat up on the headrest in the backseat, so they could see over the crowd and stand out.

"We need to get up in this party. I think it cost like ten to get in," J.B. explained.

Noticing they had already rode past the party Malachi commented, "It's right back there in the other parking lot bro. Park in that parking lot at Kroger, where everybody else turnin into."

T.C. had his music up to the max volume but somehow, they could still hear each other. "Look Mal, remember we smashed them two College Hill chicks in your basement. There they go right there," T.C. commented.

"What chicks you talking bout bro?" Malachi asked. "Right there, by the red Impala," T.C. replied.

Malachi was finally able to locate exactly who T was talking about. He set his eyes on two brown skin girls talking to each other. Malachi laughed and said, "Yeah, they went hard."

"Go head and park right there at the Kroger gas station bro," Rob said front seat navigating. "Damn! There go your old boo Kandi," he added in.

Kandi was talking to some guy who was gripping her ass as he talked to her face to face.

"I ain't tripping off her ass. All these chicks out here. Y'all think I'm tripping off her?" T.C. commented briefly irritated.

His brothers knew that he was masquerading his true feelings he had for her. J.B. thought back to the short fling him and Kandi had. He still felt bad for almost doing it to his brother's girl at the time. As T.C. parked at the gas station, Tisha who was with Kandi, waved at them from a distance.

"You shitting on em with the Maro T," a young boy from Rolling Heights shouted as he parked.

"You know how niggas from the hood stunt bro," T.C. stated. Every compliment T.C. received about his sports car boosted his ego.

"Damn, I'm salty this gas station closed. We need another relo," Rob spoke disappointed.

"We can buy one off somebody out here. Niggas out here boothing freely like we in Colorado," Malachi said.

Malachi, J.B. and Rob started to walk towards the street as T.C. was in the process of locking his car up. Looking across the street they watched a huge fight break out.

"Look like that's some down the way and Linton Terrace niggas banging," Rob stated observing the brawl.

The two hoods were fighting as of their life depended on it. Some officers ran over to the scene trying to dead the fight.

"Let's hit this party up though," T.C. said walking up. T.C. was resembling a real Rasta as a couple of his locks hung over his black shades.

"You got ya banger on you T?" Rob asked.

Thomas patted his waist signaling where his gun was at. "You know it. It's ready to bust with one in the head. You grabbed ya piece out my whip, right?" he asked in return.

"Na, I left it in the whip. You know they gone pat us down before we go on the party."

Even though his eyes were a fire truck red T.C. took his shades off so Rob could see his face clearly. "You fooling bro. You better go get your shit, it's too wild out here."

"It is wild out here, they cutting up but Rob right. Y'all already know they gone search us at the door," Malachi insinuated.

"I really don't feel safe out here without my strap, but Ima put it back in the whip. I know they ain't bout to let me in with this bitch on me," T.C. said putting his shades back on. He walked back to his Camaro and quickly stashed his Glock in the driver's panel where he could easily access it.

"Let's get in this party though," J.B. mentioned as T.C. rejoined the crew.

Walking down the street, they moved in unison like a four-man army but swagged out like they were celebrities. Walking past the different hoods that were posted up they received a lot of love.

"Aye Mal when you gone to the L and get some wreck in on that court," a young man from Linton Terrace spoke.

Malachi shifted his eyes under the low brim of his Polo hat to see who it was. "What up Peanut. I'll prolly come out there tomorrow and get it in with y'all."

"Alright bro, hit my line up," Peanut replied.

Malachi knew a lot of the Linton Terrace hoopers because he would always go to their court when Mama Kelley visited her best friend in the neighborhood.

Continuing their journey to the party they walked past the Avondale and Walnut Hills sets who were ironically mixed in with each other. Rob knew mostly all of them from living out there so many years with his father. J.B., T.C. and Malachi also seen a host of familiar faces they seen from the times past they would ride out to Rob's house.

"Rob, Rob," a couple of people called out as they walked past.

One of the dope boys from Walnut Hills had his all black Chevy parked in the right lane where everybody was at. He had all four of his car doors open playing Yo Gotti's song "Sack". A huge mob of people were gathered around the truck turning up and dancing to the lyrics of the song. The four brothers decided to partake in the turn up getting hype with the rest of the crowd. "Ay, ay, ay, ay," they all yelled out feeling the excitement of the song. A couple of people pulled out their phone to record and capture the moment. A couple of Gucci mane and Dolph songs came on immediately after the Yo Gotti song ended. A lot of the girls started twerking again when the song came on.

"Aye, they was too turnt over there!" J.B. spoke as they started to walk again.

"They definitely was. Them niggas stay on some wild shit over there," Rob implemented.

Some random dude walking past bumped into J.B.'s shoulder as he walked past. J.B. turned around pissed, stepping to the stranger immediately.

"What up bra!" J.B. shouted with his arms stretched out.

The stocky dark skin teen turned around and looked at J.B. and his brothers ready to destroy him. He replied, "I don't want no drama bro," keeping it moving in the opposite direction.

"See, that's that bullshit," T.C. said irritated. He was still looking in the direction of the teen making sure he didn't have a change of mind.

"Come on bro," Malachi yelled out to T.C. as they continued to stride.

Entering into the parking lot of the rec center it was completely full. The plaza was illuminated with overhead lighting but still gave off a dim glow. The downtown residents of Cincinnati occupied the front of the plaza. T.C. knew a handful of them because that's where he had been hustling at a majority of the past summer. A couple plugs in the downtown neighborhood had helped him get his weight up in the dope game. J.B. knew some of them from when his uncle Ricky used to stay there before he moved down south. Exchanging brief greetings with them they kept it moving to the party. The line for the party was ridiculously long stretching out down half the parking lot.

"Damn, this look like a line at Kings Island," Malachi said.

"Right! The party gone be over by the time we get up in here," T.C. added on.

Fortunately, for the brothers a pack of Woodland natives were standing in the front of the line. They were letting whoever they knew cut in line to where they were at. Preparing to go in the party they counted their money. J.B. scanned over the parking lot observing the scene one more time before they walked into the party.

"Ain't that one of them Pratt brothers we seen in the city that day all that shit popped off?" J.B. questioned getting Rob's attention.

The three of them turned around to see who J.B. was talking about.

"Yeah, that's him. That was the quiet one," Rob said observing the teenager.

T.C. stared heavily searching for his older brother Trill. "Yup, that's dude Gully. I don't see his brother Trill though," T.C. commented.

"I seen them niggas Heavy and Snake too. It looked like they was walking in the party when we was coming in the lot," Malachi spoke. Malachi wasn't too worried about them, but he wanted to make sure his brothers were on point.

"Fuck em! They know what it is," J.B. boasted aggressively. J.B. got filled with animosity as he thought about the intense warfare a couple months before.

Rob wasn't too worried about Heavy and Snake either, but Big Rob's words echoed in his head when he told him that the beef wasn't over yet.

"That a be ten dollars," the diesel bouncer told them as he patted them down. The ex Rolling Heights cop Officer Littles stood to the side of the door to help patrol the scene. He now worked for Cincinnati police department. Recognizing who they were he figured he would speak.

"How you fellas doing?" All of them walked into the party saying nothing except T.C..

"I see you work for Cincinnati now. Got ya ass up out the hood when ya partner got bodied!" T.C. spoke wiping the smirk off of officer Little's face.

T.C. was referring to when Officer Dankey got murdered by Heavy's older brother Tank a couple years prior. Thomas probably would have ignored the officer, but the heavy liquor intoxication had him on edge.

The party was lit as soon as they walked in. The party building was a nice size, but it was filled wall to wall with people. Future's song "Plug" was blasting through the enormous black audio speakers.

"It's too damn thick in here," Malachi yelled over the music.

"Yeah, it is. This gotta be the party of the year right here," Rob suggested.

With the DJ playing a mix of the hottest cuts he kept the energy at a high level. The four of them tried to stay together but the crowd was too thick to move that deep. They split off into pairs. J.B. and Rob posted on the wall while Malachi and T.C. ran through the party like they owned the building. They were split up for about a half hour. Reuniting, J.B. and Rob were getting twerk dances against the wall from some females they met in the party.

"Thomas Crawford! Thomas Crawford!" J.B. yelled out.

T.C. looked at J.B. with a mean mug on his face. "Why the hell you yelling out my government name?" T.C. was in talking distance of J.B. as the girl was still dancing on him.

"I had to get your attention before you walked off. Let me see the keys to the whip so I can get this act real quick."

"Man, hell nawww nigga! You not bout to stank my shit up! Take her ass in that backroom they got blocked off."

"Okay bro," J.B. said directing his attention back toward the girl.

"What J was talking bout?" Malachi asked as they started to walk off again.

"J over there big trippin. He gone ask me can he see the keys to the whip, so he can get some act!"

"Oh yeah, he off one. He trying have us ride home in the sex smell," Malachi mentioned laughing.

"Right! He trying have us smelling Magnums and cooch juice!"

Malachi and T.C. ended up posting up next to a posse of people smoking reefer and a clique of dude's rap battling to the left of them. Sparking a black and mild they spectated a fight break out between a group of females. T.C. still had his shades on but when he seen the faces of Heavy and Snake from a distance he was certain it was them. To his astonishment, he saw them talking to the Pratt brothers.

"Look at this shit bro. You see Heavy and Snake talking to the Pratt brothers?"

Malachi looked past the scuffle between the females spotting Heavy's figure. "I wonder what them niggas over there talking about?"

T.C. and Malachi studied the interaction between the four of them closely. Snake was doing most of the talking to Trill, the older brother. It was apparent to them that some serious negotiation was being conducted. Suddenly, they seen Heavy pull out a big wad of money and give it to Trill. Trill handed the money to Gully for him to count up. Gully nodded towards his brother as if he was signaling to his brother that the money was good. The four of them exchanged fist bumps. The Pratt brother's gold grills shined through the smirks they wore on their faces. T.C. and Malachi got a bad vibe observing the interaction between their foes. That vibe was confirmed when they seen Heavy and Snake pointing the Pratt brothers in their direction. Even amongst a room full of people the six of them made direct eye contact with each other.

"These niggas bout to be on some bullshit," Malachi confirmed pulling his jeans up as the Pratt brothers approached.

T.C. took his shades off preparing to fight if need be. Malachi glanced around to see if he saw Rob and J.B. but they were nowhere in sight.

"What up T, long time no see. Why you ain't never bring us that paper back?" Trill asked in a stern voice. Not only was Trill's grills glowing but his bald fade haircut was also.

"That shit was a misunderstanding. Heavy wasn't trying to give y'all the dough back so I was gone be short even if I did pay y'all. I ain't even have no way of contacting y'all bro," T.C. spoke trying to reason Trill.

Trill turned to his brother Gully. "You hear this nigga? Talking bout, he couldn't find us. Everybody know we be in the hood all day, every day. The same place you got fronted at is where you can find us!"

"Say what you want to. How you trying work this out right now though?" T.C. asked.

Malachi could feel the tension building up. He kept a hawk eye on Gully making sure he didn't make any ill moves. He also seen Heavy and Snake standing about fifteen feet back posted in the cut. DJ Ice was mixing Plies song "Ran off the plug" and kept spinning it back.

"Ya boy Heavy just gave me what he owed down plus interest. He said you was the one not trying to pay shit back," Trill commented with fierceness.

T.C. knew Heavy and Snake had tried to get him jammed up. "Na, that ain't even the case. We can work some shit out and keep it moving." T.C. was trying his best to dead the dilemma.

"Yeah, bro ain't trying to spin y'all," Malachi added in.

"I hear y'all but I need my fetty tonight. I ain't fucking waiting no more."

"Na, bro I can't give you that shit tonight," T.C. explained.

Dismayed at T.C.'s response, Trill turned his head to his brother then redirected his attention back to T.C.. "You can't have my shit tonight? I guess you another broke nigga hustling then." Trill's offensive remark managed to get under T.C.'s skin.

"Na, I'm not no broke nigga. I guess I just ran off on the plug twice," T.C. spoke mimicking the Plies song that was playing through the speakers.

Trill was so furious from T.C.'s response he swung a quick right hand punch on T.C.. T.C. dodged it, countering with a right hook that landed on the jaw of Trill. T.C. followed up with a straight left punch. Malachi hit Gully with a right haymaker before he could jump in the fight to help his brother. Malachi threw a left punch that hit Gully in his temple making him stumble onto the ground, fazing Gully temporarily. Meanwhile, Trill had regained his composure and was able to snuff T.C. with a couple punches himself. Locking arms with each other they both used maximum strength trying to get the advantage. Malachi ran over pushing Trill off T.C.. He would have hit Trill, but he didn't want to risk hitting T.C., since they were wrestling so wildly. The brothers were in pursuit of assaulting Trill simultaneously but the big body bouncers in black tee shirts swooped both of them up.

"Oh shit, that's Mal and T!" Rob shouted out to J.B..

Rob seen the bouncers violently escorting Malachi and T.C. out the party. Shortly after, they seen the bouncers strong arming the Pratt brothers in the same manner.

"Come on bro. Let's move up out of here!" Rob commanded.

J.B. and Rob frantically pushed through the crowd trying to get outside to their brothers. They both knew anything was liable to pop off in the parking lot.

The DJ's voice came through the speakers saying, "The party is now over. Please make your way towards the exit. I repeat the party is now over."

Making it outside, Rob and J.B. searched for Malachi and T.C. with lightning speed in the crowded parking lot. Hearing some bouncers yell out, "Go home, go home" they found them in the faces of the bouncers ready to square off with them.

-

"Y'all good?" J.B. asked checking on their welfare.

"Where them niggas at?" Rob questioned. Both Jerome and Rob were pissed off that they weren't there to help when the brawl escalated.

"I don't know where they asses at! We just had to wreck on them niggas though!" T.C. exclaimed.

"I already know. I swear to god all of us gone ice they shit when we see em!" Rob stated.

The bouncers were still yelling out to them, "Take y'all asses home!"

As more people flooded out they finally saw the bouncers bringing out the Pratt brothers. Trill had his right hand to his lip noticing that he was bleeding. The sight of him seeing his own blood made him spas out!

"Where them niggas at? Fuck fighting, we bout to pop them niggas bro!" Trill shouted out.

"Let's get them straps then!" Gully responded full of wrath. The F.M.B. squad heard everything.

"Come on y'all we gotta get to the whip!" T.C. yelled to his brothers.

All four of them ran to the Camaro parked down the street at the gas station knowing they were in a life or death situation. J.B. and T.C. out ran Malachi and Rob. Running full speed, they overheard a random girl yell out, "They bout to start shooting y'all!"

-

Spotting the Kroger gas station, they were parked at they ran a little bit harder. Everyone on the street knew something serious was about to pop off from the way they were running. Rob and Malachi seen J.B. and T.C. run into the parking lot being about ten feet ahead of them. Rob had ended up colliding and falling over some girl who couldn't move out of his way fast enough. Noticing his brother had fell, Malachi went back to check on Rob. Running back, he helped Rob up off the ground but was met by the unfortunate sight of the Pratt brothers raising their pistols up pointing at them about twenty feet away.

"What up niggas. F.M.B. this bitch!" Trill yelled out.

Gully pulled his trigger first, but his gun jammed not releasing any bullets. Trill let off two shots but didn't appear to hit anything. Nevertheless, Malachi jumped in front of Rob risking his own life for his brother's. Trill let off another shot but ran for cover with Gully as T.C. and J.B. started to return fire. T.C. and J.B. let off a handful shots causing even more pandemonium, but they stopped once they couldn't see the Pratt brothers anymore.

"Shit, shit somebody get help!" Rob yelled out desperately.

T.C. and J.B looked down to see the tragic sight of Malachi laid out in Rob's arms. His Polo shirt was covered in blood. The second shot Trill let off was going to hit Rob but was intercepted by Malachi's chest since he jumped in the way.

"Somebody help!" Rob yelled out to no end. J.B. and T.C. cried out for help also as they fell to the ground to check on Malachi. Malachi still had his eyes open but was starting to cough up blood.

"Stay up bro, stay up bro you gone be alright!" J.B. encouraged him, praying Malachi would push through.

T.C. threw the guns in the sewer knowing the cops were soon to show up. "Somebody get the fuckin ambulance!" he hollered amongst the chaos.

Malachi coughed up more blood as his eyes started to flicker in and out. "Stay up bro. You gone make it!" Rob said trying to speak life into his brother. Rob's hands were now covered in blood as he held Malachi's body in his arms.

Malachi eyes started to flicker back and forth. He managed to keep his eyes open long enough to keep sight on his brothers. "I love yall kings," he said speaking his last words.

Malachi's eyes rolled in the back of his head seconds after. Rob shut his brother's eyelids with his bloody hands. T.C., J.B. and Rob were left motionless and silent as tears of pain rolled down their face. Packs of people screamed and fell out at the sight of Malachi's slain body. The loud noise of the paramedic's vehicle increased as they got closer.

Arriving on the scene, the paramedics hopped out the ambulance van pulling out the stretcher. Lifting his body up into the vehicle they sped off down the street. Malachi was pronounced dead an hour later at UC hospital. Mama Kelley had a nervous breakdown that night when she received the news of her son's tragic murder.

-

The next day T.C., J.B. and Rob were all in solitary confinement all at their separate homes. The catastrophe of seeing Malachi pass right before their eyes had them in a paranoid state. It wasn't safe for them to be around too many people at the present time.

Grandma Lois and Grandpa Gus sat down in their living room to watch the twelve-o clock news. Malachi's murder investigation was the top story of the day.

"High school basketball star Malachi Summers was tragically gunned down last night outside of the Hartwell rec center near the

Kroger's parking lot. Police have no suspects in custody at this time. If you have any information on this investigation please call the crime stoppers number," the young Caucasian analyst reported.

They showed outside camera views of the homicide scene as she wrapped up the story. Grandpa Gus turned off the TV and Grandma Lois immediately went into prayer. T.C. hadn't told his grandparents about the bizarre events that had happened the night before.

J.B. had sat in his room all day not eating anything. Mama J had been crying all day on the verge of experiencing a nervous breakdown also like Mama Kelley did. She tried talking to her son, but he didn't want to talk to her. He had his phone off but turned it on to see if Rob or Thomas had tried to contact him. The Facebook messenger notification popped up as soon as his phone updated. He didn't respond to any messages, but he had forty-six new ones. He figured most of the messages were revolving around Malachi's homicide. He scrolled on his newsfeed seeing nothing, but statuses dedicated to Malachi telling him to rest in heaven. J.B. exited out of the social site getting ready to turn his phone back off but paused to check an incoming message.

The message was from Rob. The message read "Coming to swoop you tomorrow at eleven. Be ready." J.B. responded to the message typing "Okay." He turned his phone off feeling sick and insane in the head that he couldn't pick up the phone and call Malachi.

The next morning Rob pulled into J.B.'s driveway exactly at eleven am. He had his fro out wearing a white tee resembling a member of the classic rap group Bone Thugs n Harmony.

"What up bro," J.B. said as he got into the car.

"What up," Rob responded.

Rob was playing Maino's song "Love for my niggas" on the ride to his house. Him and J.B. shared little conversation on the drive. Pulling up to the house in Avondale, T.C. pulled up shortly after in his Camaro. T.C. had on some wheat Tim's, blue jeans and a red thermal. It looked like none of them had gotten any sleep in the past two days.

Walking in the door, Rob lit up a blunt starting the rotation. Grabbing the Xbox joystick, he went to his music archives playing Project Pat's vintage album "Mista Don't Play"

"This shit fuckin crazy man. I swear to God!" Rob said as they sat down on the massive gray sofa.

J.B. shook his head commenting, "It is man. I can't believe my fuckin brother gone."

T.C. was quiet until they passed the blunt to him. He blew the herb smoke out his nose and began to talk. "This shit all my fault. I let this shit get way out of hand. Now my mother fuckin brother dead cause of my ass." T.C. took another hit of the blunt inhaling and exhaling like he was trying to get rid of all the emotional pain.

"We all could've made better choices king but at the end of the day you not the one who pulled that trigger," J.B. clarified trying to console his brother.

"This shit unreal. Lord knows I'm the one that spose to be gone!" T.C. expressed full of sorrow.

"My nigga spose to be right here smoking this loud with us!" Rob stated.

The blunt went around a lot quicker with the absence of Malachi as it was extremely awkward for them not to be receiving or passing the smoke to him. Besides school and being on the court together, their smoke sessions is where they had bonded most at the past couple of years.

"We need to figure out what the fuck we gone do. All that damn interrogation the jakes did on us, they know for sure we not no suspects. We ain't give em no names either though so they don't got no leads as of right now," T.C. said.

"They not gone get no leads either, cuz Trill and Gully got too much clout in the hood for anybody to snitch on em. Niggas out here saying Trill still running around like he ain't did shit wrong," Rob commented annoyed.

J.B.'s eyes almost popped out of his head asking, "You fuckin serious my nigga? This nigga just gone be that cocky though. Who the fuck he think he is?"

Looking up from his IPhone Rob said, "Yeah, he that cocky. A couple people told me Gully slid out of town cuz Trill didn't want him around when some major shit pop off."

"Pop off it is! Loyalty over everything. Y'all know we good hearted, but fuck that we gotta body this nigga Trill!" T.C. confirmed furiously.

"I'm with that shit. Nigga not bout to take my brother out and think I'm not gone ride on his shit!" Rob exclaimed.

"I can for real ice his shit myself. I just need y'all to be a lookout for me," T.C. declared grabbing the blunt from J.B..

"I know his baby mama stay right there in them houses on Forest Ave. He leave her spot bout eleven every night to go to the trap house down on Blair," Rob added in.

T.C. eyes lit up! "Well that's where we gone get him at! It be dark as hell over there too where his girl stay at."

"How you gone off him though? That gun blast gone be loud as hell," J.B. said helping plot.

"Don't need the burner. Ima creep on the side of the house and take him out with the knife game, execution style," T.C. affirmed envisioning the murder out in his head.

"I'm with that shit. Shit won't be right til we body his shit," Rob confirmed boldly.

"Yup, we can use one of the dope friend's car I serve to ride out there, so we can be incognito," T.C. expressed.

Rob hit the ganja and said, "Lets off his shit! You down to ride J?" Rob asked passing the weed to him.

J.B. never thought he would be in the position of plotting to murder a man but he like his other two brothers wanted to avenge Malachi's death.

Hitting the last of the blunt for now he blew the smoke out his nostrils and said, "Fuck it, let's ride!"

-

The next night T.C. arrived at J.B.'s in his dope fiends 05 Navy blue Impala at about ten pm. J.B. came out the house in his black hoody, black jeans and old black Tim's. T.C. got out the car and got into the backseat, letting J.B. take over the driving. Rob was in the passenger's seat.

"We a hundred?" J.B. asked before he put the car into drive.

"Let's ride," Rob replied.

Rob had on an all-black long sleeve shirt, black Dickie pants and black skully over his braids. T.C. had his locks tied up in a ball on his head wearing some old black sweats and an old black long sleeve tee shirt. On the ride from Woodland to Avondale they did no talking listening to Lil Boosie's song "Retaliation" and Styles P classic "Holiday." The blunt they had lit had all of them in their own zone. T.C. sat in the back polishing the blade on his knife with an old cloth. Rob was in the front checking the clips on his gun making sure that it was ready for fire if necessary. J.B. was sure to drive careful as they got off the expressway making sure they didn't get pulled over by the police.

"Bust a left on this street coming up," Rob directed pointing forward.

J.B. cut on his left blinker signal making the turn.

"Go down the street and park behind this red car when you come back up. There it go right there. Address fifteen twenty-eight," Rob added.

T.C. pulled out his black mask with the poked-out eyes out of his pocket. He put it halfway over his head covering his dreads.

Hitting the blunt one last time he clarified, "If anything go wrong we gotta get up through sap!"

"I already know bro," J.B. replied.

"Just focus on laying Trill down. We got you if anything crazy pop off," Rob commented giving his brother surety.

Getting out of the Impala, T.C. made a short jog over across the street where he positioned himself on the side of the house behind the bushes. Kneeling down, his body was discrete from anybody on the street seeing him. The street was primarily dark other than the orange overhead spotlights put up by the city. A couple houses had their porch lights on but Trill's baby mama porch light was off, helping T.C. blend in with the scenery. J.B. and Rob had a clear view as they waited now listening to the song "Hail Mary" by 2pac.

The time was ten forty and T.C. knew he had about twenty minutes to wait for Trill to exit the house. T.C. had on his black gloves but his palms were still sweaty. The image of Malachi laying in Rob's arms bleeding to death had been stuck in his head since Friday night. Every time he seen it made him want to kill Trill even more. He wished he would have listened to Malachi when he warned him not to get into the dope game. Now Malachi was dead and T.C. was in the position of no turning back, lying in stealth mode stalking Trill.

"Where the fuck this nigga at?" Rob asked anxiously. J.B. looked at the time on the dashboard. It read eleven o six pm.

"He should be coming out any minute now," J.B. spoke.

A car rode down the street past them making Rob grip his gun tighter, but the car turned off the street where they were at. Checking the surrounding houses T.C. didn't hear or see anybody outside which comforted him slightly as he waited, although his palms were still sweaty as he took deep quiet breaths.

Suddenly, at eleven eleven pm T.C. heard the front door open. T.C. peeked over the bushes to make sure it was his target. With the quick glance he got he seen the back of Trill's bald fade. T.C. knew that Trill had his banger on him, so his moves had to be flawless. Hearing no footsteps, T.C. took another glance at the porch. Trill had paused to light up a Newport cigarette before he walked to his car. Trill's slight delay made T.C. hesitant for a short second, nevertheless, he regained his poise.

Finally, hearing him make his way down the porch, T.C. pulled his black mask over his face and gripped his knife tighter in his right hand. He waited until Trill walked about a quarter of the way to the street, so he could creep up behind him. Timing it perfectly, T.C. crept silently from the bushes having a clear angle on his target. In clear striking distance, T.C. gripped the left side of Trill's shoulder while he slid the long blade across his throat with his right hand. Trill tried to lift his hands to his throat, but he stumbled, falling to the ground where he choked out on his own blood. T.C. stood over Trill making sure he was dead.

"That's for my brother! It's still F.M.B. bitch!" T.C. fiercely expressed looking down at the dead body. T.C. threw out a couple packs of cocaine on the ground to make the crime look drug related. J.B. had already started the car seeing T.C. run from the murder scene. T.C. got in the car and J.B. wasted no time speeding off.

"Man down!" Rob said as they drove past Trill's corpse.

Driving home they sparked up another reefer joint. They knew it was no coming back from what had just happened but knew it came with the game of life they had chosen to play. They all went to their separate homes having to prepare for Malachi's funeral the next day.

-

Mt. Zion Baptist church was jam packed the next morning at ten am for the funeral service. The medium size church in Woodland wasn't hardly large enough for the multitudes that showed up to say farewell to Malachi. It seemed as if almost half of the students from Princeton high school were present. Old teachers, teammates and teenagers from different parts of the city were all present. Ziggy, Miss Regina, Mr. Smith, Coach P, Snoop, Coach Lane, Kandi and Tisha were there as well. Of course, the F.M.B. family was present except T.C., which made everyone wonder why on God's earth he wasn't there.

Malachi's family occupied the first two pews in the church. They honored the traditional funeral ritual being dressed in all black. Walking into the church, people broke down into tears seeing Malachi laid out in the shiny dark brown casket. It was a surreal scene seeing a young man dead at eighteen who had such a bright future. The emotional trauma in the sanctuary was too overwhelming for a lot of people. Miss Kelley had decided to dress her son in an all-black suit with a dark red tie. Coach Joe and Mama Kelley received numerous amounts of hugs, prayers and shed tears as people came and gave their condolences.

The church choir marched in the sanctuary single file filling up the seats behind the pulpit. They began to sing the song selection "My help cometh from the Lord". They followed up with another song selection called "Source of my Strength". Moments later Reverend Rice, the pastor of the church walked up to the podium in the pulpit after the choir finished.

"Praise the Lord children of God. It truly saddens my heart that we are gathered here for the home going service of this great young man Malachi Summers. I have been this young man's pastor since the first year of his life. Even though I am his elder, I will honor and respect the legacy he left after a brief pilgrimage of eighteen years on this Earth. Today I won't preach to you long, but I wouldn't give this young man justice if I didn't ask this chief question." Reverend Rice paused and looked at the congregation.

"How long will our young people continue to murder each other? How long will the people of our communities continue to devalue our brothers and sisters lives? When we will rise up and be the children of God that he has chosen us to be? When will we let the glory of God shine in our lives like the bright sun rays from the sky!" The pastor's voice shook the sanctuary as he convicted the hearts of many with his Martin Luther King type speech.

Rob and J.B. were listening to Reverend Rice but were zoned out in their own world. All they could think about is what they could have done to prevent Malachi's murder. The next thing on their mind was the image of T.C. slaying Trill the night before. Even though they all agreed to kill him, it still shook them up to see two men die back to back. Yet in still, the principal thought on their mind was "Where the hell was T.C. at?"

The funeral lasted about an hour and Reverend Rice gave everyone directions to the burial site. Rob and J.B. carried their brothers casket out of the church along with two other teenagers from the Woodland neighborhood.

-

After the burial everyone close to the Summer's family came and gathered at their house. Mama J had made all of the food catering for everyone. Not even twenty minutes after they had got to the house Coach Joe pulled J.B. and Rob to the side in private.

"Where the hell is Thomas at?" he asked aggressively. Looking at Coach Joe with a blank stare they gave him no response. "Y'all just gone sit here and stare at me silly. I asked y'all a damn question!" Coach Joe spoke flaring up at them.

"I honestly don't know. I was wondering the same thing," J.B. replied first.

Coach Joe looked at Rob waiting for his response. "I don't know either but if I had to take a guess, I'd say he might be at the abandoned house down on Linden Ave at the bottom of the hill."

"You talking bout the yellow one Rob?"

"Yeah, the yellow one," Rob replied.

"I'm bout to ride over there right now. I know this my son's gathering but something in my spirit telling me something not right with Thomas and to go find him right now! Coach Joe declared."

"With him not showing up today me and Rob been feeling the same way," J.B. insinuated.

Coach Joe left the house not notifying anybody he was leaving. He had told J.B. and Rob to tell Mama Kelley he would be back shortly.

Pulling up at the yellow house on Linden Ave, Coach Joe seen Thomas's Camaro parked in the street. He parked his car in the driveway of the vacant house that had been abandoned for years now. He walked up the porch steps and heard TI's song "Still ain't forgave myself" playing from behind the front door. This let him know for sure someone was in the home. He tried to look through the front window but the old grey curtains that still hung blocked any view inside. He walked back to the front door turning the doorknob, but it was locked.

"T.C., T.C., Thomas let me in here!" he yelled.

He banged on the door and yelled again but he got no response. Coach Joe was unaware that the F.M.B. crew would always use the back entrance to get in the house. By this time, he was flustered with even more anger. Raising up his size thirteen dress shoe he kicked the middle of the door three times. The door flew open on the third kick. Coach Joe walked in seeing T.C. sitting down slouched against the wall with his all black Glock pointed at his own temple. A bottle of Hennessey, a bag of pills and a loud blunt all laid on the floor surrounding him.

"Get ya ass up son!" Coach Joe shouted.

He lifted him up with both his hands making T.C. drop the gun. Coach Joe's infuriation of anger caused him to hit T.C. with two hard body shots making him drop to his knees. Coach Joe retreated deciding not to assault him anymore.

"This shit fucked up. My brother dead because of me. Everybody dead because of me!" Thomas voiced.

Rivers of tears rolled down T.C.'s face as he sat on his knees slumped over. Coach Joe knew that T.C. was pissy drunk and high but had a genuine sorrow and remorse for the drastic events. He also knew that he was seriously contemplating suicide.

"Stand up son!" Coach Joe commanded.

T.C. lifted his head up slightly moving his dreads out of his face. "I said stand up son!" he yelled grabbing him by the hand helping him up. T.C. mustered what little bit of strength he had to keep his balance on his own two. Looking at Coach Joe, T.C. seen Malachi's reflection in his dad's face causing the tears to keep rolling down his face more immensely. Coach Joe stepped to T.C. wrapping his arms around him. He knew he had taken his anger out in the wrong way by hitting him.

"I messed up. Everything my fault!" T.C. mentioned again. Coach Joe figured he must have been drinking all night because his pourers were reeking of liquor.

Coach Joe stepped back looking Thomas squarely in his eye. "It hurts like hell that my son is gone. In my forty-three years of life I've never felt a pain like this. You made some foolish decisions but you're not the one who killed my son."

Coach Joe stopped talking temporarily as the words he spoke

sunk into his soul. "Thomas, we can't bring back Malachi, but I need you to do two things for me to continue on my son's legacy."

T.C. lifted his head up a little bit more. "I promise to God, I'll do anything. Just tell me what it is!" he said staring at Coach Joe in his all black suit.

"Promise me that you'll go to college and graduate. The second thing I want you to do is start playing basketball again. I want you to make it to the NBA son. That's how I want you to carry on Mal's legacy and I believe you can do that."

The expectations and requirements Coach Joe had of him let him know that he was one person that wasn't ready to give up on him yet.

"Coach, I take it as my God given responsibility to achieve that. I promise Ima do whatever I can to make it happen. No excuses, Ima make you and Mal proud!"

Coach Joe and T.C. shook hands validating the promise T.C. had just made. They shared another father-son hug for about twenty seconds as tears rolled down both of their faces.

"Let's get out of here son," he said to T.C. Coach Joe and T.C. walked out of the house together leaving behind the gun, drugs and dope boy lifestyle.

Six Years Later

Hey, Thomas can I talk to you in my office for a minute?" Coach Ed asked him.

"Sure coach, just let me finish packing my bag up," T.C. replied.

T.C. threw his headphones and shoes into his Texas Legends sports bag. Before he began to walk into Coach Ed's office, he paused to look at himself in the mirror in his locker room cabinet. He stared at himself knowing he had came a long way. He had cut his locks and now rocked a taper haircut and a goatee. Not only had his physical appearance changed but he had changed on the inside also. Malachi's harsh death and the promise he had made to Coach Joe had redirected him down a path of positivity. Not only that but he was thankful to never get charged in the murder of Trill. The police never did any investigation assuming it was just another senseless homicide over dope.

T.C. brushed his taper a couple times and walked into Coach Ed's office. "You wanted to see me coach?"

Coach Ed looked up from the paperwork on his desk. "Yes, take a seat Thomas."

Coach Ed was the head coach for the Austin Spurs, a team in the NBA G league. He was a former NBA player who was of the Mexican origin. Coach Ed was smiling as he shuffled through some paperwork, so T.C. didn't think he had bad news but he was still anxious to hear him out.

"Thomas, let me first say that you have been playing your ass off these past two months. I can definitely say you've been a major contributor to our team's success.

T.C. smiled, feeling relieved. "Thanks coach. I just try to play my heart out every time I hit the court."

"That's evident to see. You've been damn near averaging a triple double for the past month. Twenty-eight points, nine assists and eight rebounds a game. You've been nearly unstoppable!" Coach Ed took a sip of water before continuing to talk.

"Now I'm technically not supposed to be doing this because I'm not your agent. Although, with me being your coach for these past couple years I personally wanted to tell you that the Cleveland Cavaliers want to add you to their roster to finish out their season with them. You are officially going to be a Cavalier within the next couple of days mi amigo!"

T.C. sat in the chair speechless. The goal he had been working so hard to achieve was now a reality. "I don't even know what to say coach. This almost too much for me to take in right now!"

"I know the feeling all too well, but you deserve it! I know you'll be successful in the NBA."

Coach Ed and T.C. exchanged handshakes. "Your agent should be contacting you soon Thomas."

"Okay coach!" T.C. said walking out the office full of excitement. It was the first time in a while that he truly felt proud of himself.

T.C. pulled his IPhone out of his pocket and scrolled down to Coach Joe's name. He sat on a wooden stool in the front locker because the overwhelming news had made his legs weak.

Coach Joe- What up Thomas

T.C.- I got some good news pops.

Coach Joe- What's that?

T.C.- I kept my promise. The Cavs want me to sign on with them for the last half of the season.

Coach Joe- I knew you would do it! I knew you had it in you! I'm proud of you son! Kelley, Thomas done got signed!

(Mama Kelly picks up phone)

Mama Kelly- Thomas, baby you got signed? Thank God! Lord knows you deserve this!

T.C.- Thank you mama.

Coach Joe- Were truly happy for you Thomas. You kept your word and I salute you on that. Make sure you call your Grandpa Gus and brothers asap!

T.C.- Yeah, I am as soon as I get off the phone with you. Thanks for challenging me pops and bringing the best out of me.

Coach Joe- That's what I'm supposed to do. I know Malachi is smiling on us right now. See you tomorrow son love you.

T.C.- I know he is too and love y'all too.

T.C. hung up the phone and dialed J.B. and Rob on three way. "Y'all need Cavs tickets? Yall bro just got signed with Bron and them! They gone have to trade Kyrie to Boston and send Bron off to the west coast or something, cause I'm takin that starting pg spot!"

The three young men were exuberant with excitement over the good news. All three of them decided that they would officially celebrate T.C.'s achievement when they reunited back in Cincinnati the following day.

After calling everyone, T.C. sat on the wooden stool still in a state of hysteria. He reflected over his journey after high school. He had attended a junior college in Cincinnati and ended up attending the University of Dayton where he received his degree in Business Management. Thomas had put up incredible stats while in college but was completely overlooked in the NBA draft after his senior year. Fortunately for him, he ended up getting an opportunity to try out for the Austin Spurs, an NBA G league team. Averaging almost triple double numbers midway through his second season brung him notoriety that scouts couldn't overlook. Now he was a signature away from playing in the NBA. Everybody he felt like he let down, he knew he had made proud now. Everything was perfect in his life with the exception of one thing. He wished his brother Malachi was here to share the moment with him. He shed two tears as he sat on the wooden stool. One tear was symbolic for the emotional pain that he knew would never leave him. The other tear was symbolic of the great amount of joy he felt at the present moment knowing that he hadn't let the trials and pitfalls in his life defeat him.

-

The next day T.C. pulled up to the Summer's house in his all black Chevy Tahoe playing Nipsey Hussle's album "Victory Lap". He figured everyone was waiting on him, seeing the driveway full of cars. Knocking the door, he was surprised when he seen Big Rob open it.

"Big Rob! What's up man!" he shouted with exuberance.

"I'm feeling prosperous! What up with you T?"

Big Rob and T.C. shared a passionate hug as he walked through the door. Big Rob had just come home from his prison bid a month earlier. T.C. hadn't seen him since the day he got sentenced.

"It's good to see you unc. I see you stayed on the workout tip in there," T.C. spoke referring to Big Rob's diesel frame.

He was still sporting a bald head with a thick beard. "You know I had to stay tight on there. I heard you bout to be a Cavalier. I'm proud of you T!"

"Thanks, unc. You know I'm just trying to represent."

"Well you definitely doing that. It hurt me to my core that I wasn't there for y'all these past eight years," Big Rob mentioned.

"It's all good, you here now and that's all that matter."

T.C. looked into Big Rob's eyes and knew that he was still a gangster, but his growth spiritually and mentally was undeniable.

"Is that our new Cleveland Cavalier?" Mama J said walking into the living room. Giving him a hug and kiss she yelled, "T.C. here y'all!"

Mama J, Robert, Thomas and Jerome all exchanged hugs. "So good to see you son. Y'all so grown up now," Mama J said looking at the three of them.

"How you been Mama J? I haven't see you in over a year now." T.C. spoke.

"I'm good, just grateful to be here baby," she replied.

Mama J had been cancer free for the past four years. She decided to wear a low haircut permanently now in honor of all cancer victims. She also ended up marrying Paul, the same man she dated when the F.M.B. squad was in high school.

"What up king," Rob said to T.C..

"Nothing bro, trying to live it up. I missed y'all niggas men. We then came a long way," T.C. responded.

"You right about that bro. Congrats again on your new contract bro. You and Mal was bound for the league the whole time."

"I'm just trying get in your level bro. You been ballng!" T.C. commented.

Rob had got drafted to the Tennessee Titans after his senior year at Ohio State. He occupied the role on the team as the second-string quarterback. He also had cut his braids sporting an even-Steven haircut and full beard.

"Aye though, I'm just trying to ball like y'all. Y'all playing ball and I just got a regular job," J.B. spoke downplaying his accomplishments.

"Regular my ass. You work for Google king! Ain't nothing regular about that," Rob replied.

"Right, nothing regular at all!" T.C. chimed in.

J.B. had landed an internship at Google his senior year of college. His excellent performance during his internship opened up the opportunity for him to join the company full time. Between the three brother's hectic schedules they didn't get to see one another as much but no love was ever lost between them.

"Come on y'all let's eat!" Mama Kelley yelled from the kitchen.

"Bout time ya ass got here," Grandpa Gus said to his grandson.

"How you doing son?" Coach Joe asked him.

"I'm marvelous pops," T.C. replied. He shook Grandpa Gus and Coach Joe's hand before he sat down.

Mama Kelley set the table with a large tray of her famous lasagna, salad and garlic bread. Seeing everyone at the table Mama Kelley asked Coach Joe to pray over the food.

"Everybody bow your heads please. Lord we thank you for this food we are about to intake. Please let it be well in us. We pray also thanking you for our family. Please protect and prosper us all. Amen."

After the prayer they all fellowshipped reminiscing over the precious memories of Malachi and Grandma Lois who had passed two years earlier.

-

"Damn men, I ain't been to a game since senior night six years ago," T.C. stated looking at his old school.

Rob, Jerome and Thomas were trailing the rest of the F.M.B. family as they walked in the gym on the chilly January night.

"Shit, after that hoop season ended our senior year I never came back to a game either. It took everything I had to make it through that season without Mal," Rob added.

"For real, it almost feel like we back in our senior year again. I keep on thinking bro cool ass gone pop up and enter this gym with us," J.B. stated reminiscing.

Right before they walked into the gym they passed a long white poster that read "Malachi Summers dedication game."

Strolling into the game they looked around at the surroundings that they knew all too well. They exchanged several hugs and handshakes as people started to notice who they were.

"Long time no see," Mr. Smith said approaching them in his all black Kango and leather jacket.

"What up Mr. Smith!" J.B. replied. The three of them traded strong handshakes and hugs with their former teacher.

"It's good to see you young men. I knew you all would be here for Malachi's dedication game." Mr. Smith looked exactly the same except for the strands of grey hair growing in his head.

"Yeah you know we wasn't missing this for nothing. This is certifying bro's legacy right here!" Rob commented excited.

Mr. Smith nodded his head in agreeance. "Yes, they're honoring him the right way. Seems like yesterday the four of you were in these hallways and playing on this court. I'm proud of y'all." From the look in his eyes it was evident that Mr. Smith was speaking with the sweetest sincerity.

The warning buzzer went off notifying the start of the game. The three of them and Mr. Smith walked over to the section that the rest of the F.M.B. family was at. When the game started the Princeton squad came out playing with a high amount of intensity.

"Push the ball bro!" T.C. hollered out directing the point guard.

"Hit the boards bro," Rob and J.B. yelled to Princeton's big men.

Watching the game had the whole F.M.B. family reembarking of when Malachi, T.C., Rob and J.B. were all on the court together. Mama Kelly shed some tears as she remembered her son playing on the court for the last time senior night. Coach Joe and Mama J wrapped their arms around her as they fought back tears themselves.

Big Rob was watching the game with a bittersweet feeling in his heart. It hurt him to the core that he wasn't there for the last years of their high school tenure. He figured with his presence on the streets that it was a good possibility that Malachi would still be living. Nevertheless, he was grateful to be out of prison and able to see the rest of the family at this stage in life.

-

The first two quarters flew by and Princeton dominated. With halftime beginning, Mr. Plusky the school's athletic director walked onto the court with a microphone.

"I want to thank you all for coming out tonight. As you all know tonight is a very momentous occasion for Princeton sports. We are here to dedicate and retire the jersey of Malachi Summers. He is no longer with us, but he will always be greatly remembered. As for me personally I can say he is one of the best student athletes I've ever seen. Will the parents and family of Malachi please come to mid court."

The F.M.B. family walked onto the court. Coach P and Coach Lane walked on also making the moment that much more emotional. Mr. Plusky passed the mic to Coach Joe.

"I don't have much to say but what I will say is that my son was a great young man. My wife & I raised him to be him to be the best he can be and I can honestly say that he lived every day to his fullest potential."

Coach Joe paused to hold back any tears. Mama J had her arms wrapped around Mama Kelley who was still shedding tears.

"And that's my advice to all of us here tonight, to live our lives to its max potential. It's been six years since our son was murdered but as long as we live, he will live on through us. We love you son." Coach Joe passed the mic to Coach P.

"I won't talk long because I want these three young men to have ample amount of time to speak. What I will say is that Malachi was a class act on and off the court. In my sixty-one years of living I have never seen anyone with more passion for the game of basketball. It was an honor to coach and mentor the young legend." Coach P fixed the brim of his hat as he tried passing the mic to Big Rob and Grandpa Gus. Neither of them wanted to speak though.

J.B. who was next to Grandpa Gus grabbed the microphone. Before he began to speak he looked in the crowd noticing a lot of familiar faces. Snoop, Ziggy, Miss Regina, Big Gerald and Big Sean were all in attendance along with other recognizable faces from years past.

J.B. cleared his throat before he began to talk. "I just want to first thank everyone for coming out tonight in support of my bro Mal. I never thought in a million years that I would be standing here reminiscing on past times with my brother. The three of us you see standing here plus him aren't related by blood, but we have a bond that can't be broken. That bond we share produced a lifestyle of brotherhood that's forever priceless. Through the good and bad, we stayed tighter than a pack of wolves. When I think of Mal the first thing that comes to mind is loyalty. You never had to worry about if bro was going to be there for you. You could trust him in crunch time. In fact, sometimes I trusted him more than I trusted myself. He was the true epitome of a standup guy. As far as basketball goes he was nearly impossible to stop on the hardwood. His love for the game was unmatched! I never told him this, but I used to hate to guard him, geesh!"

J.B. let out a laugh along with the crowd.

"Everyone focused on his scoring but his mere presence on the court made teams shake up. I could go on forever about my brother, my ace and my hitta. All four of us are leaders but truth be told Malachi was the leader out the crew. He was futuristic on and off the court. I love you bro and your legacy will forever live through us. To Coach Joe and Mama Kelley y'all know me, Rob or T.C. are only a phone call away."

J.B. made firm eye contact with Malachi's parents who were still were comforting each other. He passed the mic to Rob.

Rob took a glance over the crowd. "If you knew Mal then you know words alone can't express how great he was. On and off the court he was dominant, but his greatest quality was that he showed love to everybody. It was almost impossible not to love him. With that said he always demanded respect. He was solid and always knew what direction he was going. It's almost as if he had lived this life before. The night of his murder I had to experience him die in the cuff of my arms."

Rob's eyes closed as he was replayed the tragic scene in his mind. A tear rolled down the right side of his face leaving a trail. He opened his eyes back up.

"I looked at barrel of a gun and a bullet intended for me, take the life of my brother. If you want to know how deep our brotherhood was, that sums it up right there. He jumped in front of a flying bullet for me to save my life. That is the epitome of loyalty. They say we all get a guardian angel. Well mines is my brother. To continue on his legacy my brothers and I have started a nonprofit organization under his name. The organization will be geared towards helping black youth establish a positive foundation early in life. We will provide mentorship, academic programs and sporting events. Malachi was legendary and will live through us forever."

Rob passed the mic to T.C. who grabbed it with sweaty palms.

T.C. had learned how to bury the demons of his past to stay sane and move on with his life. As much as Malachi's memorial celebration manifested positivity, for T.C. it also triggered a lot of bad emotions and memories he had countless battles with over the past six years. He took a deep breath which helped sober up his mind.

"I don't deserve to be here holding this mic right now. As a twenty-four-year-old man I can stand here and say that I don't deserve to be standing here right now. I should be dead. For years after my brother's death I wrestled with the guilt for being responsible for his death."

T.C. stopped and looked around at the mounds of people in the gym. All eyes were on him and the emotional density was breathtaking in the atmosphere.

"I contemplated suicide two days after his death. I pointed a loaded Glock at my head and was inches away from pulling the trigger. If it wasn't for god's grace and that man busting the door down, I wouldn't be here."

T.C. pointed to Coach Joe so everyone could know who he was talking about.

"Malachi tried his best to stop me from going down the road of drug dealing but I was too foolish to listen. I gave up playing basketball, which at the time was the only thing that gave me peace. I got me and my brothers involved in a situation that we couldn't bounce back from. And what did I gain from it? Some fast money, a couple cars, some popularity and a little bit of street cred. What did I lose?"

Thomas held his down as he began to cry. Rob and J.B. threw their arms around their brother sympathizing with his pain.

"Hold your head bro," Rob stated encouraging him.

"I lost my brother. We lost our brother man," T.C. spoke lifting up his head. Some of the crowd had also started to cry feeling the pain that the F.M.B. family was coping with.

"Malachi was a young god and respected by everyone. When I gave up hoop to trap in the streets it hurt all my brothers, but he was the most hurt. A lot of people would often ask me who better me or him. My answer is the same now as it was back then. Malachi was better and futuristic on and off the court like J said. Every day I wish I could trade places with him. Since I can't, I dedicate every day of my life to him. Every time I step on the court I play in honor of him. Not only do I dedicate my life to him but also my son's life."

T.C. pointed to the section of the bleachers where Kandi was holding his three-year-old son. Kandi and Thomas had rekindled their relationship four years prior and were now engaged.

"Your legacy will forever be with us and live through us. Love you bro. Keep watching over us until we get there." T.C. was looking up at the ceiling feeling that Malachi was really looking down on them.

T.C. passed the mic to Mr. Plusky who now was back on the court.

"We will now retire Mr. Summers jersey which will be followed a highlight video of Malachi. We have Mr. Summers jersey plastered on the wall."

He pointed to his red and black jersey with the number twenty-four on it. His jersey hung by the other retired jerseys of Princeton alumni.

"To our scoring leader, an exceptional student athlete and great young man, it was a pleasure watching you play. You are gone but never forgotten and, in your honor, we will now retire your jersey."

The crowd started to applaud after Mr. Plusky finished talking. Everyone then focused their attention to the large projection screens set up on the gym floor.

The video featured Malachi scoring, rebounding, dribbling fancy and passing the ball off to his teammates in style. At the end of the video a post-game interview came on. The reporter in the interview asked him how he wanted to be remembered. His response was that he wanted to be remembered as a living legend. The video ended after the interview. The crowd started to clap and chant Malachi's name repeatedly. His name being chanted by the crowd was one of the best feelings anybody in the F.M.B. family had felt since he passed. His legacy was sealed as a living legend. He was gone but never forgotten.

-

Leaving the gymnasium, the three brothers headed towards the exit in the lobby.

"Watup y'all," a voice from behind them spoke.

Turning around they laid eyes on Heavy's tall frame. All of them were speechless as they seen Heavy walk towards them with a little girl by his side.

"Watup Heavy," Rob responded breaking the ice.

"Look I know I'm the last person y'all want to see but it was on my heart to come and be here. As a man I truly want to say sorry for all the bullshit that went down. I feel responsible for everything and still haven't forgave myself for his death. From the bottom of my heart I pray y'all can find a way to forgive me."

The three brothers could feel the sincerity of Heavy's apology. They knew they couldn't hold the past against him.

"Bro, apology accepted. We was all fools back then. It's unfortunate how shit turned out but all we can do is do what's right now," Rob spoke up boldly and said.

"Yeah bro, apology accepted. Looking back on it still hurt like hell but we was all young and dumb. I always will take all the blame for everything that went down," T.C. added in.

"Yeah, as black men we just got to set a better example out here for the youth. Is that your daughter bro?" J.B. asked.

Heavy looked down at the little girl who was holding his hand. "Yeah, this my baby girl. She five years old now."

"She beautiful bro. How Snake been?" Rob asked.

"Snake dead. He got killed three years ago downtown trying rob somebody," Heavy responded in a grave tone.

"Damn, sorry to hear that," Rob replied.

"Yeah, the game crazy. I'm out the streets now. I do construction work full time and focus on raising my baby girl. I'm just trying to do right," Heavy spoke.

"That's what's up bro. I'm happy for you Heavy," T.C. stated shaking his hand. J.B. and Rob also shook Heavy's hand.

"It was good seeing y'all and I'm happy for the three of y'all. All y'all legends out this way," Heavy commented. Before he left their sight, he saluted them as he walked out the door.

-

The next morning the three of them met at the court up the street from Malachi's house in Woodland.

"Damn I ain't been on this court in a minute," J.B. spoke excited as they walked onto the pavement court.

"Man what! I don't think none of us been on this court since high school!" T.C. added in.

Rob dribbled the ball through his legs and behind his back. "Aww shut T, I think I still got it. I might be coming to play for the Cavs with you!" Rob joked laughing.

"Na, Rob I think we better leave the hoopin up to T now," J.B. remarked jokingly.

"Men y'all silly. We had some classic games on this court. We used to play all night." T.C. made a jump shot after he finished his sentence.

"Yeah, we definitely did. Blood, sweat and tears on this court baby," Rob commented.

"Can you still dunk Rob?" J.B. asked curiously.

"I don't know bro. I then gained some weight, so I don't know if I can get up like I used too."

"I think I still can," J.B. said looking up at the hoop.

"Well shit, go and dunk it then. When you do dedicate that dunk to Mal," T.C. affirmed.

"You know what that's good motivation because I can't remember the last time I boomed," Jerome spoke.

J.B. backed up to the three-point line and dribbled to the hoop drop stepping and rising in the air with the ball in one hand. Soaring in the air he dunked the ball in.

"We see you J, we see you!" T.C. spoke hype.

J.B. grinned, "That's all I'm doing. That was for bro."

"Pass me that ball bro," Rob demanded. He backed up to the half court line sizing the rim up. "This for Mal." He shot the ball in the air and it spun around the rim finally falling through the net.

"Man y'all acting like y'all can't hoop no more. Y'all out here playing like y'all never left!" T.C. yelled.

Rob passed the ball to T.C.. T.C. dribbled back to the opposite three-point line on the other end of the court.

"Dayg T, you bout to gun it from there?" J.B. asked.

T.C. grinned confidently. "You know it. I can let y'all out do me."

T.C. eyed the rim on the other end of the court and took one dribble forward releasing the ball. The shot seemed like it took forever to go in. When it finally did it fell straight through the net.

"That was for bro," T.C. said gazing up in the sky.

"Good ass shot bro!" Rob shouted out.

"Can I shoot?" a little kid asked walking onto the court.

"You sure can little man. Your first shot dedicate it to Malachi," T.C. said instructing the young boy.

The little brown skin boy looked up at him and asked, "Who is Malachi?"

T.C. looking down at him answered, "The best player to ever play on this court."

The young boy dribbled towards the rim, shooting a short bank shot off the backboard looking at it go in. The three brothers ran over to the little boy giving him a high five. Turning around, they saw the same elderly man who always used to sit on the porch watching them and Malachi play. He lifted his hand in the shooting motion and smiled at them.